Also by Robert Kotlowitz

Sea Changes
The Boardwalk
Somewhere Else

His
Master's
Voice

His Master's Voice

a novel by

Robert Kotlowitz

Alfred A. Knopf   New York   1992

THIS IS A BORZOI BOOK
PUBLISHED BY ALFRED A. KNOPF, INC.

Published in the United States by Alfred A. Knopf, Inc., New
York, and simultaneously in Canada by Random House of
Canada Limited, Toronto. Distributed by Random House, Inc.,
New York.

Grateful acknowledgment is made to PolyGram International
Publishing, Inc. for permission to reprint an excerpt from "I'm
Old Fashioned" by Jerome Kern and Johnny Mercer. Copyright
1942 by PolyGram International Publishing, Inc. Copyright
renewed. Used by permission. All rights reserved.

Library of Congress Cataloging-in-Publication Data

Kotlowitz, Robert.
His master's voice / by Robert Kotlowitz.—1st ed.
p.   cm.
ISBN 0-679-40868-1
I. Title.
PS3561.0846H57   1992
813'.54—dc20
                                            91-37156
                                            CIP

Manufactured in the United States of America

FIRST EDITION

To Dorothy Olding

One

1

The August sun was up, pouring through the open window, shimmering in visible waves again. Sigmund could see them as soon as he walked into the hospital room, rising vaporously into thin air before vanishing. Ahead of him, propped in bed on his side, lay the patient. His back was turned toward Sigmund. The top sheet was folded down to his knees, his pajama shirt rolled above his waist. From his lower thighs to his navel, he was entirely naked. Above his creased behind, where there was a faint tuft of hair at the base of the spine, an ultraviolet lamp baked his flesh, the aging buttocks sagging in the strange light like deflated balloons. Sigmund's nostrils dilated a bit at the sight, a sure sign, as always, that his senses were beginning to rebel. He pulled himself up, standing rigid and holding his breath. He had seen worse in the course of his clerical rounds, far worse over the years, he told himself, but for the moment he couldn't remember where. Cancer of the colon; scabrous passage to eternity. At eleven o'clock in the morning, still so early in the day, this charged reminder of mortality wiped out all memory. It also took Sigmund's breath away. The patient, Barney Fribush, was smoking a cigar. He seemed to be half asleep. A copy of *Life* lay open at the foot of the bed. Next to it was the *Morning Sun*, still untouched.

"Barney?" Sigmund spoke in hesitant Slavic tones, in a reedy Polish voice that sounded unsure of itself. (His name had once been Zygmunt Czaferski.) "Barney?" he called again. "Are you awake? You'll burn yourself if you're not careful." Then, more urgently, "Wake up now, don't go falling asleep with a cigar in your mouth."

The baking figure stirred. Smoke rose in the morning sunlight, baroque curls floating up toward the ceiling.

"It's me. Sigmund." Sigmund removed his pince-nez in order to see his friend more clearly.

"Ah, cantor," Barney said, barely moving. "You caught me."

"You should keep the door closed," Sigmund said, still staring at Barney's buttocks. "It's not open house, you know." He forced a laugh.

"It's nothing nobody hasn't seen before."

"But they haven't seen yours." Which, for Sigmund R. Safer, was almost racy. After a pause, during which Sigmund felt himself blush, he went on. "And how do you feel?" he asked.

More smoke. "All right. Considering. Come around this side, where I can see you. Don't be so shy. It's only me. Barney."

"Here I am," Sigmund said, moving around the bed.

"Some *toches*, huh?" Barney managed a laugh as he asked this question.

"What do the doctors say?" Sigmund answered. They were now face to face, Sigmund looking stern.

"And what do the doctors know?"

A reasonable question, in Sigmund's opinion, even though they both knew what the doctors knew. (That was the easy part.) But for now he merely shrugged, looking even more severe as he stood there silently alongside the patient. He would not talk just for the sake of talking. It was a matter of principle with Sigmund never to speak unless he had something to say. He also made it a practice not to create false hopes or encourage wishful thinking, at least knowingly. As a cantor, as an ordinary working clergyman earning his living like anyone else, Sigmund solaced and comforted his congregation at services every week and by being there when they needed him, in sickness and in health. That was the least he expected of himself; and it was more than it seemed at first glance. But nurturing illusions did nobody any good. False hopes, his own and others', could be destructive. He had seen enough of that over the years.

After hesitating a moment, he moved closer to the bed, a familiar yearning beginning to tug at him. Dutifully, he tried to resist it, but the pull was too great. He wished he were home on Granada Avenue with his beautiful fish. Wherever he was these days, almost, that was what he wished for, to be settled in the little back room on Granada Avenue alone and uninterrupted with his fish. Sigmund began to hum to himself now to keep up his spirits (Barney Fribush was not the first patient he had visited this morning), something zesty from Gilbert and Sullivan, for whom he had always had a taste, thinking of his beautiful angels and black mollies swimming briskly in their spacious tanks at home, waiting for him to join them, as the sprightly little tune buzzed on inside his head.

"Speak louder, please," Barney said. "I can hardly hear you."

The humming stopped. Sigmund made a manful effort to forget his fish and focus on the patient. That was what he was there for, after all. "Wouldn't it do just as much good to expose the incision to the sun?" he asked, trying to sound authoritative as well as interested. "Wouldn't it be more natural?"

"I don't kid myself," Barney said. "The ultraviolet doesn't reach the incision. Neither would the sun. The incision is up in my *kishkes* somewhere. They use the ultraviolet for my morale, like the USO. Every morning, they broil me like this. I don't mind, it keeps me busy, it even feels good, but I don't kid myself, the heat doesn't get anywhere near the problem." Barney looked thoughtful for a moment, then went on. "But enough of me. I'm boring. It's the same old stuff, I'm sick of it. What's with you? How's Jenny? How's Amy?"

"Jenny's fine. And it's Annie, you should know that by now, an old friend like you."

"That's what I said. Annie."

But Sigmund, whose nostrils had begun to dilate again, did not feel like arguing this morning.

"And so what's with you?" Barney asked again.

"Me, I'm busy getting ready for the holidays, what else?"

"Another year. I can hardly believe it. I should live to see Yom Kippur." Barney Fribush was treasurer of Sigmund R. Safer's congregation, elected master of the budget and dispenser of financial benefits, including staff paychecks at the synagogue every other week. "And so should the House of Israel," he then added gloomily, under his breath. "With God's help, of course."

In the silence that followed, the cantor, in real pain, winced at Barney's words and their implications, forced to think—against his will—about the rebels at the House of Israel, about their fierce threats to secede and found a new congregation of their own.

They had been at it for months, ever since Passover, snapping out their demands like drill sergeants, disrupting synagogue meetings, rejecting rituals that didn't suit them, pushing others forward if it seemed convenient. They were like the BrownShirts, Sigmund thought; they were like the Nazis. They were making his life miserable, all noisy confrontations made Sigmund's life miserable, especially when they involved passionate congregational crises, of which this was only the latest in an apparently unending series once again brought to furious blood-boil by old-time colleagues and friends. Or supposed friends, he thought, naming names to himself with an unhappy look on his face. (Metzger and Sindel, that gang.) "Yom Kippur's only a month off," he finally said to Barney, lamely. "What is it, four, five weeks?"

But it was as though Barney had already forgotten the House of Israel, as though Sigmund had never spoken. "Did you hear the one about the hostess gown?" Barney asked, managing to sound both hopeful and prurient at the same time.

Sigmund stiffened again. He had an idea of what was coming, even though he wasn't quite sure what a hostess gown actually was. He hated what was coming.

"You zip it down and *du bostes.*" You zip it down and you've got it. All of it. Including the fuzzy little triangle down below. Barney began to laugh out of the corner of his mouth, choking a little on the cigar smoke. "You don't think it's so funny," Barney said, after he stopped coughing. "I should know better by now. You don't like jokes. I keep forgetting, after all these years, no blue stuff in front of the cantor. Sometimes, my friend, you're not the easiest person in the world to talk to, you're so particular." As the signer of Sigmund's paychecks, as well as his old friend, Barney Fribush felt he had the right to say this.

Sigmund, still in no mood to argue, let it pass. He always let Barney talk on, always tried to let him have the last word. That was part of the unspoken terms of their friendship. He was now staring at Barney's pelvic area, which Barney had covered with a hospital washcloth. An appendicitis scar ran like rusty sawteeth down his right side. "That's some cut," Sigmund said, with what sounded like admiration.

"This?" Barney glanced down, puffing smoke at his navel. "It's twenty years old."

Sigmund was sitting on the radiator, gazing over his shoulder every now and then at the steaming city behind him, trying to avoid the demanding presence of Barney's aging scar, his fat sunken belly button, and his soft hairless thighs, stringy with unused muscle. What did women see in Barney Fribush, anyway? What, actually, was the attraction? Because everyone knew that many were attracted. Swiveling uncomfortably as he asked himself these questions (it wasn't as though he hadn't asked them before), Sigmund could feel the sun burning a hole in his back, dead center on his spinal cord. After all these years, he had never really gotten used to the August heat in Baltimore; he had never even gotten used to the idea that he was actually living here, it was so far from what he once had in mind back in Warsaw, in another time. Baltimore, he thought vaguely, trying to distract himself. Baltimore, Maryland, in August. You set sail in life one day, battered suitcase in hand, in a dream state that seemed to go on forever, for years, for decades, and before you knew it . . . Nothing connected. Or everything connected. Sigmund wasn't sure. He had never really decided the question. But while he thought about it again, looking even more severe and abstracted as he considered the possibilities, the room grew ominously quiet. Barney's eyes were half closed. He was falling asleep again. Sigmund felt compelled to say something, if only from a sense of duty. "It was already eighty-two degrees by the time I got downtown this morning," he offered in a loud voice.

Barney opened his eyes, slowly blinking at a lizard's pace, momentarily blinded by the sun. "That's nothing," he finally answered, when he had Sigmund in focus again. "I heard from the *schvartze* orderly the Orioles won again yesterday in ninety-eight temperature. Imagine. Ninty-eight. If it keeps up, we're going to have a pennant."

"That would be nice."

"You don't really care about that, either, do you? A pennant, I mean."

"No, I don't care," Sigmund said matter-of-factly. "Why should

I care? I leave all that to the sports, of which there are always plenty. To the sports and to the children, who need it."

Barney coughed, blowing smoke at his navel again. "Well," he said, "don't underestimate it. It helps to take your mind off yourself. Baseball, I mean. Such things. You shouldn't stick your nose in the air when you hear Orioles. It gives you something to worry about that's not life and death. Every man needs that, especially these days. I don't blow it out of proportion, I know it's only baseball, but life is hard enough." At that, Sigmund could only nod in agreement. "Anyway," Barney continued, "you know me. I believe in winning."

And me, Sigmund wanted to say (for about the thousandth time), I don't even believe in God, but, naturally restraining himself, turned instead to gaze restlessly out the window again at the scorched city below, stretched to the south and the east in endless lines of redbrick row houses. There was haze everywhere, a dusty filigree rising from the harbor and the massive smokestacks of Sparrows Point, farther south, where the steel mills were. Everything still shimmered in the morning heat. A smell of rotting fish rose in the air. Baltimore, Sigmund thought. Baltimore, Maryland, in August, where nothing connected.

"Well, what's the news this morning?" Barney asked.

"I'll read you the paper," Sigmund said, turning back and reaching for the *Sun* at the foot of the bed. He was grateful to have something to do, even though he had already read the paper at breakfast.

"Just the headlines, if you don't mind. Otherwise, it's too much, I haven't got the patience."

"Allies Near Paris," Sigmund read aloud, fooling with his pince-nez.

In bed, Barney grunted approval.

"Reds Wipe Out Trapped Nazis Near Łomza," Sigmund continued, pausing a moment at the headline, as he had over his morning coffee. He knew where Łomza was, he had once been there for a wedding with his older sister, Shifra, when he was a boy. They had made the trip from Warsaw by train, an hour and a half each way. He tried to imagine the old provincial town gutted by Russian artillery fire, dead Germans littering the ground, the more dead Germans the better; then he tried to remember his sister Shifra again, but it was no use, sitting there in the hospital room with his naked friend lying supine in front of him, all that was gone, long ago.

"Don't stop," Barney said, sounding bloodthirsty.

"No Fourth Term for Roosevelt," Sigmund read, happy to move on.

"Says who?"

Sigmund scanned the paper. "Dewey. Or Dulles. One of them."

"They're talking to themselves."

"Superforts Hit Japan Twice at Kyūshū." Sigmund stumbled over the strange name.

"Kyushi?"

"In the north," Sigmund said, reading on to himself. "A fire raid." A shudder passed through him.

"Serves them right. Yellow chinks. Go on."

"Seventh Army Moves North."

And that seemed to be that for the moment. Barney grunted again, mulling over the headlines after Sigmund stopped reading. It was a lot of news to take in, it had to be sorted out, piece by piece. Seventh Army, wherever it was. Patton near Paris. Fire raids in the Orient, scorched bodies. Every morning the news had an epic quality that shook him, that shook Sigmund and everybody else. It had been like that for more than two months, ever since D day. The sheer size of it, the immensity alone, was hard to absorb; they had to work at assimilating it. Some days they could hardly keep up, some days they fell behind, trying to sort it all out. As Sigmund began to straighten out the paper, thinking about Łomza and Paris and Kyūshū again, yesterday's momentous events, a nurse walked into the room, carrying fresh towels. "You think we're about done?" she asked Barney. "Your behind is beginning to turn pink. Or violet. Something peculiar."

"Turn it off."

"Excuse me, sir," she said to Sigmund, placing the towels at the foot of the bed. Then she reached up and turned off the lamp. There was already a sweat stain under her arm.

"That's the cantor," Barney said, pointing at Sigmund with his cigar.

"I think we've met, sir," the nurse said, going on with her chores.

"Probably we have," Sigmund said, nodding coolly. Making his rounds over the years, he had come to know most of the nurses at the hospital; like the patients themselves, they came and they went in well-ordered turns; there were always plenty of new faces, especially since the war had begun. "I'll get out of your way now," Sigmund added. "I have a couple more stops to make before I'm through."

"Don't worry about me," the nurse said.

"I'll see you in a couple of days," Sigmund said to Barney, getting up from the radiator to walk to the door. "Behave yourself, now. Do what they tell you. Be a good boy." Before he could make it around the bed, the washcloth dropped from Barney's groin. Sigmund blanched. The nurse went tsk, Mr. Fribush, hiding a knowing half-smile, and began to hang up the towels. Two slack balls, hanging lazily in a leatherlike pouch, a weary penis that had seen everything (a cynic with one eye), itchy bristles slowly sprouting where there had been pubic hair before the surgeon had made his slice. Sigmund stared at this spongy swamp. There was no telling what you might run into in the hospital. You had to be prepared for anything. There were things Sigmund could tell about . . . On the other side of the bed now, he glanced back, nostrils dilated to their fullest extent. With the lamp turned off, Barney's buttocks had lost their peculiar violet glow. They were now dead-white, like the rest of him. "In a couple of days," Sigmund repeated, looking away.

"If I live."

"Don't worry, you'll live," he said, forgetting his principles for the moment. "And you'll be there for the holidays. You have to be there, you know that, you're an officer of the congregation. And the boys in the choir are wonderful this year. I have four kids from downtown again, each one special. The same alto as last year, the Scheingold kid, he'll break your heart."

Barney rolled over on his back, adjusted his pajamas, pulled up the top sheet. "Here," he said to Sigmund, handing him the cigar. "Do me a favor, put it out someplace."

Sigmund took the cigar between his thumb and forefinger, holding on to the soaking remnants daintily, as though they might be infected, feeling self-conscious standing there in front of Barney's nurse, with his neat graying hair perfectly parted, as always, his tidy European mustache hiding his long upper lip, and his pince-nez, also from Europe, resting affectedly again on the thin bridge of his nose. "Watch out for him, now," Sigmund said to the nurse, trying to sound hearty. "He's a killer."

"He knows better than to fool with me," she said, looking at Barney possessively.

"Half the time she thinks I'm Snyder next door," Barney said.

"You heard what your friend said. Now behave yourself." She stuck a thermometer in his mouth and reached for his pulse.

"So long for now," Sigmund called from the door, cigar butt in hand. "Don't take any wooden nickels."

Barney waved him away with his free hand. But he had to laugh. Wooden nickels. It was typical of the cantor. Another perpetual greenhorn from the old country—among many others just like him—who liked to chew on the Yankee vernacular as though the mere taste of it might help to make him feel like a real American. Well, if that was what it took to keep the cantor happy, Barney Fribush wouldn't argue. Not with happiness. Barney was all for happiness. But he still had to laugh.

In another moment, after fastidiously stubbing out Barney's cigar butt and dumping it in a trash can, Sigmund headed down the stairwell to the floor below, inhaling the antiseptic air all around him in short gaspy breaths, formaldehyde, ether, carbolic acid, feeling faintly queasy somewhere in midgut when the smell really hit him and wondering how the hospital staff could stand it day after day. Oh, God, he thought, trying to hold his breath as he scurried downstairs, pitying the hospital staff, pitying Barney Fribush lying pasted to his grim metal bed on the floor above, and then, as the queasiness expanded to something like full nausea, beginning to feel sorry for himself, too.

Those who serve . . .

2

Soon after moonrise that evening, the Scheingold kid began to dance with his mother in the living room of their skinny little apartment downtown. To accompany them, a radio was playing in a corner of the room on an end table. Doris Day was singing, her honey-husk of a voice perfectly suited to the dim lights, the stillness, the boy's heavy breathing, of which he was barely conscious except as a peculiar sound coming from somewhere nearby, from somewhere inside himself, he finally realized, when he began to pay attention. "Not bad, Sylvan," his mother said, as they moved together across the floor. "Suh-mooth."

He was good at it and knew it. Dancing suited him, although it was not exactly something he was likely to talk about, just like that. Some people might misunderstand, a boy talking about dancing. On this subject, at least, he kept his mouth shut. But he liked the fit of two bodies moving together against a rhythm, everything touching at once, the melody leading both of them on like a trail of gold dust spread at their feet. There was something appropriate about it, something natural and indisputably right. He sang along with Doris Day now, in a falsetto voice, into his mother's ear. They were almost the same height, Sylvan just a half-inch shorter, almost visibly catching up day by day. He led her across the floor and turned unexpectedly, grinning to himself; his mother followed expertly. Then they did it again.

"Slower, darling," she said. "It's too hot for that fancy stuff."

The room was only ten feet wide. There was a daybed set against the wall, on which Sylvan slept every night, one patchy easy chair, and the end table with the radio. In the back of the apartment, facing the alley, was his mother's bedroom, just as spare as the living room up front, except for a few miniature china dolls that stood on her dresser. There was also a bathroom and a tiny kitchen back there, where mother and son had breakfast and supper together most of the time, on a porcelain table that had begun to chip. On some evenings, when his mother worked late, Sylvan fended for himself, putting together a modest supper out of leftover bits and pieces that he ate alone. Sometimes it was only peanut butter, soggy crackers, and milk. While Sylvan ate his meal, often standing up at the sink twitching to the rhythm, the radio played the latest hits at full volume up front.

The Scheingolds lived alone. Mr. Scheingold, the Scheingold kid's father, had run away from East Baltimore years ago and left no forwarding address. (After his departure, Lillian Scheingold had made almost no effort to find him; she barely lifted a finger; good riddance was her expressed opinion, repeated many times to anybody who would listen.) Sometimes Sylvan tried to remember his father and explain his defection to himself, but hard as he tried he could remember nothing, and nothing, of course, could really be explained. Yet the truth was plain enough, it had the clarity of a lightning bolt. Sylvan Scheingold had been dumped by his old man, and so had his mother, Lillian. And that was what was called life, at least downtown in East Baltimore. If you didn't know that by a certain age, if you didn't understand that, you had it coming to you; or, at least, you did in the Scheingold kid's sophisticated judgment.

"Did you take a bath?" Lillian asked in Sylvan's ear.

"Do I smell?"

"Did I say you smell?"

"I took a bath before you came home. I even used some of your salts."

"What about your nails?"

"Impeccable." Sylvan sometimes liked to show off.

"Always take a bath before you go to choir rehearsal or any kind of public function," his mother went on, in a prim voice that she often used when offering social advice to her son. "You never know who you're going to meet. Grooming is as important for a man as a woman."

"I know who I'm going to meet."

"Still." On her cheeks were two perfect rouge marks.

"Safer, Gozlov, Volky, Bourne, and Frisch. The same bunch of grown-up gorillas at every rehearsal. Frisch has hair growing out of his ears."

"Lots of men do, darling." They did a little twirl as the song reached its climax, which left Lillian mildly breathless. "Take it easy, now," she said.

"Then there's the bunch from down here, if you're looking for animals," Sylvan went on. "Marty, Irving, Herschel, and yours truly. The thundering herd. The great unwashed. The tired and the poor. Oh, I know who I'm going to meet."

A retard set in. Doris Day was almost finished. So were Sylvan and his mother, dancing sedately together in their meager first-floor apartment in the narrow row house downtown in East Baltimore. Sylvan's skin glowed now from pleasure and light sweat. His skin was actually a profound olive tone, overlaid at the moment with a moist pink shine. The pink came from the pleasure and the sweat. The olive tone and the pink often gave Sylvan a silken, somewhat burnished look, as though someone had just rubbed him down with a chamois cloth, which some of his mother's friends pretended to envy, claiming that it made him look exotically romantic, like certain Mediterranean movie stars (Ricardo Cortez, perhaps, God forbid), while he saw it as something else, something undesirable, not to be envied, except by fools who didn't know when they were well off. Almost everybody in East Baltimore called Sylvan "Nigger." Some Polacks had shouted it for the first time while stomping him in a corner of the park one afternoon, and the name had stuck. Nigger. Nigger Scheingold. He hated it and dreamed every day of being blond.

They did a little dip then, very practiced and neat. His mother had her own plans for the evening, and she did not want to work herself up before it was really necessary. By work herself up, she meant perspiration. She was wearing a pale green summer dress with white blossoms printed on it, gardenias or camellias, something indeterminate, through which Sylvan could see the outline of her panties when she leaned over to check her leg make-up. His mother didn't wear a girdle, she didn't have to. She had the figure of a sixteen-year-old, everyone said. Fussing with her hair, which was already perfect, Lillian walked over to the radio and turned it off. "That's enough for one night," she said, as the music vanished. "If I'm not here when you get home, there's milk and some grahams."

"Mrs. Safer usually gives us something after rehearsal."

"Well, just in case." A horn blew out front. "There's Herschel's father," Lillian said. "Don't keep him waiting. Gas is gold these days."

"Hey, Nigger," a voice called.

"Have a good time tonight," he said to his mother, even though he didn't actually mean it.

"It's only Stanley Gann."

"You can still have a good time." He reached for his music, checked his olive skin in the hall mirror, shook his head in disbelief. He was surely darker than anybody white he had ever seen. Maybe if he could have a look at his runaway daddy after all these years, the burnished secret might be revealed. You could never tell. As they said, the apple didn't fall far from the tree, it was a wise son, and so on. But there wasn't even a photograph of his father in the house. There was nothing that had ever belonged to him. His mother had destroyed everything that had to do with her husband, including the very sound of his name, which Sylvan was forbidden to say aloud in his mother's presence. The horn blew again. "Let's go," the voice yelled.

Mother and son pecked each other on the cheek. There was a line stretched vertically between his mother's eyes that Sylvan recognized. Whenever his mother looked like that, she was wishing things were different. He wished things were different, too. But then, he had discovered, so did the whole world.

He rushed off, slamming the door. The car was at the curb, its motor was running. Herschel's father, sitting behind the wheel, looked put-upon. It was how he always looked sitting behind the wheel, waiting to make the long trip uptown with the boys, to the other world out in Forest Park, for choir rehearsal. Gas was gold, so was time.

3

The choir gathered for practice in the cantor's dining room. The cantor, naturally, sat at the head of the table, in a Hepplewhite chair with arms and an upholstered seat, while Volkonsky, the choir director, sat opposite him at the foot, in a similar chair, exactly like a good wife. Volkonsky, who understood questions of hierarchy and homage, who had built his entire career on an unusual ability to lead and seem to follow at the same time, also chose to wear a pince-nez on the bridge of his nose, respectfully and unfashionably, with a black satin ribbon dangling smartly below, selected especially for its aristocratic tone. (Sigmund's pince-nez did not have a black ribbon.) Massive scores lay open in front of the cantor and his director, and sharpened pencils were lined up alongside both of them, to mark any changes in notation, of which, at this point in rehearsal for the High Holidays, there were still many. The choir itself, which came together for services only this one time a year, for Rosh Hashana and Yom Kippur, was ranged around the rest of the table on ordinary dining chairs, the boys from downtown jammed between the adult men for discipline's sake (at least, that was the idea), all of them, men and boys, uncomfortably crowded into a room that was far too small to accommodate nine overheated males pressed, for the evening, by urgent artistic questions. In the living room up front, Herschel's father sat reading the sports section of the *Evening Sun*—more upbeat news about the Orioles—waiting for the rehearsal to end, while his old De Soto rested outside.

Sigmund was humming to himself at the moment, again. A cool stream of irrelevant melody, something this time by Victor Herbert, purled through him at a languid tempo. Sigmund often did this at choir rehearsal, humming to himself with his eyes half closed. It was his way of escaping boredom and the need, sometimes, to make a decision. Stern face, lugubrious gaze, lost to the real world, humming. No one in the choir ever challenged Sigmund when he was in one of his melodic trances. No one dared. Not even Volkonsky. Sigmund R. Safer was the cantor, this was his house, and they were all his paid vassals. It had been going on like this for years, in the same way. Only the individual members of the choir sometimes changed, as necessity demanded. The grown-up gorillas, the thundering herd, the great unwashed, the tired and the poor—especially the last, whose voices, at best, had a sharply limited life span.

From the foot of the table, Volkonsky watched his boss anxiously, waiting for a cue. While he waited, alert to the cantor's every sleepy move, he chewed on his lower lip, taking little nips out of the tender flesh, which hurt. (Like all true stoics, Volkonsky didn't mind the pain.) Cues, in any case, were the essence of Volkonsky's job; he had spent his entire life waiting for cues, only to pass them on to others. That had always meant an inescapable dependence on the attentiveness and respect of his colleagues and on the annual good will of each member of the choir as well, which Volkonsky had come to think of, exactly like any other second-in-command, as "his" choir rather than the cantor's, or even the House of Israel's.

A familiar restlessness set in now as they all waited for the cantor to make up his mind. Volkonsky waited, the choir waited. The cantor seemed especially remote tonight. F or F-sharp? Two voices or one? If one, which one? (Midway down the table, the Scheingold kid slid to his right, resting on one buttock, as Irving Karton's knowing fingers began to reach for his thigh. Irving Karton, who smelled faintly sour, both breath and body, was always at the Scheingold kid, always hoping to distract or embarrass him, trying to give him a hard-on in front of everyone, especially if he had been handed another unexpected solo.)

They were working on the Silent Devotion for the first morning of the Holy Days—Rosh Hashana morning—and had been at it for over an hour. It was exhausting work, painstaking in the details, that took everything out of them—the heart of the service. Silent Devotion was a prayer of the most austere, most private faith, supplicant to God, alone, offered first by the congregation in a deathly hush on their own, then repeated aloud, in gorgeous melodies, by the cantor and the choir. A little scary, they all secretly believed, especially the boys from downtown. Maybe too private, too austere, certainly not something to be fooled with. And as if that weren't enough, Silent Devotion was filled with huge abstract ideas that made them all put on serious faces, massive hefts of thought and feeling expressed in words that gleamed incomprehensibly in both English and Hebrew. Beneficent. Mighty. Revered and Sublime. Redeemer, Savior, Dominion, and Power. The Pursuit of Perfection (but not Happiness). Language that was beyond the reach of Irving Karton, Marty Schiffman, Herschel Bleiber, and Sylvan Scheingold, except in the dimmest tribal sense. And almost, as well, beyond their elders (the cantor and his director always excepted), who surrounded them at the table—the grown-up gorillas, again, Zev Gozlov, the Russian bass from Odessa; Jeffrey Bourne, the baritone, who was only half Jewish; and Sy Frisch, who sang tenor and had a bush of black hair growing out of each ear.

But it didn't matter that Sigmund R. Safer's choir barely understood the literal meaning of the Silent Devotion. No one in the congregation could tell, anyway. What mattered was that the choir have the emotional sense of it, that they have it exactly right, down to every wrenching nuance; that was what was important. Congregants at the House of Israel wept when the cantor and his choir repeated the Silent Devotion on the synagogue's great pulpit. It was one of the chief reasons they came to services, to be reminded again of how to weep together in public, sharing this age-old pleasure, which left them feeling spiritually purified, with their beloved families and friends who surrounded them on every side. It helped that the cantor had a bright lyric tenor with a never-failing sweet timbre and an extended range, a rarity that had been compared, once or twice, to John McCormack's own shining Irish voice—a voice that could be depended on to stir up certain essential emotions. And in the bargain the cantor knew how to sing, really sing, that is, not croon or moan or wail in exaggerated pain, as was the style on certain pulpits around town. (That kind of excess had always offended Sigmund.) Together on the High Holidays, when the occasion asked for it, Sigmund and the choir at the House of Israel could unman the congregation during services, bringing on the welcome release of communal tears and causing ripples of unexpected religious passion to suddenly spread throughout the vast sanctuary without warning.

The power of music—and the human voice—Sigmund sometimes thought, in a kind of religious passion himself at the idea, the giddy unsettling spiritual power of both. It seemed ennobling, somehow, to be part of that, to be central to it, even though Sigmund had always remained dubious about the efficacy of spiritual power, even though he didn't actually believe . . .

There was a sudden racket at the table, a babble of boys' voices, a couple of chairs noisily scraping the floor. Sigmund hissed angrily. He was still marking his score, which was already covered with faded notes from previous years, still humming something by Victor Herbert under his breath, almost ready to make a move. (By now, the Scheingold kid had grabbed Irving Karton's wandering fingers and bent his right thumb back as far as it would go; Irving swallowed a scream.) The cantor said something about the text, about F-sharp. That decision was finally made. There was a clearing of throats, a cough or two, the cantor sounded his pitch pipe, and in a moment Jeffrey Bourne, right ear cupped in his hand, began to sing an exquisite lament in perfect phonetic Hebrew. Within seconds, everyone quieted down. Even Irving Karton. Jeffrey Bourne's voice had the irresistible texture and color of melted chocolate (like the best chocolate, it flowed thickly and easily), and when Jeffrey Bourne sang a capella, they all listened, solemn-faced, around the table, with admiration and chronic envy, Volkonsky even reminded of evenings at the Berlin Opera during the twenties, a glorious momentary flash of his own European past that vanished almost as soon as it appeared.

The baritone opened up to full volume, still exquisitely on-pitch. As he sang, he threw his head back, letting the tones pour out in the small room. Son of a bitch, Zev Gozlov was thinking, eyes glistening with mixed emotion; true to form, like Sy Frisch and all the boys, he admired what he heard, but he wished it were the sound of his own voice filling the room. At the other end of the table, meanwhile, Sigmund stared at the chandelier hanging above him, as though he had never seen it before, then closed his eyes against the glare, deep in real thought at last. Jeffrey Bourne, he was thinking, knew how to produce a wonderful sound, the voice was gorgeous, who could deny it, but maybe, Sigmund was thinking, maybe he was growing just a little too pleased with himself. Jeffrey Bourne had that look. Self-congratulatory, self-important, self-absorbed. Sigmund had seen it all before. There had once been a tenor imported from Philadelphia for the holidays . . . Too much pride and too much greed for recognition, followed inevitably by too many demands, as well as an irresistible need to try to exceed the cantor himself. That was the unforgivable part, what inevitably caused trouble. Still, Sigmund knew when not to complain.

There was no way to follow Jeffrey Bourne when he was in full voice. Everyone understood that. After he finished, on a ringing G that could be heard in every house on the block, the group work resumed. Harmonies sluggishly found their place, balances were struck, tenor to baritone, baritone to bass, and around again in a full circle, the boys' voices contained somewhere inside the rest. Soon they were back to normal. A kind of rehearsal drudgery set in, a familiar repetitive dullness that they all dreaded, and with it Sigmund's concentration suddenly lapsed again, along with everyone else's this time. There was a false note from the Scheingold kid, immediately corrected by Volkonsky. Then Sylvan's alto, as burnished as his skin, suddenly rose in the air like a column of shining metal. Another wonderful sound, almost as wonderful as Jeffrey Bourne's. (Nigger! Irving Karton whispered, without moving his lips.) But Sylvan was off-pitch again. He could hear it himself. Again, Volkonsky corrected him. "Sit up straight," Sigmund suddenly barked at Sylvan, who was slumping in his chair while Volky talked on. "How do you expect to sound like anything when you're bent over like that?" There was a brief stir of interest among the rest of the boys at this, but as soon as Sylvan pulled himself up, torpor set in again. Over the buzz of Volky's patient voice, Sigmund could hear his wife putting out raisin buns in the kitchen. There would also be iced tea and milk for the choir. Herschel Bleiber's father, snoring lightly now in the living room, would join them for a snack, waiting for a chance to complain to the cantor that his son had fewer solos this year than last. (Herschel's father saw his son as a successor to Bobby Breen.)

A moment later the warm scent of Jenny Safer's raisin buns reached them all in the dining room. Oh, my God, they all thought, in unison. They could hardly wait. Even Sigmund grew attentive. The door to the kitchen swung open and Jenny Safer appeared, pushing a loaded tea cart into the dining room. At the sight of her, the boys gave a shout of pleasure. It was the end of Silent Devotion.

Later that night, after the choir, well stuffed for their efforts, had finally dispersed, Sigmund sat alone and uninterrupted among his fish tanks, staring fitfully at the glittering activity all around him. At last . . .

He was surrounded by four giant freshwater tanks and several smaller containers, mainly used for breeding purposes, in a back room in the Safers' shingled house; there was nothing else in the room except the chair he sat on and a small table holding fish food and cleaning equipment. Inside the tanks, swordtails and black mollies swept by in front of him, flashing in the dim aqueous light. Guppies were everywhere, eating their young. Swaying greens grew at the sandy bottom of each tank, white coral made hidden little tunnels through which the fish chased each other. Sigmund could sit for hours like this, watching, in an addictive state. His eyes craved the movement in his fish tanks. It never failed him, never let him down, never disappointed, unlike most things that were merely human. The pointless rush and sudden calms, the sweep of flicking tails through the pale green water, the pursuits and hunts, the sweet chaos that was always the same. There were nights when he couldn't get enough of it, when it got so late that Jenny finally had to call him upstairs to bed. His mind, no longer bored, floated now with the swordtails and the mollies. The water breathed aloud, strings of willowy fish excrement sank slowly to the bottom of the tanks, clouds formed and dispersed as the oxygen pumps did their noisy work.

In the next room, a drawer slammed. Annie, Sigmund thought, without moving. Annie Safer, the other house atheist. As though one in the family weren't enough, or, in this family, more than enough. And Annie—excruciating thought—didn't even believe in the Jews, she was an atheist even about history, if you could credit half of what she said. Sigmund heard her shuffling around her room, dropping her shoes, discarding clothes on the floor, banging into the furniture. Typical Annie, typical carelessness, making a mess, as though nothing or nobody else mattered. A moment passed. Slowly it became quiet again. Sigmund still sat without moving, watching his fish. But he had lost his concentration. His daughter had stolen it, leaving him vulnerable again. An echo of the evening's rehearsal sounded briefly in the room, the choir still at work, Jeffrey Bourne's baritone. Gorgeous sounds, but intrusive. Then, through the sounds, accompanied by them, an image of his old pal Barney Fribush floated up, lying so still in his hospital bed, naked to the world. (Sigmund still did not move.) The rebels at the House surfaced next, the heated faces of old friends, so-called, old colleagues, shouting angry threats at the rest of the congregation. (Metzger and Sindel, that gang.) Annie's door slammed. Sigmund heard a drawer bang shut again. At least she was home, at least she was in her own room, where she belonged.

Sigmund shifted in his chair, poking distractedly at his pince-nez. A rainbow labyrinth swam by, carrying its oxygen supply in a head cavity, then angels, swarming in a tank of their own. He turned from one to the other, without favorites, watching. Weird creatures of ineffable beauty, he thought, in an unexpected surge of poetic feeling, accidents of evolution, arbitrary byways of natural selection. Outside the mainstream, fragile part of another unreal world. A little like the Scheingold kid's voice, he decided, a little like Sylvan Scheingold's anomalous burnished alto, which, Sigmund knew, was not long for this world. When the voice broke, when the wicked hormones attacked and claimed their own, what would he be left with? Ah, Sigmund thought, his eyes craftily following another labyrinth as it darted into a coral maze, if the Scheingold kid was lucky. But Sigmund was suddenly too sleepy to worry about the matter. He could hardly keep his eyes open; and none of it really seemed to matter, when you came down to it. All those feverish human distractions; and the shapeless unreadable mass of other people's lives, including his own daughter's. He caught himself then, at the thought of Annie, who was just a seventeen-year-old kid, after all, a mere senior in high school. He was beginning to sound bilious and griping, far more than usual, far more than was acceptable, and he didn't like it.

4

Lillian Scheingold was fumbling for her house key, standing on the little white marble stoop in front of the brick row house where she and Sylvan shared their apartment. On the step below, hands in his pockets, Stanley Gann pretended to be waiting patiently. At last, Lillian turned to him, key in hand. "This is no way," Stanley said, through his teeth. Lillian didn't answer him. She was staring at a tuft of black hair curling at the open neck of his sports shirt. She had been staring at it, more or less, all evening. "I mean, we're consenting adults," Stanley added.

"I don't see that I've consented to anything," Lillian said. "Not that I recall, anyway." Lillian could also see the yellow quarter-moon suppended high above Stanley's shoulder. "It was a nice evening. Thanks."

"Can't I even come in for a sec?"

"No, you can't. My son sleeps in the front room. And he needs his rest, like all of us. But that's not the point."

"What's the point, then?"

"You can't come in just like that."

"Why not, sweetheart?"

"Because I don't allow that." Nevertheless, something familiar stirred inside her. A small wave began to crest in the pit of her stomach. Sweetheart. Two syllables only. She wanted to reach out now and touch him.

"Lillian, I'm in terrible pain." A moan escaped him.

"You can't hold me responsible."

"Let's walk over to the park."

"It's late, Stanley. I have to go to work tomorrow. So do you. And I wouldn't walk over to the park, anyway. You want to get your head bashed in?"

"Lillian."

"Listen, it was a nice evening. I enjoyed the movie. Esther Williams looks great underwater. It was nice. Let's try to keep it that way." There was the sound of tapping at one of the front windows. Lillian looked over and saw Sylvan waving her inside. A pang of resentment, which she tried to ignore, swept through her.

"Isn't that Nigger?" Stanley asked.

"His name is Sylvan," Lillian snapped. She was always indignant at "Nigger"; like her son, she hated the word. "Listen. I have to go," she added. "Thanks, Stan. It was really nice. You're a nice man. You really are."

"Lillian, please." He moaned again.

"Call me, I'd like that," she said, trying to soften her tone at last. Then she slipped inside before he could show her the condom he was hiding in the palm of his hand.

Inside, she discovered crumbs on the living-room floor. "You know better than that," Lillian said to Sylvan. "Eat crackers in the kitchen and only in the kitchen. Next thing we'll have roaches."

"You don't have to yell," he said.

"I'm not yelling. I'm just telling you."

"What'd you do tonight?"

"We went to the movies."

"What'd you see?"

"*Bathing Beauty.*"

Sylvan made a disgusted sound.

"How was rehearsal?"

"Fine."

"I don't know what fine means. Be specific."

"I got another solo. The cantor likes me. Volky likes me. They all like me out there." Watching her, bright-eyed, he said nothing about Irving Karton, about singing off-pitch, about being scolded; he never told that part of it.

"Did they find a place for you to stay?" Lillian asked.

"I forgot to ask," he said.

"Well, ask next time," she said. "It's important. If they won't let you ride on the holidays, if they insist on being that strict, you should at least stay with a nice family."

By nice, Sylvan knew that his mother meant rich. "Did Stan the Gann make a pass at you?" he asked.

"You always get around to that sooner or later, don't you?"

"Did he?"

"Stanley Gann is a perfect gentleman."

"I don't know what perfect means. Be specific."

"You mind your own business. I don't like fresh kids."

Sylvan had begun to make up his bed. As he worked, tiny pearls of sweat shone on his upper lip. A sheet flapped in the air, then floated down onto the daybed like a parachute. The bed had to be made up every night, then remade each morning before Sylvan started his day. He tucked everything in and folded down the top sheet, as Lillian had taught him, while she began to make a halfhearted attempt to remove her Woolworth's necklace.

"Give me a hand," she said. "I'm exhausted tonight. I can hardly stand up."

He moved behind his mother, staring at the faint down that lay on the nape of her neck below the hairline. He could barely make it out, it was so wispy. Sylvan reached up to unclasp the necklace, taking his time about it. What had happened tonight? he asked himself. It was the same question he asked himself every night when his mother went out with one or another of her faithful swains. (That was Sylvan's word for them, stolen from an Errol Flynn movie.) There was always somebody hanging around the apartment, waiting. What did that mean? Stan the Gann. Reuven Buchsbaum. Al Miller. A couple of new guys who were still without names. His mother was popular.

"Hurry, for God's sake," she said. "I haven't got all night."

"Here," he answered, thrusting the necklace into his mother's hand. All the 4-Fs, he thought. Joe Applefeld. Louis Breithauser. Murray Frank. Mickey Schiller. A boring collection of flat feet, mistreated hernias, heart murmurs, ulcerated intestines, myopic eyes. One of them was even pickled with psoriasis from head to toe. America's dreamboats, or nightmares, depending on how you looked at it, all of them left behind for the duration. Nobody wanted them. What kind of popularity was that?

Lillian moved away from him then, jangling the necklace. They said good night politely, Lillian taking the bathroom first. She always took the bathroom first, it was the rule. When he finally got in there, he could smell her talc and the heavy perfume she bought at the drugstore. His history teacher used the same scent. Lillian's toothbrush lay dripping on the washbasin, the toothpaste cap had fallen to the floor, there were loose hairs in the sink. She was very sloppy sometimes, usually at the end of the day, after work, when she was tired. He arranged everything neatly, screwed the top onto the toothpaste tube, hung up her washcloth after wringing it out. Then he cleaned her hairbrush until it looked like new. That was the best part of all, cleaning his mother's hairbrush. Finally, when he was finished, looking up, he met his own eyes staring back at him from the bathroom mirror. He would take care of his mother, he said to himself firmly. Nothing could be more natural or more important. He had always taken care of her, ever since his forgetful father had flown the coop and escaped to no-man's-land or wherever he was. Who better than the Scheingold kid?

5

By three o'clock in the morning, the Scheingolds, mother and son, were both sleeping like bricks in their noodle-shaped apartment downtown, each encased in ordinary dreams that they would forget as soon as they woke up, when habit would take over again and they would share a light breakfast together in their tiny kitchen and review the events of the previous evening, the way they always did before the day began.

Uptown in Forest Park, Sigmund R. Safer was less lucky. In a sleep that was not quite a sleep, hovering indecisively between one world and another, in an amorphous state approaching semiconsciousness, he suddenly moaned once or twice in his dreams, awakening his wife alongside him. It was Jenny Safer's impression, as she lay there listening in the dark, that her husband was having trouble breathing. She couldn't be sure. He was certainly making a peculiar sound, like gravel being painfully worked through a tight sieve. Jenny called to Sigmund in a worried voice, then, when he didn't respond, she began to poke him hard on the upper arm with her forefinger. She kept this up, poking hard just below the shoulder, until he seemed to settle down a bit and his breathing grew easier. In a moment, Sigmund mumbled an incomprehensible word or two, as though he were trying to reassure his wife, turned on his back, and almost immediately began to snore in a kind of adenoidal ecstasy that was now a regularized part of the Safer marital rituals, the subject of any number of corny family jokes. Instantly relieved, Jenny, too, soon fell back to sleep.

Also around the same hour, Barney Fribush's temperature finally dropped to normal for the first time since his operation, as he slept on in a nearly dreamless state in his metal hospital bed high above the steaming city. In the streets below, there was a steady rumble of trucks delivering fresh produce to the downtown markets, while overhead a dusty moon dimly illuminated the city in the west. Out in the hospital corridor, everything was quiet, but every now and then a night nurse stuck her head in the door of Barney's room to make sure that he was still there, breathing.

All seemed to be well with the patient.

Two

1

"Mr. Fribush, please." Barney's nurse was folding towels again.

"You mean to tell me you never saw one before? Come on, Belda."

"You're impossible," she said, turning her back. There was a limit, evidently, to how much even she could take. "And it's Velda. You know that. V-e-l-d-a. Velda."

"Velda. What a name. Where'd that come from?"

"I told you before, Tennessee. From my mother, from her side."

"Velda. What a name."

"Cover yourself. It's indecent."

Barney Fribush laughed and stubbed out his cigar. He was in high spirits. He glanced down at his pubis and laughed again. The doctors had just told him that he was going home within twenty-four hours. His temperature had been normal for three days, ninety-eight point six on the nose. The doctors had also told him that he was clear, that his problem was neatly detached from the colonic tissue in which it had embedded itself. That was the way one of them had worded it when they gave him the news. They had won a great victory, they added, standing in their white coats at Barney's bedside, preening in front of the patient. You sons of bitches, Barney thought to himself as they looked down at him, always bragging, you think you won a great victory, what about me? It's my asshole. Or was, until you guys struck pay dirt. But he had kept quiet, after making a terrific effort to contain himself that had finally left him exhausted. What difference did it make, anyway? His temperature was normal and he was clear. He had their word for it. He could now pick up his life where he had left off. He could go back to being like everybody else. Normal. Regular. A little of this, a little of that. As long as his mutilated colon continued to cooperate, of course. He turned toward the sun now, deciding to give his doctors the benefit of the doubt for once, and began to plan the future.

"You didn't fill out the lunch menu," Velda said, facing him again from the foot of the bed.

"I'll eat anything they've got."

"But you hate boiled fish. Last week you wouldn't touch it."

"Last week I wasn't feeling so great."

"The boiled fish is all right?"

"As long as it's kosher."

"You know everything is kosher around here."

"How do I know? You don't let me see the kitchen. Where is the kitchen, anyway? For all I know, everything is mixed up, milk and meat, and you use the same dishes for everything."

Velda didn't answer. She couldn't swear to anything when it came to the kitchen. There had been a minor scandal or two about kosher in her time at the hospital. Sometimes they were a little careless down there. They forgot the rules, they got caught up in other things. And her interest, in any case, was limited by the fact that she wasn't even a Hebrew, as everyone she knew in Tennessee called it. Still, she admired the way the sticklers for the Hebrew law insisted on their codes. They were relentless in their own behalf, they fought for their beliefs. Like Barney Fribush. Her church could use a little of that.

"Well, I'll check off the boiled fish and potato," she finally said, in a resigned voice. "You want rice pudding for dessert?"

"Ice cream sounds better."

"There isn't any ice cream today."

"I'll pay extra for it."

"You can't pay extra because there isn't any."

"Why don't you just run across the street to Arundel's and pick up a pint of peach for me?"

"I can't leave the floor, you know that. You're not the only patient I have to worry about."

"Well, if it's not ice cream, what do you suggest?" He rolled his eyes exaggeratedly at her and licked his lips.

"Stop that now. You're impossible."

"You love it."

"Pull up your pants."

"I like the breeze to get me there. It hits the spot."

"What are you talking about, there hasn't been a breeze in three days. It's ninety-two outside again."

They both looked out the window, where the city lay shimmering lazily in the celebrated summer heat. The summer heat, a new record even for Baltimore, was on the front page of the *Sun* every day now, along with the war, the Orioles, and the question of a fourth term for FDR. But Barney Fribush was indifferent to the front page this morning, as well as to the August heat. The temperature could go up to a hundred and ten for all he cared. He had other matters on his mind. His only problem had been eliminated. His colonic tissue was clear. He had won a great victory over dire fate, he was one of the few, his doctors had told him, clustered around his bed, once they stopped boasting about themselves. The future was his again. Soon he would be back to managing his affairs down at the factory, near the old B & O station over in Camden, where he made rubber heels for men's shoes, more rubber heels than anybody else on the entire Atlantic seaboard; and as soon as he had Tiger Pads under control (he was already on the phone with his plant manager twice a day), he would turn his attention back to the House of Israel, where there was always plenty to do; when it came to things to do, in fact, the House was almost as demanding as the factory. More, maybe.

At the House of Israel, he would first check out the books to make sure that the finances were still in order after his absence (you never knew in this world). Then he would have a quick look at the way seat sales were going for the holidays, not that he expected any problem. The House was always SRO for the holidays, they had to open up the auditorium in the rear of the synagogue and the small sanctuary downstairs to accommodate the swollen crowd. And, finally and unequivocally, he would turn his full attention to putting the defecting rebels in their place. The rebels were a real priority. Just thinking about them turned Barney's saliva sour, especially when he remembered that some of his oldest friends, including one or two *momsers*, true bastards he would like to give the back of his hand to, were among the leaders. (That really gave Barney Fribush indigestion, the thought of his traitorous old friends, led by Julie Metzger, first among many.) They could destroy the House of Israel with their rancor. They were already forcing everyone to choose sides, their way or the old way, no middle road, no compromise. Bullies, that's what they were, power-mad bullies. Barney would take care of them, even if the rabbi couldn't. (The rabbi! Another deep thinker, like the cantor, another airy dreamer, with his head in the clouds, who couldn't even be trusted to cross the street alone.) All in due time.

He sat up in bed. "I thought you had to go," he said to Velda, who was taking an unauthorized break in the room's single easy chair. "I thought you were so busy."

Velda gave him a dirty look that he had seen and enjoyed several times before during his hospital stay and left without a word, angrily pulling the pneumatic door to behind her as she stalked out of the room. A sweet silence followed. Velda, he thought, suddenly filled with rueful feelings of good will. One competent *shiksa*, if you asked Barney Fribush, a little tall, maybe, a little rawboned, a little too broad in the shoulders, a farm girl, after all, what could you expect; but she knew her business. And Barney Fribush really admired people who knew their business. He hated to think what might have become of Barney Fribush without Velda Reese at his side.

Barney stretched, purring a little. The morning sun almost blinded him. He welcomed it. Outside, a cloud puffed slowly along, taking five minutes to travel a single block. Another wonder. Vague sounds of traffic rose to Barney's window. His purring grew louder. He would be home on Hilton Street tomorrow, safe on his own property. It didn't matter that he would be there alone, a rich widower, and growing richer every day from the manufacture of rubber heels, with a vigilant servant his only company. He would sit up in bed at home, among all the mementos of married life, and gaze out the window at the beautiful circular lake, at beautiful Ashburton, spread out at his feet, the whole city sprawling below him on a long, softly declining hill that eventually led, miles away, to the harbor itself. There was no place better to live in Baltimore, no place else for Barney Fribush. Hilton Street with its great brick and stucco houses and its great steep terraces sitting high above Ashburton Lake and everything else. Home.

2

"I know this is presumptuous," Jenny Safer was saying into the phone a couple of days later. "I know I have no right to ask. Especially now, with your condition. But I thought, it's still another three, four weeks. And in three, four weeks . . . you know?" There was a clear note of respect in her voice, respect and diffidence and doubt, all designed to give Barney an out. She was doing her job as the wife of the cantor. Still, she hesitated.

"You can ask me anything," Barney answered from his bedroom on Hilton Street. "You know that."

After waiting a moment, Jenny rushed on. "I'm asking for the boy, for his sake. It's for the three nights, first and second Rosh Hashana and Yom Kippur. You'll hardly see him. He'll be on the pulpit with the choir almost the whole time."

"I owe God a few favors," Barney said, in a voice that seemed to turn Barney and God into active accomplices.

"Everybody has a place except the boy," she continued, sounding more confident now. "He's the last one. Volkonsky's coming here, he comes here every year, so is the baritone, you know, Jeffrey Bourne. Gozlov goes to the Berman widow on Fairview Avenue, as usual." Jenny suddenly began to laugh into the mouthpiece. "God only knows what goes on there," she added, still laughing after a hilarious pause. "Well, anyway, Frisch walks from home, two miles. The other boys have places. He's the only one left."

"I'll do it. I'll do it for you, Jenny. Not for just anybody, but for you. It's an empty house, anyway. Why shouldn't I do it? He'll have his own room and his own bath, with shower. Now tell me, I have to ask, is he clean?"

"Oh, immaculate."

"Because you know I don't put up with unclean."

"You're just home, Barney, you're still taking treatment. Are you sure it isn't asking too much?"

"Elsie is here. She runs the works. She's the boss in this house. Anyway, it's nothing. I owe God a couple of favors. I already told you. I'll do it."

"What about your daughter?"

"What about her?"

"Isn't she coming from Washington?"

"She and her husband go reformed in Chevy Chase. They only come for Passover."

"What a heart you've got, Barney."

"It's true, I know it, what a heart I've got. Don't forget it, either. Not everybody has a heart. It's a fact. Now tell me something, Jenny, are you happy?"

Jenny was silent. This wasn't the first time she had heard this question from Barney Fribush.

"Jenny? I'm talking to you. Answer my question. One favor for another. Are you happy?"

"Barney."

"Because I know what it is to be unhappy. I know how life is. Anybody can be unhappy, it doesn't have to be anybody's fault. You know what I'm talking about? Of course you know what I'm talking about. Anyway, you know where I am, sweetheart, you know who's your friend. I've been your friend since the first time I laid eyes on you."

"The boy's name is Sylvan Scheingold."

"Don't change the subject on me."

"The boy's name is Sylvan Scheingold. He has a beautiful voice, you remember him from last year. He has no father. His father ran away. He's a little dark is all."

"The one they call Nigger."

"Some of the kids do. But not us, not you."

"He's darker than Elsie. That's what I remember. Well, just so he's clean. I can't stand unclean. I don't put up with that. Jenny, are you listening to me? You're a gorgeous woman, Jenny. A knockout. I always thought so."

"Barney."

"Jenny, I don't talk this way to most people. Most women. I'm not like that. You know me."

"Make sure you get enough rest. The holidays are enough of a strain without everything else. Take care of yourself."

"Remember what I said. Think of Barney Fribush. Anybody can be unhappy, it's not a sin. I'm here. Remember that. I'm here for you."

A few minutes later, Sigmund, propped up against his pillows in bed, near the phone, said, "Then it's arranged?" He was waiting for the ten-o'clock news to come on the radio.

"I don't feel right," Jenny said, "imposing on him like this. He's just home."

"All he had to do was say no. Barney Fribush knows how to say no when he wants to. Nobody's forcing him. It's his choice. And probably a little company'll do him good." As he talked on, rationalizing, Sigmund began to sound almost cheerful.

"Well, anyway," Jenny said, hesitating again, "he's something, considering what he's been through."

"You should have seen him in the hospital naked in front of the nurses." Sigmund, overcome by the memory, shook his head in disbelief. "But at least everybody's taken care of now," he added.

"Everybody," Jenny said. "The Karton boy and Marty Schiffman are going to the Schatzes', in an attic room."

"Nobody ever says no to you. Nobody can turn you down."

"I've had a lot of practice at this, if you don't mind my saying so."

Sigmund didn't mind—not much, really—but there seemed to be a definite extra charge to this remark that he did not feel like dealing with at the moment. Jenny sometimes took him by surprise with her remarks. She could pinch. When she did, Sigmund was not always sure how to respond. Sometimes, to his amazement, a little wave of fear passed through him, a tremor that could momentarily rattle his dignity and calm, as though he were still a helpless child being scolded by his mother; but those moments were infrequent, and mostly he let them slip by and discreetly hid his real feelings for the time being. It was one of the quirks of marriage, he told himself. Every marriage had its quota. You took them as they came. In any case, Sigmund knew the danger, sometimes lethal, of constantly facing up to the truth. He let this opportunity pass, too, getting quietly out of bed and heading for the bathroom. The bathroom was always safe. "Don't forget to call me if the news comes on," he said over his shoulder, quickly slipping into the sanctum, as the whole Safer family only half jokingly referred to it.

As soon as she heard the bathroom door close behind him, Jenny moved over to her dressing table, irresistibly driven by a need to confirm—or deny—Barney Fribush's compliments. The table, which she called her "vanity" and about which she had possessive feelings, was sparely furnished with beauty aids. A couple of austere lipsticks, rouge pot, face powder, a hoarded scent from prewar Paris. Touches of each were all she ever used. A bunch of Sigmund's roses, plucked from the four hybrid tea bushes he cultivated in the Safer back yard, stood in a vase in front of her. Pinks, yellows, enameled reds—tributes to Jenny from her husband. Sitting down at the table, she began to gaze shyly at herself in the oval mirror, feeling guilty and pleased at the same time. A flicker of a smile, half ironic, wavered self-consciously at a corner of her mouth. That was all she would allow herself. A knockout, Barney Fribush had said . . . as though he hadn't been talking like that for years to half the women in the congregation.

Without thinking, then, Jenny did an uncharacteristic thing, letting her kimono fall open as she sat at her vanity. Underneath, she was naked. The sight of herself in the mirror took her by surprise. She saw the startling white gloss of her body instantly reflected back, her familiar full breasts, the slight sweet scoop at the base of her throat, and, best of all, the soft fall of her fine black hair, already hanging to her waist for the night. Jenny loved her hair; all women loved their hair, she told herself defensively. She also noted again how rosy her nipples were. That had always interested her, ever since she was a girl. Cupping a hand beneath each breast, surprised again, but not quite so surprised as a moment ago, she lifted them gently, giving herself a teasing look at the same time, as though she realized how absurd the gesture was, how flirtatious, but staying that way for another moment. Slowly, her expression became serious. She still had a few good years coming to her, was what she saw in the mirror, that and her own familiar plummy fullness intact. Nothing absurd there . . .

In the bathroom, the toilet flushed. Sigmund again. In a moment he would start to do his vocal exercises before listening to the news and going to sleep. It was the same routine every night, unless he got overinvolved with his fish. The exercises, he claimed, were essential to the well-being of his voice. Probably they were, Jenny thought, feeling expansive. Jenny was no expert when it came to singing, but she had her opinions on the subject, which she knew how to express.

When the singing began in the bathroom, not real singing but a series of mountain-climbing mi-mi-mi-mi's up and down the scale, Jenny pulled her kimono around her. Was she happy? Was anybody? It was hard to say the word "unhappy" to yourself, it rang with such a dull metallic thud that threatened to stay with you forever. If she wasn't happy, it didn't have to be anybody's fault. She had to try to remember that. Should the unlikely occasion ever really arise, she quickly added to herself, in a ladylike inner voice that she was accustomed to using interchangeably in public and private, as the cantor's wife.

On the other side of the bathroom door, Sigmund had begun to practice his trills. Trills were one of his weak spots, and he was conscientious about improving them, as he was about everything that had to do with his voice. Ah, Jenny thought, listening to her husband practice his trills in the family sanctuary . . . the nerve of Barney Fribush.

3

"Is Annie home?"

It was the following evening. Jenny was out at her weekly mah-jongg game. Sigmund, shading his eyes, peered through the screen door, out to the front porch. In one hand he carried a cardboard container filled with a squirming mass of tiny white worms. "Who is it?" he asked, trying to keep the edge out of his voice.

"Bobby." A figure out there was weaving in and out of the shadows like a prizefighter.

"Bobby who?"

"Bobby Fiorentino."

Sigmund shifted his worms to his other hand. His fish were waiting for them. He also growled quietly. The figure on the porch might just as well have replied "Benito Mussolini." "Fioren . . . ?" Sigmund began.

"Tino."

"Sorry," Sigmund said. "We already get the *Saturday Evening Post*."

Out on the porch, Bobby Fiorentino sighed and moved toward the screen door. "Is Annie home?" he asked again, closing in slowly.

There was only a slight hesitation. "No."

"You sure?"

"Now look here, young man . . ."

"I mean, the light's on in her bedroom, with all due respect."

"How do you know which one is her bedroom?"

"She told me she'd be home."

"You expect me to stand here and argue with you?"

"I'm sorry, sir. Please tell her I stopped by. The way she asked."

"I'll tell her."

"Well, I would really be grateful if you did that. Sir."

"She has a lot of friends," Sigmund said. "She knows a lot of boys." The bottom of the cardboard container was growing soggy.

Sigmund could feel the movement of the worms begin to shift. His fish . . .

"What time will she be home?"

"She didn't say."

"You really should turn off her bedroom light."

"I pay the bills around here and you don't hear me complaining."

"Oh, sure thing. I meant nothing disrespectful."

It was growing dark. Bobby Fiorentino was disappearing into the shadows on the porch. Crickets whirred frantically in the dusk. Lightning bugs were beginning to spark the night air. "You live in the neighborhood?" Sigmund called out, unable to restrain himself.

"Over in Woodlawn." There was no response to this. Sigmund didn't know anybody who lived over in Woodlawn. Nor was he ever likely to, even though it was only a couple of blocks away. Woodlawn was for others. "Well, see you again," Bobby finally said.

Sigmund remained silent. Bobby Fiorentino backed off slowly, then pivoted and took the porch steps two at a time. Heading down the street, past the Safers' perfect hedges, he looked back steadily over his shoulder, as though he were trying to fix the house and everything that went with it in his memory. Then he turned the corner onto Maine Avenue and disappeared.

There was only a moment's respite. "Daddy?" The voice came from the back of the house, from the room next to his fish.

Sigmund waited a second or two while he prepared himself. "What?" he finally answered, his shoulders tightening.

"What's going on out there?"

"Nothing."

"Who's there?"

"Nobody."

"I thought I heard voices. I know I heard voices. I'm expecting somebody."

"I'll keep an eye out."

Annie Safer, he thought guiltily, glancing over his shoulder with a reflexive gesture, as though he were expecting a physical assault from the back of the house for his perfidy. Annie Safer, he thought again, sounding wild, as usual. As wild as his sister

Shifra Czaferski, wherever she was. Annie Safer and her solicitous pal Bobby Fiorentino—could that really be it, Fi-o-ren-ti-no? A pinch of sciatica shot through Sigmund's lower back at the thought, but he persisted. Annie Safer, he said to himself for the fourth time, making a terrible clicking sound with his teeth. And Bobby F. Click. Click. The congregation would really sink their fangs into that one when they got hold of it, oh yes, as though there weren't enough agitation already at the House of Israel. Everybody loved a scandal. Even Sigmund R. Safer loved a scandal. There could never be too many. And Annie, who liked nothing better than to keep the pot boiling, would be only too happy to give them one more. Sigmund's enemies (click) would know how to use it against him, they were experts in such matters, and so would the rabbi, who was no less an expert, and always had been, in Sigmund's opinion. Over the years, through all the ongoing congregational crises, Sigmund had learned that he could always depend on the rabbi for a little treachery when the opportunity showed itself. Yes, even the rabbi, who, if you asked Sigmund, had long had his doubts about the reverend cantor when it came to certain important matters of a theological nature.

Where had Annie come from, anyway? It was one of those questions that Sigmund had been asking for a long time, ever since his daughter had learned to speak her mind. Which was just another way of saying practically forever, since in Sigmund's memory she seemed to have been born with the power of instant speech. Sometimes, when he could bear to think about it, Annie made him believe in retribution. It was horrible, but it was true. He was being punished for something and she was the punishment. But punished for what? What had he done? Standing there blindly in the hallway, clutching his frantic worms to his chest (why frantic, he wondered, in a corner of his mind, did they know that they were soon to enter into another state of being?), Sigmund finally remembered what he was being punished for. It was simple. He didn't believe in God. He didn't believe, while pretending otherwise to the rest of the world. That was it, simplicity itself; his lifelong hypocrisy, the essential part, deserving, in his view, any punishment that might be forthcoming.

At this thought, Sigmund made a confused move away from

the screen door. He backed up, rocking a little on his heels, and tried to quiet down. (He knew all the signs of approaching hysteria.) He had to remind himself now that, God aside, he still believed in the Jews, as if there were no contradiction in that, believed in them, in part, for the way they continued to believe in God themselves. For exactly that, in fact. As though He—under any one of his aliases and multiple guises—were actually out there.

Sigmund had begun to hyperventilate, a certain sign, he knew, that he was carrying this too far. He surely had better things to do than try to make a case for himself. Besides, he knew all the arguments. He had made them often enough. The personal god within; the power of the Individual Spirit; the One Life shared by everything and everyone; the ideal of the Tribe, universalized; all that and more, attitudes and rationales amassed over the years, one by one, like suits of tough spiritual armor. And at the moment, nature itself beckoned with irresistible force. The container of worms had begun to pulsate in his hand like a living, breathing lung. It was ready to explode. He made a run for the back of the house then, heading for his fish tanks, Annie Safer, his own daughter, to whom he had just lied without a moment's hesitation, Bobby Fiorentino, to whom he had also lied, quite happily, even the Jews themselves, to whom he always lied, safely out of mind for the moment.

4

"Just checking in," Sigmund said into the phone an hour or so later, still shaken by his meeting with Bobby Fiorentino. His fish were fed, the worms already digested, a squirming white host gone to a predestined death. (He could never take his eyes off the worms when his fish attacked; they actually seemed to know what was happening, it was as though they had foreseen everything.) Jenny was still out with her friends, clicking the tiles. Fi-o-ren-ti-no, Sigmund thought again, phone in hand. In Bobby's name, he could hear a sure echo of the Vatican and that whole false flamboyant crowd, flashily dressed to the nines, living like royalty, while most of the world suffered poverty and worse in austere silence. It made him shudder.

"Cantor?" Barney was sitting at his desk in the den on Hilton Street, propped up on his new air cushion, which made a suggestive noise each time he leaned forward.

"Are you feeling all right?" Sigmund asked, determined, despite his agitation, to sound like the very soul of civilized discourse. "I've been thinking about you."

"That makes two of us."

"Everything getting back to normal?"

"Nothing's happening. I'm sitting here and I can tell you nothing's happening. You know, bored?"

"And what should be happening? It's a time for convalescence."

"I sit around all day doing nothing. It's Elsie. She doesn't allow it. She's making me an invalid. She would like that." He shifted a bit on his air cushion. In his hand he held a sheaf of papers.

"And that's the way it should be," Sigmund said. "For the time being, anyway. You're no different from anybody else when it comes to convalescence. You might as well learn to enjoy it."

"Enjoy," Barney said, sounding disgusted at the idea. "Listen," he went on. "I'm sitting at my desk staring at all the bills piled up." He waved the sheaf of papers in the air. "Already, only three days home and I got a whole itemized list from the hospital. Two pages. You wouldn't believe it. A dollar for an aspirin. A dollar. Then I got the Zionist dues, the Associated, the orphans, the blind, and the old people at Levindale. It's the time of the year. It's the holidays. They know just when to go for you. They know when you're ripe. I even got the Catholic Charities, which right now I'm dropping into the wastepaper basket." Barney paused. "You hear that? The sound of the Catholic Charities dropping."

"You sound pretty good to me. Like your old self."

"I'm getting there. But it's slow. It's slow."

"Then write some checks. You can afford it." Sigmund laughed. Already he was feeling a little better just from hearing the vigor in his old friend's voice. "Are they bothering you down at the factory?" he then asked.

"They better. Half the army is marching on Tiger Pads. I got orders backed up . . ."

A wave of patriotic feeling rolled over Sigmund at Barney's statement, mixed with pride in his friend. Half the army. And even supposing that Barney was exaggerating a little, that still probably meant two million GIs. That was a lot of Tiger Pads on behalf of the war effort. Four million heels, marching for America, and all of it made possible by his friend Barney Fribush. The idea stirred Sigmund. It made him feel close to the action. "Let reason prevail," he then said in calm, professional tones. "You shouldn't push yourself too hard."

"Don't worry about me."

"Of course I worry about you, Barney."

"A man has to make a living."

"Just be reasonable," Sigmund said, trying to keep the piety out of his voice. Piety—or its cheerless simulation—was always a problem. A moment passed. "Anyway," Sigmund went on, "it's been bothering me a little, so I wanted to ask you, are you sure about the Scheingold kid?"

"What sure?"

"You know. For the holidays. The kid in the choir. It's been on my mind."

"For God's sake, I already told Jenny. I don't worry, why should you? Just so he's clean. Anyway, I got other things on my mind. I mean, wait'll I get my hands on Julie Metzger."

Sigmund took a second to think about that, although he didn't particularly want to. Julie Metzger. Norman Sindel. Larry Adelman, too, his own lawyer. The subject never seemed to go away. After a moment's silence, he said, "Don't overdo it, Barney."

"I'll wring his neck."

Sigmund said nothing as he thought of Julie Metzger, croaking.

"SOB, I'll brain him."

"Barney, restrain yourself."

"You leave it to me. Making all that trouble. And the rabbi."

"The rabbi can't help himself," Sigmund said. "He's what he is."

"I'll get my hands on all of them. You'll see. The whole rotten bunch."

What Sigmund saw was their mortal remains, the whole rotten bunch, the rabbi included, their skulls cracked open, brains extruded, necks wrung, for making so much trouble, all courtesy of Barney Fribush. "The essential thing is to rest now, Barney," he said, trying to sound as normal as possible, although it was difficult in the face of so much threatened violence. "Don't push yourself. Give yourself a little time. Let reason prevail. Head before heart. Things often work out the way you want if you just let them run their course."

"I always have to do everything myself," Barney answered, which was one of Barney's chronic complaints, at home, at the House, and down at the factory. Sigmund and everyone else had been hearing it for years. There was a long silence then, while Barney and Sigmund both considered whether they had forgotten to say anything. "Just say hello to your beautiful wife," Barney finally added. "And to your lovely daughter, too. Don't worry, I know her name. Begins with an A. You want to hear something now?" Without waiting for an answer, Barney placed the mouthpiece of the phone between his legs and leaned forward on his air cushion.

"What was that?" Sigmund shouted.

"Guess."

5

They lay side by side, staring up into the brilliant night sky, tucked away in a hidden little hollow that bordered the seventh green at Hillsdale golf course. It was only a couple of blocks away from Annie's house on Granada Avenue.

"I sure hope nobody is wandering around out there," Bobby said, raising his head and peering into the seemingly endless space that surrounded them. In the distance, he could see the lights of the houses that faced the golf course. They seemed far away, swallowed in blankness. He had always wanted to live in one of those houses. It would be like having the biggest front lawn in Baltimore.

When Bobby lay back, Annie raised his hand to her lips and kissed his palm the way she had once seen Alfred Lunt kiss Lynn Fontanne on the stage of Ford's Theater. There was an old callus at the base of Bobby's thumb, but that didn't discourage her. She kept her face buried there for a moment. "Oh," she breathed.

Bobby turned on his side, facing her, and began to trace the bridge of her nose with his forefinger. "I can't believe you're not wearing a brassiere," he said.

"Now do you believe it?" she asked, moving his hand over the front of her dress. The dress had daisies printed all over it.

Bobby exhaled slowly. "Boy," he said, "if we get caught."

"That again. If we get caught. Please, have a little pity."

"Well, suppose . . ."

"You and your guilt feelings," Annie said. "I mean, sometimes you Catholics, you're worse than the Jews when it comes to guilt. Why can't you just enjoy yourself like a normal human being? Forget your superego for once."

"My what?"

"Your control mechanism, Bobby, the thing that's always working overtime for you. Or against you. With you, I'm never sure."

"Where do you get that stuff, anyway? And leave the Catholics out of it, for once. Sometimes, Annie . . ."

"Oh, shut up," she said, taking his hand again and holding it against her.

"And what about me?" he asked, suddenly coy.

"Just take it easy," she said. "Don't be in such a hurry."

"I thought you just said . . ."

"We've got plenty of time," Annie answered. "Just try to relax a minute. Just let go." They both lay back again, staring at the sky, trying to hear each other breathe.

"I've never been able to figure anything out up there," Bobby said. "I mean, the stars and all that stuff, can you see a bear or whatever it's supposed to be?"

"Over there," she said, pointing vaguely toward the horizon.

"I don't see anything except the Milky Way, if it is the Milky Way. Is that the Milky Way over there?" He began to pat the turf alongside him with the flat of his hand. "This grass could sure use a cutting," he said in an absent-minded voice.

Without warning, Annie rolled over onto him. "What are you trying to do?" he asked, beginning to laugh. "I thought we were taking it easy."

"Oh, I love the way you smell," she said, inhaling deeply. "I just love it. Your breath, too. Breathe out now. That's right. Again. Oh, I love it."

"Pebeco," he said. "And Lifebuoy."

"Put your hand here." She was lying on her back again.

"Hmmm." His shirt was unbuttoned.

"That's right. Don't stop. Yes. Now kiss me. Kiss me as though it's the last thing you'll ever do on God's earth."

"The last thing," he whispered in a prayerful tone. A few minutes later, he sat up and began to massage the back of his neck. "Your old man'll go crazy if he finds out," he said.

"My old man again."

"Well, he will. I know. He was really suspicious the other night. I could tell. All he wanted was to get rid of me."

"Don't worry about my old man. I'll take care of him if I have to." Annie was frowning. "And anyway, it's not even that you're a Catholic."

"Who says."

"I mean, my own opinion is that where my old man is concerned, it's more that your father is a bricklayer."

"Stonemason," Bobby corrected her stiffly. "I told you before." Then, after a moment's silence, he put his fingers to his nose and began to sniff at them, exaggeratedly.

"What do you think you're doing?" she asked.

"Just testing."

"Bobby."

He was now sucking at his fingers.

"You really are disgusting," she said, trying to sound offended, but unable to keep the pleasure out of her voice. "Now cut that out," she added dutifully.

"When I get into the marines," he went on, still sniffing at his fingers, "how am I going to make it through without you?"

"You've got a whole year to worry about the marines. Don't rush things. You have to finish school first."

"How will I go on living?"

She looked at him dramatically. "You'll get along, Bobby," she said in a husky voice that might or might not have been sincere, even she didn't know. "People like you always get along."

"What does that mean?" he asked suspiciously.

"It means that you're competent, that you know what you're doing, you'll never get lost. It's a compliment."

"Oh, Annie, I do believe that I love you." He began to stroke her hair. "I really do. I love you, I love you."

"No talking. It'll spoil everything."

"Just I love you. To try it out. I never said it before. To anyone. Honest. I love you, I love you, I love you."

"Oh God," she sighed. "You're like a mule sometimes, you're so stubborn. Sometimes I can't believe it. Okay, you win. You always win. Thank you for loving me. Now stop pulling my hair."

"Do I get a prize or something for winning?"

"You always want a prize."

"Do I or don't I?"

"To you, it's a prize, that's all it ever is."

"Oh, Annie," he mumbled in her ear, falling against her. "Please. Be a pal. I need you."

"I need you," she said, mimicking him. "You're always saying that. It's getting stale. Like a broken record. Now just hold on for a second. Stop shaking like that. For God's sake, Bobby, hold on, you've got no self-control whatsoever . . ."

6

There had been a calamity a full hour into rehearsal that night, right in the middle of Silent Devotion, one that shattered the choir's routine and collective poise for the moment and made powerful demands on the cantor's—and his choir leader's—faith in the future, as well as on their abilities to improvise. What happened was simple, natural, and inevitable, but it was no less a calamity for that; and there was no way for Sigmund to be philosophical about it, at least, with much conviction, although most of the choir eventually did quite nicely on their own account, philosophically speaking.

What happened was that, reaching for a high A in a solo, one of a diminishing number this year, Herschel Bleiber's small, delicate voice, almost like a girl's, still "white," without vibrato, suddenly splintered in the Safers' dining room, a horrible sound, like a warning to them all, then smashed at the choir's feet like a piece of irreplaceable crystal. The remains lay all around the table, and, as everyone present knew, they could not be put together again. At this awful knowledge, final as death, there was a massed heartbeat, nine formidable thuds sounding as one in the Safer dining room. From now on, Herschel Bleiber would speak to the rest of the world in a new and coarser voice, one that would immediately identify him as a brazen young adult; and as he lost his special role as choir soloist and his place at the Safers' dining room table as well, he would also have to give up the pleasurable sense of being chosen, one out of many, one out of thousands, of having made his own Herschel Bleiber place in the sun, small, to be sure, tiny even, but a *place*. And the knowledge of that was an agony.

"Gosh darn!" Sigmund cried out when Herschel's voice broke, furiously banging the table with his fist and reaching, from habit, for the vernacular he enjoyed. Gosh darn! (But it could have been worse, he was thinking, it could have been the Scheingold kid.)

While the rest of the choir buzzed mournfully at the cantor's cry, Irving Karton began to laugh behind his hand. Other people's troubles often made Irving Karton laugh. He couldn't even explain it to himself, it just happened. Tough tit, he thought now, as he laughed nervously, tough titty-boom-boom. He had never liked Herschel Bleiber, anyway. He was such a perfect little prig, a perfect little Percy, and besides, he liked to lord his father's old De Soto over the rest of the boys. As though Mr. Bleiber didn't charge them all ten cents a head for each round trip from downtown. Herschel Blabber, or Fat-Ass Blubber, as Irving sometimes called him if the foul mood was on him, which was often; Irving Karton, who rarely washed or brushed his teeth and never forgave anything.

Gosh darn . . .

As the little passion play got under way in the dining room, Marty Schiffman, afraid for himself and his own voice, afraid of everything, in fact, slid down in his chair onto the base of his spine, as though he were trying to hide from destiny; he was so scared in the face of Herschel's fate that his own delicate throat muscles had already begun to constrict—temporarily, of course. As for Sylvan Scheingold, who had come to sudden full alert, all eyes and ears at Herschel's excruciating collapse, he sat erect and stiff in his chair and soon began to tap his knee against the table leg in nervous anticipation of the decisions the cantor would have to make about the redistribution of Herschel's solos. That was what interested Sylvan Scheingold, Herschel's solos. For they would certainly have to be redistributed. Alongside him now, Irving Karton giggled into his fist. Tough titty-boom-boom. And more of the same. Irving Karton, one of the great unwashed, probably the greatest, so great that Sylvan was afraid to breathe in his presence.

"Usually you have some warning," Volkonsky said from the foot of the table, in a voice that suggested that Herschel had deliberately set out to betray him. "It doesn't just sneak up on you. There are definitely signs."

"I didn't know anything," Herschel claimed stoutly, unable to say more than a word or two in his own defense. In fact, he was almost in tears, facing his colleagues, and kept glancing desperately at the living room, where his father sat on the sofa with his head buried in his hands.

"Everybody's voice goes at some time," Zev Gozlov rumbled evenly in his Oriental-Russian bass, sounding perhaps a little too equable for the occasion. Across the table, Jeffrey Bourne, for whom other people's voices were primarily objects of detached interest, like the color of their eyes or the shape of their noses, examined his fingernails in the bright overhead light. Now that the initial shock was behind them, why all the excitement? He agreed with Zev Gozlov, more or less, everybody's voice goes at some time. They both knew that all singers, sacred or profane, adult or adolescent, man or woman, ran such risks. It happened all the time—catastrophe, that is. It was almost a way of life. Remember Caruso, Jeffrey Bourne reminded himself as his nails caught the light, finished by a throat hemorrhage right in the middle of a performance.

"Excuse me," Sy Frisch said, getting up to go to the bathroom to help calm his nervous stomach. All crises affected him this way, with painful and peremptory spasms. He had no philosophy, unlike Zev Gozlov and Jeffrey Bourne, to help sustain him, no consoling rationalizations; life tended to get to Sy Frisch directly through his alimentary canal, where the vulnerable surrounding regions seemed to respond to trouble like an accordion's bellows in full action.

"Well, cantor?" Volkonsky asked politely. The ribbon of his pince-nez gleamed brightly on the lapel of his summer jacket, which he always kept on in the presence of his shirt-sleeved choir, no matter how hot it was—another mark, he thought, of elegance and aristocratic authority.

"Gosh darn it!" Sigmund clicked his teeth. But it could have been worse, he reminded himself. It could have been the Scheingold kid.

Irving Karton began to laugh again. Where did the cantor pick up such expressions? Gosh darn it. Nobody talked like that anymore. The cantor probably thought it was something obscene, something really dirty, like fuck or shit. But who could imagine the cantor saying fuck or shit? He was the cantor. It was hard enough to believe that he did them. (Did he?) In the background, like a ghostly flash, Annie Safer strode past the open door of the dining room in her daisy dress, on the way to her bedroom. (There was a grass stain under her left shoulder.) As she went by, the boys—except, of course, for the ruined Herschel Bleiber— quickly glanced at each other, sharing sudden little knowing smiles. It was the first time any of them had seen her since rehearsals had begun, the first time in a year, but she didn't even give them a second look before disappearing into the back of the house. When she was gone, Irving Karton made a dirty gesture with his forefinger under the table and out of habit reached for Sylvan's thigh. "You queer," Sylvan mumbled in return, stalling Irving with a kick to the shin. Then, after a moment of restless jockeying for position, they both quieted down under Sigmund's baleful stare.

Herschel Bleiber's father now stood behind the cantor's chair, where he had arrived uninvited. The blood had drained from his face. Everyone could hear him breathe. "You have to do something, cantor," he said in a hoarse voice that sounded like a death rattle. "You can't just leave my boy out in the cold. You have to help him."

"Daddy," Herschel said, staring at the floor. "Please."

Sigmund swiveled slowly in his chair, as though he were trying to expand to fill the space all around him, as though he were actually swelling, and peered up at Mr. Bleiber. And then peered some more, until Volkonsky began to clear his throat as a kind of cue. "You're right," Sigmund finally said to Mr. Bleiber, speaking on the very edge of his voice. "I certainly have to do something. The first thing I have to do is decide what to do with Herschel's solos. That's a problem, but it can be solved. We have other talent at this table besides Herschel Bleiber." There was a general puffing out among the boys at this unexpected remark; the cantor was not known for gratuitous compliments. "Then," Sigmund went on, still peering up at Mr. Bleiber, "I have to decide whether we have time to find someone new to fill in on the choral work. After I decide that, and assuming we find him, not a safe assumption at all, no sir, then I first have to worry about training him. Should I even try? You tell me, Mr. Bleiber. Do you perhaps know of someone? Is it worth it? We have three weeks to the holidays."

But Mr. Bleiber was not paying attention to the cantor. Mr. Bleiber never paid attention to anyone. "You have to do something about Herschel," he said again. "You can't just leave him high and dry."

"I didn't leave him high and dry," Sigmund said, gathering his words slowly. "He left himself high and dry." Sigmund gave a sharp little laugh as he spoke but pulled himself up as he heard an echo of his own voice come back at him in the room. He also heard the way he must sound to everybody at the table, full of supercilious dry rage. It was time to put an end to this. He hated this part of himself. Superciliousness. Disdain. Remoteness. "Have there been warnings?" he went on, still not quite able to control what he was saying and how he said it. "Of course, there had to be warnings. There always are."

"What can I say? You know about these things better than I do."

"I certainly do."

"If I may," Volkonsky then said to Mr. Bleiber. "Why don't you let us get on with our rehearsal? There's a lot of work to do, and the time grows short."

"Daddy, please," Herschel begged, still staring down at the floor.

After a moment's hesitation, Mr. Bleiber returned to the living room and picked up the sports section of the *Sun*. Hiding behind the paper, pretending to read, he allowed himself to feel a little guilty. Herschel's voice had cracked twice in the past week as he rehearsed in front of a mirror at home, and once the week before, and Mr. Bleiber had made his son promise not to tell anyone. Who knew, he reasoned, these matters sometimes stretched over several months before they finally resolved themselves. It had happened before with other kids. Herschel had had bad luck, the Bleibers often had bad luck. The next Bobby Breen, he told himself bitterly.

By now Sy Frisch was back in place, his stomach appeased. To meet such emergencies, which he had long ago discovered were a dime a dozen in the modern world, Sy Frisch always carried ample supplies of digestive tablets wherever he went; as a result, a mild wind now blew gently through his lower intestine, but he had it firmly under control—sphincter magic, as he thought of it. Across from him, Zev Gozlov had begun to vocalize to himself, impatient with the delay. Herschel Bleiber barely existed in his consciousness, and neither did the other boys; to him, they were mere voice boxes of a certain age, golden throats all, but not quite human. It was an entirely professional attitude. While they waited, Jeffrey Bourne, tired of gazing at his fingernails, and no less professional, tried to catch a glimpse of himself in the mirror that hung over the sideboard across the dining room. That image always reassured him; it was so clean-cut, so steadfast and reliable, so unlike the rest of the faces around the table. For Jeffrey Bourne, the half-Jew who was always more Anglo-Saxon than Semite, Herschel Bleiber's shattered voice was already forgotten. There were more where that came from, plenty of them. For the moment, rapt, he sat there at the table staring at himself, checking out various flattering angles in the glass across the room.

Ahem, Volkonsky went, modestly clearing his throat. You there, Gozlov, he meant; and you, too, Bourne, you especially. It was time to move on.

The cantor scribbled in his score books, Volkonsky now observing over his shoulder, making his own changes in his own scores. "You think that?" he asked deferentially at one point. The cantor didn't answer. "What about here?" Volkonsky suggested. "Or even here? It's almost a perfect modulation." Silence again. Minutes passed as the cantor scribbled on. Gozlov was now quiet, dreaming of the earthy possibilities that awaited him at the widow Berman's on Fairview Avenue. Sy Frisch, sitting tight, cleaned one ear with his little finger. Facing him, Jeffrey Bourne began to rehearse inside his head for an Episcopal church wedding that was scheduled for the weekend in Roland Park. And the cantor? *Verdammte* Herschel Bleiber, Sigmund cursed to himself, reverting to another vernacular as he sat there at the head of the table, still scribbling away. *Verdammte* Herschel Bleiber, he thought (even though it could have been much worse), damn Herschel Bleiber and all young boys, damn them with their sour smells (an ugly look at Irving Karton), their gargantuan stupidities (another ugly look at Irving Karton), and their ongoing, never-ending, ridiculous unpredictabilities (one sweeping dismissive glance at all the boys). They always failed you in the end by becoming something else. It was unwholesome, even if it was their nature. It should not be allowed. (A fleeting reminder, then, out of nowhere, of Bobby F., the Pope's local spy.) If Sigmund had his way . . . A trickle of spiteful sweat ran down his rib cage.

"All right," Sigmund finally announced, trying to get a grip on himself. "Attention, please." Volkonsky returned to his place at the foot of the table. The grown-up gorillas grew alert. Sy Frisch released the tiniest bit of wind, which passed unnoticed. "Page eighteen, second bar," Sigmund said, and proceeded to improvise. "Mr. Scheingold . . ." he began, in a questioning voice. "Nigger," Irving Karton muttered suavely. The redistribution of solos began. "Mr. Scheingold," Sigmund said again. The repeated sound of his name made Sylvan happy. Mr. Scheingold. His role was enlarged, his hopes fulfilled. His skin went from olive to pink. He sat up straight, spine erect. In a few minutes they were ready to continue. A beat was given by Volkonsky, who looked doubtful but loyal; there was a tortured moment of hesitation, and another, Marty Schiffman having pitch trouble (his weakness), Sy Frisch slipping behind without knowing it, Sylvan making a false entry, always ready to jump the gun (*his* weakness), until they finally managed to join forces one by one, Herschel Bleiber excepted, of course, and, slowly moving on, began to gain some strength.

The dining room soon filled with their sound. The chandelier began to sway overhead. There was a slight bothersome reverberation all around them, a matter of strange acoustics in a room designed for other activities, but they succeeded in ignoring it. On they sang, golden throats all. It came as a surprise to each of them when they realized—once again—how much strength they could gather by relinquishing themselves and becoming a part of one another. It was as though it had never happened before. Zev Gozlov's bald-eagle head was soon beaming with Slavic joy. It was what Gozlov always hungered for, sweet harmony shared. Bourne and Frisch, not natural allies in the best of times (they hardly ever exchanged a word, one way or another), tossed separate baritone and tenor melodies across the Safer dining-room table as though they were scented spring bouquets, then generously tossed them back again. Even the boys forgot themselves for the moment, almost. For Volkonsky, whose self-assurance had returned, it was a kind of bliss; for Sigmund, a triumph of self-satisfaction (and an interesting one, no tedium or procrastination tonight), even though he knew that it was temporary, that it wouldn't last more than ten minutes, if they were lucky. But ten minutes was enough, given the nature of the evening's circumstances. It was about how long any triumph could be expected to last, under any conditions.

Up front in the living room, meanwhile, Herschel Bleiber and Mr. Bleiber now sat side by side on the sofa, listening morosely to the choir rehearse the service without Herschel, and especially to Nigger Scheingold, as he took over Herschel's solos. From now on, Mr. Bleiber was thinking, in his own inimitable way, from now on there would be no more De Soto for that gang; those three little cocksuckers, Scheingold in particular, Scheingold first of all, would have to find their own way out to Forest Park from downtown, then home again, yes sirree; while in the back of the house, through all the din, the young atheist sat reading *The Razor's Edge* propped up in bed (her dirty daisy dress crumpled on the floor alongside her), deaf to the sounds up front, or pretending to be, feeling philosophical and deep, lapsing wistfully every paragraph or so into dreams of Hillsdale golf course and the hollow that lay hidden just behind the seventh green; and in the kitchen, fully enjoying the manly sounds that came from her dining room, Jenny Safer put out raisin buns and milk and set the kettle to boil for those who would want iced tea. They were having a good time out there tonight, she decided, much livelier, far more rousing than usual. That was as it should be. Pausing in her work to listen, she could easily make out the thrilling dark plumb of Zev Gozlov's bass, Jeffrey Bourne's supple creamy half-Jewish baritone, and the acid edge of Sy Frisch's high tenor. It was a wonderful mix, she thought. It was the best choir in Baltimore. Then Sigmund's familiar arching voice, riding sweetly above all the others, joined in along with the boys, every-one sounding excited. It was becoming very noisy on Granada Avenue. Jenny hoped the neighbors wouldn't mind. Nobody had ever complained, they were all very respectful of the cantor's position, but the prospect of disturbing her neighbors, the Riefs, the Tissenbaums, the Pumpians, the Sheas, Sandlers, and Dal-rymples, all those barely distinguishable families living side by side on Granada Avenue in comfort and near-perfect ease, always made Jenny Safer uncomfortable.

7

"Well, you should consider yourself lucky," Lillian was saying, "to be invited to stay in a house like that on Hilton Street."

"A house like what?" Sylvan asked, sprawled on his daybed. "You were never there. How would you know?"

"I don't like your tone of voice, young man. Watch yourself. And you know what I mean about Hilton Street, don't act dumb."

"All I mean is suppose he's not nice," Sylvan said, modulating his voice. "Suppose he's one of those old people who hates kids, who's cranky all the time."

"Don't you worry about cranky. Mrs. Safer knows exactly what she's doing. I have total faith in her."

"I wish you were coming, too."

"Well, I'm not, so that's that. Just put it out of your mind. Try to think of it as a little vacation, a little break from each other. Everybody can use a little break from time to time." Gazing from the living room into the hall mirror, hanging just five feet away, she fluffed out her hair with a quick teasing motion, then, dissatisfied with the result, began to smooth it down with the flat of her hand.

"I like it loose, the way you had it before," Sylvan said.

"I don't know," Lillian said, still gazing at herself. She fluffed her hair out again and looked unhappy.

"You really want to get away from me for a while?" Sylvan asked.

"Oh, don't talk like such a baby," she said, turning to him. "What is it, three nights? Look at the bright side. Don't be so negative all the time. Anyway, tell me about rehearsal tonight. And be specific."

There was plenty to tell, of course. The tragedy of Herschel Bleiber. The fury of Sigmund R. Safer. The triumph of Sylvan Scheingold. He told it all, some of it twice.

"Hmm," his mother responded sympathetically. "Life plays dirty tricks sometimes. Poor Herschel. I feel sorry for his parents."

"And I'm the only one who got more solos. I got them all. Marty Schiffman isn't always dependable. He goes flat sometimes. And Irving. Well, Irving . . ." For Sylvan, Irving Karton was beyond words.

"Just don't go getting a swell head."

"It's a lot of extra work. I have to learn all those new words."

Lillian thought for a moment. When she spoke up, it was as The-One-Who-Takes-Responsibility-for-Everything. "Maybe you should ask for more money," she suggested. "You certainly deserve it. Talk to the cantor. He understands those things. Mr. Fribush is treasurer. He's responsible for all the money. It's not as though we're strangers asking. Where would they be without you? And all that extra work. It's only fair."

But it wasn't money that interested Sylvan. He buried his face in his pillow. "I wish you were coming to Hilton Street with me," he said, as though he were talking to himself.

"That's enough of that," Lillian said primly. "The subject is closed. As of now. And please stop mumbling like that. Listen, I keep forgetting, did you sign up for French next term or didn't you? It's important. I want you to be comfortable in a foreign language." Like Charles Boyer, she was thinking to herself.

"I told you a hundred times, yes," Sylvan said, sitting up on the daybed and slowly stretching. His mother was standing in the middle of the living room, touching her toes now. She touched her toes regularly, twenty-five times, four times a week. There were also sit-ups and hip rotations, twenty-five times, four times a week. It was not for nothing that Lillian Scheingold didn't have to wear a girdle. "Eighteen . . . huff . . . nineteen . . ." Each time she reached down, the blood rushed to her head. "Twenty-one . . . and two . . ."

"Take it easy now," Sylvan said. "You'll give yourself a heart attack."

"And four . . ." Huffing.

"Mom."

The little rites of domesticity, à la Scheingold, continued.

Three

1

The three men slipped out of their pew just as the rabbi rose to his feet on the pulpit and proceeded to the lectern for his sermon. Their exit had been agreed upon before services began; they all knew, in fact, a full twenty-four hours before the rabbi got up to speak that they were going to walk out on him; but the knowledge had not kept them calm or given them added strength. On the contrary. They strode up the synagogue's middle aisle now in a ragged line, one of them weak in the knees from an attack of nerves. A buzz of indignation in the congregation and, here and there, mild encouragement, followed them on their way. Rebels and conspirators. The double role, daringly played out in public like this on a Saturday morning, thrilled them in one degree or another, not altogether pleasantly, however. A certain fear, of being caught—and (the essential part) punished—by a powerful, invisible, omniscient guardian, was dominant in all three. It was like being a child again and defiantly breaking the law while the law itself looked on. By arrangement, they gathered a few minutes later in the small sanctuary downstairs, unused now in the summer, in a pew facing the ark. They hardly knew how to begin after making their statement upstairs, for all the assurance they had pretended to feel before they walked out.

"And who's going to buttonhole the cantor?" Julius Metzger wanted to know, opening the exchange abruptly. He was tapping his foot on the floor in quick time and smiling unnaturally, as though he were addressing a company of possibly hostile strangers. He also had to keep his hands buried inside his prayer shawl to hide the trembling. "Somebody please tell me," he added, flicking his eyes impatiently from Norman Sindel to Larry Adelman.

"I thought you said you would." As he answered Julius Metzger, Larry Adelman looked down at his friends with a dense, unhappy expression. (Larry Adelman had always been known by everyone for his seriousness and sobriety.) "Anyway, that's how I remember it. At the last meeting. Isn't that where we left it?" All in all, Larry Adelman would have preferred to be home at the moment; but duty was duty, it always was with Larry Adelman. He had made his commitment. Let the chips fall now. Larry Adelman stood six-and-a-half-feet tall—the tallest member of the House of Israel—and walked with a slow stooping shamble that was a lifetime habit and made him look even more somber than he actually was. He waited now, unhappy, for someone to speak.

"The cantor already said. As I seem to recall." Norman Sindel, last among the triumvirate, was carrying his prayer book with his middle finger still marking the place, as though he didn't know every page of the service by heart, backward and forward. As he spoke, he kept looking over his shoulder to see if they had been followed.

"He already said what?" Julius Metzger asked.

"He wants to come with us. He wants to be part of it."

"He never said. Nobody asked. Not a single word has been exchanged." That was Larry Adelman again, speaking from his great height.

"Well, somebody get on the ball," Julius Metzger ordered. "Somebody better ask."

"I can think of more important questions at the moment," Norman Sindel said, cocking his head in an attempt to hear the rabbi's voice droning away upstairs.

"Still," Larry Adelman answered, trying to sound both patient and rational. "It has to be asked. As long as we agreed. And it's the right thing, too."

"The issue is not the cantor."

"You don't have to tell me what the issue is," Larry Adelman protested, running his fingers through the fringes of his prayer shawl. Then, after a moment, he proceeded to tell *them*. "The issue," he said, "is that the rabbi's never going to give an inch, we were fools ever to think so, and I refuse to ask again." Larry Adelman spoke in a suddenly forceful voice, even though he was notoriously shy from having been so tall all his life. Six and a half feet was not a commonplace, anywhere. In a mostly short world, he would have chosen to be more like other people, five-eight, five-nine, say, give or take. He would have liked the chance to look everybody straight in the eye for once.

"You refuse to ask what again?" Julius Metzger asked.

Norman Sindel broke in. "Somebody's coming," he said.

"Where?"

"Listen."

There was a deathly silence, broken finally by Julius Metzger. "Nobody's coming, for God's sake," he said. "What's wrong with you, anyway? Scared of your own shadow. So, Adelman, you refuse to ask what again?"

"The rabbi. For some chance at a compromise. For some acknowledgment of our feelings, our needs—of our ideals, if you want to put it that way. For some acknowledgment that we're as real as he is." As Larry Adelman spoke these words he straightened up briefly, and his eyes shone with satisfaction.

"What are we talking about, anyway?" Julius Metzger asked, sounding disgusted. He was also a little out of breath from excitement, and his hands still trembled inside his prayer shawl.

"I tell myself that I don't need the aggravation of forming a new congregation, finding a site, electing officers, going through all that, plus raising the money. Raising the money, I hate the idea." Larry Adelman sat down in the pew, looking suddenly despondent.

"All that's decided, it was decided a long time ago. We decided, you, me, Norman, everybody. What the hell's going on?"

"I'm giving you my opinion. I'm expressing myself. To me, it's a very serious matter."

"Are you thinking of backing out, by some chance?" Norman Sindel asked. "Did Barney Fribush get to you?"

"Nobody got to me," Larry answered. Sitting down, he was almost at eye level with his friends. "I'm telling you how I feel."

"Guilty is how you feel," Julius Metzger said, standing erect. "I've seen it before, hundreds of times. It'll pass." Nevertheless, he looked unsure of himself. "The question," he went on, "is when we make the move. When, not whether. It's too late for whether."

"What's the rush?" Larry asked. "We're always in such a hurry. It's not a five-alarm fire. It's a serious business. All this running around like chickens . . . We need another meeting with the rabbi, we need another meeting with the board. We owe it to ourselves."

"The rabbi's not talking to us anymore," Julius said. "You just said it yourself. He said his piece once. You heard him, we all heard him. We want men and women sitting together, we can go to the Methodists across the street. We want a little English in the service, ditto. You heard him. By him, we're apostates. It's either-or, it's no to everything. The board will back him down the line. It has to. It's not our board anymore."

"Tell me, Julie," Larry said in a pained voice, drawing each word out as though it were a thorn, "and you, too, Norman," he went on, careful not to offend by omission. "You think it's worth it, all this, you think it's worth risking the ruin of two congregations just because we don't get everything we want?"

"What ruin? What two congregations?"

"The House of Israel, it's obvious, and the new one. Our new one."

"How ruin? I see a little disruption, maybe. And if there's a little disruption, it's not the end of the world. But ruin? Don't exaggerate."

"A split here will cut their support in half, I call that ruin, and, on the other hand, who knows how many will follow us to a new place, how many members we'll get? Nothing is sure."

"We've discussed that until I'm blue in the face," Julius Metzger said. "Enough. The only question now is when. When?"

"End of the year," Larry Adelman said, sighing.

"Sooner," Norman Sindel said. "Otherwise, we'll lose the momentum."

"I say right before Rosh Hashana," Julius Metzger said. "I say the sooner the better. Within the month. That'll show him."

"Not before the High Holidays," Larry said. "We can't do that to old friends. It'll send a terrible signal to everyone. It's bad enough walking out on the rabbi the way we just did. Already I regret it. Do we have to act like barbarians?"

"Is Halperin coming with us or isn't he?" Julius Metzger asked, ignoring Larry's question.

"One day it's yes, the next no," Norman said. "His business is not so hot at the moment."

"You have to get a firm commitment. By check, not mouth. Don't let him slip away. And the Sherover brothers, too. You got one, you got all five."

"I don't feel so sure about the whole thing anymore," Larry Adelman went on, still agonizing. "It goes against the grain. It's not natural."

"I could have predicted," Julius Metzger said. "I could see it coming a mile away. Not natural. Against the grain. The trouble with you is you're too softhearted. Always were. Going way back. You've got too many screw-pulls, Adelman."

"That's just the point," Larry almost shouted, suddenly fervent. "Scruples! That's exactly it, the right word. What else is it all about?" But when he saw the same blank expression settle on Julius's and Norman's faces at the question, the same blunt indifference, if not downright weariness, his heart shrank inside his huge chest and he decided to take a different tack. "All I mean," he went on, trying to sound reasonable again, "is that it raises important questions, making a new congregation, it's not like establishing another country club, it's not just a little social thing."

"Little social thing," Julius said, with a derisive note. "Nobody ever said it was a little social thing. You're the first one who said it. From your mouth, remember. Anyway, it's all decided. It's been decided for weeks. And you know it. From now on, it's just tactics, like Patton or one of those guys overseas, it's just like that, a war, whether it suits you or not."

"So who tackles the cantor?" Norman Sindel asked after a brief silence, returning to the subject.

"The cantor's not all that important," Julius said. "I mean he's not top priority. Cantors come a dime a dozen."

"I'll take it on," Larry Adelman offered, rising to his feet in the pew. He was flushed from Julius's rebuff—he could feel a pulse beating erratically somewhere behind his left ear—and also from the awkward effort of trying to act like a leader. "The cantor and I are old friends," he went on, as though he were offering a piece of news to Julius and Norman, something they had never known before. "I'm his lawyer, after all, he'll at least hear me out. Just tell me what I can offer, give me the range and all the benefits, too. I have to have it exact. And Julie, everybody is important, everybody counts. That's what I think. You should understand that, so there's no doubt."

"Nobody said no," Norman put in. "Nobody ever said no."

"So where were we?" Julius asked, smiling unnaturally at his friends again.

The conspirators went on with their conversation for a few more minutes, standing together self-consciously in the small sanctuary in front of the ark, all three washed by a strange purple-and-yellow light that filtered through the stained-glass windows lining one side of the room, so absorbed by their exchange that they didn't even notice the glow they cast as they faced each other. The subject of Barney Fribush came up again, at length; the cantor and the rabbi, too; all those irritating ongoing things, repeatedly. Still they talked in the now-golden light, turning in on themselves and the future, slowly spinning in perfect circles that they could all track in their sleep.

2

Upstairs in the main sanctuary, while this subversive exchange was taking place in the small sanctuary below, the rabbi continued to deliver his sermon. It was very abstract, in the accustomed way, sailing serenely over the heads of most of the congregants, who, unlike Julius Metzger, Norman Sindel, and Larry Adelman, had chosen to stay in their seats and bravely sweat it out in the terrific heat. Not that there was such a crowd in the synagogue this morning; it was still August, still the dog days, and half the congregation was away on vacation in Atlantic City and other seaside places. As always, the rabbi was undaunted. The size of the congregation never bothered him. He could perform in front of a hundred as easily as a thousand. Only his will and the sound of his own voice counted. Splitting already anciently split hairs; sometimes declaiming, sometimes ranting; clarifying an occasional obscure point for those who knew how to appreciate one; and failing, in his philosophic and intellectual pretensions, to hold the attention of more than a dozen ardent believers, if that many. In short, there was nothing new.

Sigmund was seated behind the rabbi, flanking the ark in his beloved high-backed chair, a kind of clerical throne that had been carved by hand when the House was built. He was dozing on the pulpit with his eyes open, pupils vaguely fixed through his pince-nez on the congregation scattered below him. No tunes wandered silently, for a change, inside his head, no daydreams clouded the landscape of his brain; he was, for all practical purposes, in a totally mindless state. Sleeping with his eyes open while the rabbi hectored the House of Israel was one of Sigmund's cherished tricks, like humming, designed to ward off the old enemy tedium and its well-known effects. Sigmund had long ago cunningly rationalized his Saturday-morning naps. Sermons were an old story to him, especially the rabbi's. There was one every week, fifty-two weeks a year, plus holidays; and not a surprise among them. So why bother? And his own Saturday-morning service, he reminded himself each week, was hard labor in any terms. Its demands could break a man. What it came down to was one long merciless aria, lasting at least an hour, with minor breaks here and there to let the cantor catch his breath, full of punishing tessitura and moods that changed with volatile suddenness; in Sigmund's opinion, the relentless equivalent of an entire opera by Giuseppe Verdi or even Richard Wagner. And there were other exhausting factors at work this particular morning that made a doze essential.

Sigmund had seen the conspirators rise from their seats as one. He had seen them exchange nervous eye signals with one another, and then, after a moment's shuffling hesitation, in which the fate of the world seemed to hang in the balance to Sigmund, walk out on the rabbi's sermon. He had felt it as an affront, of course, as a kind of malevolent physical shock. Almost everyone had, except the rabbi, who was made of highly weatherproof material that left him immune to almost any emotional assault. It had also disturbed Sigmund's sense of possibilities, of what could and could not be done, of what was permitted, especially in the House. That ragged run up the aisle! The childishness of it, the cold-blooded nerve, the crassness! It was what he might have expected from Julius Metzger and his old crony Norman Sindel, from those two. They were acting exactly in character. But Larry Adelman? His sympathetic pal (one of the few), his sensitive, sensible, shambling old friend, his own lawyer, privy to many of his life's secrets, who was known to weep on occasion at the misfortune of others and who sometimes beat his breast in empathy and pain in the presence of human suffering? (Sigmund had no answers to that one; wherever you turned these days, he told himself in his iciest tones, it was increasingly clear that unnatural things were happening.) As a result of the episode, an air of crisis filled the sanctuary again, as it had all summer, a tension in the congregation that had been increasing from week to week, touching Sigmund with a sense of nervous foreboding that made him feel even sleepier than usual today. But at the lectern it hardly mattered. At the lectern, it was like any other Saturday morning. Standing there positioned several feet above his congregation, the rabbi talked on, lavishly spilling arcane ideas into a human void, never acknowledging the reality at the House of Israel, the possibility of dissolution and destruction that they all recognized with fear and a certain horror, operating, as always, on the fragile theory that what he didn't publicly acknowledge didn't and couldn't exist.

In his half-sleep now, Sigmund took in a loud rasping breath. At the sound, he instantly came awake. His head shot up; he blinked forcefully a few times, poking at his glasses and hoping that no one had noticed. (Few had; out front, most of the congregation was also half-conscious.) A moment passed while Sigmund pulled himself together. He appeared abashed but dignified, staring straight ahead, trying to pretend to listen to what the rabbi was saying. The rabbi's words were painfully abstruse, but it was clear that the morning's harangue was almost over. There had been the statement of theme, the challenge to congregants, development, further development, clever rationalization of the improbable, and, now approaching, Sigmund could tell with a joyous little leap of his blood pressure, the inevitable climax, the threadbare synthesis, which answered all questions while raising none.

It was going to be noisy, as usual. The rabbi's tiny fist already shook in the air. He was red in the face, above his austere goatee. He rose on the soles of his feet, to gain a little height, and came down hard on his heels. The final points were being passionately made. The congregation stirred, as though a wind were blowing through it; everyone was fully awake now. God's meaning was everywhere, the rabbi was shouting—while Sigmund yawned—contained in everything. By everything, the congregation understood that the rabbi meant everything Jewish, and Jewish only, a connection—or disconnection—that often made Sigmund's nerve ends pinch in protest and pain. That was the message today, that was always the message, more or less, at the House of Israel. Everything else, the rabbi disdained. The congregation stirred again; the wind blew all around them. Willingly, they bent their heads in submission.

But soon enough the rabbi began to run down. That was one thing they could always depend on. His body sagged a bit, he stopped shouting. As he moved on to his coda—subdued now, placating, as soft-voiced as a pigeon cooing—Sigmund began to clear phlegm from his throat, preparing to follow the rabbi in the service. Phlegm always seemed to collect in his throat when he dozed upright on the pulpit. It was a physiological reality, like yawning. Once he had cleared the phlegm from his throat, other disagreeable noises followed. Sigmund blew his nose, coughed once or twice into his fist; there was another rasping snort—all in behalf of his voice. After this, the rabbi finally paused, waiting for the racket to subside behind him. For a moment, he held the bridge of his nose between his thumb and forefinger, eyes unhappily cast down—the pose of stricken authority. But it was over almost before it had begun. The strange noises stopped. Sigmund's nasal passages miraculously cleared, the laryngeal ducts opened wide. In another moment, restored, the rabbi finished speaking. All was quiet, except for a faint whisper of relief from the congregation. It was over, for another week. Ignoring Sigmund, who was busy pocketing his handkerchief, the rabbi retreated to his own hand-carved throne, symmetrically positioned on the opposite side of the pulpit, and took his seat, looking very imposing for such a tiny man. (No matter his size, everyone at the House of Israel recognized the force of the rabbi's will and the intensity of his self-regard.) At this cue, offered week in and week out over the years by his colleague, Sigmund rose to his feet, ignoring the rabbi in his turn, and, carrying his pitch pipe hidden in his hand, made his way to the altar. There, with a sudden majestic swish of his great black robes, while the congregation settled back in their pews, wiping the perspiration from their brows, he turned to face the ark.

For Sigmund, it was the moment . . . the only moment. The demanding heart of the Saturday-morning service belonged to the cantor, not the rabbi; and when Sigmund opened his mouth and began to sing, after blowing his little pipe for reassurance, it was with a clear sense that he didn't have to prove anything (including God's meaning; among all those other rabbinical things) beyond the validity and power of his own gift. That, of course, would require continuing proof, in any congregation.

3

"The way I figure it, I should have been at the House for services today," Barney said from his bed. "For sure." He had already had three phone calls describing the morning's events, with varying degrees of accuracy, and he was still trying to imagine how it must have been. The effort had ruined his lunch, little as it amounted to, and he could still taste the bittersweet aftermath of the peach ice cream that Elsie had served him as a treat. Such treats, Barney told himself, he probably did not need. He meant Julie Metzger, Norman Sindel, and Larry Adelman.

"The doctor won't allow it," Elsie said in her most precise accent, of which she had several. "You heard him."

"Well, I figured. No harm in figuring. I feel all right. Good enough."

"One more week. That's all. What's one more week?"

"I'm rarin'," he said, making an aggressive, guttural sound, but his heart wasn't really in it. There was a lot of pain this morning, more than usual; the sharp, steady, dark kind, which no medication seemed to be able to relieve. He had been warned by his doctors about occasions like this; not quite relapses, more like reminders, powerful ones. "I could have walked there this morning," he persisted bravely. "And they could have used me, too."

"The doctor says no. You heard him. And he's the Man."

There was a brief silence while Barney turned on his side. He waited a moment, testing the position. It was little help.

"If I fall asleep," he said, "be sure to wake me in time for the game. Where's the portable, anyway? Don't let me miss the game. It's very important. Two more and we're in."

"Don't forget, it's Sabbaday, you have to call To-ba and whassisname down in Chubby Chase."

"Tonight. When the rates change."

"Well, don't forget, she waits for your call. It's Sabbaday, your own daughter." As though Barney and his own daughter hadn't been speaking to each other every day since he came home from the hospital, and some days more than once.

Barney closed his eyes for a moment against the pain. "How long you think this war is going to last?" he asked, to keep the conversation going.

"You're asking me? How would I know? Ask Mr. Roosevelt."

"Things are coming to a head. I can feel it in my bones. It's in the air. Who knows, maybe by winter . . ."

"Well, don't look at me. Nobody tells me anything."

"Half of Tiger Pads goes to the war effort."

"You have to do your part, like the rest of the folks."

"Nobody can say Barney Fribush doesn't do his part."

"Oh, no, sir," Elsie said, looking for a less formidable topic to discuss. "Nobody says that. Anyway, don't forget Mizz Mazer called again yesterday. She wants to come see you, she says."

"You know the rules, Elsie. No widows."

"You have to have some company. You can't just stay around here alone all the time without your own kind to talk to."

Barney closed his eyes again and counted to three. "We're going to have some company," he said as soon as he finished counting.

Elsie was silent.

Barney opened his eyes. "For the holidays," he said. "In a couple of weeks."

"Is that so?"

"The Scheingold kid," Barney said in an innocent voice. "For Rosh Hashana and Yom Kippur. For the High Holidays."

"Is that so?" Elsie said again, also sounding innocent. "And what's the Scheingold kid?" she added after a moment. "I never heard of a Scheingold kid. How come I never heard of a Scheingold kid?"

"He's in the choir at the House," Barney explained patiently. "He's the star. He lives downtown in East Baltimore, he's a poor boy, almost an orphan, but he's spotless, you can depend on it. He needs a place to sleep for the holidays so he can walk to the synagogue."

"And this is the only place he could find in all of Forest Park?"

Barney rolled his eyes. "I just thought. The cantor's wife asked me to do it. Mrs. Safer asked. It's a favor I'm doing. You know what I mean. You know exactly."

"What I know is you just thought this place is a hotel or something."

"Come on now, Elsie."

"Well, isn't that the truth? You just thought this place was a hotel."

"And what difference does it make what I thought? As though what I think ever counts. You've got your mind made up already. You've always got your mind made up. You don't even know what I'm talking about and you've got all the answers. Well, forget it. We'll talk about it another time. It can wait." Barney groaned. "And this position you've got me in is murder. Give me a hand, for God's sake. It hurts laying here like this."

"Well, this is no hotel," Elsie said, helping to prop him up. "Mrs. Safer knows better than that."

"You leave Mrs. Safer out of it," Barney said, letting vaguely guilty feelings wash over him at the mention of Mrs. Safer's name. A few minutes went by in silence again. "Now listen," Barney said when he was finally comfortable in bed. "I want you to get Mr. Metzger on the phone."

"I thought you were on the outs with Mr. Metz-gah."

"I want to give him a piece of my mind. He's been asking for it. I want to make a little trouble for him."

"That's your middle name. Trouble."

"Quit giving me a hard time. I want to have a little fun, for God's sake. It's coming to me. Now make the call. I got a notion to chew his ass out."

Elsie put her hand over her mouth and pretended shock. "Sinful," she said in a reproachful voice, trying to stare Barney down. "Sinful and wicked. On Sabbaday, too. I didn't light Friday candles last night so you could go around cussing all the day long."

"When did I cuss? What did I say?"

"Mr. Metz-gah is a human being just like the rest of us."

Barney laughed at this description.

"Okay, now," Elsie said, giving in. "You want the phone near the bed?"

"Yes. And don't forget to wake me up for the game. I don't want to miss it. Just two more and we've got it."

"You're already awake."

"In case."

"In case," she repeated, standing alongside Barney's bed, watching him without moving.

There was another moment or two of silence, after which Barney began to drift off, having just about forgotten Julius Metzger and his telephone call, having just about forgotten almost everything. "Hurry up, now," he ordered Elsie in a muffled voice, nodding off while she stayed in place, keeping an eye on him. "Don't make me wait all day. For God's sake." Not even knowing what he was saying, not even knowing he was saying anything. He was worn-out from the morning's pain and from the exchange with Elsie. He was exhausted. It was almost like being in the hospital, struggling with Velda Reese or one of those pesky white-coated residents who looked about fourteen years old and were always ready to clamp an icy stethoscope onto your chest and damn near shock the life out of you. Worse even.

4

They were dancing again downtown that evening. Mother and son moved together across the skinny living room in each other's arms. The Glenn Miller Orchestra, featuring Tex Beneke, was playing "Moonlight Serenade," which was one of Lillian's favorites. She was dressed to go out. It was Saturday night, when everybody went out. This evening, it was going to be Mickey Schiller, whom Lillian liked. Unfortunately, Mickey Schiller was already married, although currently living apart from his wife, who had been one of Lillian's classmates all through grade school. Already, that seemed about a million years ago.

"Don't be such an eager beaver," she said, as Sylvan pushed the beat along, ahead instead of on top of it. "Relax." She was wearing her green dress with the white blossoms again, along with brown-and-white spectators bought at a special discount at the department store on Howard Street where she sold ladies' underwear. Lillian couldn't remember whether Mickey Schiller had ever seen her in the green dress. She hoped not. She wanted him to see her tonight as though it were the first time.

"Henny Schiller tells me his father is going out with Marty Schiffman's sister, Irene," Sylvan said in a single breath.

"Who asked Henny Schiller?" Lillian answered.

He took her around the floor again, doing a soft, slow spin. "I just thought you'd like to know," he said.

"I already know."

"Well, you know what I mean."

"No, I don't know what you mean. You always think I know what you mean. What do you mean?"

Sylvan didn't answer. He wasn't sure what to say. What did he mean? Anyway, "Moonlight Serenade" was winding down. It sounded sad. It made Sylvan feel full of regret. The last spiraling woodwind chords depressed him. They clearly said "The End."

"That's enough," he said, pulling apart from his mother, who had already begun to straighten her dress and touch up her hair. "Where are you going tonight?" he asked, as the disc jockey began to yammer again on the radio.

"Probably the movies."

"Henny Schiller tells me there's a party over at the Spectors'."

"Henny Schiller seems to know everything all of a sudden."

"Well, I can't help it, that's what he told me."

"Tell him I wasn't invited."

"Well, maybe Henny's father was."

"I'm not in the mood for a party, anyway, if you have to know. I need an air-cooled movie tonight."

The doorbell rang. Sylvan answered it.

"Hi, Nigger." It was Mickey Schiller, freshly shaven. Sylvan could smell his lemony after-shave coming right through the open doorway. "Where's your mother?" Mickey Schiller asked.

"Come on in," his mother called enthusiastically, from way back in her little bedroom. "I'll just be a minute." How had she gotten back there so fast? Sylvan didn't move. Standing there as though he had weights on his feet, he blocked the doorway.

"Well," Mickey Schiller said, smiling at Sylvan like a guy who thinks he's going to hit a home run.

"She'll be out in a minute," Sylvan said and closed the door half way, leaving Mickey Schiller waiting outside on the white marble stoop. About thirty seconds passed. Then Lillian came out, all sweetness and charm and forced laughter with Mickey Schiller and sour reproachful looks at Sylvan when she saw what was going on, and within another minute or two, they were on their way, both of them talking at the same time as Mickey guided Lillian by the elbow to his beat-up old Ford, which was parked across the street. Lillian's Woolworth necklace was in place again. She smelled of her heavy drugstore scent. And her hair needed a trim, Sylvan decided, watching them move off together. He would tell his mother about her hair at breakfast; he would make a complaint, for her own good. He always told her things like that, for her own good. He hid behind the window shade in the living room and watched them drive away. The old Ford made a lot of noise heading down the street. Mickey Schiller's car needed a new muffler. He would complain about that, too.

"In the Mood" was playing on the radio. That was all right with Sylvan Scheingold. Sylvan liked Glenn Miller, although he liked Glenn Miller better when there were no vocals. The vocals, in Sylvan's knowledgeable opinion, tended to be dopey or else whiny, and sometimes both at the same time. Well, "In the Mood" certainly didn't have any vocals, so why make a fuss? In a moment or two, Sylvan slowly began to sugar-foot around the room to the music, making faces at himself. In the mood, da-da-dee-da-da, narrowing his eyes to slits. As he passed the hall mirror, opening his eyes and hopping to the count, he caught a familiar glimpse of how dark and shadowy he was. It always came as a surprise. A regular *schvar*, he thought, doubling over his lower lip, a Sylvan Scheingold specialty, and footing it over to the daybed. In the mood, da-da-dee-da-da, faster now. One-two-one-two, one, one, one-two. Narrowing his eyes again. Then he began to pretend that he was doing a lindy, the way it was done over on Pennsylvania Avenue near the Royal Theater, in one of those forbidden upstairs ballrooms where the floor shook under the dancers' feet, first swinging somebody straight out in a crazy whirl that came right back to him, right into his capable arms, then, after doing it again, tiring quickly. In another moment, he went back to the sugar foot. In the mood . . . Sugar foot was even more demanding than the lindy. It really concentrated the energy, it took everything you had, but you could do it by yourself, you didn't need a partner, although a partner always helped. The record played on, the room turned a little. One-two . . . Saturday night, dancing alone. Solo. And nobody watching, nobody applauding. At this barren realization, he reached over in the middle of a step and switched off the radio, suddenly throwing himself down on the daybed against a pillow. Breathing hard and feeling for his heart, which seemed to swell uncontrollably beneath his palm, he lay back and decided to give himself over to daydreams. He often did this when his mother went out on a date. It was better than dancing alone. This time, it took a couple of minutes to get into gear—he had to wait for his heart to smooth out and his breath to settle—but he was soon off, winging it again.

Solos in the choir, he dreamed, starting slowly and familiarly. More solos and more, there could never be enough, plus especially kind words from Volky and the cantor, who were very stingy with praise. (That was always the first dream.) Then the discovery that underneath the make-up he was really blond, like Van Johnson. He lingered a moment on that, it was especially nice. Then wild acclaim at the House of Israel, out in Forest Park, where everybody had a house of his own, a front lawn, a back yard, a garage, and a car. Followed by an accidental meeting with Mr. Louis B. Mayer in the lobby of the Lord Baltimore Hotel and instant stardom at MGM, singing his heart out in Technicolor with Judy Garland and that gang. Or this one, his mother married to the richest Jew in Maryland, he didn't even have to be a Jew, rich was good enough, a mansion out in the Valley, someplace like that, where there were horses and a swimming pool and a tennis court or two, as well as a lot of maids dressed in black-and-white uniforms who never rested. Good-bye East Baltimore, good-bye daybed, good-bye Patterson Park, where you took your life in your hands if you were dumb enough to set foot inside, good-bye Polacks (oh, yes), farewell Irving Karton, Marty Schiffman, and all the other envious great unwashed, the sour-smelling thundering herd, who were all trying to pass themselves off as real human beings. (As though they could fool the world.) Good-bye. Good-bye. Good-bye. There weren't enough good-byes for all the good-byes Sylvan Scheingold had to say. Then good-bye Nigger again, yes, and then, best of all, in a loud welcoming voice, hello to that tall natty blond fellow standing over there in the middle distance, smiling so oddly at Sylvan, oddly yet not at all strangely, more charming, like an old buddy almost, an old pal, beckoning to him in an eager friendly way that left no doubts, wearing his smart floppy air force officer's cap at just the right angle, and his sharp summer uniform, decorated with rows of colorful medals lined up just below a silvery D.S.C. Yes, best of all, hello to Daddy, hello to Daddy Scheingold home on furlough at last, whoever, whatever, wherever. Yes.

So he dreamed.

5

When it was almost dark and *shabbos* was really over, Sigmund invited his wife out for a spin. They often did this on Saturday night as a pick-me-up after the rigors of Sigmund's Saturday-morning service, more rigorous this morning, considering everything that had happened, than ever before. Nevertheless, they both felt a little guilty about wasting gas on pleasure drives, even though gas coupons were no problem for Sigmund as a clergyman. Sigmund and Jenny were among those worthy citizens who carefully obeyed civilian war regulations. What the government required, they complied with. Without complaints, they did their share. Their only lapse had been the wholesale purchase of a gross of two-ply toilet paper right after Pearl Harbor, when a certain hysteria had swept over everybody for a few weeks. The rolls of paper, along with a couple of five-pound sacks of sugar, had been hoarded for years down in the basement of the Safer house, awaiting apocalypse, and, of course, had yet to be touched; nor would they ever be, since they were already half mildewed from the underground damp.

Sometimes on Saturday night Sigmund and Jenny headed out for Reisterstown Road, driving as far as the town of Reisterstown itself, where, amidst a rural clutter of unfamiliar stores and strange cattle-feed silos, they made a careful U-turn on the busy highway and dutifully headed back home. It was not one of their favorite routes; too much truck traffic mainly. Often, when the pastoral itch was on Sigmund, they visited the Vanderbilt heir's farm, closer in, where they treated themselves to homemade ice cream at a roadside stand, which Jenny especially enjoyed because they often ran into a few old friends who were out doing the same thing. At Emerson Farms, Sigmund also had a chance to stroke the rich Vanderbilt cows over the freshly painted white fence, which always aroused sweet bucolic feelings in him. What hard massive skulls they had, a little startling at first touch, like huge impenetrable bricks. But sooner or later the fat nagging flies that seemed to come with farm life and cows everywhere drove the Safers back to their car and the road home. They were always covered with bites when they finally reached Granada Avenue. Still, the contact was salutary, however brief. Sigmund always looked forward to it, and he continued to believe that it was very generous, very trusting of the Vanderbilts to allow the public to stroke their cows like that over the white fence. It showed the proper democratic spirit.

Tonight Sigmund was tuning up his blue Chevy at the curb—good as new, he thought pridefully, even though it predated Pearl Harbor by a couple of years—while trying to decide where they should go. He was impatient. He was always impatient when Jenny kept him waiting. It seemed a presumption on her part, or even a kind of challenge, a nervy one (and the effects of the morning's rigors, which Sigmund had not yet assessed or shared with Jenny, didn't help). "Come on," he shouted impolitely toward the porch, where he could see Annie Safer sprawled on the old metal glider, trying to read her book in the dimming light. He had left his pince-nez upstairs on his dresser and was wearing his special driving glasses, with their perfectly conventional metallic frames. Not only did they make him look younger, they made him feel younger, too, when he caught a glimpse of himself in the front-hall mirror on his way out the door; not bad, he thought, for a Saturday-evening spin through the countryside in the company of his wife . . . And where was she? What was keeping her? "Come on," he shouted again at the house, this time feeling a puff of fury at being kept waiting.

Upstairs in their bedroom, Jenny was putting on lipstick, a little rouge, a touch of powder, and a spray of Paris scent, as though they were going to a party at which she had to look her best. Each Saturday evening, whatever the destination, she prepared for their miniature excursions in the same way, grooming herself patiently at her under-utilized vanity, only half admiring what she saw in the mirror. Jenny never seemed to be entirely sure of herself and how she looked, as so many of her friends were; her confidence, unlike theirs, came and went, unpredictably, from one day to the next; it had always been like that, ever since she was a girl. (It was one of her charms, if only she knew it.) A knockout, Barney Fribush had said. Still . . . When she heard Sigmund's shout, she blotted her lipstick with a Kleenex and examined herself in the mirror for the last time. She approved of what she saw tonight—thin arched nose, fine black hair in an impeccable bun, full body, red lips; everything was in order, it would do. There was another shout from the street. "I'm coming, I'm coming," she muttered to herself, not even aware that she was talking out loud, as she headed down the stairs.

"Will you be here when we get back?" she asked her daughter when she reached the porch.

"Maybe," Annie said, looking up from her book.

"What do you mean, maybe?"

"Well, I sort of have a date."

"You can't sort of have a date. You either have one or you don't."

"Then I have one. Okay? But I haven't decided whether I want to go out. It's too hot, I'm not sure I feel like it."

"If you go out, make sure the front door is locked."

"I'll be here when you get home. I'm not going anywhere. So stop worrying."

"If you do."

"Enjoy yourself, Mother." Annie twitched away, making the glider creak rustily.

"Why don't you come with us for a change?"

"Another time. Thanks."

"You'll ruin your eyes reading in this light."

"Mo-ther."

"All right. Have it your way. They're your eyes. Just don't forget to lock the door if you go out."

From the curb, Sigmund was shouting again, sounding really irritable this time. Jenny, after having the last word with Annie, headed down the walk toward the car, hesitating a moment as she plucked some dead leaves from the hedges in passing. "I've wasted half a gallon waiting for you," Sigmund complained loudly, as Jenny got into the front seat alongside him. "The hedges can wait."

"Who told you to keep the motor running?" she said. "You know better than that."

"I wouldn't have kept the motor running if I knew it was going to take you this long. What is it, that you have to keep me waiting all the time?"

"I don't have to keep you waiting all the time. You're imagining things again. It's all in your head."

Sigmund, who hated to be told he was ever imagining things, put the Chevy in gear, making a terrible grinding noise, and on a perverse impulse headed toward Forest Park Avenue, rolling for the moment west-northwest.

"Where are we going?" Jenny asked.

"Another direction, for a change. I'm tired of the same old scenery. Maybe to Catonsville. Or Ellicott City. We haven't been to Ellicott City in years."

"What's in Ellicott City?"

"We'll see when we get there."

"What about Liberty Road? That's always nice."

"We were just on Liberty Road."

"In June."

"Well, it's too late now. You should have spoken up sooner."

Sigmund and Jenny rode along together, tight-lipped for a mile or two, looking neither right nor left, but as they sat rigidly alongside each other without speaking, cool air rushing in through the open windows in powerful drafts that almost took their breath away, they slowly began to return to themselves and, in time, to each other. It didn't take long. The silence helped. So did the comforting motion of the Chevy, the neat little sway it had on the road that was so soothing and buoyant at the same time; and besides, bickering had always made them feel ashamed in the other's presence. Bickering was unworthy and therefore beneath them. When Sigmund and Jenny heard their friends bicker, they turned away in embarrassment.

"This is much nicer," Jenny finally said, making the opening move as they passed the Children's Hospital along the way. "You were right to head in this direction."

"It's not too late to take Liberty Road," Sigmund answered, feeling suddenly conciliatory at Jenny's words. "So we'll waste a little gas. Why not? It's coming to us. Would you like to take Liberty Road?"

"I'm perfectly happy where we are. This is just right."

"You sure now?"

"It's perfect."

They continued out into the country, heading west, silent again but almost fully at ease now with each other, riding into strange, alien land that lay impassively all around them, gazing solemnly into the darkening light at the mysterious farmland and the thick crops growing there, corn and tomatoes, squash, beans, watermelon, rich Maryland produce. A fuzzy moon hung a couple of feet above the Chevy's right fender. Overhead, a few stars shone dimly through the humidity. It felt like rain; everything already seemed a little damp. Late-summer evenings were often like this in Baltimore, filled with haze and lingering moisture, dense with heat that refused to lighten. Here and there they could still see a few farmers at work in their fields, bent figures that appeared cut in two at the waist. A young boy with a crisp blond crew cut drove a tractor next to Sigmund and Jenny for a few hundred yards, waving at them soberly before turning off into a pasture filled with haystacks; and every now and then they could also make out the figures of overalled men sitting quietly on their front porches, stout strong women rocking at their sides, fanning themselves in the August heat. Sigmund eyed them warily as he drove along. Like Jenny, he felt a foreigner to all this. He could never quite get over the feeling, riding out in the open country away from Forest Park, that he was a guest and a stranger here, doomed, probably, to be a guest and a stranger forever. (Wasn't that perhaps the essential history of the Jews, he asked himself, writ small?) It was not like stroking a cow over the fence at Emerson Farms with all the other strangers; it lacked the innocence of that sweet experience.

At the wheel, Sigmund suddenly spoke up. "What do you think," he began, making a sweeping gesture that seemed to take in the whole countryside, "what do you think these farmers would say if they knew I was a Jew riding by?"

"What a question," Jenny said, after a moment's uncomfortable consideration.

"Well, think about it. What would they say?"

"How would I know? And isn't it two Jews riding by?"

"All right, two Jews. Now think."

"Pshaw?"

"What?"

"That's how farmers talk, isn't it? Pshaw? Or holy smoke?"

"Come on, Jenny," Sigmund said. "Be serious."

"What should they say?"

"That's exactly what I'm asking you. And I don't have any answer. And you know why? Because I don't know any farmers, I don't know any gentiles. That's the whole point I'm trying to make. All I know are Jews." Then he thought of Bobby Fiorentino. Bobby Fiorentino was certainly a gentile, direct from the source. Did Jenny even know he existed?

"You know George Haney," she said. "You know Milton Holliday."

"They don't count the way I mean. George and Milton, we share a hobby, that's all, it's an accident. All we talk about is tropical fish. I mean something else. Something entirely different. I'm talking about everyday gentiles. You know?"

"George Haney seems pretty everyday to me. Milton Holliday, too."

"Don't act so thick."

Jenny pretended to think for a moment. "Well," she finally said, "it would probably not be flattering."

"You think so?"

"Probably."

"Something not nice? Something insulting? Or threatening?"

"Probably. Sad to say."

"Well, I bet they don't know any Jews, either."

"Maybe, maybe not. I mean, how could they, living out in the sticks like this."

"I always knew in Poland, when I was a boy. I always knew what they thought."

"Well, in Poland. Everybody knows about that."

"I have dreams about Poland," Sigmund went on.

Jenny waited alongside him without speaking, her scent floating up into the night air. Sitting there, waiting for Sigmund to explain himself, she began to make a silent linen count as she gazed through the windshield, straight ahead, where the Chevy's headlights swept the empty road in front of them.

"I see my sisters in my dreams. I see Bronya and Shifra, both of them." Sigmund turned to see how Jenny was taking this. She looked impassive. "I see them waving to me from their graves," he went on, braking the car a little, "calling to me to join them. It's all in slow motion, like sleepwalking. Calling to me from their graves in the Jewish cemetery in Warsaw. What do you think of that? I'm only a little boy in the dream, maybe ten years old. Younger, even. I just started having these dreams."

"Sigi," Jenny finally said. How many extra sheets would she need for the holidays? Pillowcases? Hand towels and washcloths? The house would be crowded with choir members, with demanding types like Samuel Volkonsky and Jeffrey Bourne.

"It's true," Sigmund said. "I dreamed that the other night, the second time."

"You don't know that your sisters are dead," Jenny then said. "You don't even know where they are. You don't know any of those things. They could be in Russia or someplace like that. With all that's going on . . . You should try to put it out of your mind. It's useless to worry."

"I don't want to put it out of my mind. I like the dream. It doesn't make me unhappy. I see my sisters, after all. And anyway, I don't have any control over my dreams. Nobody has."

Jenny twitched.

"There must be a lot of people around the world having dreams like that these days," Sigmund went on pensively.

"I hope not. I know I don't."

"Sometimes I see the casualty list from the *Sun* papers in my dreams." He glanced at her again to see how she was taking this. "I can recite you names," he added.

"Never mind."

"Baylor. Roy. Dean. Baetjer. I'm not even sure how to pronounce that one."

"Sigi, please."

"Steele. Coursey. Goldstein. Taylor. I know it sounds terrible, but I look for the Jewish names first, then all the rest."

Jenny looked away.

"Not all of them are dead," Sigmund went on, unperturbed. "Some are just wounded. Warnick. Fanslick. Chehowski. Dye." He shook his head at the irony of PFC Dye's name, and added, "Some are MIA."

"MIA?" Jenny said after a moment. "Is that missing in action?"

"Yes. Or lost. Or maybe prisoners."

"Your sisters are MIA."

He looked at her in surprise. "Yes," he said. "That could certainly be the case."

"Think of it that way."

"My sisters are MIA," Sigmund said, as though he were testing the idea. "Like a lot of people. Like a lot of Jews." Like my own daughter, he added to himself, wincing at the thought.

They drove on in silence, taking a series of winding curves that demanded all of Sigmund's attention at the wheel. He managed them carefully, swerving gently with the Chevy at each turn. Several moments passed without conversation. Jenny was wishing that they had taken Liberty Road tonight. She should have insisted. She always gave in too easily. Maybe on Liberty Road, where there were distractions like real neighborhoods and drive-ins and even billboards along the way, not rustic at all, they would have been talking about other things. Jenny couldn't always be sure what was on her husband's mind. She wasn't always sure that even he knew. Sigmund was sometimes wayward. (Not sometimes, often!) And now, she reminded herself, morbid as well, given the evening's conversation. He sometimes (often!) seemed to be possessed by a hummingbird's nervous flutter; he liked to hover over strange landscapes, comfortably suspended in midair, observing from above. He was like a bird, she thought, like a small-boned, quick-eyed bird, with a beautiful silvery voice, always at the ready. A bird, she thought again, a small quick bird, touched by sadness . . .

"Well," Sigmund finally said, heading straight ahead again, "there's always plenty to dream about in this world. You can depend on that."

"And you're a dreamer, too," Jenny said, knowing that her words would please him. "Awake or asleep."

"I always was," he answered without hesitation. "My sisters used to tease me about that. A dreamer, awake or asleep, yes."

"And you're an *artiste*, too," she added pointedly.

"Being an *artiste* is part of being a dreamer."

Who knew better than Jenny Safer? "You should really be singing in opera," she said. "I always thought that."

"Operetta. I know my limits."

"You have an unusual talent. You should never forget that."

"For Friml. Romberg. Victor Herbert. Maybe a little Mozart, too, where you have to have the long breath, but not the heavy stuff," Sigmund said. "The truth is, I did what I could with what I had. Not what I wanted, maybe, but what I could. I didn't have a penny when I landed here, after I ran away from Warsaw. I didn't know north from south, I didn't know my thing from my elbow. I only knew that I had to change Czaferski to Safer. And a lucky thing, too, for all of us that I knew to do that. I thought I was a goner when I got to America. Missing in action. That was me. I had to do what I could, take the first real offer. The first real offer turned out to be the only offer. Then I got stuck in all this. You think I had a calling? I never meant to be a cantor. It just happened. Circumstances made it happen. It wasn't like the Ten Commandments, laying down the law. I had other things in mind. I was thinking of another life."

"Well, you're very sensitive," said his wife, "everybody knows that. I mean, you know it, too. So it shouldn't come as a surprise."

"What shouldn't?" Sigmund asked.

"Your dreams," she said, with an air of finality.

On the way back, they didn't talk much. They had nothing more to say for the moment. Sigmund had spoken his piece in carefully selected words, nothing too extreme, and Jenny had listened in a patient, dignified, wifely way—her way. Now she willed a silence between them; she had heard enough for one evening, she told herself. But at the same time, as they drove along without talking, she began to wonder again—vaguely, abstractly—about her happiness, that far-fetched and absurd question that Barney Fribush had planted in her mind like an insidious creeper. And as for happiness, Jenny began, very slowly, her head resting easily on the back of the car seat, as for happiness, so what? It was Jenny's opinion that everyone worried far too much about happiness. Men and women both. And that was a waste of cherished time, it was nonproductive. Happiness was like a tide, she thought, you took it as it came in and said good-bye when it went out. It was that simple. And either way, it didn't last. That was the only way to think about happiness. Elusive. Ephemeral. The slippery thing . . . And, she went on thinking, unable to resist, as for Barney Fribush himself . . .

Jenny sat up and stared out the window, ruffled at the thought of Barney Fribush. She would put him out of her mind. She was good at that, she never thought about what she didn't want to think about, and it was time, in any case, to consider the practical matter of sleeping arrangements for the holidays. The matter of sleeping arrangements was as important as a linen count or even happiness. It had to be dealt with, the sooner the better. So she began, methodically clearing her mind of all extraneous abstract matters, of everything that was irrelevant and nonproductive. Sleeping arrangements, she thought, concentrating hard on it . . . Volky could have the small room off the kitchen again, she decided. The small room suited him, with its little fold-away cot, its tiny chest of drawers, and its single chair. It was on the right scale, it was modest but neat; he wouldn't bother anybody back there, off the kitchen. And Jeffrey Bourne? Jenny felt a twinge of resistance as she thought of Jeffrey Bourne. Jeffrey Bourne was not such a simple matter. All baritones were lecherous, was Jenny Safer's basic proposition. Consider Lawrence Tibbett. Think of John Charles Thomas. And there were others she could name, whose derring-do popped up in the newspapers from time to time, disguised in libel-proof gossip items. Even Nelson Eddy. Jenny, of course, wasn't thinking about herself, she was thinking about Annie. She always seemed to be thinking about Annie. It was by now a lifetime habit, even though she had begun to doubt whether Annie any longer wanted or needed her protection. She felt another twinge, stronger, followed by a long, deep internal sigh. . . . Maybe they could fix up the loft over the garage for

Jeffrey Bourne, get him out of the house, and Annie out of harm's way. It was like a steam bath up there, with its unfinished ceiling, no insulation at all, but when you considered the undesirable possibilities . . .

The country air rushed in, smelling of cropped hay and manure and, here and there, fresh-cut grass. While Sigmund drove a little faster, they passed the same modest farms, the same rickety slanting barns, the hen coops, the silent watchful animals and blue Maryland hills silhouetted against the night sky. The humidity still hung heavy and low, they could actually feel the moisture, but the moon had risen a considerable distance without the Safers being aware of it. Every now and then another car sped by, going in the other direction, but there was hardly any real traffic to speak of. Getting closer to home, Sigmund slowed the pace. It was nice rolling along like this. He wished they could go on forever, rolling along, speaking their minds to each other when they felt like it. And the Chevy was a real honey, in tiptop condition. Of course, Sigmund had seen to that. He was prideful of that. Suddenly, he grew eager for Granada Avenue.

A few minutes later, after parking in front of the house, he raced around the front of the car and opened Jenny's door for her. Jenny liked small chivalric gestures, and so did he; they made a point of trying to maintain them, without too much fuss. "It was very nice tonight," she said, holding on to his hand as she stepped out on the curb. She sounded a little dreamy. "Just what the doctor ordered."

"Sometimes it does wonders," Sigmund said cheerfully.

"Come," Jenny said, heading up the walk toward the porch. "We'll have some iced tea and brownies. I made some for you. I put nuts inside. They're crispy, your way."

"Good," he said.

"And those glasses become you," she added, with a sly little smile at her husband. "You should wear that style all the time."

6

"It wouldn't hurt you to read something every now and then." It was Annie Safer speaking. She had gone out after all, as she always did when Bobby Fiorentino called. She was standing on a darkened street corner across from the Forest Park High School track field, which she had just finished circling for the third time. As she spoke, she shifted her weight from one leg to the other. Her shins hurt. Bobby Fiorentino liked to walk fast.

"Such as?" Bobby Fiorentino asked, sounding bored.

"You could read the book I'm reading. *The Razor's Edge*. Ever hear of *The Razor's Edge*? Or you could try *The Fountainhead*. You'd probably like *The Fountainhead*. It's just crazy enough. The fascist hero has orange hair."

"I never heard of orange hair."

"Well, he's an architect."

"I'm not a reader, Annie. You should know that by now. I never was a reader."

"There's always a first time."

"You sound like my mother. She keeps talking like that. There's always a first time. Better late than ever. A stitch in time." As he spoke, Bobby took a hefty swing with an imaginary bat, as though that might clear the air. He swung so hard that he felt a momentary muscle spasm in his right shoulder.

"It's 'better late than *never*,' Bobby."

"And stop correcting me all the time. It gets my goat."

"Well, sometimes you're lazy. For a guy with brains. I think you have brains. That's one of your things. You don't think you're very smart."

"Well, I'm not as smart as you, that's for sure."

"Oh, don't give me that stuff."

"I'm not giving you any stuff, with all your big words and books and some of your ideas. Holy Christ, some of your ideas." Bobby took another swing with his imaginary bat, holding back a little this time.

"I can't help it. I'm a thinking person. I was raised that way."

"Oh, I-was-raised-that-way," he said in a prissy voice. "If that's where thinking gets you."

"What are you talking about, anyway? What ails you tonight?"

"I mean, you don't even believe in God."

"I might have known."

"A sin against nature."

"And that's exactly why I could never be a Catholic."

"Who asked you to be a Catholic? Did I ask you to be a Catholic?"

"You believe everything you're told. Whatever the Church says, you lap it up."

"Because it's the truth."

"You don't know any more about the truth than I do. At least I admit that I don't know."

"I'm talking about God."

"You're talking about Jesus Christ. Jesus Christ isn't God. Who could believe that Jesus Christ was God?"

"Bite your tongue," he said, quickly making the sign of the cross over her.

"Oh, how did we get on this, anyway? It's so god-awful boring."

"I don't like being bored any more than you do."

"Well, then, why don't you read a book for a change?"

"Okay, I'll read a book. I'll read a book if you just shut up for two minutes. It's enough talk for one night. You hear me? *Basta . . .*"

They had been arguing like that all evening, as they often did.

7

Before he went to sleep that night, Sigmund spent a half-hour alone with his fish, the time drifting slowly past, like the lazy angels and labyrinths that swept in front of him in close lingering formations. When they saw him, or felt his familiar shadow suddenly hovering over them, looming darkly in the cloudy water, some responded by resting their snouts against the glass wall of the tanks, staring out at Sigmund, eyes popping, while others instantly rose to the surface, mouths up, eagerly waiting to be fed. Sigmund did the chores patiently, moving in a slow, deliberate way, by the numbers. He loved the normality of it, the repetition and set rules, one arm sweeping the water up to his elbow, his shirt sleeve rolled almost to his shoulder, cleaning, feeding, checking temperature and oxygenation levels. It was useful work, he felt, no small thing, and he could see the results almost instantly. Everything brightened up, the cloudy water dissipated, his fish seemed to move with new energy at his direction, under his control.

Sigmund felt a little tired from the evening's drive—that was the point, he reminded himself—but he also felt pleasantly calm after telling Jenny his dreams. He liked telling Jenny his dreams, just for the telling. Dreams were magic, the most mysterious magic of all; it was right to share them. But clearly it helped in another way, too. It took the edge off the fears that seemed to surface so easily these days. Fears of dissolution at the House, of deception by his friends, and of the recurring appearances of his insistent Jewish sisters, willful as ever, rising from their imaginary Polish graves to tempt young Zsygmunt Czaferski to join them. It would take more than a single telling to get rid of that one—all its smothering power and the way it gripped him, and all its chilling pleasure, too. Dreams, he thought, sitting in the ethereal green light that came from his fish tanks, dimly remembering Warsaw and other half-forgotten places from another time. Dreams, the spooky soap operas of agitated souls.

A little sleepily now, he watched one labyrinth chase another. The fish fluttered through some coral construction and disappeared in the back of the tank. He knew that upstairs Jenny was probably taking off her light make-up at this moment. She was always very careful about her make-up. There was never any mess in their bedroom. Sigmund liked the scent that Jenny used these days. *Femme de France.* Imported just before the war. Touches of it on the lobes of her ears, at the hollowed base of her neck, and sometimes, when she was feeling imaginative and bold, on the nipples themselves, just a drop or two, nothing excessive. Then he reminded himself that Annie was out; she had left them a terse note containing two words only, "back late"; the old patronizing noblesse oblige of children growing up. Who was she with? Where was she?

Stirring into action again, Sigmund checked the oxygen level in the tanks for the last time, thinking as he worked of Jenny Safer, upstairs in their room, hair down to her waist, reading in bed probably, in her own slow, stately, word-by-word, sentence-by-sentence fashion, something by Pearl S. Buck or John P. Marquand, smelling faintly of Paris, where she had never been, and of Europe, where her husband's dreams were so handily manufactured these days. It was late. It had been a long day; Saturday always was. He had better hurry, before they both fell asleep.

"Do you think . . ." he began a few minutes later, standing in front of Jenny upstairs at the foot of their bed. In his left hand, he held his driving glasses; his right arm, where the sleeve was rolled up, was still wet.

At his question, Jenny nodded agreeably and began to remove her earrings, then turned in bed to dim her reading lamp. The room instantly became suffused by a pale pink light that touched everything. Even the curtains looked pink when Jenny turned down her lamp. For a moment, neither spoke. The soft rosiness enveloped them. "I can smell fish food," Jenny said in a distant voice.

"Probably," Sigmund answered, also sounding faraway. He began to undress.

"Don't forget your shoes again," Jenny said, stroking her hair. "I almost broke a leg tripping over them last night."

"Sorry," Sigmund said, lining up his shoes neatly on the floor. It seemed to take forever, this simple little action, one shoe in line with the other, out of his wife's way. Then, feeling pleasantly enervated, he got into bed alongside Jenny and, after hesitating a second, leaned over and began to count her ribs.

"One," he said, poking at her with his wet forefinger, just as she had poked at him to awaken him from his dreams. "For the money."

"Two," he then said. "For the show." He had learned the little rhyme when Annie was a child, without ever understanding a word of it.

"Three," he said. "To get ready."

A moment passed while he cleared his throat; he had forgotten to gargle with salt water tonight.

Jenny had begun to laugh. "You know how ticklish I am," she said into his ear. "It's your mustache. And I've got a little prickly heat there, too. Which doesn't help."

Four. Five.

He liked to hear the sound of his wife laughing. It didn't happen often enough. He was laughing, too, he discovered, he who had just climbed the stairs to their room, who did everything, with such a grave and chaste face. A European mustache; new metal eyeglasses, the latest thing; Jenny's perfect arching ribs; her skin. And one kiss then, their usual quota; one kiss only, accompanied by a feeling of gently increasing urgency and a certain pleasurable amount of writhing about, mostly by Sigmund, who was not at all the reluctant lover tonight.

8

She was shaking him by the shoulders. "Sweetheart? Sylvan?" she was saying. "You fell asleep with your clothes on," she said.

When he opened his eyes, he blinked twice. "What time is it?" he asked. He struggled to sit up, trying to remember when he had fallen asleep. He made a long drawn-out sound that lasted until he felt in control of himself. "Did I leave all the lights on?" he asked.

"You must have conked out," Lillian said, sounding amused. "Were you drinking or something?" She was obviously in a cheerful mood.

"Drinking?" Then he smiled, too. He was still trying to remember.

"You'd better put on some pajamas."

"I was dreaming," he said, forgetting to ask about Mickey Schiller.

"The whole world is dreaming," Lillian answered, glancing at herself in the hall mirror.

"No, I really was."

"I believe you. Now come on, get into bed. It's after midnight."

They went through all the prescribed motions then, considerate of the other's presence, Lillian taking the bathroom first, as usual, Sylvan wandering back and forth like a sleepwalker on the narrow living-room floor, waiting his turn, still trying to remember how he had fallen asleep with his clothes on, and why.

9

At three o'clock in the morning, Barney Fribush awoke. A thick pall of already forgotten dreams hung over him. All his life, Barney had had trouble remembering his dreams. Even as a child. It was as though he had always lived on the thin crust of awareness, at the very edge of his consciousness. He lay in bed now, listening for a sound. There was nothing. His anus began to itch. A healthy symptom, he decided. Several minutes passed. At last, a car sped along Hilton Street, out front. The reflection of its headlights fanned across the ceiling, then vanished. Another minute passed. Barney turned on his side, turned back, unable to find a comfortable position for himself. A needle of pain shot through his crotch. He thought that one just like it had probably awakened him. He waited for it to subside, then waited some more, finally reaching for his medication on the bedside table.

I am alive, he told himself forcefully, as though he were trying to convince a roomful of white-coated skeptics, listening to his own heartbeat in the dark and reminding himself, from lifetime habit, of everything he had to do tomorrow. That didn't take long, the list was still short. Then, swallowing his pills and sipping some dusty water, he said it again.

I am alive.

Four

1

"Hello there, cantor."

It was Velda Reese, calling to Sigmund from down the hall a few days later; they had become "new" friends, associates almost, having begun to acknowledge each other on Sigmund's hospital visits soon after Barney Fribush's discharge, chatting together amiably whenever they met on their rounds to help pass the time and, especially, to exchange professional information. Velda was carrying a clipboard clasped in her arms, keys dangled from her uniform pocket, her cap was set straight on her head. Velda loved her cap; she had worked hard enough for it. She waved now, looking cheerful.

Sigmund nodded heavily in her direction. He could hardly stay awake this morning. Hospital visits and clerical rounds were often debilitating. There was something in the air, beyond the nause-ating smells that hovered everywhere, a powerful sense of fore-boding, of menace, urgency, and worse, no matter how cheerful the nurses tried to look. All hospitals, in Sigmund's experience, were haunted by it. Besides, the day was already fiercely hot, near-hallucinatory in its power, and he had not slept well. Dreams kept breaking through his light slumber, the familiar ones, once at midnight and again just before he finally awoke at dawn, leaving him breathlessly disoriented as he lay in bed counting the hours and waiting for the morning light to show itself. His sisters, Bronya and Shifra, beckoning to him from their Polish graves. Outside, it was already eighty-eight degrees. News of the heat was still on the front page of the *Sun*, along with the war, the Orioles, and the future of FDR. Nothing had changed.

"How's our friend look to you?" Velda asked, suddenly swaying in front of Sigmund in her immaculate white oxfords. It was always her first question when they met.

"Full of vinegar," Sigmund said. He thought of Barney, snapping orders to his factory manager over the phone, complaining about accumulated bills, cursing the rebels at the House of Israel whenever the subject came up in his exchanges with Sigmund. Did they think they could beat Barney Fribush at his own game? Julie Metzger and that gang? "Vinegar" was just the word.

"Such a shrimp," Velda said, shaking her head, and Sigmund had to agree. Barney *was* a shrimp, but one who always seemed to occupy a lot of space, as though it were coming to him. (The world, Sigmund sometimes believed, was filled with shrimps trying to act like sharks.) As they faced each other with friendly smiles in the broad corridor, Sigmund, like Barney, also had to look up at Velda. (Most men did.) But Velda was so hugely real, so without pose or pretense, that Sigmund was unfazed. He saw, at an unnatural angle, wide-set eyes, a frizz of blond hair, a mouth that was fire-red with lipstick, and, finally, supporting it all, broad, reliable, strong shoulders. No, Velda Reese did not intimidate Sigmund R. Safer. To Sigmund, she was a benign apparition.

An orderly loped by, pushing an empty stretcher. "Hey, Velda," he called in a sleepy voice, "how you doin'?" Sounds of early lunch carts came rattling down the hall. There were vague overtones of ether in the air, seeping down from a floor upstairs, where the operating rooms were located, a scurry of late-morning work all around them. Sigmund yawned again, although Velda's tall, authoritative presence was slowly bringing him to full alert. At Sigmund's request, Velda began to report on the Freedman boy's tonsil operation. The Freedman boy's father sat on the board of the House of Israel. The Freedman boy was already eating ice cream, Velda said, glancing at her clipboard. He was going home in two days, it was standard stuff. Sigmund then went down the list of his congregants, checking off the names with Velda. He had learned that Velda knew a lot about what was going on in the hospital, whether it involved her directly or not, and was both generous and discreet about sharing her information, never giving too much away or withholding news unreasonably. She helped him use his visiting time wisely.

"Mind if I share something with you?" Velda asked, when they came to the end of the list.

"Shoot," Sigmund said, looking up into her eyes and blinking.

Velda didn't hesitate. "What would you say if I told you I was going to work for Mr. Eff?" she asked.

Sigmund was confused for a moment. Mr. Eff? Then he understood. "Is it so?" he asked, sounding doubtful.

"Yes."

"You want my opinion?"

"What would you say?"

Sigmund plunged in. "You're thinking of leaving the hospital?" he asked. "You'd give all this up? Your job? Your security? With the nurse shortage and the war, would they let you? And what do you want with him?"

"Take it easy, now. I'm talking about two weeks, on my vacation time. I'm talking two weeks only. Mr. Eff says he could use a little assistance."

"He's already got a housekeeper, Elsie. She runs the place."

"But she just cleans the house, right?"

"She does everything. She's in charge."

"Well, that's not what we're talking about." There was a pause, Velda fidgeting. "She's colored, isn't she?" she then asked.

"Listen, she's been with him for fifteen, twenty years," Sigmund answered. "She was there before his wife died. She helped to raise his daughter."

"One of those," Velda said.

"Yes," Sigmund acknowledged. "She even speaks a little Yiddish by now. But what do you want to give up your vacation for? Don't you need a vacation like everybody else?"

"Barney says he could use me, and he probably can."

Barney, Sigmund thought with a pang. All of a sudden it was Barney.

"I know this postoperative thing," Velda went on. "It's always the same. You can be flat on your back again, just like that." She snapped her fingers in Sigmund's face. "I wouldn't be doing any housework, nothing like that," she added. "It would be straightout nursing business. In uniform, too, so nobody gets confused. And between you and me, I could use the money."

"Far be it from me, Velda."

"You don't think I should do it."

"I didn't say that."

"You might as well."

"Look, it's none of my business, but why don't you just run down to Ocean City like a good girl and have some fun?"

"And where'd you get the idea I was a good girl, cantor?" Velda said, grinning at him.

At least, she had the delicacy to add the "cantor," Sigmund thought. "You're telling me you're not a good girl?" Sigmund asked, feeling daring.

"You know what they say about nurses," Velda said. "Anyway," she went on, dropping the flirtatious tone, "I think I can handle all that. Elsie, I mean. I'll bring her something nice. A handkerchief, maybe, with edging and her initials on it. It's for the Holy Days he wants me. Soon. He just bears watching," Velda added, in her proper nurse's voice. "All postoperative patients do. And I've got a soft spot."

"Well, it's all right with me. Who am I, after all? You do what you want. You're a big girl."

"You betcha," she said, pulling herself up to her full height. "And thanks for your patience, thanks for the advice," she added, looking gratefully down at Sigmund.

Sigmund watched her turn and head along the corridor, off on her rounds. Her starchy white uniform had a nice high sheen to it, and it lay over her buttocks in a crisp fold that had not yet been wilted by the heat. As she walked away from him, Sigmund could see the cleft between the cheeks, the neat little valley, the little glen of iniquity, appear and disappear with her nurse's stride. "That's somethin', revrun," the orderly said, deadpan, on his way back with another stretcher; he didn't even bother to look at Sigmund as he spoke. "Yes," Sigmund heard himself say, and blushed. Some days, it seemed, everybody thought they could say anything they wanted to the cantor and get away with it. Sigmund stood there without moving until the orderly disappeared into a storage room. Then he took off his pince-nez and stared into the middle distance, trying to look dignified. Finally, as the lunch cart appeared, smelling of stewed fruit, Sigmund headed for the stairwell and walked down one flight, feeling his usual queasiness, momentarily overcome by it, as he got a powerful whiff of carbolic acid in his nostrils.

He hadn't quite finished his morning duties. He had promised Mary Goldman a visit. She had been in the hospital for almost a week and he still hadn't seen her. Mary Goldman had diabetes. Sometimes, her system went awry. She was here to be controlled. (That's what Velda had told him.) After Mary, he would visit Albert Sallens, undergoing tests for auricular fibrillation, who would want to complain about the rabbi—his habit whenever he was alone with the cantor—while chewing on a ham sandwich smuggled in to him by his secretary, as though Sigmund had neither eyes nor ears in his head; then the Freedman boy (for his father's sake), minus his tonsils; ending the morning with a brief appearance at the bedside of Lew Mittelman, whose chronic stomach pains and black stools had yet to be diagnosed, although there were plenty of theories about them among the hospital staff. It seemed to Sigmund, as he turned into the corridor, trying to hold his breath against the acrid smell, that there were always more men in the hospital than women. It had always seemed that way to him. Men got sick, for whatever reason, from whatever cause; women nursed them. Then the men died, leaving the women to life.

"What do you know?" Mary Goldman cried out, as Sigmund came through the door after gently knocking. "The cantor, at last!" But Sigmund barely heard her. He was yawning again, preparing to go slack. Also, his nostrils had begun to dilate. Approaching Mary's bed, he took off his pince-nez so he wouldn't have to look Mary in the eye. That way, sitting blindly alongside her, facing into the sun, he could pretend to listen to what Mary Goldman had to say, which was always a bit too much for Sigmund's comfort, and think about Velda Reese and other pleasantly voluptuous matters at the same time, without feeling guilty. In any case, he wouldn't stay longer than ten minutes. For medical reasons, for professional clerical reasons, for reasons of simple humanity, ten minutes was always his limit.

2

Barney was wandering around the house on Hilton Street, touching things. He had been at it for two days, touching things in every room in the house. It was his way of taking emotional inventory, checking that everything was in place, exactly where he had left it, undisturbed during his absence in the hospital—just the way Barney wanted to feel about himself.

The house was full of objects, large and small, most of them on display. That had seemed to be the whole point originally. What was not on display, except for the Stieff silverware and the mounds of English china hidden away in breakfronts and cabinets, lay piled in untidy heaps up in the attic, which was just too damned stuffy at this time of year for Barney to venture into (even if he hadn't just had an operation), or else rested downstairs in the cement basement, where the air in summer was cool and faintly chalky. (He'd get to those another time, after his full recuperation.) The number of things in the house always amazed him. And the quality. His wife had known what she was doing. Everybody always said that. The ormolu clock, ugly, maybe, in Barney's opinion, but still one-of-a-kind (or so he had been told), ticking away the wrong time on the mantel; the matching pair of massive silver candlesticks, standing in the center of the dining-room table, supposedly out of some French castle from the Loire, wherever that was; the vases, the sconces, the mirrors, the glass bowls of all sizes and colors, the tiny footed candy dishes, also silver, so refined, so delicate, polished to a high shine over the years by Elsie. His wife had known all about that.

At the moment, Barney was running his finger over the glistening walnut concert grand that took up an entire corner of the vast living room, where he had never felt entirely at home. (The living room had belonged to his wife and her friends.) "Knabe," it read over the lid, in huge, curling letters that swirled in all directions. Elsie had really done a job on it. Smooth. Beautiful. Brown and big. Worthy of Paderewski or somebody in that class. It was a shame that nobody played it. Or ever had. Not even Barney's daughter, Toby, who had turned out to be tone-deaf and immune to the charms of music. Barney himself wasn't so crazy about music, either, at least the way some people he knew were, in the Bock, Beehaven, and Brooms way, as he loved to call it when he was around those people, just to needle them for their grim high-mindedness. For Barney, music, like most other things, was not quite enough in itself. It had to be attached to something else to make its full impact, preferably to words that were emotional and strong, that meant something, something he could get hold of, something, in fact, like the Silent Devotion, as passionately delivered in the high silvery tones of Cantor Safer, backed by the massed forces of the House of Israel choir, men and boys. When that kind of match took place, so full of sweet impenetrable mystery, so incomprehensible to Barney in any ordinary terms, it could really shake him, almost sweep him away, in the same way that sexual pleasure did. (He was one of those who wept in the synagogue at the sounds the choir made.) That was real power, as Barney knew, worthy of a man's honest respect. When it took hold, it did not let go easily.

But the piano, the glistening giant Knabe with the yellowing keys, what was it, what was any piano, standing alone and unplayed in the corner of an unused room?

The clock marked late afternoon, dead time. Barney was due for some special medication soon, to be ministered by Elsie when she finished her housework. He was just killing the hour, touching things. He wished he were down at the factory, giving orders in a loud voice. They could use a little of that down at Tiger Pads, after his absence. They probably even missed it. It went with the job. Orders. Commands. The rumble of the boss growling! The roar of Barney Fribush's voice! The unchallenged authority! He missed all that, too. It was important to him. He liked to shout. He liked to shout at people. Why did some people object to that? What was so wrong with shouting at people?

All these objects surrounding him, all these things. He kept touching them. That was what they were there for, to be looked at and to be touched. Sooner or later, of course, if he wanted to be realistic about it, they would all go to his daughter and whassisname, over in Chevy Chase. Sooner or later, they would have it all. But not yet. Certainly not yet. Barney was not quite ready for that. Naturally, Elsie would get an odd piece all her own, too. She deserved it, at the very least. He would choose it himself, he wouldn't leave the decision to his daughter and whassisname, it would be something special, special and costly, that Barney Fribush himself had selected. (And maybe he'd leave the Knabe to the cantor, it didn't seem such a bad idea; in fact, it seemed somehow wholly appropriate.) Barney could hear Elsie now, running his wife's old vacuum cleaner upstairs, probably over his bedroom carpet again. Since he had been sick, she had taken to vacuuming his bedroom twice a day, and sometimes even more if he let her get away with it, as though the source of his illness lay hidden somewhere inside the carpeting, waiting to be sucked into the cleaner and eliminated. Yes, sooner or later she would get something special, he would make sure of that. Something that would help to make up for everything.

He paused a moment on his rounds and stood still in the middle of his vast living room. He was feeling better today. No question. Yesterday's fatigue and unexpected pain had lifted somewhat, like a heavy fog slowly moving out to sea; in its place he felt a touch of new energy, a need for action, for something to do, on a small scale, of course. Whom could he call? Where could he make some innocent mischief, have a little teasing fun that might dispel the late-afternoon gloom? There were plenty of names that came to mind, Barney had a long list of them. But who? He dropped into a velour armchair (he couldn't remember whether he had ever sat in it before) and began to pluck at the soft fabric. The room was now in deep shade. Upstairs, Elsie went on with her cleaning. She was probably talking to herself at the same time. It was one of her habits. Why not? Barney talked to himself sometimes, probably everybody did. (Barney then remembered that a few tiles in his shower needed grouting. He would have to remind Elsie to call the handyman. Elsie took care of all those things.)

Sitting there vacantly, in a chair he may never have sat in before, waiting for the day to end, also waiting for the supreme moment when he could smoke his first and only cigar of the day, all the doctor allowed him until further notice, plucking unconsciously at the strange soft velour until it began to shine, Barney thought of Julie Metzger and instantly discarded him. He did not want to call Julie Metzger; he did not want to talk to Julie Metzger today. He would save Julie Metzger for another time. He thought of Norman Sindel and Larry Adelman. Same thing. He didn't have quite the energy for that, or the patience. Velda Reese came to mind, as she often did. But Velda Reese was on duty, and the hospital was strict about personal calls during duty hours. Well, he would see her for the Holy Days. She would take care of him in his own home. She would act tough and efficient, as always, just what he needed. It would be a houseful, all right, for the Holy Days. That pleased Barney. It made him happy to think about Velda Reese and the Scheingold kid sharing his generosity. What else was he rich for? Why make money in the first place, if not to create a little happiness, a touch of joy among those who could use it? Was Jenny Safer happy? he asked himself then, almost without a transition. Was she? He would make it his business to find out. He already had an opinion on the subject, he had made that clear to her over the phone; but Barney always had an opinion on every subject. He began to brood about these matters now in his armchair, amidst all the objects and things, waiting for Elsie to tell him the moment had come for his special medication. He did not look forward to it. The afternoon wore slowly on. Things dimmed in the dusky light, the house grew quiet. Since his wife's death, Barney often sat alone on Hilton Street and brooded like this in silence, pretending that he was really thinking.

3

After only a day in bed, Sigmund had had enough. It was airless and musty in the bedroom upstairs, the sheets were damp and sticky and the windows heavily shaded, the way they had been when Annie, aged nine, had had the measles. (The shades were Jenny's idea.) He could even smell his own dried sweat faintly polluting the air. A small pitcher of salt water, with tired-looking dust motes floating in it, stood on the bedside table, alongside some pills for catarrh and a bottle of aspirin. He was surrounded by all the accouterments that accompany a minor ailment, including, among reading material, the necessary entertainment to break the monotony of the endless hours, a copy of Ernie Pyle's latest book (more encounters with GIs, America's noblest breed), plus a brief narrative of President Roosevelt's privileged childhood, about which Sigmund could never get enough, as well as an old Franz Werfel epic that Sigmund had somehow missed when it was first published. That was in case he got tired of one or the other, so he could pick and choose among the three volumes, as he liked to do.

Every now and then, as the future seemed to loom larger and more forbidding than usual, Sigmund took to his bed for a few days. It didn't happen often—it was rare, in fact—but he had been at it since he was a child. Over the years, naturally, he had become something of an expert at this minor art form. To make it all look real, he had early learned how to complain convincingly about illness, about suffering pain, about fatigue and weariness, with just the right note of pathos that never seemed to ring too loud. (It was essential not to overdo it, the first lesson went, to avoid suspicion of malingering.) When he was a child in Poland, this meant mainly stomachaches, to suggest the possibility of appendicitis and, from there, peritonitis, about which everyone tended to panic and, as a result, give him everything he wanted, spoiling him forever as a patient. Sick now, on Granada Avenue, meant the vocal cords, the throat, the larynx, and the nasal passages, everything contained within his skeleton from the chest up. There lay the family jewels, capital for old age, security for the present. If the vocal cords went . . . It was unthinkable, of course, although Sigmund managed to think about it a lot, like all singers, chilled by a kind of true and persistent terror at the prospect.

The Holy Days approached. That was the daunting future that loomed large for Sigmund R. Safer and everybody else. For the Holy Days, Sigmund R. Safer had to be perfect for himself and for his congregation. The House of Israel would put up with nothing less. Why should it? One way to help assure perfection was to avoid the distractions of the world in the days preceding the arrival of the New Year. Sigmund was no fool. He knew how to protect himself from distraction. He had known for years. Stay in bed and avoid other people, where the real threats lay. Their rebellious demands, their needs, their urgent voices, cries of woe, envy, jealousy, spite—the whole ragged bugle call of duty endlessly beckoning. It was one of the first lessons he had learned in life, one of the few permanent lessons, and his visit to the hospital yesterday had only confirmed it.

He had been asked for advice by Velda Reese, who clearly wanted only to hear the sound of her own Amazon's voice, and he had responded to his new friend in good faith. Of course, it had made no difference. Velda was going to do exactly what she wanted to do, like everybody else, whatever Sigmund suggested. Then Mary Goldman had assaulted him from her diabetic bed with a kind of noisy malice on every subject, every subject for Mary Goldman being other people's ongoing inadequacies and chronic misdemeanors. Given such a range, there was more than enough for Mary Goldman to natter about. Al Sallens, true to character, had bitterly attacked the rabbi for fanaticism and false pride, as he ate, this time, a bacon, lettuce, and tomato sandwich, imported from the outside. While he talked and ate, droplets of bacon fat fell onto the paper napkin on his tray, leaving long greasy stains that dried slowly in the heat. Pig food. Slop. Poi-

sonous trichinosis. And arrogance and hypocrisy. Sitting alongside Al Sallens, sniffing the pungent alien odor of bacon, Sigmund
felt his soul shrivel.

Then Lew Mittelman . . . but Lew Mittelman was another story.
Lew Mittelman was serious business. When Sigmund opened the
door to Lew's room, he recognized an excremental odor that made
him cringe. Holding back a moment, he had to gather his strength
and force himself to go through with the visit. Inside, Lew was
lying flat on his back with his eyes closed, receiving fluids and
sugar intravenously through a tube stuck into his lower arm. There
was also a rubber tube that led into his nostrils from a jar hanging
overhead. Sigmund didn't stay long. He didn't speak, either. He
held on for a minute or two, eyes misting, then hurried away
when he felt the nausea coming on. Hours after the visit to Lew
Mittelman, the excremental odor still with him, Sigmund, feeling
a twinge, and then another in his left shoulder, decided to crawl
into his own bed, complaining to Jenny in the age-old way about
his newly discovered symptoms.

That was twenty-four hours ago. Now, struggling to throw off
the top sheet, he had to remind himself again of his duty to
himself—to his vulnerable psyche and to his voice. Especially his
voice, the source of all blessings. He had turned the remaining
choir rehearsal for the week over to Volkonsky, who would conduct it—quite content to be on his own at last—in a basement
room of the synagogue. "Keep an eye on the boys," Sigmund had
told him over the phone, sotto voce. "Don't let them get away
with anything, with Bleiber gone. Especially Scheingold. Watch
him. Work him hard." Sigmund had also decided to give up the
Sabbath service for the weekend. It would hardly be a loss. There
was no bar mitzvah, nothing that needed special attention. All
he had to do now was focus, in temporary peace and quiet, on
the midnight service that heralded the Holy Days, then on the
New Year itself, and finally on the Day of Days, the twenty-four
hours of austere breast-beating atonement, on which everything
that was essential to mankind was decided, for better or worse,
for the next twelve months. Yom Kippur, Sigmund thought
gloomily, when you paid your spiritual dues in public, while

everyone else watched the transaction, when the Kol Nidre alone, which opened the service, the one prayer that everyone considered their own personal possession, had to be sung three times in immediate succession, and each time differently. It was almost inhuman. No one knew what it took out of him. He was a vacuum for weeks afterward, physically and emotionally. Sometimes it took Sigmund a full month to get back to himself after Yom Kippur.

He lay flat in bed now, having finally willed himself into a few additional aches and pains, including his left shoulder again, which began to throb gently, as though on call. The Ernie Pyle book had quickly grown tiresome; the charm of the American soldier was not enhanced by sentimentality. President Roosevelt's childhood could be saved for another day; and the Werfel needed a kind of concentration, an imaginative plunge into an exotic past, that he was not capable of on a heat-encrusted summer afternoon in Baltimore, Maryland. He looked at his radio longingly. He depended on the radio to help him follow the war. The radio, along with the *Sun* papers, delivered him unscathed into the heart of poor, suffering Europe (from which he had had such a narrow escape), guiding him along each changing battle line, each widening front, almost as though he were actually there himself; but, of course, with no danger, no threat to Sigmund R. Safer personally. First Army, Third, Fifth, Seventh, they were almost like old friends now. He wished them well, he cheered them on, he was ardent on their behalf. All those new place names and unexpected adventures; all those heroic leaders and their confident presences. And then the price of it all, dramatized for the world (and Sigmund) every day in the casualty lists that appeared so prominently in the paper, along with a picture or two of the victims, impeccably posed as though for a class yearbook. Just this morning, Hoyt, Kerr, Junemann, Kinlein, Legg, Drum, and Levi, a relatively short one, for once. Thank God, thank God.

"Are you all right?" It was Jenny, standing in the doorway.

"Better," he said, putting on a careworn face.

Jenny walked over to the bed and placed the back of her hand against his forehead. "Feels normal to me," she said.

"I don't think I have a temperature. Or if I have, it went away this morning." He looked up at her with dull eyes; he wished she would keep the back of her hand on his forehead.

"Maybe you shouldn't conduct services this weekend," Jenny said.

"That's probably a good idea," he said in a bland voice.

"Are you up to some cold salmon tonight?"

He was starving. "I like cold salmon in the summer."

"Want me to make the bed again?"

"Don't worry yourself about it."

"Well, I should be getting over to the A & P."

"Go ahead, I'm all right. Maybe I'll listen to the radio a little."

"You want anything special?"

He thought for a moment. "Maybe the new *Life*, if it's in. And pick up some of that fish food in the green box. You know the kind. Large size."

"You sure you'll be all right? Annie'll probably be home any minute." Jenny looked at her watch.

"I'm fine. It's just the shooting pain." What would he do with Annie? She was one of the distractions he was trying to avoid.

"You haven't even touched your gargle water," Jenny said.

"Later."

Jenny picked up the bottle of aspirin and checked its contents. "All right, dear heart," she then said. "I'm off."

Dear heart, he said to himself, holding the phrase close for a moment. Dear heart. But it was not easy to say it back.

"I won't be long."

"Don't worry about me," Sigmund said. Then she left, the house buried in a deep silence, the whole neighborhood at this time of day stuporous and immobile in the heat. Jenny knew exactly what to do in these circumstances, glancing upstairs at their shaded bedroom window as she got into the blue Chevy. Even Sigmund's fish were no use to him at such a time. But she could be patient. Patience was something Jenny understood. She had been through more or less the same exercise in the weeks before the Holy Days more times than she could remember.

4

"And another thing," Sigmund was saying. "Don't ever try to lead the leader. It's a terrible habit, especially for a musician."

Standing alongside him at the Chickering in the Safer living room, the Scheingold kid shuffled from one foot to the other. He had been on his feet for more than an hour, doing what the cantor called "solfeggio," then doing it again and again, without mercy. For the honor of taking over all but one of Herschel Bleiber's solos, Sylvan had been invited—ordered, he thought, was more like it—to give up a couple of Sunday afternoons for special lessons in vocalizing and performance diction, a-e-i-o-u, plus the consonants, which were very important, the cantor insisted. As though Sylvan didn't know how to sing, as though he had never opened his mouth before. All this collaborative effort was accompanied by a barrage of vaguely culture-oriented lectures, an abstract ongoing hectoring by Sigmund that had the sole effect on Sylvan of swelling his resistance to Sigmund's every word. It was like yeast irresistibly rising in the oven. All the cantor had to do was start talking and Sylvan went deaf. Sunday afternoon, for God's sake! Sylvan had to take two streetcars to get out to Granada Avenue, on a day when streetcars ran infrequently, then repeat the trip in reverse to get home. It took an hour each way, four streetcars in all; the scenery was dull, it was just sad old Baltimore sitting out there beyond the window, the city half dead with the Sunday blues. Today he was lucky, sort of. His mother was out for some fun at Gwynn Oak Amusement Park, in the company of Mickey Schiller, and they would pick him up at the cantor's in Mickey's car on their way downtown. Gwynn Oak was on the outskirts of Woodlawn, a mile away. It was already four o'clock. Where were they?

"Are you listening to me?" Sigmund asked from the keyboard. He had been up from his sickbed for twenty-four hours and was feeling almost fit. (He always left open the option of a minor relapse, however, should things out in the great world get too hot again.)

"My feet hurt," Sylvan said.

"Your feet hurt? Is that what's on your mind, your feet?"

Sylvan let out a long sigh and leaned into the curve of the baby grand. Little plaster busts of Schubert, Mozart, and Mendelssohn were lined up in front of him.

Sigmund banged out a chord. He banged out everything on the piano, all unmodulated bombast; the piano was not really his instrument. The louder he played, the louder the Scheingold kid had to sing, which didn't displease Sigmund, because at the moment he wanted volume. (He could play as loud as he had to this afternoon; Jenny was down the street, visiting a neighbor.) "And remember," he said to his pupil, "noise is not music." Sylvan grunted. He had heard that one before. Noise was not music. What did the cantor know, with that banging? Anyway, Sylvan was beginning to have his doubts about music, which he had yet to express to anyone. Solos aside, he had his doubts about singing, too. (He had his doubts about a lot of things, including Lillian Scheingold and Mickey Schiller, out playing together at Gwynn Oak Amusement Park and other places.) What was so wonderful about singing? You opened your mouth and out came a column of controlled sound. The sound seemed to affect some people peculiarly. Deep emotion showed itself, tears sometimes, and gratitude often. It was very strange. The sound of his own voice as he sang out could even do that to Sylvan himself, although he would never admit it to anyone. It would be like talking about dancing.

"Are you listening to me?" Sigmund asked.

Sylvan nodded.

"You've got a look on your face that's a million miles away."

Sylvan stared over the cantor's head, toward the front door. Somebody was out there on the porch. He could hear footsteps. His mother? Mickey Schiller and his lemony smell? Stan the Gann was better than Mickey Schiller, in Sylvan's opinion. At least he was single. "Quiet out there," Sigmund yelled. Sylvan heard the rusty sound of a glider in motion, a couple of whispering voices, stifled laughter. He had an audience.

"You haven't got long, you know," Sigmund said.

"Long for what?" Another lecture, Sylvan thought, going blank.

"Your voice, that's what. This is probably your last holidays at the House. What happened to Herschel Bleiber will happen to you. It will happen to all of you. You don't believe it, do you? None of you ever believe it."

"I believe it."

"It'll happen to you. Rest assured. In the old days, they used to cut off the testicles and that was that, a soprano was a soprano for life. In your case, an alto."

"Eunuchs," Sylvan said.

"That's right, eunuchs. Castrati, they called them. But only in church, not Jews. Jews didn't do that. It took the sex away, you couldn't tell what was singing or who. Anyway, it happened to me what happened to Herschel, only I had the misfortune to come back in a few years with a voice that was bigger and better." Sigmund gave an ironic laugh at the idea of his "misfortune."

"I hope I lose my voice forever," Sylvan said, leaning even harder into the piano. "The alto, I mean. I wouldn't mind that."

"Your mouth to God's ear," Sigmund then answered, under his breath.

They returned to work for a few more minutes, trying to get each note centered the way the cantor demanded. It was not easy. Sylvan had had a glass of milk before taking the streetcar uptown, and, just as the cantor always warned, it had created a little mucus in his throat. No dairy products and no meat before singing was the rule. "Not from the roof of your mouth and not from the nose," the cantor said. "You want to sound like Lily Pons? You have a tendency from the nose. Now, diaphragm, diaphragm. Keep going." Sylvan kept going, thinking about his diaphragm. Arpeggios. Scales. Even grace notes, exaggerated for emotional effect. Hearing his voice come back at him in the living room, he began to feel that maybe he was doing better. It all sounded almost inevitable. It was as the cantor always said, practice helped, practice was essential. It helped his pitch and his projection, it made his voice rounder and stronger, it also gave him confidence, but it was a lot of work, layers of dulling repetition, hours of heady concentration, more than he had ever bargained for.

The cantor looked pleased. He stopped acting so cranky, stopped barking orders, although there were flare-ups; and as soon as he seemed to acknowledge success, or hint at it, Sylvan, too, began to feel more kindly. He almost forgot that his feet hurt, almost forgot that it was Sunday afternoon, smiled at Mendelssohn (Felix, the beloved), Mozart (mighty midget), and Schubert (pudgy little genius who couldn't even finish . . .), then smiled— once—at the cantor. (Maybe someday, he thought, there'd be a plaster bust of the Scheingold kid on the cantor's piano. Another star. Sylvan the sonorous. Nigger nebbish.) Seeing the smile, Sigmund had an idea. "A little Kern," he suggested. "One of those gorgeous melodies, nicer than Romberg, more up-to-date, know what I mean?" He riffled the sheet music on the piano, humming to himself. "You like Kern?" he asked. Which one was Kern? Sylvan asked himself. He hoped it wasn't going to be one of those "One Alone" numbers that used language that went out with Shakespeare. "One Alone, to be thine own . . ." or something like that.

"Here," Sigmund said, indicating some music in front of him. "Long Ago and Far Away," Sylvan read. "You know it?" the cantor asked. "I saw the movie," Sylvan said, trying to remember which movie it was as his spirits began to sink again. The cantor struck a chord, holding it with the damper pedal until it was nothing but moist pulp. Couldn't he hear himself? Sylvan wondered. Noise was not music. He cleared his throat of mucus. "Now . . ." Sigmund said, counting one-two-three-four. Sylvan began to sing in a tentative voice, moving behind the cantor so he could read the words over his shoulder. "No, no, no, no," the cantor cried out, banging his foot hard on the pedal. "Not lon-goggo. Long, stop, ago. Get it? Long a-go. Two words. Three syllables." They tried it again. It was tricky. "And far away. I dreamed a dream one day . . ." And so on, while Sylvan, as he sang, careful of his diction and his pitch, examined the perfect round balding spot on the crown of the cantor's head, saw there a few vulnerable wisps, a thin whorl of vanishing hair, a couple of unexpected freckles, then a crusty-looking mole that took on an astonishing presence the longer Sylvan looked at it.

The cantor played on, each note like a trumpet blast, while Sylvan continued to sight-read, still staring at the cantor's bald spot, at his amazing mole. The tune was nice. It grew on you. Like Sylvan's stubbornness, it had a real swell to it. As Sylvan's alto scaled upward, not quite full volume, a shadow tiptoed across his vision, through the hallway. He looked up. It was Annie Safer, on her way to the back of the house from the porch. As she tiptoed, she rolled her eyes in exaggerated disbelief, making sure that Sylvan could see her. Sylvan stumbled, went flat, recovered. Then he lost his place. The words made no sense, anyway. As for Annie Safer . . . He stopped singing. "Gosh darn it," the cantor complained. "What's wrong with you? You were doing so well."

"I'm tired," Sylvan said, turning away.

"You said that before." The cantor turned to look up at Sylvan. "Maybe you don't get enough sleep. Kids your age. Is that it? Do you get enough sleep?"

"You asked me and I already told you," Sylvan said in a nervy voice.

"You're feeling sorry for yourself. I can hear it in every word. And you're getting fresh with me, too. I don't like fresh. You don't think Irving Karton and Marty Schiffman wouldn't give their right arm for a chance like this?"

"I've been standing on my feet for two hours."

There was the sound of a toilet flushing. In a minute, Annie came tiptoeing back. This time she said, "Hi, Daddy."

"Who's that?" Sigmund asked, turning around to investigate.

"Me."

"I thought you went for a swim."

"We did."

There was a pause. "Who's we?"

"Bobby."

Then Sigmund struck the loudest chord of the afternoon. Sylvan jumped. The screen door slammed. "Enough," Sigmund shouted, bouncing on the piano bench. Special class was over.

5

"You like the racer dip?" Mickey Schiller asked, in a voice that was meant to sound interested. He was sitting up front in the beat-up old Ford, alongside Lillian, who had taken over the wheel from him as a special treat. They were on their way downtown, after picking Sylvan up at the cantor's.

"It's all right," Sylvan said from the back seat, hanging on to the hand strap. One of the windows next to him had a crack in it. Mickey Schiller was probably too cheap to get it fixed. Sylvan knew the type. They seemed to be irresistibly drawn to his mother. He would have to lodge a complaint.

"Sure you're not scared?" Mickey Schiller asked. "Henny's scared. He won't go on the racer dip."

"No, I'm not scared. None of that stuff scares me," Sylvan said, puffing up his voice. But Henny Schiller was scared of almost everything, like Marty Schiffman. Didn't his father know that? Maybe Sylvan should tell him.

"It's the whip that gets to me," Mickey Schiller went on, shivering for effect. "When you start coming around those corners at a hundred miles an hour, I feel like I'm exploding. Like my head's blowing off. I hate that."

Sylvan had a picture of his mother and Mickey Schiller spinning around a corner on the whip together, jammed against each other one moment, flying apart the next, holding on to the safety bar for dear life. In the picture, his mother was screaming.

"Lillian, careful now," Mickey then said, in a whole other voice, pitched half an octave lower. "Don't let the wheels get caught in the trolley tracks."

"I'm doing my best," she said, concentrating on the road.

"We took one of those little pedal-boat rides, too," Mickey said, returning to Sylvan and changing his voice again. "You think you're going to cool off out on the lake, but all you do is work up a good sweat pumping away like that. You're lucky if they don't break down on you, things are made so cheap these days."

"I pedaled more than you did," Lillian said, glancing at Mickey.

Sylvan was silent. He was examining the back of their heads. The back of their heads—of everybody's head—suddenly seemed to be very interesting. He had never noticed that before this afternoon's session at the cantor's. They were like fingerprints, each one unique.

"The whole place is going to the dogs, if you ask me," Mickey continued. "Trash all over the place. Paint coming off everything. The food is lousy, it could kill you. And I don't like the element."

"It wasn't so bad, honey," Lillian said. "It took care of the afternoon."

Honey.

"I wouldn't go to Gwynn Oak if you paid me," Sylvan said, exaggerating only a little. He waited a moment to let this sink in, then added, "It's for dumb *goyim* who don't know any better."

No one seemed to hear him. "Lillian," Mickey said, using his serious adult voice again, "when you get to Lake Drive, head straight down Mount Royal past the B & O and keep going, you follow me?"

"What's for supper?" Sylvan asked. The back of his mother's head, where the center of the whorl was, was particularly interesting because it was so perfect.

Lillian glanced at Mickey again.

"I finished the chicken in the Frigidaire," Sylvan said, "so we don't have to worry about that anymore." On the other hand, the back of Mickey Schiller's head, when you examined it really closely . . .

"I thought you'd fix yourself a couple of hot dogs," Lillian said. "We can pick up some baked beans on the way."

"What about you? You never eat hot dogs."

Lillian waited a moment before answering. "Actually, we were planning to have a bite at Sussman and Lev," she said, turning down Mount Royal, "and then take in a picture."

The Ford poked along noisily for a block or two, the muffler barking. "I don't feel like baked beans tonight," Sylvan finally said, staring hard at the back of Mickey Schiller's lopsided head, trying to create a field of force there that he would be able to control forever.

"Sylvan," Mickey said, turning around in his seat and making a noticeable effort to appear sympathetic. Mickey Schiller's sideburns were definitely too long, Sylvan decided, staring back at him, and the silver-plated identification bracelet dangling on his left wrist was definitely too much. Also, he had five-o'clock shadow. Maybe he would tell Mickey Schiller that his son Henny was scared of everything.

"What is it?" Sylvan answered, trying to look Mickey Schiller in the eye without blinking.

"Don't make it hard for your mother," Mickey said, facing front again.

"Honey," Lillian said in a soothing voice.

Honey again. Which one was honey?

"I'll tell you what, just drop me off at the house. I'll find something to eat. There's some pretzels somewhere. Or maybe I'll just go to the Rubinsteins'. They're always telling me their house is open to me."

"Don't be that way, sweetheart," Lillian said. "It's just Sunday supper. Try to give a little. You're good at that."

"I'm glad I'm good at something."

"Sylvan."

"Because I'm going to lose my voice soon. Just like Herschel Bleiber, just like everybody else. And when I lose my voice, I'll be nothing."

"Sylvan." The car wobbled to the left.

"Nothing," he repeated. "And the cantor thinks so, too."

"I don't believe that," Lillian said.

"Just ask him. He'll tell you."

"What's he talking about, anyway?" Mickey said, out of the side of his mouth.

"You'll lose your voice in the normal course of events," Lillian said, ignoring Mickey's question. "Everybody expects that."

"Unless they cut off my testicles," Sylvan muttered.

"Now you just calm down back there," Lillian said in a tight voice. The vertical line was rigidly set between her eyes, and she kept glancing anxiously in the rearview mirror, trying to get a glimpse of Sylvan.

"You want to come to Sussman and Lev with us?" Mickey asked, sounding as though each word were a stone in his mouth. "The three of us could have a bite together."

"I hate Sussman and Lev."

"Well, you can't say I didn't try," Mickey said, throwing up his hands.

"Okay, now let's get serious," Lillian said. "What do you want for supper?"

"I'll skip supper or I'll go to the Rubinsteins'."

"You won't skip supper and you're not going to the Rubinsteins'." There was a bright hot flash in Lillian's voice that had begun to excite both Sylvan and Mickey. Sylvan drummed his fingers on the car seat.

"I'll fix some spaghetti," he said.

"Spaghetti is too heavy in heat like this. You know we never have spaghetti in the summer. Oh, God, the summer," Lillian cried out. "I hate the summer."

"Don't aggravate yourself while you're driving," Mickey said, looking concerned. He began to stroke her arm.

"My mother doesn't like to be touched like that," Sylvan said, resting his chin on the back of the front seat.

"Sylvan!"

"You don't."

"Nobody asked you. It's none of your business. What's got into you, anyway?"

"You always say you can't stand it when people try to touch you." He sat up straight again.

"Listen," Mickey said. "Why don't we just kill the plans for tonight? It's not the end of the world. We'll go to a picture on Tuesday night, I can wait till Tuesday night."

"No," Lillian said firmly.

"Really," Mickey said. "I mean it."

"No."

"You know," Mickey said, "I actually did promise Henny tonight."

There was a long pause. "Promise him what?" Lillian finally asked.

"A little of my time. You know what I mean."

"What's going on here, anyway?" Lillian asked, changing gear with a loud noise. "I thought . . ." She punched the horn with her fist.

"Take it easy now."

"You guys . . ." she started. "Both of you."

"I really did promise Henny. Honest. It's my wife, too. She's always looking for something to build a case against me. When I forget Henny, it just plays into her hands. Believe me."

"I believe you, all right," Lillian said, staring straight ahead. "Now," she went on, "why don't you just quit while you're winning?"

"I'm sometimes forgetful. My memory's not so hot."

"I said quit now."

A few minutes later, Lillian slowly began to circle the park downtown on the way to their tiny apartment. The moon was already up, the gray sky streaked with crazy summer pinks. Neighbors clustered on their white stoops trying to get some air, or on funny little beach chairs set out on the pavement. "Everybody's out tonight," Lillian said, absent-mindedly pulling up to the curb. She braked the car and turned off the ignition while the neighbors stared at them. The neighbors liked to stare at Lillian because she was so popular. "Well," she said, taking a deep breath. "At least I got us all here in one piece."

"You did great," Mickey said. "You *are* great." He hopped out of the car and ran around to the driver's side. He opened the door and Lillian slid out. "Tuesday night," he said. "The picture changes on Tuesday."

"Okay. If that's what you want. Tuesday night."

"Come on." Sylvan was calling from the stoop of their house. "You've got the key."

"Just so you don't go around making too many promises you forget to keep," Lillian said, turning to Mickey at the curb. She hoped the remark, which she knew was petty and clumsy, and maybe even mean-spirited, had the right sarcastic edge. She hoped it hit home.

Mickey lowered his eyes. "It was a great day," he said. "It really was. I'll make it up to you. I promise. You'll see."

6

"I don't think we ever met," Sigmund said, striding across the front porch a few minutes after the Scheingold kid had left with his mother and Mickey Schiller.

Bobby Fiorentino jumped to his feet. "We met. Sir. We met last week."

"Funny, I don't remember you. There's always so many boys around, I can hardly keep track. What's your name?"

"Fiorentino. Bobby Fiorentino. Remember, here on the porch?"

All those sweet Mediterranean vowels—even Sigmund had to admit they were sweet—which Sigmund was not used to except when doing his vocal exercises, all those *o*'s and *e*'s and *i*'s, began to bob around in Sigmund's head like so many tiny corks, disarming him with their buoyancy. He'd better watch himself, he thought. He didn't want to be disarmed. And he was susceptible. His natural tendency was toward peace and harmony, toward conciliation; that was his true temperament. But everyone knew that from the delicious blue waters of the Mediterranean it was only a short hop to the so-called Eternal City and the Vatican and all that, and from the Vatican . . . maybe it was better not to even think about it. Maybe it was better just to draw the line here and now, you on your side, me on mine. "I would say it's almost suppertime," Sigmund remarked, narrowing his eyes. He heard a click. It was the sound of his own teeth coming together.

"What is wrong with you, Daddy?" It was Annie, swinging back and forth on the glider. A sandal dangled from one foot, its strap broken, and she was trying to hide a cigarette in the palm of her hand. Sigmund disapproved of Annie's smoking.

"And what should be wrong with me?" Sigmund asked, nostrils already beginning to flare. Without knowing it, he had struck a faintly operatic pose as he asked the question, one hand resting lightly on his hip, like a Neapolitan tenor, head thrown back, right foot turned out. He might have been getting ready to render "La donna è mobile," which he had been known to croon falsetto around the house from time to time. A moment passed as he glared at Annie. Smoke curled from inside her palm. The glider swung back and forth, creaking. She looks like Shifra, Sigmund was thinking, considering Annie indignantly. My daughter is beginning to look like my sister, a double retribution, with that wild, self-absorbed expression on her face, feeding on itself, as though she can't wait for anything, as though it's all coming to her. Sigmund gave a little snort as he gazed at his daughter and slowly resumed a more normal posture. One Shifra in a lifetime was enough. The whole family in Poland had agreed on that.

"I'm really on my way," Bobby Fiorentino said, dancing on the balls of his feet. "It's getting near supper time for me."

"Oh, so you have supper over in Woodlawn, too?" Sigmund regretted the question as soon as it was out of his mouth. The stupidity of it made him cringe. If he claimed not to know who Bobby Fiorentino was, how could he possibly know where he lived?

Bobby laughed. Then laughed again. "Guess so," he said, still dancing. "The whole world has supper, it's a fact of life."

"What is wrong with you, Daddy?" Annie asked again. "And stand still, Bobby, stop twitching around like that."

"Your mother's due home any minute," Sigmund said, pretending to check his watch. "Maybe you'd better get the table set." Annie even had Shifra's pouty lower lip, he saw, examining his daughter's features with sudden objective clarity. And everybody knew that a pouty lower lip meant eternal demands and eternal dissatisfaction, whether in meager Poland or bountiful America. She had begun to look just like his sister, he thought again, taking care this time to remind himself that nothing could be more natural. Annie Safer and Shifra Czaferski. Shifra and Annie. It was part of his punishment for not believing. It was the inescapable heart of retribution. "Tell me, young man," Sigmund then said, turning back to Bobby Fiorentino. He could hardly wait. "What do you think of the persecution of the Jews?"

"Daddy!"

"Shush."

"Please!"

"I want to know. I have a right to an answer. I want to hear a gentile's opinion."

"Sir," Bobby said.

"Never mind the sir. Just give me a straight answer."

"The persecution," Bobby said.

"That's right," Sigmund answered.

"Don't pay any attention to him," Annie said, stubbing out her cigarette and throwing it over the porch railing. "I don't know what's wrong with him."

"I'll show you what's wrong with me," Sigmund said, nostrils flaring again. "And be so kind, don't turn my lawn into a garbage dump. If you have to smoke . . ."

"Maybe you'd better go," Annie said to Bobby.

He didn't have to be told twice. "It is supper time in Woodlawn," Bobby crooned in a whisper, moving off.

"Call me," Annie said. Then, as Bobby headed down the street, checking out the perfect hedges and taking ferocious swings with his imaginary bat, Annie turned back to her father. They stared at each other guiltily for a moment. Sigmund's shoulders sagged. His whole body sagged. That's what comes from drawing the line, he told himself wearily. You on your side, me on mine. He took off his pince-nez and waited.

"Now what was that all about?" Annie finally asked, in a sad, quiet voice, hardly hers, that Sigmund heard as sullen.

Sigmund shrugged before answering. "I want to know what the Christians think about the persecution of the Jews," he said. "Why not, with what's going on everywhere." Without his glasses, Sigmund saw Annie's face as a blur. It made it easier to confront her. "It's on my mind," he went on. "It's important to me. I want to know."

"Then why don't you ask one of them?"

"I just did. And he ran away. He couldn't wait to get away from me."

"I don't mean my friends, Daddy. Ask one of your own. Pick on somebody your own size, like your fish pal, the one who lives over in Walbrook with his mother, George Whoever . . ."

"About George Haney I don't have to ask," Sigmund said, pulling himself up. "And don't you say anything against George Haney. I know George Haney. George Haney is a gentleman. It's not George Haney, it's the others I'm worried about. I want to know about your Italian friend. Bobby. Whatever his name is. Your friend."

"My friend?" Annie asked. "Oh, Daddy, Bobby is more than a friend."

"And what does that mean?" Sigmund answered. "What is 'more than a friend'?" Annie was silent. Her father waited, his heart turning over at her declaration. It didn't even have to be true, it was enough that she had said it. "Annie," he said in a suddenly placating voice. He waited another moment, then held out his hand to her, unable to keep himself back.

Annie set the glider going again, ignoring the question and Sigmund's gesture. "You can't do that to my friends," she said after a moment, not looking at him. "Saying anything that comes into your head, just like that."

"That's what I'm trying to tell you, it wasn't just anything. I said what was on my mind." His hand was now back at his side. "I said what I felt."

"It's humiliating," Annie said.

"If it humiliated you, I'm sorry. I wouldn't ever want to do that to you. It was a moment. Everybody has moments."

She looked up at him. "When did you have your last checkup?" she asked.

"My what?"

"Your last checkup. You know what I mean."

Sigmund rose on his toes. "You think I've got something in my bloodstream? Is that it? A bad liver, maybe? Something we can blame on me? It's not so simple."

"Maybe you should give Dr. Rapoport a call."

"Dr. Rapoport," Sigmund said, waving the name away. "Listen, Annie, I have these dreams. You know anything about dreams? Do you ever have dreams?"

"Just as I thought," Annie said, as though she were talking to herself. Then, speaking up: "If you're bothered by dreams, you should see a psychiatrist. They know about dreams. They specialize in dreams."

"Psychiatrists are for crazy people."

"Come on, Daddy, nobody believes that anymore. The whole world knows about dreams . . . Isn't Harry Forcher's son a psychiatrist? Call Harry Forcher's son."

"I keep seeing my sisters. In my dreams. In Poland."

"A century ago."

"A century ago?" Sigmund took a step forward, hands clenched.

"I'm speaking figuratively. Good Lord, do I have to spell everything out, word for word?"

"A century ago," Sigmund said again.

"Oh, Daddy, forget it. It was another world. Let go."

"What do you know about it, you never even ask."

"Oh, I know, all right. How could I miss? I mean, look at you. You still look as though you're just passing through. A tourist. A visitor from Mars. With those fancy glasses . . ."

Sigmund raised himself to his full height, swung his pince-nez in the air, and looked down his nose at the blur seated below him. Had she finished with him? Now was the moment for peace and harmony, now was the time to show his true temperament. He awaited another assault.

"And a Catholic, too," Sigmund then heard himself say, feeling not at all peaceful.

"Who?"

"That boy."

"I might have known." She shook her head as though agreeing with herself. "That boy. He comes to see me, and you tell him I'm not home. That's right. I know all about it. Insulting us that way, as though we're retarded or something. So what if he's Catholic? Big deal. Catholics live, too. Yes, they do. Whatever you think. You go around worrying about the Jews, he goes around worrying about the Catholics."

"A Catholic. They're murdering the Jews. You don't care about that, either. A century ago and right now, still, this minute."

"I refuse to discuss this," Annie said, reaching down to fix her sandal. "It's totally irrational. I refuse to discuss anything on an irrational level."

"All right, you're supposed to be the smart one in the family," Sigmund said. "So listen to me for a minute . . ." He paused to consider his words. After a moment of intense thought, he went on. "I don't know what's happening to me, Annie," he finally said.

"And Bobby's not a boy," Annie said, as though Sigmund had not spoken. She was busy struggling with the broken strap on her sandal. "I resent it when you call him that."

"Listen to me, now," Sigmund persisted in a louder voice. "I'm trying to tell you something. I have these dreams. I've been wanting to discuss them with you, but you're always in such a hurry."

Annie was silent.

"There's too much going on," Sigmund added, quieting down. "You know what I'm saying? Too much, everywhere. And between you and me, the truth, I don't even believe in God, either." At last, he had said it. It was out. He slipped on his pince-nez. Annie came into focus.

"I'm not surprised," Annie said, sighing after a moment. "I guessed that a long time ago. I think I've always known it. But be careful. It's dynamite, what you say. If you don't believe, don't go around talking about it."

"It's between you and me. Not even your mother . . ."

"Because they'll get you right between the eyes. Your pals at the House. They'll nail you. The whole congo." Which was Annie's word for the congregation.

"I only talk to you, Annie. Nobody else knows."

"Well, just make sure."

"Anyway, it's not for conversation. It's not for words. For a cantor, naturally, it's forbidden. For any Jew." Sigmund paused a moment, looking for a way to escape. He did not want to talk about the House, he did not want to talk about God. He was sorry he had brought it up. If he had to go on living without God, he would. He was no stranger to that. He had lived without God for years. And Annie? Her friend? Her more-than-a-friend? "Well," he said, turning back to her. "Do I really seem too fancy to you? Should I get rid of my mustache?"

"Oh, Daddy," Annie said, trying to end the exchange by getting up and going into the house.

"Well, it's true," Sigmund said, feeling relieved as he followed Annie into the front hall. The argument was over, they would soon be friends again. Nothing had been said that couldn't be unsaid.

"You're not the first to complain about such matters," he went on, still following her. "My glasses, too. My glasses and my mustache. Too fancy. It's true."

7

"By my count, that makes four."

"That many?"

"There's you. Them. And me. That makes four."

"You're absolutely right, it does make four." Barney lay on his stomach in bed, while Elsie swabbed his anus with special medication. He was trying to sound surprised at her calculations.

"That means big work. For me."

"Careful, darling. That stuff burns."

"It is not a pretty picture."

"Don't look."

"I have to look to see."

"Well, the Scheingold kid will only be here for a couple of nights," Barney pointed out. "It's nothing."

"Three nights. Three days."

"And Miss Reese will be here strictly on a professional basis for two weeks. And those are doctor's orders, remember." The last statement, of course, was created on the spot to serve Barney's convenience.

"She still has to eat."

"Don't you worry about Miss Reese. She knows how to take care of herself. Miss Reese is a pro."

"That still makes four. I'm not used to so many." The phone rang. "Now, don't you move," Elsie said. "Stay there. I'm not finished with you." She picked up the phone and during the brief exchange that followed reached for a pencil and a piece of paper. "Just spell it, please," she said in her Mayfair voice, "and go slow. Right. Right." Very chirpy. "This is Elsie, how are you? Right. Sure thing. First he has to nap. Sure thing. Sure thing." She hung up.

"Und zo?" Barney asked, facedown on the bed.

"Mr. Metz-gah," she said, suddenly back to normal.

"What's he want?"

"Mr. Metz-gah doesn't tell me what he wants. You call him back later."

"That's the message?"

"That's what he said."

"Up to no good."

"Well, you know better than me."

He certainly did. In the silence that followed, Barney thought again about the walkout at the House. Metzger himself, Sindel, and Adelman on the run from the rabbi—already notorious, a legend in six days. And a clear warning, he knew, of things to come. God help me, he thought, stirring in pain and silently muttering a Yiddish curse so vile he was afraid to say the words aloud.

"Aren't you finished with me yet?" he finally asked, in an angry voice.

"One more touch." Elsie swabbed a last time.

"Phew," he said, writhing on the bed.

"They say if it don't hurt, it don't mean nothin'."

"I'm sick of it."

Elsie screwed the top back onto the medication bottle and threw away the swabbing stick, after examining it closely. "Now," she said.

"Can I turn over?"

"Five minutes."

"Read me about the Orioles." Barney reached out and tossed her the sports section of the *Sun*, which was lying at his side.

Elsie rustled the paper as though she were shaking the dust out of it. "Now, let me see. Hmmm. Big headline this morning. You ready? De-feat came again yesterday to the hap-less Roy-als," she read, "as the O-ri-oles went on to take one more con-test . . ."

8

"Mummy."

Mummy. That was always a bad sign. Or a good one, she could never really be sure. "I'm here in the kitchen," Jenny called.

Annie sidled in and leaned against the Frigidaire, casually crossing one sandaled foot in front of the other. Her strap was still broken. "Why are you working like that in this heat?" she asked.

"I'm not working, I'm passing the time." Jenny was making chicken salad, very slowly. It was eleven o'clock in the morning. A half-finished glass of iced tea rested on the counter in front of her.

"Where's Daddy?"

"He's at the House. I think. Some meeting. There's always some meeting."

"He runs around a lot. Too much, if you ask me."

"It's good for him to keep busy. It's good for everybody. It makes the blood go." Jenny dipped a spoon into a mayonnaise jar, hesitating. "After all this time, I'm never sure how much."

"Try less," Annie said. "It doesn't have to be so thick."

"Daddy likes mayonnaise."

"A little less, Mummy."

Jenny followed her daughter's instructions, then turned to the celery stalks, which she began to chop up with a neat, steady action. "I didn't even know you were home," she said, as she worked. "You've been like a mouse all morning."

"I've just been hanging around my room. Reading, stuff like that. The heat's beginning to get to me." She uncrossed her feet and began to scratch an instep with the heel of her other foot.

"The heat's getting to everybody. It's the worst I remember. But I say that every year."

"When did Daddy have his last checkup?" Annie suddenly asked.

Jenny looked up from her work. "What kind of checkup?" she asked, eyes alert.

"You know, Dr. Rapoport."

"Dr. Rapoport. Who knows, a year, two maybe. Why?"

"I think he needs a checkup. You, too, for that matter. We all neglect ourselves. Me included. We all need checkups every year. Anyway," she said, looking down at her feet, "he seems a little peaked."

Jenny pretended to be thinking about Annie's comments and began to toss the celery bits into a bowl with the pieces of chicken and the mayonnaise; then, after that was done, she wiped her hands on her apron, taking her time about it.

"Well, he does," Annie said, as though her mother had put up an argument. She glanced at Jenny. "He looks peaked. No color. And he says some pretty strange things, too. I've heard him."

"What's so unusual about that?" Jenny asked. "You know your father as well as I do. Sometimes he says strange things. So? But it hasn't been an easy summer. It never is. And you know this is the hardest part of the year for Daddy. Everything coming around at once. The holidays. The choir. They just lost one of the kids. And there's trouble at the House. You know all that."

"Well . . ." Annie began.

"It's just the way things go," Jenny said, sipping at her iced tea. "It's always like this. What do they call it, the pressure of events? And the war, too. The war, that's another thing. Anyway, it's nice that you care."

"I guess I'm ready for school to begin," Annie said.

"I never heard you talk like that before."

"The summer seemed longer than usual."

"You should have had a job. I told you that in June."

"You're right, but this'll be my last summer of freedom. Next year . . ."

"Oh, don't talk silly. Your last summer of freedom."

Annie yawned behind her hand, then stretched to her full height, arms overhead. She was wearing her dress with the daisies on it. Underneath, she was wearing only pants. Jenny watched her out of the corner of her eye, working her lips a little as Annie's body pulled taut. "That dress is at least a size too small for you," Jenny couldn't help saying.

"This old thing?" Annie pulled at the waistline.

"Why don't you get rid of it? Give it to somebody. Hand it down. It's time." Jenny made a pretense of being busy again with the mixing bowl. "I'll deliver your message to Daddy," she finally said. "You're probably right. We probably all need checkups."

"It's just that Daddy seems a little worn-out. You know what I mean."

"It's what I said, everything coming around at once."

"Let me give you a hand with that. I can do it as well as you."

Jenny paused a moment, surprised but pleased. "Be my guest," she said, shoving the bowl in Annie's direction.

Mummy.

9

"And in my absence?" Sigmund asked, sitting in an empty office at the House of Israel, going over business with his choir director. That was how the cantor worked at the House during the week; if he was lucky enough to find an empty desk somewhere, he grabbed it for himself.

"It went very well," Volkonsky answered. "Very well, indeed." He could barely suppress a smile at the memory of it.

Sigmund noticed the smile and decided to let it pass. If his choir director wanted to pretend that the cantor had not been missed, Sigmund would let him. It couldn't be easy always to take second billing, Sigmund thought, with a touch of sympathy for Volky, which quickly passed, too. Anyway, everybody everywhere surely took second billing to somebody at some time. "Tell me," Sigmund said. "The Scheingold kid first."

"Pretty good," Volkonsky said. "He's picking up Bleiber's stuff in no time. The kid's smart. But we know that. No trouble there."

"Well, I'm coaching him, of course."

"Of course. And it shows in everything. His voice is fuller. Richer, too. I mean, it's always been rich, but it's even richer now. Nice advance in projection and diction, also."

"I've been concentrating on that, so I'm not surprised. And the rest?"

"Frisch has nasal congestion. The voice is pinched, too tight. He has to watch himself. Gozlov is a little temperamental. You know, the usual."

"Jeffrey Bourne?"

"A dream."

Sigmund was silent for a moment, thinking it over. "And the other boys?" he asked.

"Oh, you know," Volkonsky said. "Again the usual. Up and down."

"Well, I'm glad to say that I'm back to my old self," Sigmund said. "I'll be there tonight, in person, in my own dining room."

"I assumed."

"Well, I will." As though a doubt had been expressed.

"Cantor, I heard a tenor at the Mount Vernon Methodist last week, oh, my." Volkonsky blew a kiss in Sigmund's direction. "It was something, let me tell you."

"You go to church like that?"

"To scout. I drop in. You never know what you're going to hear."

Sigmund was jealous. If the truth be known, he liked to go to church, too, for reasons of music, of course, in the cause of Art and Aesthetics. If the truth be further known, he preferred a good old Catholic high mass of the kind he used to sneak into occasionally when he was a boy in Warsaw, vast, resonant, assured, deliciously fragrant with mysterious foreign scents, with all the sensory stops pulled full out and the giant organ blasting away on behalf of the faith. The Catholics really knew how to do it, they understood those things, they were masters. Nevertheless, as the boss, he thought he should warn Volkonsky. "You should be careful," he said. "There's no telling who you might run into in one of those places. They find you there, they'll never forgive you, they'll hold it against you for life." And against me, too, he added to himself.

Volkonsky suppressed a smile again. "Don't worry about me, I'm very careful. I'm always discreet. Anyway, I'm just doing it for my work, it's all in the line of business."

"I know why you're doing it. You don't have to explain to me."

"Also," Volkonsky went on, edging forward in his chair as he finally got to the point, "the Civic Opera asked me to take over the chorus next season. In the spring." He looked away when he said this.

"You don't say." For the third time that morning, Sigmund was swept by a current of jealousy. It made him very unhappy.

"Three operas, as usual. One Puccini, probably *Butterfly*, a double bill of something or other to be decided, I hope not modern, and *Aida*."

"*Aida*, that's all?" With just the right sarcastic touch.

"Can you imagine Bourne as Amonasro?"

"Better Amonasro than Aida."

They both laughed at this, a little.

"Well, that all sounds very nice," Sigmund said, taking a suddenly avuncular tone. "A real step forward for you. As long as it doesn't interfere . . ."

"Don't worry."

"I leave the worrying to you, my friend."

"I can handle both. Easily. Civic and the House."

"I always wanted to sing opera," Sigmund then said, without knowing he was going to say it.

Volkonsky carefully considered his response to this, eyes cast down. "Well, Verdi is a little heavy, don't you think?" he asked. "I mean, Radames calls for almost a *helden*."

Sigmund could no longer bear it. "I'm not applying for a job," he snapped. "What do you think I am? Why would I apply for a job? I already have a job. I can't mix the two, anyway. Oil and water. The House is the House, it's a jealous master."

"Of course," Volkonsky said, smooth as silk now that the message was delivered. "I know that very well."

"For you, too. Remember that. Be careful."

"Right."

"Because I can't defend you if you get caught in church."

"Of course not."

"Well, I'm in a hurry, I'm on my way downtown for lunch," Sigmund said in a businesslike tone, getting up from the empty desk. Radames, he thought irritably. Pinkerton. The bitter stuff of old dreams. "I'll see you at rehearsal tonight." They both began to adjust their pince-nez at the same moment.

"Frisch worries me a little," Volkonsky said.

To hell with Frisch, Sigmund thought, reaching for his skinny leather briefcase, which contained a few copies of the latest tropical-fish journals and a couple of music scores for stuffing.

"His voice is very tight," Volkonsky went on. "He chokes up. I've seen that before with tenors."

So have I, thought Sigmund, more times than you. He had begun to sulk. It was another thing he hated in himself. Sulking. Jealousy. Sarcasm. His worst sides.

10

Hidden away in a red leather booth near the kitchen at Ballow's a half-hour later, Sigmund and his friend Larry Adelman faced each other at lunch over kosher corned-beef and tongue sandwiches, both on rye. Sigmund's tongue sandwich, two inches thick, also contained cole slaw and Russian dressing to help sweeten it. Larry Adelman's corned beef, substantially thinner, was just that, with a generous layer of yellow mustard running thickly from crust to crust that Larry had added himself. There was also iced coffee and a cream soda resting between them, as well as a couple of huge pickles, just out of the barrel, smelling powerfully of brine. Larry had taken his jacket off, loosened his tie and undone the top button of his shirt. Sweat ran down his fleshy cheeks, streak marks dirtied his face. He was breathing hard.

"You'll make yourself sick," Sigmund was saying. "Carrying on in this heat. Too much emotion, Larry. It's not good. You should learn how to take things as they come." As though Sigmund R. Safer were one of those who knew how to take things as they came.

"It's the way I am," Larry Adelman said. "The heat has nothing to do with it. Does a leopard change its spots? So I bleed. I suffer. That's my way." As though everybody didn't know what Larry Adelman's way was.

"It's not worth it," Sigmund said, picking up his sandwich again. The Russian dressing dripped onto his paper napkin. "Don't forget," Sigmund went on, grabbing another napkin, "you have a duty to yourself. And to Mildred and the children, especially. Remember that. It's your first responsibility." But Sigmund's voice wavered. His heart wasn't really in what he was saying. He was going through the motions with his friend, sounding more pious than he liked, even unctuous, but pleased at their exchange and trying to hide his pleasure. Despite the digression (not the first), Larry Adelman was making him an offer. He had been at it for a quarter of an hour. Sigmund wasn't sure whether the offer interested him, but the making of it did. It had certainly taken the edge off his meeting with Volkonsky. It had taken the edge off everything. It had made him feel almost cheerful.

"The way I see it," Larry Adelman said, still single-mindedly digressing, "everything is worth a man's full attention in this world. Everything is important. Big, little, it doesn't matter. That's what I believe. That's how I was raised . . ."

"A godly belief," Sigmund put in, raising his eyes to Ballow's tin ceiling and blushing at his own presumption, "directly out of the rabbinic tradition, which states that everything and everybody, regardless, counts equally in this world." And exactly where, Sigmund asked himself, did such an assertion appear in the rabbinic tradition? As far as he knew, he had just invented it himself.

"Yes, godly enough, I guess," Larry repeated, modestly shaking his head.

"And everybody respects you for it, Larry. Your integrity, that's how people know you. Nobody fools with Larry Adelman when it comes to integrity. But you can carry those things too far, you know."

"How far is too far? If I didn't believe that everything was important, I'd never get involved with this thing in the first place."

This time Sigmund didn't answer. His friend was wandering too far from the subject. He was worried that Larry had lost his way. He would have to shepherd him a little, shoulder him firmly back into line.

"It's not as though it's such a simple thing," Larry said. He bit into a pickle and made a face.

Again, Sigmund remained silent.

"To keep at it out of conviction," Larry continued, "in the face of all the opposition. Half of my old friends don't talk to me anymore. They turn away when they see me coming. To them, I'm a pariah. You don't know what that's like, it takes everything you've got to face that and then some, heart and soul."

Finally, Sigmund responded. "You've got plenty of both," he said. "Heart and soul. You always did. Just don't make yourself sick over it. That's all I'm suggesting. People have been known to die of their convictions."

"Then what do you think?" Larry sat back in the booth, settling in. "What's your first reaction?"

Sigmund pretended to be deep in thought. They were back on track at last, and he would have to make sure that they stayed there. What was his first reaction? Keep making me an offer, he was thinking. I like it. That was his first reaction. The feeling of treachery came later. What he said was, "It's a very interesting proposition. I never thought. I mean, you've taken me completely by surprise." Which was literally true. "It's not every day," Sigmund went on, struggling to find his real thoughts. "There are important issues here, things that count." He began to think about them for the first time that morning.

"You would really help make it go," Larry said. "You would be a major asset to a new congregation. If you decided to come with us, your name alone would help assure a success."

"I don't know that my name's worth all that much," Sigmund heard himself say, with a sharp flutter of insincerity. Where had that remark come from?

Larry looked up from his sandwich, which was soggy with mustard. "Your voice, then," he said in a patient tone. "You know that everybody admires your voice. You're the best in Baltimore. There's no competition. You're too modest."

"Maybe I am. Sometimes," Sigmund said, flushing with pleasure. But he felt he had lost some ground unnecessarily. He felt that he had put himself on the defensive. It was often like that for Sigmund when it came to a negotiation. He had never quite found the right tone for a negotiation; negotiations often made him feel uncomfortably like a child again, one who needed approval more than success.

"Just tell me," Larry Adelman said, straightening up expectantly in the red leather booth. He took another bite of his sandwich, which was beginning to fall apart in his hands, then sipped at his cream soda. Sitting there across from Sigmund, he was a full head taller than his friend. "Just tell me exactly how you feel about it now, between the two of us. First reaction. Be frank. I won't hold you to anything."

Sigmund began to measure out his words again. "For one thing," he began slowly, "I'm very honored to be asked." Speaking this elementary truth, however self-effacing, helped to increase his confidence. "Anybody would be," he went on. "I know what it means and I appreciate it. I also know the thought and the planning that's gone into all this. Tremendous. You can't underestimate that. So given all that, how serious you are, how important the new congregation could be in this city, all that, I owe you and I owe myself the time to think it through with the proper care and attention." The conclusion, perhaps, was a little more diminuendo than he had intended (that, of course, was what came of being surprised), but it wasn't bad, it would serve.

"That makes sense," Larry said affably. "At least it's serious, and serious is always good."

"You know, I haven't had all that much success with my pulpits," Sigmund found himself saying, in a confidential tone. "I don't mean my personal success, of course. I've had plenty of that. As much as any man could ask for. What I'm talking about is the congregations themselves." Sigmund, after hurrying to correct any wrong impression his words might have left, now waited for Larry to respond, but Larry, in no rush, just sat there, chewing thoughtfully on his corned beef. "You know what I mean?" Sigmund asked in a small voice, sorry that he had brought the matter up.

"I'm not sure that I do," Larry Adelman said. "Explain it to me."

"Well," Sigmund started, wondering where all this was taking him. "My first pulpit in this country, in Paterson, New Jersey, collapsed when the silk mills went under. You know Paterson, New Jersey? A terrible thing. That was in 1928. And there was plenty of money there, too, before it happened. Paterson was one rich town, full of big shots. Then it just evaporated when the silk mills went. Down the drain. Finished. A bankrupt town, a bankrupt temple. They still owe me three months' salary. Jenny and I were down to our last hundred dollars. It was a question whether we would eat."

Larry Adelman stared at his friend without expression, waiting for Sigmund to continue.

"Then afterwards there was New Rochelle," Sigmund went on, his voice tighter. "The last one, the one before this. New Rochelle, New York. In Westchester, on the Long Island Sound. More big shots. Bigger even. That crashed in 1931, right after the stock market. The same story. Nothing but misery. They owed me a month. They still do. They always will. Counting Paterson, New Jersey, I'll always be four months behind." Sigmund gave a hard little laugh at his joke. "I was lucky that the House of Israel came to my rescue," he finished.

"I never knew all that," Larry said, shaking his head. "I never heard it before. You see, you never know, even your own lawyer. I guess you could say you've been on the run all this time from one defaulting congregation after another."

"Not I could say. I was."

"Terrible."

"So that experience, between you and me, makes me want to think very seriously about our conversation. That experience is not something I want to repeat."

"I can understand that," Larry said. "Who needs troubles like that? But times are different these days. This pulpit is not going to crash."

"But first there has to be a pulpit."

"Don't you worry about that. There'll be a pulpit."

"And the rabbi?" Sigmund asked after a moment.

"What about the rabbi?"

"Are you still talking? Is there a discussion going on? Is it really hopeless, the split, I mean? It's not as though he ever tells me anything."

"He said his piece to us. To Julie and me, in private. Then he said it again officially at a full board. You were there. You heard. All that beautiful diction, all those great big fat words. I hate to talk this way, it's unbecoming to a grown man. But there it is. You can't get near him. You can't reach him."

"As you said, can a leopard change its spots?"

"Maybe I shouldn't knock it. When you think about it, that

kind of stiffness, whatever it is, stubbornness, has kept the Jews alive for a long time . . ."

"It's like the Catholics," Sigmund said, his eyes clouding over. "It's a force."

"About the Catholics, I can't say. I don't know many Catholics, except for a couple of clients."

"I know a few," Sigmund said. "George Haney, who breeds fish, he's a Catholic." As is Annie Safer's friend, Bobby F., he thought, but there was no point in bringing up Bobby F. over lunch at Ballow's.

Larry pointed at his cream soda, signaling the waitress. "I know I shouldn't," he said to Sigmund. "But I love the stuff."

"Cream soda, I don't even know what it is."

"It's all sugar, like everything that's good."

"And tongue," Sigmund said, gazing at his plate unhappily. "It's disgusting, when you think about it."

"No more than most things. All animal organs, in fact."

"Maybe it's worth another try with the rabbi, Larry. What do you think? After all, there's nothing to lose."

"Not me. I won't go through that again. He treats us as though we're not there. I've only got two cheeks and I've already turned both."

They were silent for a moment, playing with the remains of their sandwiches.

"You know," Larry Adelman said, "I'm not really one of those unquestioning types, the way you might think. I'm not like Mildred, for example, who never asks a question, my own wife. I mean, to be frank, sometimes I have my doubts. You know?"

A familiar chill came over Sigmund. He had heard this before from Larry Adelman, and others, usually in the days just before Yom Kippur, and he didn't want to hear it again, not today, anyway. In the days just before Yom Kippur, Sigmund had discovered, the human spirit sometimes rebelled, faced with the merciless prospect of having to confront its own destiny in public. "You mean . . ." he began, halfheartedly.

"I mean about God," Larry said, sounding defiant. "I mean sometimes I'm not sure I'm a believer. As simple as that. It's been going on for years. I can't seem to get it behind me."

"Don't eat yourself up," Sigmund said in a controlled voice. "It's a normal thing. You're not alone. Everybody struggles with that. If they tell you otherwise, they're liars. The important thing is that you want to believe."

"I look around me."

"Every man does."

"I mean," Larry went on. He began to mop the back of his neck with his handkerchief. "I mean, it's not as though death isn't enough of a punishment, enough of a price to pay for life. Eternity, oblivion, oblivion for eternity, what a prospect. But life itself . . . Oh, well, why go on? What can I say? You tell me."

"I can't tell you anything. You know that."

"We pay a terrible price for being human. All of us, Catholics, too."

Sigmund sighed. He should have known this was coming. He should have known Larry Adelman better. There were Spinozas everywhere in the days before Yom Kippur.

"All right," Larry Adelman suddenly said, sounding renewed. "Back to reality." He pocketed his handkerchief. "We're able to offer you a three-year contract, no strings, and twenty percent more than the House. Plus insurance for Jenny, in case, God forbid."

"It's generous."

"And don't forget, think of it as an adventure, too. A spiritual adventure. We'll be building something new. It's not just dollars and cents. It's not cut and dried. It's an open experiment, a new way. Don't underestimate that at our time of life."

"I don't underestimate it. But at the same time, it's a very serious thing, as I said, and I have to think about it seriously."

"Talk it over with Jenny."

"Whatever I decide is okay with Jenny."

"And don't discuss it with Fribush."

"Barney is an old friend. Barney was my first supporter at the House, after I came from New Rochelle. It was Barney who came to audition me and gave his blessing."

"Just don't let him make the decision for you, that's all I ask. He'd like nothing better than to see us come running home with our tail between our legs. He's laughing at us all the time, and Barney Fribush's laugh goes a long way."

"He has a right, Larry. You know that. And Barney's a sick man."

"He can still do damage."

"Barney is treasurer of the House. What do you expect?"

Larry shrugged. "Well, I'll just leave all that to Julius," he said. "Barney, I mean. They're a good match for each other."

"Frankly, Larry, Julie Metzger is not one of my favorites, and never was. It's only fair that you know that."

"Look, it can't be perfect, can it? We'll always have the likes of Julie Metzger and Barney Fribush to remind us of that. Wherever we are. It's even-Steven. It's a draw."

The two friends laughed. Larry Adelman, whose shirt was now soaked through, despite the fans that blew over every table, finished his second cream soda. "At least we didn't run into anybody we know," he said, looking around warily. "It's probably better if nobody sees us talking together."

"What do we have to hide?"

"I really like the corned beef here."

"You eat too much of that stuff. You're putting on weight again."

"I know deli is *dreck*, but I have a big frame to fill."

Larry patted his stomach lovingly and reached for the check. He read it carefully, working a toothpick in his mouth. Sigmund waited while Larry paid up. By now, Ballow's was more than half empty, everybody on his way back to work. Sigmund rarely had a lunch date, the way businessmen did. Usually he ate at home, scraps, decorated with parsley, that Jenny put together, or a quick sandwich at the hospital cafeteria on the days he made his rounds. Eat and run was the rule. A serious lunch, with conversation, was a clear improvement. It was the way the rest of the world lived. Why not Sigmund R. Safer, too?

11

That night, the cantor and his choir director faced each other across the length of the dining-room table again. It was back to normal after Sigmund's brief rest in bed, and their second meeting of the day. Between them, on either side of the table, stood several empty chairs. The choir was riddled by absentees tonight, even though the Holy Days were almost on them. This happened every year, a kind of mass nervous defection just before the battle. Marty Schiffman had poison ivy, his annual curse. At this very moment, he was stuck at home down in East Baltimore, around the corner from the Scheingold apartment, scrubbing away at the inside of his elbow with primitive brown soap, gazing with a kind of perverse affection at the familiar tiny blisters that covered his lower arm. He knew that it would take a full ten days to clear up, and that he would have to return to rehearsal before he was fully cured. Sy Frisch the tenor and Gozlov the Russian bass were also absent, Frisch suffering from a chronic postnasal drip that needed careful attention and Gozlov out enjoying himself for the evening by self-imposed right of seniority. As the oldest member of the choir in terms of service, Gozlov felt that he was due an occasional evening to himself, without excuse. That left Jeffrey Bourne as the only adult voice, and Irving Karton and Sylvan Scheingold seated across from him. (The boys had come uptown together by streetcar, and Volkonsky had promised them a lift home.) Herschel Bleiber had not been replaced. Sigmund had never made the effort. The Scheingold kid would have to carry the burden. He was the star. But it didn't leave Sigmund a lot to work with for the evening.

Not that it mattered much. It was clear that Volkonsky had done his job well during Sigmund's brief absence the week before. Everyone was prepared. Everyone knew not only their own solos, but everyone else's, in case. In case! They dreamed of catastrophe for each other, catastrophe without permanent effect, however, just enough to give them a chance to grab another solo for themselves in time for the Holy Days. After the Holy Days were behind them, they wished each other well as they disappeared back into their own lives for the rest of the year. Sylvan was singing Marty's part tonight, besides his own. Jeffrey Bourne did both Gozlov's and Frisch's, eerily pitching his supple voice up and down the scale into the bass or tenor range, as needed, making everybody laugh. Even Sigmund, who was recovering from the inevitable heartburn that had followed his lunch with Larry Adelman, laughed.

At one point, Irving Karton reached out to grip Sylvan's thigh in the middle of a solo. By now the gesture was habit, he didn't even know he was doing it. But there was too much space between the chairs tonight. "Nigger," Irving muttered under his breath, but without heart. "Again!" Sigmund ordered Sylvan, who was more than happy to repeat the disputed phrase in his solo and hear the sound of his own voice ringing in his ears. And again, Sigmund ordered; then once more, again. Later, they all sang together, sounding thin and undernourished, Volkonsky waving his arms lethargically from the foot of the table. It hardly made a difference. They were really just walking through their parts, no matter how peremptory, how urgent, Sigmund tried to appear. They knew that everything was in order. They knew what they had to do. If anything, they were over-rehearsed.

Meanwhile, downtown, locked in the family bathroom, Marty Schiffman began to scratch his arm energetically as soon as he had finished scrubbing with the primitive brown soap; a moan of pain and agonized pleasure escaped him. Gozlov, the bass from Odessa, visiting the widow Berman on Fairview Avenue a bit prematurely, shared a box of chocolates with her on her sun porch, making insinuating remarks with each creamy bite that kept the widow in stitches. At home, a couple of miles away, Sy Frisch inhaled steam from a boiling kettle with a towel draped over his head, and rubbed his tender stomach with a gentle counterclockwise motion designed to ease the intestinal turmoil. In the Safer house, duets followed solos. Group work dominated, without enthusiasm. Sigmund's little pitch pipe sounded in the dining room. The voices were raised and lowered. In the kitchen, Jenny Safer set out raisin buns, iced tea, and milk. Annie was out. In the back of the house, next to Annie's room, Sigmund's fish waited to be fed. A fresh box of white worms pulsed on a table near the tanks. Up front, Irving Karton, frustrated, silently reviewed a catalogue of various obscenities to be tried out on friends and enemies at the first opportunity; across the table, Jeffrey Bourne carried on playfully, which was not quite his usual style; and Volkonsky, nattering away, began to lecture Sylvan Scheingold about the finer points of his present solo, as Sylvan slid down in his chair onto the base of his spine and slowly closed his eyes from sudden weariness.

It was another hot rehearsal night, very boring in Sigmund's estimation. Nevertheless, he had Larry Adelman's interesting offer to chew on, while the singing continued halfheartedly. Already, it had helped to inflate his confidence and bring him back to himself. For a moment or two, he even allowed himself to feel complacent. Later in the evening, he continued to think about the offer as he sat in front of his tanks, happily watching his fish go through their familiar pointless motions.

Five

1

Outside the House of Israel, at the bottom of the steep granite steps that led to the main sanctuary, the congregation gathered at the end of Saturday services. It was ritual, the last of the morning, and purely communal in nature, entirely social. All the rousing hymns were done with, the weekly Torah portion recited in sad-joyous Oriental tones, the scrolls solemnly replaced in the ark, the rabbi's crisp and sterile sermon delivered and half digested by the congregation, while Sigmund R. Safer dozed behind him in the usual way, making strange noises as he nodded off on his golden throne. Now, at noon, it was over, another Sabbath morning, this one without incident.

In the terrible midday glare, Barney Fribush, who had special dispensation from the rabbi to drive to synagogue on Saturday during his convalescence, was being led to his car by his servant. They walked slowly along the pavement together, arm in arm, while Barney tossed loud greetings to his right and left, indiscriminately, hobbling a bit with the effort of walking again and trying to disguise the hobble. But he was back, hobble or not. He was back where he belonged, treasurer of the House, and the idea charged him with unexpected energy. Through the greetings, Elsie, who was wearing the shining white uniform that she always reserved for public appearances with Barney, nodded approvingly, with a little self-satisfied expression around her mouth, at all the old friends who were so glad to see Barney back in place. Elsie loved all this sociability with a kind of innocent greed. The enthusiastic hellos, the obvious affection, the hearty smiles, the exaggerated displays of welcome—they were meant as much for her, she felt, as for Barney Fribush. They belonged to Elsie Thaymes, too. If Elsie had her way, she would have gone to services arm in arm with her boss every Saturday morning, wearing her shining white uniform.

A small crowd filled the pavement around them: the towering Adelmans, Larry and Mildred, worrying with their friends the Sahlmans about Larry's concerns for the congregation's future; Julius Metzger, alone as always (his wife, Rose, rarely left the Metzger house since her hysterectomy and never went to synagogue), stalking the crowd at the curb for possible rebel recruits, for new defectors to join the movement, while his old friend Barney kept a frigid eye on him; Norman and Irene Sindel, amateur intrigants; a couple of servicemen on leave for the weekend, flanked by their grateful parents; the rabbi's delicate wife, who had arrived an hour before the end of services, as she often did; and others, including a collection of timid German refugees on their best behavior and a tiny but intense cluster of House intellectuals who always stuck together like magnetic filings, one appeals court judge, one professor of physics from the University of Maryland, and a long-suffering dentist. Also standing around in the crowd were three of the five Sherover brothers, without their wives for the morning, hovering over one another like fat pashas, their plump young sons, olive-skinned and soft, clinging to their father's trouser legs and whining for lunch. Among the others, too, was Jenny Safer, who was carrying a moist handkerchief rolled up in one hand to use against an expected onslaught of rose fever, touching everyone as she approached with her faint Parisian scent, a becoming aura of lilac and talc, her glistening hair pulled tight into an implacable bun that was like a challenge to the world. At least, that was how some saw it, as a challenge. It had taken Jenny an hour to do her hair this morning—too much time, she thought fretfully, too much time and effort, and for what; maybe she should just cut it and go with the fashion for once.

"Don't hold me so close," Barney complained to Elsie as he hobbled along. (Where the hell was Metzger? He couldn't lose him now.) "For God's sake," he then added in a loud voice, "I'm not a cripple."

Elsie instantly let go of his arm, looking affronted. She accepted orders, even scoldings from Barney, but not in front of strangers and never in public. She counted to two before answering, her mouth open. "You see that little ole gray car sittin' over there?" she asked, assuming another exaggerated accent that Barney hated, while pointing across Garrison Boulevard at the massive Fribush Buick parked at the curb. The self-satisfied, somewhat prissy expression vanished, and something stringent and hard appeared in its place. "Yes," Barney answered, instantly regretting his complaints and trying to sound humble. "Thass where I'll be," Elsie said. "Jes in case you can't find yo way." She headed across the wide street, over the trolley tracks, leaving Barney standing on the pavement alone, blinded by the sheen of her white uniform, feeling momentarily lost. When Elsie got a bug in her head . . .

He was interrupted by a couple of unfamiliar voices. It was the Copelands, newcomers from Wilmington or Trenton, he couldn't remember which, stopping by to whisper good wishes to him in their well-bred voices. Yes, yes, Barney said, smiling agreeably at them. I'm here, feeling wonderful, that's all that counts. The Sahlmans also passed by. The Sahlmans were unreliable, in Barney's opinion; he suspected them of defecting. They were always hanging around with the wrong crowd, the Adelmans, the Sindels, Julius Metzger, the others. "Ho, Barney," Hy Sahlman called, as though that said everything. "Ho," Barney answered, with a brusque wave. Then the Oppenheims from Hesse, to whom he made a little self-conscious bow, hoping that he looked as sophisticated and cosmopolitan as they. Barney never felt quite sure of himself with the congregation's German refugees, all of whom had such beautiful manners and were also clearly profoundly cultured, always talking in their woeful accents about music and literature and such matters. The Oppenheims returned his bow, smiling sadly, and politely moved off, hand in hand.

Barney waited only a moment then before making a move to maneuver himself alongside Jenny Safer, who was waiting, as she always waited on Saturday morning, for Sigmund to change into his civvies from his pulpit dress, including the white sneakers he wore against the fatigue that came from standing so long. Jenny was positioned only a few yards away on the pavement, looking self-conscious and preoccupied, as she often did in the presence of the congregation. Barney worked his way patiently in her direction, he could hear himself breathing with the effort, making all the amenities along the way, showing pleasure at seeing everyone. In a moment, he would surprise her. There were certain people Barney always liked to surprise. But he was in no rush. All good things took time. He took a deep breath. In just a minute or two . . .

"Barney, you scared me," Jenny said.

"I didn't mean to bump you. The sidewalk is so crowded."

She stepped back a bit. "Let me have a look at you," she said, examining him as though she were growing nearsighted.

"I'm a new man," he said. "I feel wonderful. Don't I look like a new man?" He was trying not to fall over, as he changed position alongside her.

Jenny was still examining him at arm's length.

"It's true," Barney said, seeing Jenny hesitate. "I'm clear. The doctors say I'm a new man."

"A healthy man is good enough."

"Oh, my darling," Barney Fribush then said, in a voice that could be heard only by Jenny Safer. At his words, she flushed and turned away, pressing the ball of her handkerchief to her mouth. "And that's just a token of how I really feel," he added. "You hear me? Why don't you look me in the eye?"

"Barney, please."

"The truth is always in the eyes."

"The truth," she said.

"I'm your friend, Jenny. Be kind. Don't put me off." But despite his talk about the truth, he wasn't even looking at her as he spoke. They were each looking away. Barney had suddenly lost Julius Metzger in the rush of words and emotion and was craning his neck to find him in the crowd.

"Barney, please," Jenny said, decisively turning back to him. "You'll only make trouble for me."

"Don't be so jumpy," he said, still looking for his old friend. "Try to relax a little. It's only innocent fun. One man. One woman. Innocent fun that makes me feel alive. Would I make trouble for you?" Without answering his own question, he paused a moment, then continued. "Listen, Jenny," he said in a tone that seemed to come from deep inside his chest. This time, alerted by the urgency in his voice, Jenny looked him in the eye. "Don't let Sigi do it," he said. "Don't let him."

"Do what?" she asked.

"You know what. Don't let him."

"I don't know what, Barney. What are you talking about?"

Barney changed position again, regaining a little of his balance. "They want him to scaramouche," he said. "Metzger and that gang. They want him to go along with them. I know from reliable sources."

"Where did you hear that? I don't believe it. Sigi never said a word."

"It's true. I know. I have spies. He's keeping it from you."

Jenny was silent, thinking about it.

"I'm your friend, Jenny. Believe me," Barney said. "I know what I know. Keep an eye on him. Don't let him do it. It would be terrible. It would be a tragedy. I'm depending on you. We all are."

The congregants swirled by. Julius Metzger hovered at the edges, in sight again. Elsie waited across the street, alongside the Buick. Never in front of strangers, Barney reminded himself irritably, catching a glimpse of her. Never in public. Upstairs, in his little dressing room, Sigmund changed his clothes. So did the rabbi, in the room next door.

"Well, at least everything's set for the choir," Barney said to Jenny, sounding suddenly close to normal again, as though everything had been resolved. "Thanks to you."

"It's not me. It's you who's doing a good deed. That's what we depend on every year. It's thanks to you."

"A stranger. A boy I don't even know. I owe God."

"You won't be sorry, Barney. You'll see. He'll bring some life to the house."

"My nurse is coming, too. Velda. From the hospital. She's coming for two weeks."

"Take all the help you can get. You can't have enough."

"All I'm missing is you."

"Me," Jenny said, looking around anxiously. But Barney had

seen to it that they were standing alone. No one could hear them.

"There goes that Metzger *momser*," Barney said. "With Sindel and his wife, two dead fish. That's some belly he's getting on him."

"I never liked him," Jenny said.

Barney growled. "One bite, Jenny. Please. Then I'll behave myself."

Jenny moved aside.

"You know how I feel," he persisted, even though he could hardly wait to get behind the wheel of the Buick and head for home.

"You're like a child," she answered. "If you see it, you want it. If you want it, you grab. What's wrong with all those beautiful ladies over there, widows like Sophie Harmon or Rina Meyers, look at them, beauties, and you . . ."

"I already had one sermon this morning."

"It's not a sermon, Barney. You have to stop it. At least, for my sake."

"For your sake," he repeated.

They were overwhelmed then by a hive of buzzing Wassermans, parents and all six children, zeroing in for a few greetings. Jenny and Barney pulled apart with false smiles, turning around to offer good will and friendly concern, clucking over the Wasserman twins, now aged five, acknowledging the heat, applauding the Orioles with Sol Wasserman, listening to their stomachs rumble for lunch, along with everyone else's, rumbling greedily for fish and chicken and fruit salad, soggy from the can, the same old syrupy junk pile that raised the sugar count and depressed the spirits every Saturday afternoon. Across the street, the trim little Methodist church, where only English was spoken at services and men and women sat together in perfect harmony, stood quietly under a giant elm, its brown late-summer lawn stretching neatly toward Garrison Boulevard. No one gave it a second thought. By now the crowd was much thinner, but a few stayed on, still lingering sociably. That was how it went every Saturday.

"Hey, Barn. Old pal!"

Old pal. It was Julius Metzger, at last. Julie, with the growing potbelly. Barney waited a moment. "Well?" he asked as Julie came up to him.

"I need some time with you," Julie said, giving Jenny a curt nod as he spoke.

"Call me," Barney said. "You got my number."

"Yeah," Julie said, beginning to laugh, "I got your number all right." Then he laughed some more. "I'll call you later in the day," he went on. "God knows, I been trying. We need to talk. You know, Barn, thank God, you look like a million bucks. You do. We should all look so good." As they stood there together on the curb, Barney's legs almost giving way beneath him, Julie Metzger moved toward him and, coming close, as close as he could get, began to stroke Barney's arm. He couldn't help himself. He couldn't keep from touching. He always had to stroke, to press in and fasten on, even to pinch a little, as though to assure himself that there was real flesh and blood there, just like his old friend Barn, who was subject to exactly the same need.

2

When the sanctuary was empty, as it was now, when it was once again a cavernous void after services, without human presence or echoes to disturb it, in which you could hear a pin drop from one end of the great hall to the other, then Sigmund sometimes thought that he could almost feel all around him the skittish presence of something-or-other, call it what you like, in which, of course, he did not believe and about which he did not speak, hiding itself shyly, as always, behind the skirts of eternity, waiting to be discovered. G-d. The evanescent thing. The divine continuum. So Sigmund whispered to himself, every now and then, in a soft voice full of Polish accents; so he spoke. But that was only sometimes, and it always passed, like all fancies, as it had already passed today.

In his dressing room upstairs now, Sigmund was tying his shoelaces. The cushioned sneakers that he wore for services were lined up neatly in front of him. He was hurrying so that Jenny would not have to wait outside too long, standing alone on the pavement, as he always imagined. After a satisfied grunt, he finished making a tight knot in his laces. When he sat up, he was a little breathless. Raising his eyes, he saw the rabbi standing in the doorway.

"Cantor."

"Rabbi."

The rabbi appeared to smile. Sigmund wasn't sure. You could never really tell with the rabbi. "There's a small matter," the rabbi said.

Sigmund got to his feet and reached for his jacket, which was hanging on a hook behind the door. "Yes, rabbi," he said dutifully, squaring his shoulders as he put on his jacket. "What can I do for you?" Then he turned to face him, looking down at the tiny but erect figure, at the dark smoky glasses hiding the already remote eyes, at the pampered goatee, the graying hair impeccably linking goatee to sideburns and so on; the rabbi's facial hair was another physical dimension entirely, decorative, protective, virile.

"Normally I wouldn't bring this up," the rabbi said, touching his fly without thinking. "Normally, I would let it pass. Another problem, so what, how many problems have we faced together over the years? It's hard to even count them, much less remember. Wouldn't you say? Anyway," he went on, in a suddenly grave voice, "the point I want to make is that we're facing critical challenges to the House at the moment, actual threats to our very existence, all of us, you and I particularly"—here his voice grew even more somber—"and we must all be beyond suspicion, particularly careful about what we do and say as regards our beloved congregation."

Sigmund nodded in agreement. There was nothing the rabbi had said that he could argue with. It was exactly as he described it. Fraught. Nevertheless . . . "What is it?" Sigmund asked in a wary voice. Was it perhaps Annie Safer?

"It has to do with the choir."

Sigmund showed surprise. "The choir?" he asked.

"The choir." The rabbi leaned against the doorjamb, as though he had decided to settle in.

"People are not happy?" Sigmund asked, somewhat bewildered. "People are complaining?"

"No, nothing like that."

Sigmund waited for the rabbi to go on. Sometimes the rabbi was excessively circuitous, especially when he was standing face to face with another human presence. Face to face was not his normal way. "What's the matter with the choir?" Sigmund finally had to ask.

"It refers to Joshua Bourne."

"Joshua Bourne?"

"The one with the Presbyterian father."

"You mean Jeffrey Bourne," Sigmund said, staring hard at the rabbi's thick shadowy glasses, in which he could see nothing but his own dim reflection.

"Jeffrey Bourne, then."

"And?" Sigmund drew out the word while he took off his pince-nez, dangling his glasses affectedly between his thumb and forefinger, already beginning to posture a little as he waited for the rabbi to continue. It was not as though they hadn't had this conversation before in other years and reached a truce of sorts. It was not as though everything hadn't already been said, many times over. A sense of outrage swept over Sigmund.

"I'm sure you understand the problem," the rabbi said. "It's not so strange, after all."

Sigmund shook his head stubbornly. "No, I don't understand the problem. What is there to understand?"

"It's the same old group, the old-timers, the heart of the congregation, and the same old question," the rabbi said, sighing deeply at this catalogue. "They're uncomfortable with Jeffrey Bourne in the choir. As they have always been. As they have a right to be."

"Rabbi, we settled this a long time ago."

"Questions like this are never really settled. You know that."

"This one is certainly settled for me. You and I settled it years ago."

"Well," the rabbi said, coughing lightly into his fist, "the congregation doesn't agree. The old-timers don't see it that way at all. And I tend to agree with them. You know that I've always taken a certain stance as to ritual and tradition at the House of Israel. That stance represents my most powerful beliefs. And I have never wavered. I never will. Do I have to explain that to you, of all people?"

"What are you suggesting?"

"Only what is reasonable. Get rid of the problem. Bourne is only a half-Jew. His father is a Presbyterian. The old-timers don't think he should be in our choir. I agree."

"It's two weeks to Rosh Hashana, rabbi."

"I'm sure you would know how to handle that. No one better than you, after all."

"I already lost one choir member," Sigmund said, making an extra effort not to give ground. It would be terrible to give ground at this moment. "The Bleiber boy's voice is gone. I can't afford to lose another, especially when it's the best. And Bourne is the best. It's a great voice. Make no mistake. And besides, his mother is a Jew. That's the part that counts, isn't it? If your mother is a Jew, you're a Jew. That's rabbinic tradition. What the old-timers want is unfitting. It is inappropriate. And, if you'll forgive me, it's also ugly."

"Come, cantor, everything in proportion."

"Rabbi, it is inappropriate."

Again, the rabbi took a deep breath as he shifted his position against the doorjamb. "Cantor," he began, with a kind of slow smoldering impatience that everyone at the House of Israel had faced at one time or another. "The synagogue is exposed to the very real possibility of dissolution. Nothing could be more serious. You know that as well as I do, and if you don't, you certainly should. I must be an example. On the pulpit and off. I must be as faithful to my congregation as possible."

"Of course, you must be faithful. But my choir has nothing to do with your fidelity."

"Cantor, I am not the issue in this conversation."

"Rabbi, you're making demands on me that I can't fulfill. I have obligations to the choir and I take them seriously. Just as I have obligations to the House, and, it goes without saying, to you, too."

"I would be happier," the rabbi said, without hesitating, "if I could feel a little more sure of those obligations."

Sigmund rose on his toes, courage now steaming up. "You have never had any reason to doubt me," he said.

The rabbi turned. "Think about what I said." He moved away, his back to Sigmund. "You will make it very unpleasant for both of us if Bourne stays. If you insist. What is it, for God's sake, a baritone, a performer, not even a Jew."

"For shame."

The rabbi started down the narrow staircase, then stopped a moment and looked back at Sigmund. "And you would be doing yourself a favor," he said, "if you thought more carefully about the way you speak to your rabbi."

Sigmund waited a few minutes, until he felt that the rabbi was

safely out of the synagogue; then, after waiting another few minutes to get himself under control, he followed him down the
stairs. Jeffrey Bourne, he thought, with a certain amount of con-
tempt. A cool one, all right, Narcissus among the lily pads. But
it didn't matter what Jeffrey Bourne was, he had to be defended.
A human principle was involved. Justice, it was called. There was
a ring to that, a kind of powerful resonance coming after his
exchange with the rabbi, that thrilled Sigmund, that made his
pulse race with a kind of manic throb, and as he made his way
down the stairs, stepping carefully, his resolution began to swell.
He would defend Jeffrey Bourne, as vanity-soaked as he was. He
would save him from the wrath of the old-timers, from the vengeance of the rabbi and all the other rigid Pharisees, even if he
didn't like him. Silently, he promised himself.

Outside, Jenny was waiting for him at the curb. When he came
up to her, he kissed her lightly on the cheek, "You're shaking,"
she said. "Why are you shaking? Are you all right?"

"Of course I'm all right," he answered, giving her a peculiar
look.

A few members of the congregation then complimented him
on the morning's service. The pale fishy Sindels, almost vanishing
into the sunlight behind them; the Wasserman hive, buzzing all
around him. Yes, Sigmund responded, beaming unnaturally at
their compliments. Yes. But he didn't feel unnatural. He loved
the honeypot of flattery and always sought it out. (There was
enough of the other kind, enough wounding criticism, he could
depend on that.) Also at the curb, Julius Metzger was standing
alongside Barney Fribush, tugging at his jacket sleeve, stroking
his arm. To Sigmund, standing just a few feet away, Barney seemed
agitated. He was scowling at Julius Metzger, objecting, trying to
pull away, as Elsie began to call to him impatiently from across
the street. Then the Sherovers, all three of them, clasped Sigmund
to their chests, one after the other, Bimi, Benny, and the youngest,
Barry, who swallowed a belch as he held on to the cantor, praising
him. The rabbi was gone by now, heading toward Ashburton Lake
with his dainty wife at his side. So were the German refugees,
with their impeccable manners, and the House intellectuals, dis-

persed to their books and journals for the rest of the day. Then the Sherovers left with their plump ravenous sons; Barney Fribush hobbled across the street, leaving Julius Metzger stranded at the curb; all the remaining God-drenched congregants were moving off, heading for home and the special peace of Saturday afternoon, shedding their morning piety step by step on the blazing sidewalks, storing it away for another week, as though it were a kind of nourishing spiritual mulch that would feed all their needs. Sigmund would do the same, as soon as he calmed down, as soon as he stopped shaking—Sigmund and Jenny together.

For shame, he had said.

3

"Is your ma home?" It was Mickey Schiller, accompanied by his sharp after-shave smell, facing the Scheingold kid on the white marble stoop downtown early that Saturday evening.

"Ma?"

"You know, your mother."

"My mother." Sylvan waited on the doorstep, pondering the question. His mother. "She's gone out," he finally said.

"You know where?" Mickey Schiller certainly was not shy with questions.

"I don't know where, but she's there with Stanley Gann."

Mickey Schiller ran his fingers through his hair nervously. "Any idea what time she left?" he asked.

"A half-hour ago, forty-five minutes, something like that."

"Say when she'll be back?"

"Late, I think. Yeah, late."

Mickey Schiller thought for a moment, then tried a smile. "Any message for me?"

"Let's see," Sylvan said, pretending to scramble through a pile of notes on a table that stood near the door. "Hmm," he said in an important voice. "Nothing I see."

"Never mind," Mickey said, thoughtful again. "Tell me something," he then added. "You like rummy?"

"It's all right."

"Feel like a hand?"

"Of rummy?"

Mickey was already across the threshold and inside the front hall. "We'll play a hand or two. Penny a point. We'll kill a little time that way. What the hell."

"I don't have any money," Sylvan said.

"Don't worry about it. I'll stake you. You're good. Where are the cards?"

"I can't pay you back. I don't have any money."

"Look, kid, I won't bite. Honest. I got a little time to kill. It's no big deal. Gimme a break. Let's play a few hands."

Sylvan turned without a question and headed for the back of the apartment, moved by what seemed to be an irresistible force contained in the unwelcome presence of Mickey Schiller. There was nothing he could do against it. Once in the kitchen, he pulled out a deck of cards from the porcelain table drawer and began to set them up on the peeling tabletop. The sooner he got this over with, the better. His supper dishes sat in the sink, unwashed. His laundry was stuffed in a bag on the floor. His plan for the evening was to listen to "The Hit Parade," maybe practice a little for tomorrow's coaching session with the cantor, then afterward definitely take a walk to Rosofsky's candy store for an ice-cream cone. He didn't even like cards. "Maybe you'd better check the deck," Sylvan said to Mickey, who was already sitting across from him, in Lillian's usual place. "There's always something missing." He couldn't keep from yawning.

As Mickey carefully turned each card over before arranging them in piles, Sylvan, still yawning, brushed some supper crumbs off the table onto the floor. Then, in another moment, they began to play. "How's Henny doing?" Sylvan asked, to make a little conversation and help keep himself awake. "Henny," Mickey said, as though he had never heard the name before. He was looking at his cards with a concerned expression, "Hmmm. . . probably playing with himself at this very minute. All kids play with themselves."

The truth, Sylvan thought, a little taken aback at Mickey Schiller's answer. He threw away a nine of spades.

"And what am I supposed to do with that?" Mickey asked, gazing at the nine of spades with overt hostility.

Sylvan shrugged noncommittally and sat back in his chair, waiting for Mickey Schiller to make a move. It took a long time. Finally, Mickey pulled a card from the pile resting between them on the table and instantly discarded it. "Never saw such a mess," he said.

The game then went on for a few minutes indecisively. "Kids all call you Nigger?" Mickey asked, hiding behind his cards.

"I don't want to talk about it."

"Sorry." There was a silence. "It won't happen again," Mickey added.

Another minute passed. Sylvan began to grind his teeth. "Want a glass of water?" he finally asked, in an effort to stop himself.

"Got anything more interesting?" Mickey said.

"More interesting?"

"You know, a beer or something."

"We never have beer in this house," Sylvan said.

"You don't know what you're missing," Mickey said, disapprovingly.

Suppose Mickey Schiller wanted to play cards all night? Sylvan asked himself. Or even for a couple of hours. If he did, it would ruin his plans. Sylvan didn't like to have his plans disrupted. He was just like Lillian in that. About plans, both Sylvan and Lillian were very orderly. When things were disorderly, when there was a touch of anarchy in the air, they couldn't even go to the bathroom.

"Your ma ever talk about me?" Mickey asked, trying to sound indifferent. Sylvan looked with longing at the dirty dishes. "She mentions you," he said. "What she say?" "You know, Mickey liked the movie better than I did, stuff like that." Mickey looked at Sylvan from under his brows. "That's it?" he asked. "Far as I know," Sylvan said, smiling weakly. "Hmmm," Mickey said. Then Mickey took the hand, making a note on a little sheet of paper he lifted from his shirt pocket, and began to shuffle the deck again. He shuffled by riffling the cards up and down like a waterfall, a trick that Sylvan admired and had never been able to master. Then Mickey dealt them, counting out each card under his breath. As he dealt, his identification bracelet flashed in the kitchen light.

"You like singing?" Mickey asked, fanning his cards out.

"I better," Sylvan said, and laughed, making little croaking sounds, like a sick frog.

"It must be nice to have talent. I wish I had talent."

"You want mine?" Sylvan laughed again.

"You think it's funny now to make jokes about it. You wait and see. Someday you won't laugh so fast. All my life, I wished I had talent. All my life, I wanted to do something I could put my name to. And now look at me."

Sylvan thought about that. Put the way Mickey Schiller put it, it was a new idea. Voice by Sylvan Scheingold. Singing by ditto.

"Now," Mickey went on, "I'm struggling just to keep a roof over my head."

Who told you to leave your wife? Sylvan wanted to ask. Instead, he said, "How come you're not in the army?"

Mickey looked up. "I only have one kidney. Congenital. They don't take you with one kidney."

One kidney, Sylvan thought. How many kidneys were you supposed to have?

"Take that, my friend," Mickey then said, tossing out a jack of hearts.

Sylvan swept it in, unable to restrain a grin. "Just what I had in mind," he said.

"Anyway," Mickey said, making a mental note to remember about jacks, "as I was saying, the world is your oyster if you got talent."

"It's not all that great."

"I didn't say great. I meant opportunity. You know what I'm talking about?"

"Sure. Everybody's always telling me."

But Mickey looked skeptical.

They played in silence, on and off. The only sound was of snapping cards. Occasionally, waiting for Mickey Schiller to make a move, Sylvan rehearsed one of his choir solos inside his head. He was good at that, he was used to doing two things at once. Now, his jaws had begun to ache from grinding his teeth. He moved them from side to side, slowly, to relax them. The game went on. It took Mickey Schiller a long time to make up his mind how to play his cards. He was full of hesitations and doubts and small protesting sounds at the way the rummy god was dealing with him tonight. In twenty minutes, which passed like an hour for Sylvan, Mickey Schiller managed to lose a quarter. "I see the time's beginning to fly," he said, checking his watch. "And I got an appointment on Baltimore Street."

"Can't be late," Sylvan said. "It wouldn't be nice."

"I liked this," Mickey said. "It really killed the time. Did you like it?"

"Sure."

"You play real good. Smart." Mickey tapped his temple with his forefinger. "I'd sure like to play again. It's an idea. You owe me one. Tell you what, let's get a regular game going."

Then Sylvan was almost sorry he had lied to Mickey Schiller. Lillian wasn't out with Stan the Gann, she was at her girlfriend's, Ida Milnick, who was expecting, for a baby shower.

"I like you," Mickey went on. "We ought to be friends. Smart's smart. We should get a regular game going."

"Yeah," Sylvan said, standing up and putting his hands in his pockets.

Mickey headed for the front door. "Don't start playing with yourself, now," he said. "It gets to be a habit and you can't stop. Ever see some of the old cockers over in the park, sitting around with their hands in their pockets, playing with themselves?"

Sylvan hardly went to the park anymore. You had to be crazy to go to the park. "Sometimes," he said, to be polite.

"Well, don't get like them," Mickey said over his shoulder. "I'm older than you. I know a few things. More than a few. Everybody needs an older man he can depend on. A mentor, they call them. I'll be your mentor. Why the hell not? There's lots of things I could tell you. You want me to be your mentor?"

"If it doesn't cost anything," Sylvan said, watching Mickey Schiller move down the marble steps outside.

"Ice in the winter," Mickey mumbled under his breath, one eyebrow raised, looking back at Sylvan, who was now framed in the doorway, with the setting sun hitting him square in the eyes. "Just like Henny," Mickey went on, louder now. "All you kids. Same thing. Same jokes. I mean, I don't know who you kids think you are." But Mickey spoke almost good-naturedly, sounding only a little put-out. "Well," he continued, "thanks for the game. Tell Lillian I was asking for her. Tell her I was around. I'll call to-morrow. We're supposed to do something together in the after-noon. Tell her I was here. She'll like that. Take care of that quarter, now. Don't get any big ideas. And take your hands out of your pockets. It don't look right."

Don't, Sylvan thought. That was how peasants talked.

Then Mickey Schiller finally headed up the street, hurrying to his appointment. Sylvan rushed to the radio in the corner of the living room to turn on "The Hit Parade" and the boring voice of Joan Edwards. All the singers on "The Hit Parade" were boring, but it wasn't the singing that was important on "The Hit Parade," it was the competition. The competition held Sylvan in terrific suspense, all through the "Lucky Strike Goes to War" commercials and the boring singing. What song would be third? Coming in third didn't count. Second? Placing second was a dead loss. Only America's favorite really counted. Number one on "The Hit Parade." That was what was important. Only first interested Sylvan Scheingold.

4

"I think your old man's a little nuts."

"Everybody's old man is a little nuts. Mine's no exception."

"Tell me, young man, what do you think about the persecution of the Jews?"

"That's enough, Bobby. Only children mimic. And monkeys. That's why it's called aping, and it's definitely crude."

"You think I'm an ape?"

"Oh, stop it."

"You know," Bobby said after a moment, "I've started studying for the marines exam. For your information."

"The marines exam? What's there to study? They must be dying for suckers like you."

"You have to be a whiz at math and things like that. You have to know algebra to know how to aim right."

"The war'll be over by then."

"I hope not. I want a crack, like everybody else."

"All you guys. You don't know when you're well off. You can live without the marines, Bobby."

"But I can't live without you."

"Please."

"Oh, my dolling, I cahn't live without you. I'm frightfully desperate, old chepp."

"What's that supposed to be?"

"It's the way they talk in the book you gave me. Mr. Mawgam."

"It's Maugham, you dummy."

"I know, I know. I'm just kidding. Where's your sense of humor? Anyway, let's talk about what you'll do without me when I'm gone."

"I'll sit at home and knit socks for you. What else should I do?"

"You know what I mean. Feelings, that kind of thing. Let's talk about how you feel."

"About you, right? You want to get me to say things I don't really believe. I know that game."

"Half of it's in the saying, Annie. Just say it and you'll begin to mean it. It's true. You'll see."

"I don't pretend that way. I know what I mean. I always know."

"Annie, I do believe that I love you."

"Jesus Christ."

"Come on, say it. 'Bobby, I do believe that I love you.' It's easy, you'll see."

"Oh, lay off. Let's have some fun for a change. They all say you better have fun now because when you get older . . ."

"That won't happen to you and me."

"That's what your mother and father thought, and mine, too. Just look at them, and everybody else."

"Who cares about everybody else? And my mother and father still have fun. They even still do it. I happen to know. Anyway, your old man's a little nuts. The things he comes out with. No offense, Annie. But my old man would never talk that way. I never heard anybody talk that way."

5

As promised, Julius Metzger called Barney. He called him within two hours of their meeting in front of the House after the morning's service. He could hardly wait. "I told you I was going to call," Julius said, while Barney started to complain in a sleepy voice about being awakened from his afternoon nap.

"Jesus Christ. . ." Barney began.

"We need to talk," Julius interrupted.

Barney turned grouchy suddenly, barking his complaints over the phone in harsh syllables, but Julius, who was no stranger to grouchiness, persisted. "I'll call you back," Barney said. "I'm still half asleep. Christ."

"No, no, no," Julius Metzger answered, pushing hard. It was Julius's habit to push hard. He wanted to see Barney soon, that very evening, in fact. And he had just the place.

"I can't go all the way out to the club," Barney said, although he was feeling better than he had that morning, when, for a moment or two, he felt as though he might pass out in front of the whole congregation, right on the sidewalk on Garrison Boulevard. "I'm not ready for that. I already had my social quota for the day. Doctor's orders."

"I'll pick you up in my car, we'll drive out, have a drink, then right away, home to bed," Julius said. "You won't have to lift a finger."

Barney hesitated, a serious mistake where Julius Metzger was concerned. "It'll do you good," Julius said, pressing on. "You'll see familiar faces, a change of scenery. Everybody needs a change of scenery. And you'll be in bed by nine. I promise you." Julius was always making promises, too.

"And what about my dinner?"

"We'll have two turkey clubs with a couple of drinks, anything you want, then home."

"I can't digest the chow mein they serve out there."

"So you won't have the chow mein."

"It can't wait?"

"Come on, Barn, be a sport. We need to talk."

In the end, Barney had been unable to refuse his old friend. Simple animal curiosity—and the challenge of facing down the adversary—won out. And about one thing Julius Metzger was certainly right. They needed to talk. They had a lot to say to each other. It was time. Now, early in the evening, they faced each other across a round metal table, seated on cushioned metal chairs beneath a striped umbrella on the terrace at the club. The sun still hung over the horizon far in the west. A few clouds sailed slowly along overhead. Otherwise, the sky was clear, as it had been for most of the summer. At the moment, Barney and Julius were both silent. Below them, at the bottom of the terrace, a few teen-age girls were still swimming in the pool. Barney and Julius watched them with serious faces, their club sandwiches sitting half eaten in front of them. There were also a couple of drinks on the table. The girls swam a few lengths, halfheartedly pretending to race each other, then climbed out of the pool dripping chlorine water on the concrete and tugging at their two-piece bathing suits, the latest models. Barney could hear the snap of the artificial fabric against their flesh.

"The Shamer girl should shave her pubic hair," Julius said, with an air of distaste.

Barney shrugged but said nothing. Even though it was something of a blur down there at the pool, you didn't get a chance to catch a sight like that every day. Why complain?

"They're not so careful these days," Julius continued, keeping an eye on the pool. "They don't watch themselves the way they used to, because they don't have to pay so much attention to their persons."

"What persons?" Barney asked.

"To themselves and to the boys. All the real boys are in the service. You don't have to shave your pubic hair for what's left behind. You don't have to be so careful about things like that anymore."

"You think so?" Barney asked. He had never thought about it. It was an unexpected idea, a little startling, people being less careful about the way they behaved because of the war. The war seemed to be everywhere, changing the world, changing Barney Fribush, too. You could never really get away from it, it moved in so many unexpected directions. Pubic hair. Who would have thought? "They're careful about those things in the hospital," Barney said, scratching himself in the groin. "It's still only half grown-in down there. Makes my thing look twice as long, for a change. And it itches, goddamit," he added, continuing to scratch himself.

"And what about the rest of it?" Julius asked, after a discreet silence.

"The rest of what?"

"You know, the cut, the operation." He couldn't bring himself to say the dread word aloud.

"Safe and sound."

"All clear?"

"Everything gone. Safe and sound."

"No pain?"

"Sure there's pain. Moving my bowels, medication, that kind of stuff. What do you expect?"

"You're a lucky man, Barn."

"Don't tell me. Don't say it out loud."

"Well, I'm telling you. You're a lucky man. You always were. Even when we all had the strike, and everybody else had to . . ."

"Oh, the strike," Barney said. "I forgot all about it."

"Well, I didn't."

"Jesus, I go to sleep one night a happy man and wake up the next morning with a payroll twenty percent bigger. Don't tell me about luck."

"The rest of us had to bring the goons in. You were the only one who didn't have to bring the goons in."

"Well, that was the price. Twenty percent. You always have to pay the price."

"And the price is going up," Julius said. "The price is always going up. Wait till this war is over. You ain't seen nothing."

"I should live to see the war finished. I should live to see Hitler hang by his balls. I should live to see everybody home safe, fighting the unions. Yeah, I'd settle for a whole life of fighting the unions just to see the war over."

The Shamer girl did another dive. Her friends applauded her. Barney watched her carefully as she climbed out of the pool. This time he put on his glasses. Julius was right. She needed to groom herself. It wasn't right, a sixteen-year-old, seventeen, maybe, running around the club with her pubic hair showing like that. Decorum was important. For everybody, Barney thought, glaring for a moment at Julius Metzger. Somebody should pay attention to such things. Somebody should care. . . . Behind Barney and Julius, a buffet dinner was being served in the club dining room. It was still too early for the smart crowd, the couples who came to dance away the evening, but a few clusters of families were already sitting together, glumly eating Saturday-night chow mein.

"I'm going to have another Scotch," Julius said, signaling the waiter. "How about it?"

Barney took a bite of his sandwich.

"Another one for me," Julius said as the waiter came up. "And go light on the water this time, Joseph."

Joseph nodded. "And for you, Mr. Fraybush?" he asked.

"Okay, you twisted my arm," Barney said, pretending to sound put-upon. "But forget the water this time. Just ice. Okay?"

"Forgive me, sir, for speaking up, but you sure do look like your old self again," Joseph said, holding his round drinks tray against his chest reverently.

"Thank you, Joseph. It does me good to hear you say that."

"Yes, sir, it makes us all happy to see you out here having a good time again, sir."

"Well, it makes me happy to be here."

"It ain't never the same without you, Mr. Fraybush."

"Joseph," Julius said edgily, "I get very thirsty sitting around like this in the heat."

"Coming up, sir," Joseph said, and moved off to the bar.

"You see?" Julius said. "It's what I always say. Everybody likes Barney Fribush. Everybody cares about him. As though Barney Fribush didn't know that."

"Okay, Metzger," Barney said, grinning. "What's the deal?"

"The deal?"

"You didn't ask me out here to talk about pubic hair."

Julius waited a moment before answering. "No, I didn't," he said.

"So?" Barney said, still grinning.

Julius was silent.

"Well, if you won't answer my question," Barney went on, "I'll answer it myself. You got me out here to talk about the House of Israel. Isn't that so?"

"That's about right," Julius said, lighting up a cigar. "Want one?" he asked, holding out his leather case.

"I already had my cigar for the day, thanks. And what do you have to say about the House of Israel?"

Julius puffed at his cigar to get it going. "Maybe a couple thousand words," he said. "It's worth a couple thousand words, yes?"

"The House of Israel is worth a couple million words," Barney said, sticking out his chest. "As long as they're good."

"I don't disagree with that."

"You wouldn't know it from the way you act. You and your cronies."

"Barney." Julius looked hurt.

"You think we should kid ourselves? At our age? You and me?"

"Not so fast, Barney. We got a lot to talk about. One step at a time." Peevish little smoke puffs rose in the air.

"You promised me home by nine."

"Don't be such a stickler, for God's sake. It's not even eight o'clock. What's the rush?"

"I'll tell you what's the rush. You know how I feel about the House of Israel?"

"Sure, I know."

"You know how important it is to me?"

"It's important to me, too."

"We're not talking about you. We're talking about me, Barney Fribush."

Julius shifted uncomfortably on the metal chair.

"You're a spoiler, Julie. That's your trouble, you're a spoiler."

"Drink up and I'll drive you home, if you're going to take that attitude."

"Uh-uh, too late for that. You wanted this, you got it."

"I didn't invite you out here to be insulted. It's a habit of yours. It's a bad habit, Barney."

"I like to get things out in the open."

"Yeah, I know all about you."

"Not as much as you think. So don't be too sure of yourself."

A few minutes passed while the two of them sulked on the terrace, trying to avoid the other's eyes. What each of them had just said was the literal truth. They knew all about each other, but not quite as much as they thought; and what they knew, they had known for almost a half-century. Finally, Julius spoke, clearing his throat. He couldn't stand the silence. "You've never been exactly the easiest guy in the world to get along with, Barn."

"And the same to you, my friend."

"Aw, come on. After all these years."

"Say your piece, Julie."

"Okay," Julius said, nodding somberly. "We're going. You know that, don't you? And don't interrupt me now. Another habit. And the rabbi only has himself to blame."

"I've heard that song before," Barney crooned.

"And you'll hear it again. I just want to make sure you hear it from me."

At that moment, Joseph set two fresh drinks in front of them, hovering a moment as he wiped up some wet spots on the table. "Okay, then," Julius continued, swallowing half his drink as Joseph moved off. "Where was I? What was I talking about? Yeah, the rabbi. Anyway, he's the one who forced our hand, he made us do what we're doing. You think anybody wants to go out and build a new synagogue? You think we're crazy, we don't have something better to do? He forced us. He's the spoiler, if you're looking for a spoiler. The rabbi."

"Go build a new synagogue. I wish you luck."

"We will. We are."

"So what are we doing here, eating a lousy club sandwich?"

"I have something to say to you."

"You already said plenty, my friend."

"Listen, Barn." But the words wouldn't come, Julius couldn't get a sound out. Instead, he sipped at the rest of his Scotch for a minute or two, then finished it with one swallow. He sat back, easing himself into a comfortable position, legs splayed, hands folded over his stomach, and began to watch the swimmers again at the bottom of the terrace. By now, the sun had dipped below the horizon. The whole western boundary of the club, where the hills were, seemed to be shining with green and gold emanations. On the other side, where the golf course spread out to the east as far as they could see, a great yellow-green wave of heat shimmered in the air. Still, it seemed that the heat was beginning to go, they could all feel it, a soft cooling wind was springing up all around them, and there was even a dark cloud or two floating in from the south, from the bay. Behind Barney and Julius, the dining room had suddenly become full; a long line snaked toward the buffet. Julius raised his left hand slowly, as though he were making a silent benediction, and Joseph, standing behind an umbrella nearby, scurried off for another couple of drinks.

The friends sat in silence. The Shamer girl was diving again. When she came up for air, she treaded water in the middle of the pool and adjusted her bra at the same time. "She doesn't even wear a bathing cap," Julius said.

"It's the new style."

"Natural, you mean."

"Right, natural. Natural means you can see the belly button and the hair. *Pupik* and all. Nipples are probably next, then God only knows what." Barney laughed.

"It's the war," Julius said.

"With you, everything's the war."

Julius made a face. "You going to argue with that, too? For God's sake, Barn, everything *is* the war. Here and everywhere else. Last week, a hundred thousand Jews disappeared in Poland, and nobody knows where."

"I read three hundred thousand."

"All right, three hundred thousand. There aren't any Jews in

Europe sitting around the club having a drink like this. You can be sure of that."

"We're lucky, Julie."

"That's what I was saying before, when you tried to take my head off."

"All I said was with you, everything's the war."

"I remember what you said," Julius answered, nodding vaguely as Joseph set two more Scotches in front of them.

"I didn't order this," Barney said. "Who ordered this?"

"I ordered it," Julius said. "You're my guest."

"I'm only allowed one a night. Doctor's orders. One cigar, one drink. I already had two."

"Excuse me, Mr. Fraybush," Joseph said, still standing by. "It won't do you no harm once in a while."

"Another county heard from," Barney said, looking up at Joseph accusingly. "Well, at least bring me enough ice so I can dilute it," he added. "Otherwise, I'll be on my ass and you'll be the one who's responsible."

"Yes, sir."

"Oh, Jesus," Julius said. "The band is starting to set up already."

"I can't stand the racket," Barney said. "Especially when that kid gets his hands on the drums."

"Listen, Barn," Julius began again, but without finishing what he had to say. Above them, the sky was now a pale mauve and perceptibly changing color from moment to moment. Half the sun had already disappeared. The dark clouds had moved in closer, and more followed. Joseph set a glass filled with ice cubes in front of them.

"How come you're not in the army?" Barney asked, swirling the cubes with his finger.

"Me?" Joseph said.

"Of course, you."

"Mr. Fraybush, I'm fifty-seven years old."

"You're fifty-seven years old?" Julius asked. "You're kidding us. You look about forty. Jesus, with you people you can never tell. I mean, how come you never seem to grow old?"

"I'm proud of my appearance, sir. I'm proud of how I look. I am fifty-seven years old. Fifty-eight on February tenth."

"Well, you look about forty," Barney said, drinking deep. "As Mr. Metzger here was just saying."

"Listen, Joseph," Julius said, squinting into the distance. "I think Mrs. Sheer is trying to get your attention over there. See, sitting alone over there, by the band? Isn't that Mrs. Sheer trying to catch your eye?"

Joseph glanced over his shoulder in Mrs. Sheer's direction. "Guess I better snap to, on the double," he said, moving off. A moment passed. Julius puffed at his cigar. Barney took off his glasses, then put them on again. "If you ask me," Julius said, "it's time those kids got out of the pool. It's getting chilly."

"It doesn't matter so much when you're young."

"Come on, Barn, none of that. We're young. If that's what you mean."

"To Methuselah maybe, we're young. To the Shamer girl, well, I hate to even say it."

"You can say it."

"I already forgot."

Their third drink sat in front of them, almost empty. Barney now began to nibble at a few potato chips. "Barn," Julius started, lazily sliding down in his chair.

"What is it?" Barney answered.

"I have something to say to you."

"So say it."

"You don't give me a chance."

"Well, I don't want to talk about the war."

"Who said anything about the war?"

"You did. You brought it up. You always want to talk about the war."

"I never said a word about the war. It was your idea."

"My idea." Barney yawned. "Cissy Sheer is waving to you over there. I knew it the first time. Near the band. Pay attention."

"Cissy Sheer."

"I knew she was waving to you. Let's go on over and give her a good goose."

Julius was draining his glass.

"I remember Cissy in the third grade," Barney went on. "A *pisher*. But tough."

"Where's her husband? What's his name, Herbert, Hubert, something."

"Prostate, I think. I remember talk about prostate."

Julius tried to blow a smoke ring with his cigar, but as soon as it was out of his mouth it wavered and broke in two. "Wouldn't you just like to be in Paris now?" he asked.

"I never was in Paris."

"Who was in Paris? Not me. I mean now, with the army, when it's all going wild the way it is."

"Who needs you in Paris, Metzger? Nobody over twenty-one is allowed in Paris, anyway. It's the French law of the country."

The two friends began to laugh, Barney chewing on an ice cube. "I was twenty-one once," he said. "I can even remember." Julius got to his feet slowly. "What are you doing?" Barney asked. "I got to say just one hello to Cissy Sheer. I hate to see anybody sitting alone. Come on, let's just say hello."

"She used to sit next to me in the third grade."

"Oh, Jesus, there goes the band already, and it's not even dark yet."

The bandleader was strapping on his accordion. There was a thump from the percussion, the sound of a sour saxophone practicing lame scales. Through the noise, the friends made their way over to Cissy, who was sitting under an umbrella at another little metal table with a tumbler of gin and a plate of chicken salad in front of her.

"Well, boys," she shouted, as they found chairs and sat down on either side of her. "I was getting ready to send up smoke signals."

"Hi, Cissy. How's things?"

"Things are great. What's up with you, Julie?"

"What could be up with me?"

"I could name a thing or two." Cissy drank half her gin after making this remark, looking from Barney to Julius, smiling slyly the whole time.

"Aw, Cissy, come on," Julius said, finally understanding. "Don't try to scare us. We just sat down."

"You scare too easy," she said. "You always did. How about you, Barn? You scare easy?"

Barney pretended to shiver.

"Look at your friend," Cissy said to Julius. "Look how scared he is."

Joseph was suddenly at their table with two drinks.

"Who ordered these?" Barney asked.

"I did," Cissy said. "If you're going to sit with me while I finish this rotten chicken salad, we might as well have some fun. Anyway, three lonely people, what the hell, as the saying goes. Rose is home, yes?"

Julius had to think for a moment. "Yes," he finally said, remembering who Rose was.

Cissy nodded, looking relieved, opened her mouth to speak, then seemed to think better of it. "So, Barn," she began again, a moment later, "they tell me you just got out from under the knife. That's no joke, the knife, but what they tell me is true, everybody says so, you're looking very handsome, very swave, somebody must be taking good care of you."

"I'm coming along. No complaints."

"That's a good boy, now. Complaining never helped anything. That's a fact. So . . . how's about a peek at the scar for old Cissy. I won't tell a soul."

"Cissy. Jesus. Sometimes."

Cissy began to laugh. "It wouldn't be the first I've seen of that variety," she said. "You've seen one, you've seen them all." She was still laughing.

"How's Herbert?" Julius asked politely.

"Herbert," Cissy said, peering into her gin.

"How is he?" Julius asked.

"You really want to know, he spends half his life going to the toilet. Zip down, zip up. They're going to have to cut. That's what they say. I can't stand it anymore, he's up a dozen times a night, tinkling."

"Ah, Cissy."

"What?"

But Julius had already forgotten what he wanted to say. Something about Herbert's prostate, something comforting, something personal. But for now it escaped him, it was gone right out of his head, as though he had never thought of it in the first place. He took out his handkerchief and dabbed at his forehead, while Cissy drank her gin. After she finished it, she had another. Then Julius and Barney, joining in, got through their fourth Scotch, the laughs spilling over in the fresh evening breeze, time vanishing with the sun, their memories also beginning to go as the minutes mysteriously evaporated. A few moments later, during a lull, the Shamer girl walked past their table, still in her bathing suit. She was banging one ear with the palm of her hand. Julius and Barney stared at her crotch. Barney shook his head. "Fellas," Cissy scolded.

Inside the clubhouse, the buffet line was twenty feet long. A few couples were already dancing on the terrace in front of them. "I'll walk alone, because to tell you the truth . . ." Cissy held out her wrist to show them her new watch. Thirtieth anniversary, she told them. Could you believe it, a gift from Herbert. It was studded with tiny diamonds. Thirty years. Hot stuff, Julius said, examining the watch. You're a lucky woman, Cissy. I hope you know that.

"By him," Barney said, "everybody's lucky."

After another lull, during which they all silently gathered strength for what might come, Barney began to describe his stay at the hospital, just to have something to contribute to the conversation, not complaining, in deference to Cissy, and leaving out certain unacceptable details involving the operation itself, also in deference to Cissy, such as the ridiculous and humiliating position he had been strapped into before they slipped the ether mask over his face; while Julius, a moment later, and a little incoherently, he couldn't seem to get the chronology or the figures right, told them about the latest real estate transaction that had just been completed down on Redwood Street, which was going to make another cool million, maybe more, for the Sherover clan, Bimi, Benny, Barry, Shimi, and Malcolm. As though they needed it, Julius added, with a little snort. Right, Cissy echoed, tossing her head indignantly, as though those guys needed another penny, what would they do with all that money, anyway? They pondered this question in silence for a moment, but let it pass, knowing full well that this was a conundrum that needed no answer from anyone, ever, for who could ever have too much money? There was a bit of gossip then about a couple of old friends who had been caught together at some mischief or other, which made the three of them laugh, too loudly, even though they had heard it all before, then Julius, rising to his feet almost in slow motion, invited Cissy out for a spin on the dance floor.

Now why didn't I think of that? Barney asked himself reprovingly as he watched the pair of them walk off, without so much as a by-your-leave. Nevertheless, he leaned forward and gave a little whistle of approval between two fingers, then settled back in his chair to watch. At first, at least in Barney's opinion, Cissy and Julius seemed a bit self-conscious together. There was too much pointless smiling, as though they thought the whole world was looking at them and making a judgment. And if it had been Barney out there with Cissy (Barney told himself), he would never have left her standing like a bump on a log on the other side of the band, gazing anxiously all around her at the other dancers. But soon enough, Cissy and Julius finally managed to get together. They were not a perfect fit, Barney decided, Cissy a half-inch taller than her partner, as she had always been, going back to grade school; but what was a half-inch in this life of ours, and who was a perfect fit out there, or anywhere else? Actually (Barney thought to himself, generously sipping from another Scotch that Joseph had just put in front of him), they didn't look so bad now that they had finally gotten started, and the band was playing almost in unison, for once, not bad at all, considering that they probably hadn't danced together in at least a quarter of a century. A quarter of a century, he thought again, brought up straight in his chair at the idea. That was how he counted his time now, in century fractions, large ones. And so did all his friends.

Cissy and Julius passed by in each other's arms, Cissy vaguely pink, and gold, with her ash-blond hair highlighted quite effectively by the pastel lanterns hanging overhead, which were bobbing gently in the fresh breeze as they shed their pale light on the dancers, and Julius corseted and suddenly trim and chin up, apparently ready for anything. That was Julius Metzger all over, how he had always been, gut sucked in (it was getting harder every year, with his swelling belly), barrel chest thrust out, chin up, ready for anything. Barney began to tap his foot to the music, "Saturday Night Is the Loneliest Night," watching his old friends Cissy Sheer and Julius Metzger dance by in a lovely pink-and-gold haze, tugging at each other solemnly as they trotted along with a serious look on their faces. One, two, Barney counted, eyeing the dance floor appraisingly. In the dreamy lights, his friends looked almost romantic. So did everyone else, pulling each other along in such a somber way, trying to keep up with the beat. Barney couldn't keep his foot still. One, two, tap, tap. And so on, to the percussion beat, which was beginning to give him a headache. Nothing ever changed, Barney told himself, wishing he were out there on the dance floor with Cissy Sheer. Nothing ever changed, he quickly added, except what counted.

Later, after the dark clouds sailing up from the bay had settled directly overhead and a brief squall had taken them all by surprise, dampening everyone who was sitting out on the club terrace, leaving tiny puddles on the dance floor, long after Joseph had served the last drinks at their table and Julius had signed the check, when they unexpectedly found themselves paying guests at the Ro-Dell Roadside Cottages, way out near Westminster, somewhere along Reisterstown Road, Barney had a moment of pure retributive terror. If he didn't behave himself, heaven would wreak vengeance, lightning would strike again. . . . But it hardly had a chance to take hold. Inside their little one-room cottage, while Julius was busy in the bathroom, making a lot of noise, and Cissy sat on the bed picking at a hangnail, Barney leaned forward slowly on a wooden chair and, thinking his way through the process step by step, putting terror aside for the moment, began to untie the laces of each shoe. It seemed to take a half-hour. By the time he finished and sat up again, temples throbbing from the unusual pressure, vision a little blurred, Cissy Sheer was standing over him, a couple of inches away, wearing only her stockings, garter belt, and high heels. Barney began to make a humming noise deep inside his throat. He stared at her garter belt and her rib cage. There was a dim scar running down her right side, just like his own. "Cissy, Cissy," he then called in a dreamlike whisper, exactly as he had in the third grade once, begging for help in a spelling test. At the sound of his voice, which rose to her like a thin wisp of smoke, Cissy wheeled in front of him and started to sing "A Pretty Girl Is Like a Melody" in a husky voice, balancing the turn by holding out her arms like a showgirl and trying out a vamplike pose for a moment, then made for the bed. Barney rose to follow, dropping his clothes on the worn linoleum, stumbling over his shoes.

"Come, darling," Cissy called over her shoulder. The seam of her left stocking was crooked.

Then Julius came out of the bathroom wearing his boxer shorts and ankle socks. Through the bathroom door, Barney could see his girdle hanging over the shower rail.

"Get back in there," Barney ordered. "What do you think this is?" On an end table, a dim blue light screwed into the metal figure of a mermaid, glowed.

"I want to watch," Julius said. "If you're going first. That's the deal."

"What are you talking about?" Cissy asked. "There's no deal. Nobody watches Cissy Sheer. Get back in there until I'm ready for you."

There was a moment's hesitation while Julius stood there, shyly looking from Barney to Cissy and back, as though he were trying to make up his mind about how serious they were, then he turned and did as he was told, closing the bathroom door behind him without a word.

Barney waited there, thinking long and hard about what to do. He thought of his doctor. He thought of his operation. He even thought of Velda Reese. Then he climbed into bed alongside Cissy and stretched out on his back, arms held straight at his sides. He was shivering. "That's a good boy, now," Cissy said, bending over to examine the stubble at his pelvis. "Are you comfortable?" she went on, running her finger over it. "It's important that you're comfortable in your condition. How long does it take for this to grow in, anyway? God, you're so skinny." Then she straddled him efficiently while he groaned, reached over and turned out the blue light on the end table, while he groaned again, louder this time, then began to heave away in the sudden darkness, her sturdy legs, encased in their crooked stockings, tightly flanking Barney's thighs. Between them, the powerful smell of gin mixed uneasily with Scotch. Outside their window, the Ro-Dell Roadside sign blinked on and off, pink and green. Part of the window shade was torn. "Cissy, Cissy," Barney called, still groaning. "Yes. Yes." By the fourth "Yes," it was over. When he looked up in the sulfurous dark, Cissy Sheer was sitting on top of him, her face a few inches away, looking befogged, ash-blond hair falling over her forehead. They stayed that way for a moment or two, then she reached over and turned on the light. A blue pallor suddenly covered everything—flesh, furniture, discarded clothes. Such extravagant blue breasts, Barney thought with a kind of dull detachment, examining the strange unembarrassed woman sitting above him, such extravagant mammoth baggage to have to carry around for half a century, so much for one woman, just as a pain wrenched through his pelvis, once, twice, of a kind he was now very familiar with.

"Please, darling," he said, tensing his jaw. Another groan escaped him.

"Okay, okay," Cissy said, recognizing the problem and clambering off him in a clumsy way that started the pain again.

"Oh, God," he said.

She stood alongside the bed, stroking him absentmindedly, her new diamond watch glittering in the blue light. "Whose idea was this joint, anyway?" she asked, staring at the soiled bedspread that they hadn't even bothered to turn down. "Chenille," she said, wavering above him on her high heels, legs slightly parted, stroking him. "I hate chenille."

Much later, on his way back to Hilton Street, after they had made sure that Cissy got home all right out near Park Heights Avenue, Julius turned to Barney in the car and, hyperventilating noisily, said, "Listen, Barn, all kidding aside, and I mean it, why don't you come with us and be our first president?" It was the longest sentence Julius Metzger had spoken in at least an hour.

"Our first president," Barney said in a bemused voice. "Hmmm."
He waited a moment, trying to assimilate Julius's suggestion. It
only confirmed what he already knew; you couldn't put anything
past that gang, there was nothing they wouldn't try. "What do
you want with a president, you don't even have a rabbi yet?" he
said. "And what are you going to do for a rabbi, anyway? What
rabbi would go with you?"

"Come on, Barn, don't be that way. Pay attention to the subject
for once. I'm not talking about rabbis, I'm talking about us, you
and me. In the Jewish religion, you don't even need a rabbi. In
the Jewish religion, all you need is a congregation. With God,
it's every man for himself." Julius was suddenly very talkative.

"The first president," Barney said again, without expression.

"That's what I wanted to say to you all night, when you didn't
give me a chance." Julius took a deep breath, followed by a few
stabbing ones. "That's what they authorized me to say," he went
on, without identifying who "they" were. "We need you. That's
what I'm supposed to say. You're the man. It's a compliment, you
know, more than a compliment, don't look like that, don't make
faces. Anyway, a great president. Why not? Everybody agrees
with that. Think what we could all accomplish together. A great
president. How about it, Barn? Give me the word."

Barney said nothing. He was still bemused. Bemused and suspicious and ready to laugh in Julius's face. But he didn't want to
talk. He certainly didn't want to talk to Julius Metzger. He had
nothing to say, in any case. Fools were better off keeping their
mouths shut. He was such a fool he could hardly find the running
board of Julius's car when they reached the house on Hilton Street.
The Scotch had turned sour in his mouth. It lined his palate, his
gums, his tongue, it even filled the crevasses between his teeth.
And he could still smell Cissy's gin, to say nothing of other Cissy
things. Up at the house, at the moment, in her own wing downstairs, Elsie was waiting at her bedroom window, thin-lipped; and
Barney knew it, he could make out a familiar, half-hidden shadow
waiting quietly there. It was after midnight, he knew, long after,
maybe even after one.

So what, he thought, pulling himself up slowly as he began to climb the steps to the house. Behind him he heard Julius call out, "Don't forget, Barn. Don't forget what I said. It's not just drunk talk. I was authorized. It's the real thing." Barney waved him away in the dark, laughing to himself. Then Julius gunned the motor, making a racket in the quiet street, and drove off. There was a sudden silence. Behind Barney, the lake gleamed with fresh rainwater, silver ripples broke the surface. The first president, Barney thought, counting the steps. Like George Washington. He laughed again. From her bedroom window, Elsie continued to watch him. Barney waved to her, still laughing. It was very late. It had to be sometime after one. Doctor's orders, he thought. Heaven's vengeance. For a moment, he seemed to be floating. Already, the first wave of a hangover was beginning to sweep over him. It took all his strength to stay on his feet, get inside the house, climb the stairs, and keep his club sandwich down as he crawled into bed.

6

The carburetor sounded funny to Sigmund, and funny, in that context, could only mean ominous. Sigmund revved the motor. A hoarse rattle came from somewhere behind him. He did it again and the car began to shudder. Flaring his nostrils, he reached for the ignition and turned it off. Gosh darn it, he muttered irritably (but without passion). His honey was not so sweet tonight. She had failed him. It was not like her. Maybe he hadn't been paying enough attention, what with everything else that was on his mind these days. Maybe she needed one of those twenty-four-hour specials that the Squicerini brothers were so expert at. Squicerini brother, to be exact, ever since Vince, the younger one, had been hauled off to the ETO in the Quartermaster Corps, where he was now redballing it madly somewhere in France, leaving behind hairy Pasquale to run the garage on Garrison Boulevard almost single-handedly. Pasquale was the solution. He would know what to do. The Squicerinis had always taken good care of the blue Chevy. Pasquale's hand was sure, and overcharges were minimal. Sigmund was clergy, as he had to keep reminding himself.

"Forget it," he yelled up to the porch when he saw Jenny heading his way. "The car's on the blink."

"Oh, dear," Jenny said, pausing on the porch steps.

"We'll take a walk," Sigmund said, getting out of the car. "It's not the end of the world."

"What's wrong?"

"I think it's the carburetor."

"It won't go?" She began to head for the pavement again.

"Nothing serious. She coughs and shakes. One quick check-up is all it'll need. Pasquale'll do it."

"Oh, dear," Jenny said again. She had been looking forward to their Saturday-night spin.

"Come, we'll take a walk instead. It's a beautiful night. We could use the exercise."

"If we're going to take a walk, I'd better put on a different pair of shoes."

Sigmund waited for her on the pavement. He was in no hurry tonight. They had no special place to go, they could take their time. Standing there in the dusk, with Granada Avenue, in its mildly stuporous state, stretching all around him, he began to examine the perfect hedges that lined the sidewalk in front of the house and, eyes sweeping right and left, rigidly critical, could find no faults. They were ruler-straight, boxed and symmetrical, perfectly even front and back and clipped flat on top, as he had often seen them pictured in *Better Homes and Gardens*. Neat hedges were clearly what was called for in America; they set the tone. Sigmund gave himself an A-plus for hedges. Next he checked the new fir standing upright and conical in the center of the tiny front lawn and decided that it, too, was flourishing. Why shouldn't it, Sigmund tended it like a lover every day, standing guard himself for hours on end when it was first planted, to assure a sufficient flow of water into the root hole. Another A-plus. The flowers themselves, the extravagant blossoms, bordered the side of the house, as well as the back yard, small as it was. Tulips, of course, in the spring, crayon-colored and waxen, but sturdy and somehow very Dutch in both spirit and appearance, with beautiful bell-shaped blooms supported by thick waving stalks. A touch of forsythia in the front, earlier on, to herald the arrival of the ravishing Baltimore spring (along with most of his neighbors), a brave burst of tiny yellow petals that always made Sigmund want to open his mouth and start singing something from Gilbert and Sullivan. Then roses in June and July, roses all summer and into October and even beyond, hardy little pink buds that came up by the dozen, fragile crimson blooms the size of half-dollar pieces, and vast, heavy giants, Sigmund's hybrids, thick as peonies, almost like cabbage heads, some of them voluptuously scenting Jenny's dressing table in their bedroom, as well as the back of the house, the two rooms downstairs where his fish swam and his daughter Annie slept (with one eye open, Sigmund sometimes thought).

Somebody had picked Annie up just twenty minutes ago, whisking her off to an air-cooled movie or someplace, without even a "May I?" to her father. There was always somebody. Sigmund could depend on that. Bobby Fiorentino wasn't the only one. He just thought he was. Boys came and went, they always had, at Annie Safer's powerful whim, which seemed to have a peculiar life of its own. Whim and fickleness, in fact, sometimes seemed to Sigmund to be twin family traits, undesirable ones, natural faults of character, something genetic, perhaps, on the Safer side. Or Czaferski side, he corrected himself. His sister Shifra was notoriously fickle, no one had ever questioned that, with her never-ending succession of radical boyfriends, one after the other; and for all her bluestocking tendencies, so was Bronya, given half the chance. (At the thought of his fickle sisters, Sigmund began to snap his fingers impatiently.) And Sigmund himself? Was he any different? Hadn't he deserted them all by running away exactly a year to the day after his father's death? And it wasn't merely an impulsive gesture; he had carefully planned the whole adventure in secret, sometimes hiding the plans even from himself. In his pocket, when he ran away, he had a steamship ticket to New York, the Polish equivalent of two hundred dollars, and, packed in an old suitcase, along with his clothes, a few novels, mostly Russian, which carried the romantic scent of his adolescent illusions between their covers—Artzybashev, Lermontov, Goncharov, Sudermann, Zola. There was also his passport, in the name of Zygmunt Czaferski. Behind him in tired old medieval Poland, where the future disappeared before it even came into sight, he had left his older sister, Shifra, and her wayward ways, his younger sister, Bronya, and her intellectual opinions, as well as their bereaved mother and her complaisant new husband, Hermann, a total stranger from Galicia, who after the marriage instantly made himself at home in the Czaferski Warsaw apartment, as though he were the host and Sigmund and his sisters the guests, and did not even have the grace or ordinary delicacy to close the conjugal bedroom door after they all went to sleep at night. It was too much to bear, it was the breaking point, the sound of his own mother in bed with a stranger, the midnight sounds of *her* fickleness; and he had fled.

Yes, Sigmund knew all about fickleness. Standing there in the deathly stillness of Granada Avenue, examining his miniature landscape, his squared-off hedges, his upright fir tree, his new late-summer blooms, his estate (all A-plus, he decided), he knew that he was an expert on the matter. It was not so complicated, after all. (Even Larry Adelman, making his offer, had known how to tap into it.)

Jenny came walking toward him, wearing flat-heeled shoes. She carried a shoulder bag, and her hair was pulled taut. (Her hair was so long that it had to be washed by professionals once a week at Miller's Beauty Parlor.) A handsome woman, Sigmund thought, partly from habit, eyeing her with a touch of condescension and husbandly pride, handsomer than his sisters, if he was going to be fair, more comely, softer, more womanly, although not at all intellectual, like Shifra or Bronya, or, for that matter, her own daughter; not at all educated in any serious way, not at all a thinker. Could he talk about Lermontov or Emile Zola to Jenny? Or make a joke about his sisters' Marxist lovers? Or his daughter's tough American candor, as he had diagnosed it? He had never tried. Handsome. Comely. Soft. The thought touched his vanity. It flattered him. He had always been susceptible to good-looking people. He preferred them. He frequently judged a book, so to speak, by its cover; beauty was only skin deep, they said, but that was often one of its attractions.

Without speaking, the Safers came together at the foot of the path and slowly headed up Granada Avenue, Jenny one foot behind Sigmund. He walked faster, she remained one foot behind. He slowed down, the same. A kind of unspoken scientific principle, involving marital balances the world over, seemed to be at work. After they had walked two full blocks in total silence, Sigmund said, "Whatever I do, you're one foot behind me. Always one foot."

"Is this any better?" she asked, joining him as they turned a corner.

He grunted at the figure walking alongside him, indicating reluctant approval. "It's still warm," he said after a moment.

"They're calling for showers."

Sigmund looked up. "There's not a cloud in the sky."

"By midnight," she said. "It's coming from the south."

"We could use a little. The hose isn't enough for my roses."

"We had a few drops yesterday."

"A couple of inches is what we need."

"Barney Fribush tells me . . ." Jenny began.

Sigmund looked at Jenny sharply. Her eyes were watering a little from her rose fever. He always had to remind himself that rose fever had nothing to do with roses. It was just a name. Thank God for that. He would hate to have to feel guilty about his roses. "What does Barney Fribush tell you?" he snapped.

"Don't be so jumpy. You're always ready to fly off . . ."

"What does Barney Fribush tell you?" he repeated.

"He tells me that the apostates want you to come with them. Julie and that bunch."

Sigmund hid his surprise. "That shows how much Barney Fribush knows," he said. "What could he know about it, anyway? He's their enemy. You think they would tell him anything? And 'apostate' is a serious word, Jenny. If you're going to use a word like that, you should be careful who you're talking to."

"I'm talking to my husband."

"You know what I mean," Sigmund said. Then, after a moment's resistance, he admitted that Larry Adelman had broached the subject over lunch at Ballow's just the other day.

"And you didn't tell me?" Jenny asked. She dabbed at her nose with her handkerchief.

"It didn't seem important at the time."

"Didn't seem important? Sigi! Tell me exactly what he said."

"Flattery," Sigmund said, relieved at last to use the word. "That's what he said."

"Tell me."

"Oh, you know, a lot of stuff about my voice. I loved it, of course. And the drawing power of my name, I loved that, too. And about being old friends, family almost. And the challenge, too, naturally, and then something about me being smart enough, liberal is what he meant, for anything that might come up."

"And what might come up?"

"You know, men and women sitting together, maybe an organ

in the synagogue, a little more English in the service, a lot more, in fact, maybe even women reading from the Torah on the pulpit. Someday, maybe. You know all that."

"I don't want to sit with men in the synagogue," Jenny said.

"I thought you always said . . ."

"I changed my mind. I wouldn't want to sit next to Barney Fribush, I can tell you that."

"Who says you have to sit next to Barney Fribush? Barney Fribush's staying at the House. You think Barney Fribush wants to sit next to you?"

"Okay, okay."

"Sometimes, Jenny."

"I said okay."

They turned another corner and headed down Maine Avenue. "You won't believe this," Sigmund then offered casually, "but you know what the rabbi said this morning? I should fire Jeffrey Bourne." Sigmund began to bristle as he spoke.

"I thought that was dead and buried a long time ago."

"Jenny, for the last time, I can't keep talking over my shoulder." She caught up with him.

"As though Bourne's mother isn't Jewish," Sigmund said.

"You said no, I hope."

"Of course I said no."

"Don't let him force the issue."

"He knows how I feel about the matter. I told him a thing or two."

"I felt a drop," Jenny said, stopping a moment.

"There's not a cloud in the sky," Sigmund said, looking up.

"I can't help that. I felt a drop."

They continued walking, side by side.

"Be firm," Jenny said.

"Don't worry. I let him know exactly how I felt. Can you imagine the nerve?" Sigmund paused a moment, still bristling. "Anyway, Larry Adelman broached the subject," he said.

"And?"

"I said thank you, I'll think about it."

"What does Larry Adelman have to lose?" Jenny said under her breath. Then, "Were you just being polite or were you serious?"

"I was both. Why not? That's the way those conversations go."

"If you want my opinion . . . Do you want my opinion?"

"Of course I want your opinion."

"Your life is at the House."

"I'm not married to the House. I still have a few choices left."

"Not so loud."

"Well, I do," he said in a softer voice. "I still have choices."

"I don't like the way you're beginning to sound. If you want to know the truth. And remember, we still have Annie to think about."

Annie. "What does Annie have to do with it?" he asked. But he knew the answer to that one.

"She starts college next fall. Remember?"

"Don't patronize me, please. Do me that favor. They're offering twenty percent more money. Plus other things, like insurance. Think about that a little."

"They don't even have a name yet, so how can you believe . . ."

"A name. That's the least of it."

"Or a site. Or even a rabbi. They don't have anything to offer except disloyalty and bad manners."

To this, Sigmund said nothing.

"Will they give you a lifetime guarantee? Will they promise tenure?"

"Who gets a lifetime guarantee?"

"You've got one now. You know that. Even with the ups and downs. Even with the rabbi."

Again, Sigmund was silent. He didn't enjoy arguing with Jenny. He never had. She always seemed to be able to push him to the end of a limb, where he didn't want to be, stuck there to defend questionable points in which he might or might not believe. She was very tenacious about that, and without a doubt she knew how to keep him at full attention. All the women who had surrounded him throughout his life had known how to keep him at full attention.

A breeze had come up while they were talking, gently sweeping the dust into the air. Sigmund coughed and blew his nose. Jenny began to sniffle. "I just felt a drop, too," Sigmund said, holding out his hand. They were now walking on Hillsdale Avenue, the vast blankness of the golf course across the street sheering away like an abyss in the darkness. Sigmund could see the tops of the trees begin to bend in the wind. "Better step on it," he said, increasing the pace.

They began to hurry toward Forest Park Avenue, where they would turn back toward Granada and home, having made a full circle. Up there, ahead of them, two figures ran across the street from the golf course, into the wind. Sigmund stared and blew his nose again. He couldn't afford to have street dust accumulate on his vocal cords. There was no telling what street dust might carry. He would gargle with warm salt water as soon as he got home. That would do the trick. "I know that walk," he said to Jenny.

"It's that Italian boy from Woodlawn," Jenny said. So she knew about Bobby Fiorentino. And she had never said anything. Not a word. "They must have been out for a stroll," she added.

But Annie and Bobby Fiorentino were already turning the corner. They didn't hear Sigmund as he tried to call to them, they were hurrying on, moving fast. After a moment's hesitation, Sigmund and Jenny continued their own walk, also moving fast, but silent now, on the way home, staring into the void across the street as a little rain began to fall. Sigmund was thinking about his fickle sisters and his fickle mother, Shifra and her radical lovers, Bronya and her opinions on everything, his bereaved mother who could hardly wait to remarry. It all seemed to go together somehow, it connected somewhere, if he could only find the right fit. Then he thought of Annie again. Annie Safer and her more-than-a-friend Bobby Fiorentino, the boy from Woodlawn, who surely believed in many gods, at least three if Sigmund had it right, Father, Son, and the Other Thing, who worshiped icons and human idols as well, at least 365 of them, probably more, like lucky charms, a dead saint for every day of the year. He turned to Jenny. Thinking about his daughter was unbearable. So was thinking about icons and human idols. As Jenny walked along beside him, striding now, as the wind blew more heavily, her face was expressionless. Did she know his thoughts, even when he was silent? Could Jenny actually hear him think? Sometimes he believed that. Often, in fact. Together, they began to move faster in the rain. Thick drops fell from the darkened sky.

Forbear! he told himself, in the commanding inner voice that he sometimes used to swell his assurance. Be generous! Act rational! It was the twentieth century. It was the modern world. The past was dead.

Long live the past!

Six

1

"Why? Because I want it, that's why."

"Because you want it. Look at you, bags under your eyes, skin like a sheep dipped in . . ." Elsie aimed the swab and Barney yelped. "That's good," she said, trying again.

"Have some pity," he begged.

"You just lay there now. You got no pity for your own self, why should I? And what's To-ba going to think when she gets here with whassisname?"

To-ba—Toby to the rest of the world—and her husband, Irwin Fedder, sometimes dropped in from Chevy Chase for an hour or so on a Sunday afternoon to visit Barney. With her father's illness, these visits to Baltimore had become more frequent. Toby was devoted; she worried about her father, living alone in the big house on Hilton Street. "So I had a little fun," Barney said, feeling not at all comfortable at the prospect of his daughter's visit today.

"Drunk as a coot."

Barney laughed at the memory, a little too heartily to please Elsie.

"One more time," she said.

"Go easy now. Please."

Again she swabbed him. This time Barney lay silent. The sun poured into his room. The Sunday papers were strewn all over the bed, the funnies rumpled beneath him as he lay there on his stomach. It was almost noon. He had awakened feeling like the Oklahoma dust bowl before the rains came. That was how he put it to himself when he tried to open his eyes. His thirst was unbearable. He had already drunk a quart of cold water out of the Frigidaire and followed that by gobbling down some cold spaghetti he had found on one of the shelves. As soon as he saw the spaghetti, slowly stiffening in the frigid air, he felt a craving at the very center of his physical self that did not let go until he had finished the whole plate. He had eaten so fast and so greedily that loose spaghetti strands littered the floor at his feet. Nevertheless, his energy seemed to have disappeared down a chute. He could barely move a limb. His upper arms were like liquid. He would get through the day by placing one foot in front of the other, slowly, pausing deliberately at each step until he was sure that he was going to make it.

Lying on his stomach, waiting for the burning to subside, Barney fell into a half-doze. He thought he could see Cissy Sheer's ash-blond hair floating all around him in the sunlight, like wisps of wayward clouds. He could see her straddling him in her garter belt and stockings, ash-blond hair falling lazily over her face, he could see her wavering in front of him on her high heels, blowing a lock of ash-blond hair out of her eyes. Then he could see Julius Metzger running around the one-room Ro-Dell cottage in his boxer shorts and ankle socks. Julius never did get to take off his socks; but somehow he made it seem that there was nothing unusual about it. Maybe he lived like that all the time. Maybe he wore his socks when he got into bed every night with his wife, Rose. It wouldn't surprise Barney, he had heard of stranger things. Barney opened his eyes and blinked. Instantly, the memories began to congeal in the powerful light. They were like small open cuts just before the scab forms. All Barney had to do was cleanse the wounds and let them heal. That was why he had told Elsie they were going to have a picnic. A picnic—his own—would help everything heal. When she began to question him, he interrupted her by making his statement. "Because I want it, that's why." Then, liking the sound of it, perhaps because it echoed the unabashed truth about himself, he said it again. "Because I want it." Reason enough for Barney Fribush.

Before his swabbing, Barney had grabbed the phone next to the bed and made a few calls. He lay propped against a bank of pillows. Beneath him was his air cushion. Velda Reese, first. The picnic would give her a chance to look around the premises, he told her. She could familiarize herself with the house. It would be fun. Yes, Velda responded in a thoughtful voice from her room near the hospital. It sounded nice. Yes, she said again, dolefully appraising the condition of her frizzy hair in the mirror, she liked picnics, although it was certainly short notice. What the hell, Barney said. We don't have to stand on ceremony with each other. We know each other too well for that. All right, Velda said. But I look like a witch this morning, she added, don't say I didn't warn you. Then the Scheingold kid, and his mother, too. It would give them a chance to look around the house, just like Velda, and, not to put too fine a point on it, it would also give Barney a chance to have a look at the Scheingold kid and his mother.

"But I have a date," Lillian said, thrown off-guard by the call. She was pleased at the attention, but she began to think that Mr. Fribush sounded a little crazy, the way he was forcing himself on her, as though nothing were more urgent than her presence on Hilton Street that afternoon.

"What kind of date?" Barney asked.

"With a friend named Mickey Schiller," she said, trying to pull herself together.

"Bring him along."

"Hmmm," Lillian said, considering the offer. There could be ramifications with Mickey Schiller. Who knew? He wasn't entirely dependable socially. "Well, maybe. Actually, we could pick Sylvan up at the cantor's on the way."

"At the cantor's? What's the cantor got to do with it?"

After all the explanations, Lillian agreed to come with Mickey Schiller, and Sylvan could get a lift with the cantor and his wife, who were also on Barney's guest list. Listening to Barney's inquisition, she sighed. She was sitting at her little kitchen table down in East Baltimore, drinking a second cup of coffee. She wasn't even dressed yet. Outside on the marble stoop, Sylvan sat reading the Sunday papers in the sun, waiting to take the streetcar uptown for his weekly coaching session. Lillian had slept late, after another insistent evening with Stanley Gann, who had dropped in, unasked, at Ida Milnick's baby shower as they were all opening their fortune cookies.

"So," Barney went on decisively, as though he were buying raw materials for his factory downtown. "Five o'clock. A picnic. Nothing fancy. You don't have to stand on ceremony."

"Yes," Lillian said, "that's very kind of you," remembering her

manners at last and thinking about the emptiness of Sunday afternoons. She hadn't been to a picnic since high school.

The Safers followed. "Jenny?" Barney began. But as soon as
Jenny heard Barney's voice, she became all business. He might as
well have been trying to sell her life insurance. If he started
anything on the phone, she would hang up. Barney had gone far
enough yesterday after services. Five o'clock? she asked, as though
she and Sigmund had several other engagements to choose from
for the late afternoon. A picnic. And bring Amy, Barney said,
behaving himself. The more, the merrier. It's only hot dogs.
There's always enough on the platter. Bring Amy.

"Why?" Barney repeated after Jenny had asked again. "Because
I want it, that's why." Then he laughed like a boy.

Elsie had her orders. Two dozen franks, fat ones. A salami for
whassisname, who claimed franks were poison. Cold slaw, as
Barney called it, with plenty of wet stuff. Potato salad. Paper
plates, they would picnic in the back yard. Pretzels, too, the thick
chewy kind that could stop up a windpipe. And a couple of cases
of Coke. On second thought, make it Pepsi. Joe Ranshoff, who
bottled Pepsi for the Baltimore area, a gold mine, was a member
of the House.

When the medication dried, Barney got dressed.

"Where you going?" Elsie asked, watching him put on an orange
sports shirt.

"There's a committee meeting at the House. There always is
on Sunday."

"When you going to start taking care of yourself?"

"Look at me," he said, flexing a meager bicep. "I'm in perfect
shape." The effort almost made him drop.

"If you saw what I saw," Elsie said.

Barney turned away. "Do me a favor and don't tell me," he said
after a moment. "These things take time. Give it a chance. Now,
where are the car keys?"

"Never mind the car keys, I'll drive you. Not gorgeous, I can
tell you."

"How could it be gorgeous so soon? Healing takes time. That's
why I asked Miss Reese, so she can concentrate on that for a
couple of weeks. It'll save you."

"Oh, yeah," Elsie said.

"You don't have to drive me."

"Yes, I do. While you're having your meeting, I can shop. Then I'll pick you up."

"Well, let's go. I'm late."

"A picnic."

"What is it, for crying out loud, boiling a couple dozen hot dogs."

"Huh," Elsie said.

2

Sigmund was sitting behind the wheel of his honey, trying to turn the motor over with gentle little thrusts of the ignition key. Something was wrong, no doubt about it. The blue Chevy was still resisting his efforts. It made hoarse noises, choking sounds, rocking back and forth when the engine caught as though it were in pain. His darling was sick. He had better call the garage. Pasquale would take care of her.

"Need a hand?"

It was Bobby Fiorentino, appearing on the curb out of nowhere. Bobby F., on a scorching Sunday morning. He was wearing a black suit, a white shirt, and black shoes with fading pink crepe soles that looked like chewed bubble gum. Also a speckled red tie, bulging below his Adam's apple with an extravagant Windsor knot.

"I can't seem to figure out what the trouble is," Sigmund said, as though he were some sort of automotive expert. He was trying to keep his eyes off Bobby's red tie. It was not easy.

Bobby walked around to Sigmund's side and peered through the open window. Sigmund could smell Vitalis. "Mind if I give it a try?" Bobby Fiorentino asked. "Sir? I'm pretty good at this stuff."

It would be boorish to turn his back on Bobby Fiorentino at this moment, Sigmund felt. Forbear, he had told himself just last night, on the way back from his walk with Jenny. Be generous. The opportunity had arisen soon enough. Sigmund got out of the car, Bobby slid in behind the wheel. His Neapolitan curls were brushed so they shone. Sigmund stood shyly alongside the car, staring at the serious, immaculate profile positioned in front of him in the driver's seat, blunt-faced and chunky in its black suit, Italian chunky.

Bobby Fiorentino turned the ignition over a couple of times, biting his lower lip as he considered the possibilities. He pressed the accelerator, checked the gauges, pondered the information registering on the dashboard. Then he pondered some more. "I think I have an idea what's going on," he finally said, listening to the complaining noises that came from the Chevy. "But I better have a look inside."

Sigmund moved away as Bobby got out of the car. Bobby took off his jacket and tossed it onto the front seat. His white shirt was dazzling in the morning sun, perfectly ironed and starched. After a moment, he maneuvered around Sigmund and, squaring his shoulders and hitching up his pants, headed for the front of the Chevy.

Sigmund forbore and remained silent.

Bobby Fiorentino lifted the hood of Sigmund's honey and peered inside. He looked more serious than ever. After another moment, he stuck his head in. Sigmund could hear a buzzing sound of concentration coming from Bobby as he made his probe. Bobby moved slowly, working mostly through his fingertips, touching the valves, pulling easily at wires, as though he were old pals with each one of them, even sniffing a spark plug at one point, with a connoisseur's expression on his face. Then he repeated each move, just as slowly the second time. Sigmund wished that Bobby Fiorentino would hurry up. He had responsibilities at the House this morning. He had committee meetings. If the Chevy wouldn't move, he'd have to walk.

After a few minutes, Bobby Fiorentino straightened up and said, "Would you mind getting behind the wheel and turning the motor over a couple of times? Easy like?"

Sigmund got back into the car, making sure that he didn't sit on Bobby's jacket, and did as he was told. "That's good," Bobby Fiorentino called out, looking pleased. "That's real good. Now one more time." Sigmund followed Bobby's order and waited. There was another humming noise, this time mechanical and sweet. The engine buzzed along, really humming. "Okay," Bobby Fiorentino said. "You can stop her for a while." He stuck his head down into the engine again, staying there for a minute or two.

"Okay," he called again in a muffled voice. "Now give her the gun."

Sigmund checked the gear shift, turned on the ignition, stepped lightly on the accelerator. It certainly made a sweet sound.

"I guess that's about it," Bobby said, suddenly standing alongside Sigmund, after having slammed the hood shut. He was wiping his hands on an immaculate white handkerchief. "It's not such a big deal. All she needs are some plugs and maybe an oil change. Definitely an oil change. The oil is definitely filthy. You really have to pay attention to those things. They don't take care of themselves. She'll be all right for a couple of days. She'll go okay now, but still."

After this long speech, Sigmund and Bobby stared at each other. "I'm grateful for your help," Sigmund finally said, carefully handing Bobby his jacket. "I'm never any good with these things, I'm so clumsy with machinery."

"It's nothing," Bobby answered, his face about three inches from Sigmund's as he slipped his jacket on. "Just basic stuff." Vitalis and scented curls filled the car window. A white shirt and red speckled tie. "You know," Bobby went on, with a hesitant half-smile, "with all respect, I never noticed how much Annie looks like you. I never noticed that before."

"Well, why shouldn't she," Sigmund said, pulling back a little. "I'm her father."

"I just never noticed before."

"Actually, she looks just like my sister. I have a sister in Poland. I have two, in fact. Did Annie ever tell you that?"

"No, she didn't. We're not very intimate about things like that."

"Oh, you're not," Sigmund said, stiffening at the word. Then, after a moment's silence, he said, "You're certainly all dressed up this morning."

"I'm on my way home from church."

Sigmund looked stern. "Isn't this the long way round?" he asked, staring through the windshield.

"I promised Annie I'd drop by on my way home from church." Bobby began to dance on the balls of his feet.

"Well, she's in there somewhere," Sigmund said, still looking stern, but proud of how he was holding on. "She's probably out in the back yard getting a suntan. She likes to sit in the sun. She does it all the time. Now listen, I have to be at the synagogue in about five minutes for a meeting, so if you don't mind . . ."

"Yes, sir." Bobby Fiorentino stopped dancing and backed away. Then he saluted Sigmund smartly. "I enjoyed our conversation. I really did. Know what I mean? Sir?" He saluted again.

"Stop doing that," Sigmund said, starting up the motor. "That military stuff makes me nervous."

"Spark plugs and oil," Bobby said. "Definitely oil. Don't forget. You have to watch those things."

"Okay," Sigmund said. "And thanks again. I envy people who are mechanically oriented. I was never any good at that."

"At your service. Anytime, sir." His right hand moved at his side, but he managed to restrain himself.

Very carefully, then, Sigmund moved the Chevy out onto Granada Avenue, while Bobby waved him off. After taking a full five minutes to drive the half-mile to the House, as though he were afraid the car might not make it if he went too fast, he parked it across the street from the synagogue. It still sounded sweet, still hummed pleasantly. Bobby F. had done his job. Sigmund had to hand him that. What was right was right, give the devil his due. In front of Sigmund, as he slowly got out of his car, reluctant to leave it to itself at the curb, the great granite mass of the House loomed in the heated blue air. It was not like the Methodist church that faced it. No tidy landscaping softened its stony outline. No blue firs, no handsome elms, no lawn. And no spire, no tower, reached toward heaven. All that distinguished it, besides its size, were two immense copper domes capping its rooftop on each side, like ancient twin skulls, just where it should have begun to soar. It was as though it were trying to make a statement about human limitations, as though it were determined not to overreach itself, to remain of this world, here and now, earthbound.

Sigmund began to climb the steps to the synagogue offices. It was an effort, they were so steep. What did Bobby Fiorentino think about the persecution of the Jews? Sigmund asked himself, beginning to find the climb more effortful than usual. Did he even know where Poland was? Had he ever heard of Warsaw? Good questions for Bobby F., especially on a Sunday morning after church. Vitalis and black curls. White shirt, red speckled tie, pink crepe soles. Black suit.

Spotless for Christ.

3

Inside the House, several committee meetings were under way simultaneously—Cemetery, Ushers, and Membership. It was the usual Sunday pattern, made urgent by the approach of the Holy Days, when all meetings would be suspended for a few weeks. Cemetery and Ushers had gathered in empty classrooms in the school wing, while Membership, of which Barney was a part, was sitting in the adult study hall downstairs next to the small sanctuary, the committee spread out at a long sweeping table that ran for at least twenty feet, from one end of the room to the other. Huge books, relics of Saturday-afternoon brooding, were piled at one end of the table. Glass-fronted bookcases lined the walls. A lingering odor filled the room, an airlessness made up of dust, crumbling book covers, yellowing pages, forgotten leaves withering in a huge vase, as well as an unemptied spittoon sitting in one corner, the bane of the good ladies of the Sisterhood, who wanted it eliminated altogether from the premises. Spittoons were for primitive old men from another time.

Sitting at the table, Barney Fribush could hardly contain himself. Immense yawns split his face. His body ached. All he could think about was fatigue and sleep and the true meaning of a hangover, which he had never quite understood before, even though he was no novice when it came to alcohol. But he forced himself to listen to the other members, trying to look attentive and concentrated when they spoke their piece; sitting up straight in his chair, he wanted everybody to note Barney Fribush's quick recovery. On the other side of the table, Norman Sindel was reading a list of family names aloud. New members. Eight in all for the month; not bad for the dog days of August, when half the world was in Atlantic City. Now, Barney thought, growling a little to himself, it would be interesting to see if Norman Sindel walked off with a copy of the new list himself, hidden in his jacket pocket, as he had walked off with all the previous monthly lists, including the one overall list that contained the names of every member of the House of Israel and the amount of their annual contributions. In that way, accumulating names and lists and contributions, the rebels continued their secret solicitations on the path to independence and a new congregation.

The door opened to the study hall. A small fine-boned head peaked around the corner, eyes eager and diffident at the same time. Sigmund R. Safer. Reasonably fresh from his business with the pride of Italian mechanicos, Robert Fiorentino, who had spent most of the morning, if Sigmund understood it right, down on his knees in his black suit in church, curly head bowed, begging to be allowed to go on with life without fear of eternal damnation for his sins. "Sorry," Sigmund said to the committee members, closing the door behind him as he came into the study hall. "Cemetery ran a little late. We had a problem. Do I have your permission to enter?" Sigmund smiled facetiously at his colleagues.

The five faces at the table stared at him. Norman Sindel, report in hand, looking truculent at the interruption. Larry Adelman, Sigmund's giant friend and booster, slumping in his usual posture of despair. Nat Berlin, who rarely spoke, nodding sleepily. Reuben Sacks, periodontist and one of the House intellectuals, who, while waiting for Sigmund to find a place, took the opportunity to dip into one of the huge volumes that lay close at hand, filled with double-columned pages, footnoted, the footnotes footnoted, refined, excruciatingly detailed, just as Rube preferred it. And Barney Fribush, of course, who had momentarily returned, with an effort of will that was almost painful, from the dread clutches of fatigue to the enlivening prospect of his picnic later in the afternoon.

"And what was the problem?" Larry Adelman asked Sigmund, breaking the silence and sounding as though the answer to his question were the last thing that interested him.

Sigmund sat down at the table, looking serious now. "The four acres on Dickeyville Road," he said. "Same old thing."

"For God's sake," Norman Sindel said, impatiently rustling the sheet of paper in his hand.

"You mean it's still not resolved?" Barney asked, forgetting his picnic for the moment.

"It's resolved," Sigmund said.

"Tell us," Reuben Sacks said, looking up from his book.

"We'll make an offer."

"Well, I should hope so," Barney said.

"There are some people on Cemetery, I won't mention names," Sigmund went on, "who believe we have enough land out there to bury our dead for another hundred years. They should worry about what happens after we're all gone."

"Well, dead is dead," Barney said cryptically. "I mean, when you're gone, you're gone."

"We're offering four hundred dollars an acre," Sigmund told them, ignoring Barney's remark. "It's not exactly a bargain, they say, but it could be worse."

"We should have bought last year," Barney said. "I warned them that land was going up, like everything else."

"It will give us a nice expanse in the back," Sigmund continued, "where the woods are now. It'll open everything up."

"What's the estimate per acre?"

"Rube?" Barney asked. "You're the expert."

"Expert I'm not," Reuben Sacks said. "But the last I read I think it was sixty bodies per acre. I read somewhere that's the national average."

Nat Berlin, still silent, shuddered at this piece of information. Larry Adelman groaned quietly.

"Two hundred and forty," Barney Fribush said, after a quick calculation. "That should get us near enough to doomsday."

"Well, at least the committee finally accomplished something," Sigmund said. "It'll only take a couple of weeks to settle it. That's what they say, anyway."

"Can I proceed now with our own committee business?" Norman Sindel asked in a mincing voice.

"Sorry," Sigmund said.

"He's just going over the new members," Barney said, nodding to Sigmund.

"Massing, Coleman, Shuger, and Zentz," Norman read out. "That's it for the month."

"Pretty good for this time of year."

"Is Zentz the pharmacist on Liberty Heights?"

"That's the one. With three daughters."

"We have a lot of pharmacists in the congregation, considering."

"Considering what?"

"I don't know. There just seem to be a lot of pharmacists all of a sudden."

"Think of it like dentists," Barney said, nodding respectfully at Reuben Sacks.

Nat Berlin laughed at this without making a sound.

"Have all the acknowledgments gone out?" Larry Adelman asked.

"They're in the works now," Norman said.

"I'm handling that," Reuben Sacks said, continuing to pore over the treatise in front of him while he listened to the discussion with one ear. His glasses were pushed up over his forehead, as his forefinger traced the small print, line by line.

"Well, if that's it," Larry said, looking around at the committee, "and we're all in agreement, then put it in the minutes, Norman."

The meeting wound down. The voices quieted. Everybody was getting hungry. It was time for lunch. Barney made a motion to close the session. Norman Sindel seconded it and slipped a copy of the new members list into his jacket pocket. There was some shuffling around; Larry Adelman stretched his enormous bulk, his arms reaching out right and left. Then, one by one, they rose to their feet, except for Reuben Sacks, who continued with his studies. As they all understood, Rube was in the grip of an abstract ethical problem, a somber question of righteous moral behavior (with which he was always comfortable), first stated eight hundred years ago by a rabbinical scholar in Toledo, Spain, then fattened century by century with added commentaries of ever-increasing subtlety; by now, many of them were almost incomprehensible, they were so dense with explication, but that didn't keep Rube from trying to memorize them, point by point, as they passed beneath his finger. He mumbled them under his breath, waving his friends off without looking up from the text. During office hours, they all knew, Rube was just as relentless on behalf of his patients' gums.

"I'll see you later in the day," Barney said to Sigmund as they left the room together.

"What do you mean, later in the day?"

"You're coming to my house. I'm having a picnic."

"A picnic?"

"A picnic in my back yard. Why not? You never heard of a picnic?"

"I'll have to check with Jenny."

"I already did. Five o'clock. You're all set."

"A picnic," Sigmund said.

Larry Adelman suddenly loomed above them. Both Sigmund and Barney looked up. (A Goliath, Barney thought, with the soul of a maiden.) At the same moment, Julius Metzger walked up, looking surprised to see them all standing together outside the study hall. Greetings were exchanged in a mumble. Barney looked at Julius, Julius gazed back noncommittally, both reddening as the blond ghost of Cissy Sheer rose between them. Larry Adelman said something about new members, something positive and for-ward-looking, and they all had to agree with him. After another moment of mumbled exchanges filled with embarrassment, the four of them began to move in a self-conscious phalanx toward the synagogue offices. First they sidled through the small sanc-tuary, flooded now with an effulgent yellow-and-gold light that poured through the open windows. Behind them, as they walked up the aisle together, the purple velvet curtains decorating the ark gleamed. Dust motes floated everywhere, clearly visible. Along the aisle, a few prayer books lay on the floor in a crooked pile. Julius Metzger gave an impatient cry when he saw them, kissing each one like a distracted lover as he bent over to pick them up and place them in a pew, perfectly lined up. "Terrible," he mut-tered. "On the floor. It shouldn't be allowed."

"Where did you come from all of a sudden?" Barney asked.

Julius looked offended. "I had an Ushers meeting," he said. "I'm a member, you know that." He kissed one last prayer book before moving on.

Once outside the small sanctuary, they all headed for the offices upstairs, moving in a straight line now. Barney led the way; Julius tagged after him, then Sigmund followed, with Larry Adelman at his heels. Larry Adelman was bent from the waist, as though he could feel a stomach cramp coming on; his knees wavered a little.

Nobody spoke, but almost at the same moment, as they climbed the stairs, a vague but sure feeling of entrapment began to come over both Barney and Sigmund. There was a sudden perceptible sense that the four of them had not come together through mere coincidence—not this Sunday morning. A plan was afoot. Something unpleasant and out of their control. Julius and Larry had the focused air of predators. They stuck ruthlessly to their prey, Julius to Barney, Larry to Sigmund. Sigmund could even hear Larry's breathing growing heavy behind him. When they entered the offices, Barney gave Sigmund the eye. Sigmund knew that look. What's going on with these jokers? Barney was signaling, raising a cynical brow. What the hell's happening?

The answer came soon enough. After greeting Jeanette, the synagogue secretary, who was sitting behind her desk looking sour, Julius turned to Barney and cried out, "That was serious what I said last night. Don't forget it. Whatever else happened last night, that was serious."

"I can hear you without shouting," Barney answered in an irascible voice. "And this is the wrong place, you should know that. Use a little *sachel*."

"I only wanted to make sure you understood," Julius said, quieting down. "Whatever's between us."

Barney made a disgusted sound. "You can call me," he said, "like everybody else. You can call me tomorrow morning down at the factory. I'm going in for a couple of hours. And try acting like a *mensch* for once. It won't kill you. And you can tell that to Sindel, too, stealing private information right off the Membership Committee table."

They turned away from each other then, they could hardly wait to escape, Julius reddening again with suppressed fury and grumbling at the floor, Barney, as a distraction, trying to make weak jokes to Jeanette, who, like Barney, was in no mood for jokes; she never was on a Sunday morning. A moment passed, then Larry leaned down, as though an important idea had just occurred to him, and whispered heavily into Sigmund's ear.

"I don't want you to forget what we talked about."

Sigmund managed to look blank when he heard this, but a

flush of renewed embarrassment flooded his cheeks. He could feel the heat of his own blood. He tried to pull away. What was wrong with this gang? They were like spoiled children. Stupid, too. Didn't they know there was a time for everything?

"You know what I mean," Larry said, sounding miserable. Sigmund nodded brusquely and made a move toward Barney, who stood just a few feet away. He was still flushed. After a moment of shared confusion, Julius and Larry finally began to move off together. "We'll talk," Larry called over his shoulder. "Yeah," Julius added. "We'll all talk again." They could hardly wait to get away. There was no touching, no stroking this morning. They had done their duty, out in the open, and now they were sprung.

A few minutes later, speaking softly so Jeanette wouldn't hear him, Barney said to Sigmund, "Okay, you heard what Metzger said to me, and I heard what Adelman said to you. What was that all about?" He would have it now from Sigmund himself.

Sigmund didn't hesitate. He was sick of thinking about it. "They want me to come with them," he said. "They made me an offer." As he spoke, he felt better immediately. All feelings of betrayal and Safer fickleness vanished.

"Is that so?" Barney said. "Tell me more."

"There's nothing more. That's it. They made me an offer."

"Adelman?"

"Adelman."

"And what was the offer, if you don't mind?"

"Well, twenty percent more salary. Other things, too."

"Like what?"

"More insurance."

"How much more insurance?"

"Another ten."

"Another ten. Not bad. Did they show you a contract?"

"Be serious, Barn."

"What did you tell them?"

"I told them I was flattered."

Barney nodded. He knew the simple truth when he heard it. He also knew his man, going back to the time when he had made the trek to New Rochelle, to audition Sigmund R. Safer at a service at his old synagogue for the job of cantor at the House. Even then, Barney could tell that Sigmund was wholly transparent. At their first meeting, over a supper of Jenny's special pot roast, he could see right through him. As plain and simple as a canary, Barney thought, and still thought, just a simple old songbird that needed to be fed and watered and petted occasionally, which Barney liked to do because he felt responsible for Sigmund R. Safer. "So they made you an offer," Barney said. "Actually, I already knew from my spies. That makes two of us. It's pathetic."

"What do you mean, two of us?"

"They want you for the cantor and me for the president."

"You for the president?"

"What's wrong, you don't think I'm good enough for the job?" Barney was half grinning.

"You know what I mean, Barney. It's a surprise, that's all."

"Making me the first president, the founding father, would solve a lot of problems for them. The same goes for you."

"What did you say to them?"

"I didn't say anything. I'm smarter than that. It's pathetic."

"You'll have to say something."

"I'll keep them guessing. That always suits me. It's my style. I don't like to commit myself, anyway. I don't like to rush. Where have I got to rush to? And that's my advice to you. Don't rush anything. Ever. Slow. Always slow. All good things . . . You get my point? I'll keep them guessing as long as it makes me happy. You should, too."

"Happy," Sigmund said, shying from the word.

"Right, what else? So, five o'clock, and come on time. We'll celebrate my recovery."

They said good-bye. Outside, where the Methodist congregation, twenty-eight strong this morning, was lined up on the street after services, waiting to shake the hand of their pastor, Elsie Thaymes was waiting for Barney, the big Buick loaded with picnic food, including a couple of cases of Pepsi-Cola, out of respect for Joe Ranshoff. Barney moved off slowly through the office door, more slowly than he intended, paying attention to himself, placing one foot carefully in front of the other. Sigmund's

forehead creased as he watched his friend go. There was something about his walk, a twinge that showed at every step. It made
Barney open out his left thigh as he moved forward, unnaturally,
as though something burned there.

The door to the street opened, and Barney disappeared through
it, heading for his car. The small Methodist congregation began
to disperse. Sigmund turned back to the office. To distract himself,
to forget about Barney and Larry and Metzger, too, he would try
to make Jeanette smile. It was a game they all played. Jeanette
had rarely been seen to smile on a Sunday morning. While Sigmund cracked terrible jokes, like Barney before him, getting the
punch lines all wrong, Jeanette sniffled into a moist handkerchief
at her desk. She was put-upon, was what she had been trying to
say to them all for almost a dozen years; the congregation was
unfair. Nobody wanted to work on Sunday morning. That she
didn't work on Friday afternoon, all day Saturday, and Sunday
afternoon made no difference; the rhythm of her life was thrown
off because she was a Jew. Ah, Jeanette, a little smile, Sigmund
begged, but without making a sound. Then, suddenly, Jeanette
got busy at her Remington. Tap, tap, tap, her fingers went, in
their clever way. Sigmund felt another presence behind him, while
Jeanette pretended to be at work, and, turning, came eye to eye
(at almost a thirty-degree angle) with the rabbi.

"Oh-ho, cantor," the rabbi said, looking up at Sigmund through
his thick glasses and rubbing the side of his nose with his forefinger, as though searching for signs of a disease.

"Yes, rabbi, good morning."

"And good morning to you on this beautiful day," the rabbi
said, moving around Sigmund. "It should only hold for the holidays. And so," he continued, without a pause, "we have come to
a friendly meeting of the minds?"

Sigmund thought a moment. "I'm not sure, rabbi . . ."

"The little matter between you and me. The little matter we
talked about."

Sigmund was silent, waiting. He would make the rabbi work
a little. He would give nothing away.

"Jeffrey Berg?" The rabbi's fingers reached for his thyroid to test for swollen glands, while Sigmund's nostrils flared. "Yes, cantor?"

Sigmund knew that the rabbi had deliberately confused Jeffrey Bourne's name again. He was always doing things like that when it was to his advantage. Sigmund felt something pull tight: the iron knot of resentment. "I don't get it, rabbi," he said. "Speaking frankly."

Then the rabbi looked angry. His dim eyes snapped a warning. He rose on his toes, and so did Sigmund. They rocked like that a moment or two, face to face, barely able to hold themselves back. It was over in a few seconds (but not before Jeanette smiled a faint smile at last). Both came to earth at the same moment. Sigmund backed away a foot or two in order to see better. The rabbi stood his ground, glaring.

Then the blood in Sigmund's upper arms seemed to thicken. The old shooting pain began again. The left shoulder and the right, more than twinges, more than an annoyance, more like the mad dog Satan with the pitchfork in the Ben-Gay ads. It was enough for one morning. Italians. Traitorous old friends. Rabbis. This one, for example, standing in front of him, still glaring as though he were getting ready to hurl a few thunderbolts. And it wasn't even one o'clock, the day wasn't even half over.

4

She would look her best, because she always looked her best when she was out in the world, away from the hospital. It was just another obligation in life, of which there were already so many. That was why the blond frizz was important. To help her look her best, it had to be worked at, like everything else. Each tight curl, even the microscopic ones, had to be pulled at, pinched, unrolled, lengthened, made straight. Above all, made straight. Straight was Velda's ideal, encouraged at home in Tennessee, where frizz had come to her hidden away in her mother's genes. Straight, of course, was for white folks. It was an emblem, especially for white folks out on Hilton Street, even if they were Hebrews, even if they were used to a little frizz among themselves, here and here.

Velda pulled at a yellow curl, and held it between two fingers. When she relaxed her grip, it sprang back into a frizz. There were thousands of them, each one full of a lifetime's stubbornness. How often had she tried to change their nature? She should know better by now. She did know better, but she kept trying. It was a silly pact she had made with herself when she was a girl, to keep trying, to keep trying in everything.

A picnic would kill the rest of the day. It would create a nice late-afternoon hum full of pleasant overtones. And Sunday was always so hard to get through when she was off duty, she had made so few friends in Baltimore. She would get to see the house on Hilton Street, the room she would live in for two weeks, and the famous Elsie, fierce guardian of the palace gates, the unknown dragon lady. But there was no point in rushing all that. There would be plenty of time for Elsie when Velda arrived for her stay, gift in hand. For the moment, she would just act like herself in Elsie's presence, be as straightforward as she really was, say what was on her mind. Barney would help. He was pretty straightforward himself. The point was that she would let nothing get to her this afternoon. It was her day off. She only had one each week. And when you worked in a hospital where everything, without exception, was serious business, a day off was a day off. You owed it your best.

She gazed in the mirror. Her lipstick looked hard, her hair too short. She never seemed to be able to get any of that quite right. And it was too late for repairs. Frizz was frizz. It had a life of its own. Velda made a little jokey face at herself, pulling her lips down. Then she smiled. When she thought about herself, it was easy for her to smile. The hospital was serious. The doctors were serious. Barney Fribush was serious. So, probably, was the dragon lady of the house. But Velda Reese, in her own eyes, was always worth a jokey smile.

5

"Mi, mi, mi, mi, mi. If I had to carry on like that on a Sunday afternoon, I'd go right out of my frigging mind."

"Stop it, Bobby, you know I hate that kind of language."

"We're very sensitive these days, aren't we?"

"Don't give me that we business. *I'm* the way *I* always was."

They were sitting next to each other on the rusty glider, out on the front porch, thigh to thigh. When they spoke they kept their voices low, meant for each other alone. From inside the Safer house, in the living room a few feet away, they could hear the Scheingold kid doing his Sunday vocal exercises while his teacher banged away on the piano alongside him. It was very hot again. The sky was filled with ragged clouds through which the sun easily burned a searing path. The heat had been going on for so long now that they hardly felt it anymore. A circle of fire had settled around their lives in the course of the summer, and they had grown comfortable inside it. The glider moved back and forth, creaking faintly, stirring a small breeze. They controlled its swing with their feet, pushing off together, then braking without thinking about it. Bobby's hand was on Annie's knee.

"You know, the truth is that I'm never bored when I'm with you. And everybody knows how easy I get bored."

"Thanks. That's nice to hear."

"You don't have to sound sarcastic about it."

"I wasn't being sarcastic. I meant it. It's nice to be complimented."

"See what I mean?"

"Oh, Bobby."

"I try your patience, don't I? I get on your nerves. I've been noticing that more and more lately."

"Patience is not my long suit. It never was."

"You know I love you."

Annie made a move to get up, but Bobby, prepared, held her in place by the elbow. "Come on, now," he said. "Don't be like that. You'd think I was insulting you or something."

"I told you a hundred times I'm not ready for that kind of talk."

"A little quiet out there, please. Have a little respect." It was a familiar voice, calling in a foreign accent from the living room.

"You know, I think your old man is beginning to like me," Bobby whispered.

"I wouldn't depend on it."

"You'll see. He was very nice to me this morning when I helped him with his car. Mi, mi, mi, mi, it would drive me crazy. So how about it, let's go to a movie or something."

"I told you, I have to go to Mr. Fribush's. I promised my mother."

"There's still a couple of hours."

"I'm happy right where I am."

A few moments passed. Inside the living room, the Scheingold kid began to sing "I'm Old Fashioned."

"You know, I've never been in a house on Hilton Street," Bobby said. "I don't know any Fribushes. They're not for the likes of the Fiorentinos."

"Don't start feeling sorry for yourself."

"I've never been in one of those Jewish houses."

"What's a Jewish house got to do with it? This is a Jewish house. What are you getting at, anyway?"

"Don't get your bowels in an uproar. I was just making a simple point. I've never been in a house on Hilton Street."

"Big deal. And I've never been in a house on Charles Street."

"Well, neither have I."

"But not because you're Jewish."

"I never said I was Jewish."

"Oh, God."

"All I said was that I've never been in a house on Hilton Street."

"All right," Annie said, "if it's so important, then you can come with me. You'll be my guest. It's only a picnic. Nobody'll care. It's your big chance."

"You know I wasn't invited."

"I'm inviting you. Okay? It's only a picnic in the back yard."

"You think so?"

"Yes, I think so."

Bobby began to rub his jaw. "Maybe I will. You sure now? I've never been in a house on Hilton Street. You think I need to shave again?"

Annie examined his beard. "You'll do," she said, turning his head from side to side. "It's Sunday, you don't have to be absolutely perfect."

"Because I can run home and use my electric."

"Forget it. It's not a big deal." She let go of him.

The sound of scales rising a little off-pitch came from inside the house. The Scheingold kid had come to the end of "I'm Old Fashioned."

"It would drive me out of my mind," Bobby said, putting his fingers in his ears.

"Don't worry, nobody's asking you to join the choir."

"Mi, mi, mi, mi, mi."

"You said that before. The trouble with you is you have a one-track mind."

"You're telling me."

"Stop it, Bobby." She pushed his hand away and gave a powerful shove with her feet that set the glider creaking, back and forth. "You have no control over yourself," she said. "It's your worst fault." She moved a few inches away from him.

"Oh, divine lady."

"Cut it out, now."

"You're my divine lady, you're a goddess from above. You sure I don't have to shave?"

Annie made an indecisive gesture. There was a murmur of voices inside the house.

"Why didn't you say so in the first place?" Bobby asked. "I'm going home to shave. It's only the electric. I'll change my clothes, too. I'll bring my old man's car so we don't have to tag along with your mom and dad."

"You do that."

Bobby got to his feet. "Don't forget me while I'm gone," he said. "You know what they say. Out of sight."

"I know all about it."

"What time?"

"Five."

"You know," he said, looking down at her, "I don't like it when you sulk the way you are, but I do like the way it makes you look. When you're sulking like that, it gives you a certain something."

"Thanks a lot. Now how about it, let me have a little peace and quiet."

"Oowie," Bobby cried out, spreading his arms like wings as he jumped down the porch steps. "I know when I'm not wanted. Yes, sir. What goes on in that head of yours I'll never understand. That's what keeps me coming back, I guess. That and a couple of other things."

"You louse," she called out halfheartedly, flouncing a little on the glider. Bobby headed for home, laughing.

6

Upstairs, inside the deep-shaded room where her husband sometimes hid from the world, Jenny Safer was trying to nap. She lay back against a bank of high pillows in her light summer slip, hair loosened to her waist, shining like a silken waterfall. Jenny was concentrating on sleep, perhaps too intensely, in anticipation of Barney Fribush's picnic. A half-hour would be enough to carry her through the rest of the day. It would keep her looking fresh and make sure that she remained alert to the world. Yet sleep did not come.

The sound of the Safers' piano rose to her room. She heard Sigmund bang out some chords, then begin to deliver one of his lectures in a dim voice. (Poor Scheingold kid, she thought, sympathetically.) She heard the peculiar accent float up the stairwell, the sudden unexpected emphases, the exaggerated attack that sometimes caused people to misread Sigmund. She had heard it all before, of course. It was one of the ongoing themes of her life. Sometimes it still embarrassed her when they were out in public among strangers, Sigmund's abrupt Slavic tones, his reedy Polish voice. Strangers sometimes resisted it, pulling back at the strangeness of it. But more often it brought Jenny the seductive comfort of familiarity, it was a sound that she knew better than her own voice; and besides, everybody in Baltimore—everybody Jenny cared about—knew the way Sigmund talked, he was famous for it, the children at the House even mimicked him behind his back, with a kind of affectionate playfulness. His master's voice, she thought, longing for sleep, one of a very special kind out of the entrails of dying old Europe.

Then Jenny heard the sound of the Scheingold kid's alto suddenly spiraling upward with a burnished metallic shine. Mi, mi, mi, mi, mi. Sylvan's alto was the real thing, just as Sigmund claimed. It sang out now, doing mere exercises, mechanical repetitions that brought little pleasure. But these classes wouldn't go on forever. Once the Holy Days were past, they would vanish, along with the choir and their rehearsals on Granada Avenue; no more raisin buns, no more iced tea and milk. Sunday afternoon would resume its trancelike state. Sigmund would go back to performing weddings of varying degrees of elaborateness. Burials and memorial services would go on as they always had; everybody at the House made a practice of remembering the dead in public. Maybe by then Sigmund would calm down. He usually did after the Holy Days. But Jenny had begun to doubt. It was as though Sigmund were running a fever. Maybe Annie was right. She saw something, too. An alien charge was racing through her husband's veins, something Jenny didn't quite recognize, had never seen before, and it left her bewildered.

A lot of it was the war. That much Jenny knew. Sigmund's morbid dreams, his nagging sisters, and the Jews, too; always the Jews. But the rest? A new job? Severance from the House, at their age, which could only mean a kind of permanent exile from the very things, like old friends, they depended on most? Jenny did not want to face that. She could not bear disruption of any kind. Life was meant to go on in the same old ways, and for Jenny Safer that meant serenity and calm. It was one of her ideals.

Sylvan's voice rose again, this time in melody. I'm old-fashioned, he sang. I love the moonlight. I love the old-fashioned things. That was more comfortable, Jenny thought. Sylvan's voice sent a pleasant shiver through her. It was the way it should be. Melody solaced. The human voice caressed. The sound of rain, Sylvan sang, upon the windowpane. Old-fashioned things. Serenity and calm. Jenny closed her eyes, hearing no ironies.

The minutes passed. The lesson continued. Still, Jenny did not sleep. She knew now that sleep was hopeless, she was as wide awake as she ever was. If she couldn't sleep, she'd do something useful. Useful was good, useful was productive. After staring at the ceiling for another few minutes, she finally got out of bed and, taking off her slip, began to try on some clothes. (That was always useful.) First, she pulled a dirndl skirt from the closet. Slipping it on, she examined herself in the full-length mirror, turning sideways, pulling in her stomach, then letting it go slack. Too unbecoming, she concluded with a touch of unhappiness, it made her look ten pounds heavier. Then she put on a halter dress, in which, she immediately saw, her unsupported breasts rested like water wings. That would never do, either. (And whom, the question suddenly occurred to her, was she doing all this for, Sigmund R. Safer, herself, or perhaps even Barney Fribush?) Moving over to her vanity, feeling defeated, she could see the outline of her nipples, those interesting phenomena, through the thin bright cotton of her dress. She gazed at them a moment, then, in a sudden surge of restlessness and renewed dissatisfaction, turned away from the mirror, getting up with a self-deprecating shrug. It all felt too much like self-love to her, staring enraptured for minutes on end at one's own image in the mirror. It was not an emotion she admired. Self-love was for other, vainer women; most other women, perhaps; not for Jenny Safer. But sometimes she couldn't resist it.

Jenny moved to the bedroom and raised the shade. A blinding shaft of sunlight stabbed her. Granada Avenue was immobilized again, enclosed in its circle of fire, as torpid as a dreaming lizard in the August heat. Nothing human seemed to move out there. Vaguely, she could hear the old glider creak downstairs on the porch. Then she saw Bobby Fiorentino jump off the front steps, pretending to be flying. Another one for Annie, she thought calmly. Jenny had never had to worry about Annie having enough boys; or about herself, either, when it came to that. She heard her daughter call something to Bobby. The sound was muffled. When Bobby heard Annie, he gave a hoot of mocking laughter. Then he began to run down the street. Jenny watched him go. She was still wearing last year's halter dress. Last year's dress made her arms and upper body look especially full. That was why she had bought it in the first place. She began to brush out her hair with long, slow strokes, preparing to put it up in a tight bun. Downstairs, the music continued.

7

"A little quiet out there, please."

Once the voices on the porch subsided, Sigmund rippled off an arpeggio by way of acknowledgment. That would hold them, he thought, both Annie Safer and Bobby Fiorentino. Maybe it would keep them quiet, too. They seemed to have so much to talk about all the time. But the sloppy cascade was full of wrong notes, and Sigmund clearly heard every one of them. It was painful, it was always painful. (A day of wrong notes, he judged harshly, thinking about his confrontations at the House and the strange way his blood seemed to be moving at a snail's pace.) Nevertheless, he loved to hear himself play the piano, he loved the sounds he made. He banged a chord now, listening for a jarring note. No, he was no Paderewski, no Rachmaninoff. Who was? He wasn't even José Iturbi, who banged a lot, too, and was making a fortune these days doing sentimental vaudeville turns in the movies.

"I think that's probably enough exercises for one afternoon," he said, suddenly catering to his own weariness. After the morning's exertions, the class with the Scheingold kid had tired him even more, but in a whole other way, without strain or tension, just wearing him down, like all hard work.

Standing alongside the piano, fingering the bust of Schubert, Sylvan heaved a sigh of relief and shifted on his feet. He, too, was tired.

"I know you don't like exercises," Sigmund said, reaching for some sheet music. "It's only natural. But the voice is a muscle, and if it's not exercised regularly, it goes soft, like any other muscle. I bet you didn't know that, did you? The voice is just like that muscle in your arm, your bicep. Without exercise, there's nothing."

Then I'll settle for nothing, Sylvan wanted to say, but decided against it. He was very bored, too.

"A little Kern?" Sigmund then asked, without waiting for an answer. "You deserve a treat. We both do."

They exchanged a few words about the song, ideas about tempo and phrasing, matters on which they did not always agree, and in a moment, after Sylvan had moved behind Sigmund so that he could read the lyrics, Sigmund began to play the score at the proper volume, for a change, and with all the notes in place. It was a relief.

"I'm old-fashioned," Sylvan sang over Sigmund's shoulder, gazing again at the thin whorl of hair resting at the very crown of Sigmund's head and the amazing mole that lay dead center there, invisible to its owner. "I love the moonlight . . . I love the old-fashioned things . . ."

The song spun on, Sylvan neatly reaching for the rising notes in a half-voice, finally enjoying himself as the music came back at him. Up, up, the melody climbed, but staying well within Sylvan's range. This was easy, this was fun. It was like having his own "Hit Parade." "The sound of rain, upon the windowpane . . ." It had sweep and a sweetness, too. And it was modest. It made no inhuman claims. It wasn't like the Silent Devotion, it did not reach for the unreachable. "The calming songs that April sings . . ." Lovely, lovely. Sigmund hummed along with his protégé, feeling suddenly tender toward Sylvan as he accompanied him with unusual discretion. "Let it out now," he shouted, "all the way, with a long breath," and almost in the next instant Sylvan's voice, suddenly enlarged, became so substantial, so real, that Sigmund felt it as a visceral presence, something powerful and precious that might be emerging from his own body. Music, Sigmund thought giddily, hardly able to restrain himself at the piano. It was a kind of rapture, it cured everything. He began to bang again, from excitement.

A few bars later, the song ended, on a sad, remote note that hung for a second or two in the air. The silence that followed lasted only a moment. "How about some iced tea?" Sigmund asked, trying to sound matter-of-fact, almost afraid to look at

Sylvan for the grateful tears in his eyes. "Maybe we should take a break," he added. "No use overdoing it." Which was how it always was when it came to pleasure.

In another minute, facing each other in the living room like strangers, Sigmund and Sylvan were both considering, with some anxiety, what they might have to talk about. It was not easy, suddenly launched at Sigmund's whim into unexpected social roles like this. Without the piano between them, without a score to share, even without Sigmund's amazing mole to ponder, they were once again merely two isolated entities thrust back into their own private worlds. It left them mute. Sylvan sipped his iced tea politely and nibbled at one of Jenny's brownies, wishing the afternoon away, willing himself elsewhere. He was wearing immaculate white ducks, considered appropriate by Lillian for Barney Fribush's picnic. He also had on a short-sleeved navy-blue sports shirt decorated with shining white buttons. Sewn onto the pocket of his shirt was the emblem of a sailboat tacking at full speed. This striking combination of blue and white only emphasized Sylvan's coloring, heightening the pink tones that ran just below the surface of his skin, burnishing the dark lustrous mix, which already had a strange shine of its own. Lillian knew what she was doing when she chose her son's clothing. She wanted her son to be noticed, and, once noticed, never forgotten. Now he sat carefully in the upright wooden chair that Sigmund had offered him, spine erect, fastidiously eating his brownie and sipping his iced tea from a tall glass. It would not do to spot his white ducks. They were the only pair he had. The one other time he had worn them this summer was in the local Fourth of July parade, when Sylvan and a thousand other kids had marched along Baltimore Street waving tiny American flags to the unsteady beat of the downtown firemen's band, which at ten o'clock in the morning was already woozy from beer.

What should I talk about? Sylvan asked himself, his mind a perfect blank. It often was, in school, at choir rehearsal, and at other threatening public gatherings, when it simply dried up or vanished defensively into a kind of cold-blooded hibernation until the threat of exposure passed. He would wait for his cues from the cantor. The cantor would know what to talk about. It was his living room. But Sigmund himself wasn't doing much better. Watching Sylvan sitting there, plate in his lap, with what appeared to be total aplomb, Sigmund began to consider possible subjects for conversation, feeling a touch of panic setting in. There was the heat, of course, there always was. There was the war, another time, not today. There was FDR and the fourth term. There was also the Orioles, they were very dependable these days as a subject of discourse, so Sigmund understood, although what Sigmund had to say about the Orioles could be contained within a ten-second exchange. Minutes passed, and still not a word.

Suddenly, Sigmund spoke up. He could hardly bear the silence another moment. "So tell me, Sylvan, what do you want to do with your life?" he asked, letting an ice cube melt comfortably in his mouth. Both their larynges were dry from the singing lesson. "I don't want to seem nosy about the matter," Sigmund added, fussing with his tea. "I know it's none of my business, but it's an important question for a young man to ask himself. The most important."

Sylvan nodded in agreement, slowly. Young man. That was new. And agreeable. At fourteen, he was usually the kid in conversations like this. And everybody was always asking him the same thing, what do you want to do with your life, kid, insistent about it, too, as though maybe they were really asking themselves the same question, as though they were still looking for an answer to their own lives.

"Do you have any idea yet?" Sigmund asked.

"I want to be a movie star," Sylvan said, flashing a white-toothed smile to keep from being taken too solemnly. He had decided long ago that he hated solemnity.

"A movie star," Sigmund repeated in a toneless voice. He shook his head. Was he being made fun of? "Be serious, now, Sylvan," he said. "Life is no joking matter, you know." Sylvan put on his long face, it wasn't hard, feeling the muscles in his jaw begin to tense. There they were, sitting face to face in the Safer living room for the first time, and within five minutes they had come to this without even trying. First solfeggio, mi, mi, mi, then the beautiful mysteries of Jerome Kern, now serious talk about life. His life. It was Sunday afternoon, didn't the cantor know anything? "I don't know what I want to do with my life," Sylvan said, taking a huge bite out of his brownie.

The corners of Sigmund's mouth turned down. "It's America," he said disapprovingly. "Easy come, easy go. A wisecrack's as good as a commandment. Tomorrow's another day. Everything can wait. I can tell you, I always knew what I wanted to do with my life. I had to. Everybody had to. You kids today are lucky."

"And you wanted to be a cantor?" Sylvan's mouth was still full of brownie, but he easily managed the sarcasm, even though he half hoped the cantor hadn't noticed.

"No," Sigmund said, without hesitating. "I didn't want to be a cantor. I wanted to sing opera."

Sylvan thought about that. It put the cantor in a whole new and interesting light. An opera singer. "Is that more serious than the movies?" he asked, smiling a little but still sounding sarcastic.

"Yes," Sigmund said. "I think it is."

"But everybody likes the movies."

"What everybody likes is merely popular. You should know that by now. You're old enough to understand. I'm not talking popular, I'm talking serious."

That word. It was inescapable when you were talking to an adult. Everything was serious. Sylvan yawned behind his hand. Adults wanted all the answers in black and white, and they wanted them now. Was it because they themselves were getting crowded for time?

"Have you ever been to the opera?" Sigmund asked, mindlessly rubbing his shoulder. The pain there reached to his buttocks, a hot wire running the length of his torso.

"No," Sylvan said. "It costs five dollars for a seat. I don't have that kind of money."

"Then I'll take you," Sigmund said. "We'll go for the spring season. My treat. It'll do you good. I'll start you with *Aida*, one of the big ones. A lot of spectacle, like the movies. Better than the movies."

"I know *Aida*." Sylvan began to hum an aria.

"That's not *Aida*," Sigmund said. "That's *Carmen*. That's the Flower Song."

"I knew it was something like that."

"It's not *Aida*. It's not even Italian. Bizet wrote it. Did you ever hear of Bizet? Georges Bizet. With an *s* on the George. He was a Jew. (Sigmund was guessing.) A French Jew. There were a lot of Jewish composers in France in those days. Offenbach. Ever hear of him? Meyerbeer. And so on. We'll go in the spring."

There was another silence. They seemed to have exhausted the subject of opera. A stillness began to fill the room again. Sylvan coughed politely. "Tell me," Sigmund asked, breaking in again, "how are you making out downtown?"

"I make out fine. It's where I live."

"I know it's where you live. That's the point."

Sylvan coughed again.

"You can't tell me that conditions are so wonderful down there," Sigmund went on, in an apologetic tone. "Let's not kid ourselves. I mean all the Polacks and the others. It's tough stuff. I know Polacks. You don't have to tell me. With the Polacks, unless you're the Virgin Mary herself . . . But I'm not making judgments about downtown. Don't misunderstand me. I'm just suggesting there are other ways to live."

"You mean Forest Park," Sylvan said.

"Well, yes. For one. Forest Park."

"You have to be rich to live in Forest Park."

"You don't have to be rich. Forget rich. Everybody always thinks rich. We're not talking about money. We're talking about ambition."

"I know what we're talking about," Sylvan said, sounding nervy to himself. "And it's not so bad downtown. It's not as bad as you make out. At least there's always something happening, there's a lot going on, the whole world's right there outside your window." Sylvan paused, tilting his head ironically to one side as though he were listening for the quaint sound of a cicada out on Granada Avenue, or a passing car, perhaps, one among a half-dozen others that might drive by in the course of the afternoon. Of course he understood very well what Sigmund was talking about, just as he had said, who wouldn't understand, it was what they dreamed about downtown all the time, escape, flight, running away; but it was nobody's business out in Forest Park.

"I know your home is special," Sigmund went on, appearing to choose his words a little more carefully now in the face of those disdainful eyes staring back at him. "I know everything is on your mother's shoulders. She has to be a very strong woman. It can't be easy, with all that responsibility."

"My mother does all right," Sylvan said, bristling.

Sigmund pulled himself up in his chair. "I'm saying this all wrong," he said. "If it sounded too personal, I apologize. But I know what it's like, believe me. I know what it's like not to have a father. When there's no man in the house, when there's no father around, it's hard, it's like living in a world that's only half there."

I'm a man in the house, Sylvan said to himself, deliberately choosing to misunderstand Sigmund. He fidgeted for a moment, taking another nervous bite out of his brownie. With adults, whatever they seemed to be talking about, whatever they pretended, it always came down to the same thing, to his father. Maybe the two of them, the cantor and himself, should get back to solfeggio or Jerome Kern, where they belonged. This conversation was going nowhere. All conversations about his father went nowhere. There was nowhere to go.

"Well, of course, I never had a son of my own," Sigmund said.

There was certainly no answer to that.

"Every man would like to have a son."

Tell that to Poppa Scheingold, Sylvan thought. Then, "What time is it?" he asked sharply.

Sigmund checked his watch. "Four-thirty. A little after. Maybe we should start thinking about getting a move on." But he continued to sit where he was, as though they had all the time in the world. "This is a sensitive question," Sigmund suddenly said. "And don't answer it if you don't want to," he added, waving his own words away. "But do you ever feel the need to talk to somebody older, you know, an older man, there are always things you can't talk about with friends, or even your mother? You know what I mean?"

"You mean a mentor?" Sylvan asked, sitting up even straighter, his shoulder blades thrust back in his navy-blue shirt.

"Well, yes, as a matter of fact, somebody you can trust."

"There are plenty of mentors around."

"There are?"

"There's always somebody," Sylvan said casually.

"If that's true," Sigmund said, "you're a lucky boy. That wasn't my experience in life. No, sir." A dreamy look came over Sigmund's face. "Anyway," he went on, "it was on my mind. I just thought."

"What?"

"I just thought"—his cheeks reddened slightly—"I just thought you should feel that you can depend on me if you need advice or anything like that, you know what I mean, some guidance or . . ." He faltered suddenly.

"Sure," Sylvan said.

"Well," Sigmund said, looking wildly around as he finally got up. Not for the first time that day, he felt as though he were being dismissed. "Maybe you'd like to help me feed my fish before we go," he went on, unable to let the conversation end. "I've got a killer on the loose in there. A Siamese thing. I have to get rid of him. Maybe I could set you up downtown with a couple of starter fish and a little tank of your own. How would you like that? Then we'd be sharing a hobby."

Before Sylvan could answer, they were interrupted by Jenny. "We should be getting ready to go," she called from upstairs. "Does Sylvan want to wash up? Where's Annie?"

"Out here," Annie yelled from the porch.

Sigmund peered through the living-room window, out to the porch. Annie was swinging back and forth on the glider. "You mean you've been sitting out there listening in all this time?" Sigmund asked. He sounded spiteful even to himself.

"Oh, Daddy, what do you think I am?"

"Eavesdropping," he said.

"I didn't hear a word," she said. "And who cares, anyway? You're always ready to think the worst about me."

"Listening in," he said.

"Sigi?" It was Jenny again. "Barney said five o'clock."

"Let's go, then," Sigmund said, turning back to the room. "Finish your iced tea," he added to Sylvan.

"I'm finished," Sylvan said, putting down his glass. He got to his feet and carefully brushed brownie crumbs from his lap. One of them had left a tiny brown stain, barely visible, on his white ducks, disturbing his sense of propriety and order. He kept glancing down at it fretfully, as though if he stared long and hard enough it might vanish.

Jenny came down the stairs, wearing her yellow halter dress, with proper support this time. "Everybody ready?" she asked, taking in Sigmund and Sylvan with a glance. Her hair was pulled tight in the usual bun, her lips were bright red with a new lipstick she was trying out, and she smelled of Paris. When she turned around to look for her pocketbook, swirling in a slow, controlled motion, Sigmund could make out the faint cleavage of her buttocks, just as though she were wearing Velda Reese's white nurse's uniform. At the sight of his wife standing there, resplendent in her yellow halter dress, Sigmund shook his head a few times in a bemused way, as though he were trying to clear it, while Sylvan stood quietly aside, eyes cast down, finally ready to do exactly as he was told.

Within five minutes, after hearing of Annie's independent plans for the picnic—the air smoking again with Sigmund's indignation, but this time a little tired and forced, as though he thought it were merely expected of him—they were on their way, Sigmund, the handsome Jenny, and in the back seat of the blue Chevy the Scheingold kid.

8

Lillian was driving Mickey's beat-up old car again, at his pleasure, naturally. She liked to drive and was always after him for
another chance. With her hands gripping the wheel and Mickey
seated authoritatively alongside her, a current of power seemed
to run through Lillian, transmitted directly from the noisy engine
through the floor of the car into the accelerator, which was now
throbbing pleasantly under her right foot. Actually, Lillian was
saving to buy her own car with pittances put away every week
from her salary at the department store.

"Keep it steady, now," Mickey said, pressing his own right foot
down without knowing it. Mickey was one of those sympathetic
drivers.

"Who's driving this thing, anyway?"

"Just stay off the trolley tracks. They're treacherous."

Lillian steered a half-foot to the right, then straightened the
car out.

"That's better," he said. "Just keep to the right. Look," he went
on, without a pause, "I don't want to sound like a whiner or
anything, I hate a whiner, but we don't have to stay too long, do
we? I mean, it's Sunday, I don't want to waste the rest of the
afternoon."

"You didn't have to come, you know. You're not doing anybody
a favor."

"I'm not complaining, I'm just asking. Don't be so touchy all
the time."

"The answer to your question is, we'll see when we get there.
I'm looking forward to it, as a matter of fact. It was nice of the
old man to ask us."

"No complaints."

She glanced at him. "You could use a haircut, you know."

Mickey stroked the back of his neck with his open palm. "Maybe a little," he said. "Maybe a trim."

"Well, too late now. No use crying."

"I like the sideburns long. My face can handle it." He began to stroke his jaw.

She glanced at him again. "I don't know," she said. "They're *very* long. They make you look like George Raft."

"I've been told that before. Listen, Lillian."

She stopped for a red light, racing the motor.

"Don't do that, it wastes gas. I'm low on coupons as it is."

The light changed and they drove on.

"I want you to marry me," he said, staring straight ahead through the windshield.

Lillian waited three seconds, then three more, before answering. "I would think one wife at a time is enough," she finally said in a careful voice.

"I mean after the divorce comes through, of course."

"She said yes?" Lillian asked slowly. "She's agreed to a divorce? You never told me that."

"She will, she will. I got her right here in my palm." He opened up his hand and held it out to Lillian as though his wife rested there in thrall.

"Well," Lillian said, after waiting still another three seconds. "I'm pretty cozy where I am, you know. I've put a lot of effort into that. Making a home. My son. My life is plenty complicated as it is." Suddenly, she wasn't at all sure what she was saying.

"I'll make it simple for you. I'll make it easy," Mickey said.

"You know what I mean."

"So what do you say?"

"Thank you, my friend. I'm really honored."

"That's it?"

"For now."

"I love you, Lillian. What else can I say? I love you."

The car swerved a bit. "Now you made me miss the turnoff," Lillian said. "I'll have to make a circle to come around. You're distracting me, Mickey. When we get back to Hilton Street, keep an eye out for thirty-five-oh-one."

"Thirty-five-oh-one. Okay. We won't stay long, will we?"

"We'll see."

"I'll be a father for Sylvan. I'm good at that. I think he likes me. That kid could use a father."

"He already has a father."

"You could have a divorce like that, one, two, three, if you wanted."

"We'll talk about it."

"Just so you know how I feel. I want to be sure of that." He touched her arm, rubbing the flesh below the inside elbow with his thumb. "Lillian," he said, as emotion choked him.

She turned into Hilton Street, driving slowly. "What's the number of that house up there?" she asked.

"Thrity-seven-oh-three," he said, glancing up but still stroking her arm.

"Must be the next block."

"Your skin is like satin."

"Hmm," she said, pulling up to the curb absent-mindedly. "Am I close enough?" she asked, trying to measure the distance from the curb. Parking was not one of Lillian's gifts.

Mickey nodded. "But not to me," he said, moving in.

"You're taking advantage, Mickey. Come on, it's Sunday afternoon, get into your party mood."

"I want you to wear my identification bracelet," he said, reaching for his wrist.

"No gifts, please. Nothing personal. We're just beginning to have a conversation. We've hardly said a word. Don't assume anything."

"Just my bracelet. A token."

"There's no such thing as just a token between adults. I put on your bracelet and the whole world says I'm yours."

Mickey smiled. "What's so bad about that?" he asked.

"I'm not yours."

"Lillian." He began to breathe deeply, in a deliberate way.

"Oh, come on, Mickey," she said. "Let's have some fun. Get out of the car."

"We're the first ones. There's nobody else here."

"Come on. I want to see the house. I've always wanted to have a look at one of these places."

"I delivered some furniture once on Hilton Street. Maybe to this very house. Years ago, when I was a kid in high school. Making an extra buck."

"You used to deliver furniture? I never knew that."

"I've been around. Listen, I'll make you happy. I swear. That's all I want. I'll do anything for you. Just give me the chance. I love you, Lillian. I want you to marry me." By now, he sensed the onslaught of a stomachache.

"So I heard," Lillian said, trying to keep it light, but her voice no longer sounded like her own to her. A lot had been said. Maybe too much. Her pulse was racing in a ridiculous way. She stepped out of the car. "Come on, Mickey, try to get in the mood," she called to him. "It's a party."

9

Barney was mixing some ancient rum he had found in the back of a closet with a little of Joe Ranshoff's Pepsi-Cola, having decided to relieve his problem with a hair of the dog. Fatigue still gripped him after his committee meeting at the House, his mouth was painfully dry, and he had a tic in his left eyelid. Hangover, he thought, with a generous edge of self-contempt. Hangovers were supposed to be for other people, not Barney Fribush.

Barney and Elsie had been busy ever since they had gotten back to Hilton Street at noon, setting up a long folding table in the back yard that had been stored in the basement for years, putting out paper plates, paper napkins, paper cups, and a set of fake silverware. Everything was a little musty from having been stashed away for so long. After fooling around with the picnic paraphernalia for an hour or so, Elsie doing the heavy work, they set about rearranging the lawn furniture. "There aren't enough chairs," Barney kept complaining, trying to hide his tic from Elsie as he watched her move the pieces around. "Only six people can sit down at one time."

"There's the whole inside of the house," Elsie said, wiping the chairs off with a damp rag. They did look a little skimpy, as Barney claimed, spotted around like that, but it was probably the best they could do with what they had.

"It's a picnic," Barney went on, still complaining. "Nobody wants to be inside at a picnic. That's the whole point."

"You going to make trouble if somebody chooses to sit inside in the sun parlor?"

"Get a couple of Toby's old camp blankets. We'll put them out on the grass. The young people can sit on the blankets."

"And make a mess," Elsie said, moving off to the house, where there was still plenty of work to do.

Barney sipped at the rum and Pepsi. It was syrupy sweet, but nice. It would help to wipe out last night's Scotch marathon, and other things, too, if hair of the dog could be trusted. He began to stroll around the back yard, jiggling the ice in his glass, taking his time. Out there, cosseted by the late-afternoon Sunday silence, filled with the sweet anticipation of giving his own party in his own home, he almost began to feel like himself again: forceful and manly, forthright, four-square. A rock. Barney's yard, with its small-scaled landscape and narrow vistas, only enhanced the feeling. It grounded him, like one of the giant oaks facing the lake out front; it kept him down-to-earth and matter-of-fact, even though it wasn't much of a back yard, a mere quarter of an acre or less, enclosed by well-tended shrubbery that was carefully shaped to block the view of the alleyway that ran, Baltimore-style, behind all the houses on Hilton Street. (It was the steep terraces up front, overlooking Ashburton, that counted on Hilton Street.) Besides the shrubbery, Barney had planted a small prized magnolia tree in one corner of the yard, which offered tenuous shade to the canvas beach chairs that he and Elsie had just positioned nearby; a garden plot of formidable simplicity running along one side of the lawn, containing a few pallid rosebushes, a stunted tulip bed, and something indeterminate marking the border; and a concrete birdbath, filled now with dank water that looked rusty. Few birds had ever been seen by Barney watering themselves, as they were supposed to, in his back yard bath. He blamed this on the cat that lived three doors down in the Shapiro house and was always on the loose. Also in the back yard, set dead center in the lawn, was a modest fishpond, six feet in diameter and six inches deep, one of Barney's wife's occasional follies, in which rather unhealthy-looking goldfish swam in hapless circles searching for food. Barney made a point of keeping a daily count of his goldfish, suspecting the Shapiro cat of malevolent intent there, too.

Barney ambled around the lawn, carrying a growing sense of well-being with him as he awaited his guests. Life was all right, after all; certainly, it was all right enough, for the moment. He must not be greedy, he told himself. Who enjoyed more of life's pleasures than Barney Fribush? (No one came to mind.) The rum helped. The stuff was magic. New energy surfaced with each sip, even his tic was easing as he almost finished off the glass. He was beginning to feel like a master again, master of his own fate, in control of the world around him. How many of his pals could say that? (No answer to that came to mind, either.) In front of him, above the folding table, a couple of flies buzzed threateningly around the cole slaw. Barney waved them away with one hand, making the usual growling noises, and covered the slaw with paper napkins. Then he covered the bowls of potato chips and salad, as well, critically eyeing the soggy hot-dog rolls and varieties of mustards and relishes that were set beside them. The hot dogs themselves, the huge fat franks, waited in the kitchen to be boiled by Elsie in her largest pot, once the guests arrived. Beyond the table, on the lawn, bottles of Pepsi and a few beers sat in a metal tub filled with large chunks of melting ice. It was not quite a feast, Barney told himself, but it was not meant to be. It was a picnic, where people were supposed to relax and take it easy. An informal occasion, for fun. Nobody would go hungry.

The screen door to the kitchen opened. "Company," Elsie called in a tired-of-it-all voice, moving aside to make way for a couple of strangers. Barney put his hand up to his eyes to shade them from the sun and stared at his guests framed in the doorway. A few seconds passed. Who were they? Then, without pause, there was a swift social rush, willed by Barney, a cry of welcome, also Barney's, and a bustle of movement that grounded itself at the foot of the kitchen steps, where Barney, Lillian Scheingold, and Mickey Schiller came together in a more or less cordial triangle, blushing slightly and avoiding each other's eyes as they fumbled for an introduction.

"Mickey Schiller." Mickey's bracelet jangled on his wrist as he reached out to shake Barney's hand, and, reddening even more, he had a sudden incongruous sense as he faced his host, an instant intuitive flash of self-awareness, unusual for Mickey, that his side-burns, as Lillian had pointed out, were definitely too long for the occasion.

"Pleased," Barney said, coming to the same conclusion at exactly the same moment as he examined Mickey's hair. Zoot suit, he found himself thinking.

"I'm Sylvan's mother," Lillian said, "Lillian Scheingold."

"Of course," Barney answered. "I could tell at a glance. Sylvan's mother."

At Barney's dubious but interested look, Lillian began to explain at length, but Barney stopped her. "I know, I know," he said. "You don't have to tell me twice. Sylvan's mother. I'm glad you're here. Make yourself at home. It's all yours, the whole works. What you don't see, yell for. We've got everything. If you want hard stuff, there's some rum, and there's some gin. You want some gin? Elsie," he shouted up to the kitchen, "how about a little Dixie Belle out here for our guests?" Then, as the three of them began to move around the lawn together, Barney pointing out the landmarks, Velda Reese arrived.

"My nurse," Barney said proprietorially, introducing them all and reaching up to peck Velda on the cheek. The uncomfortable triangle opened up, a symmetry of couples set in as Velda joined them. This made it easier for everybody, two and two. Velda, of course, was the tallest of the group, and certainly the most powerful-looking. Her yellow frizz was in perfect place. Her height and her great strapping shoulders gave her an immediate authority, which Velda herself often doubted. She looked nervous, in fact, as she faced them all, as nervous as Lillian. While the two women eyed each other hesitantly, already nostalgic for their own places downtown, they exchanged tight little smiles. "How'd you get here, anyway, darling?" Barney asked.

"Streetcar," Velda said, still smiling. Barney had never called her "darling" before. "I had to transfer twice. That trip's no joke from my part of the world."

"I should have made other arrangements," Barney said, looking mildly stricken. "You should have reminded me. That was dumb." But whether on Barney's part or her own, Barney didn't say.

Then Elsie reappeared and whispered something in Barney's ear, sneaking a quick look at Velda at the same moment, which Velda returned.

"What do you mean?" Barney asked.

"I mean there ain't no Dixie Belle." This time, in a loud energized cry.

Barney winced. His wife had lost the battle of "ain't" years ago.

"Well," he began to shout, "just call Vito's and have them send over a couple of pints. Tell them to send it rush rush. Listen, Velda," he said, turning back to his guests as Elsie made her way back to the kitchen, lips moving silently as she scolded Barney to herself, "I want you to feel at home. I want you to look around the house, take it all in, you, too, Mrs. Scheingold, and Mr. Scheingold, make yourselves at home, we'll have gin before you can snap your fingers. Help yourself, the hot dogs'll be ready in a couple of minutes, and"—something familiar catching his eye in the middle distance—"about time, here's my daughter from Chevy Chase with her . . ." He could almost never say the word.

Toby and Irwin Fedder appeared in the back yard suddenly, having avoided the big house altogether, coming around the side from the terrace out front, from the Hilton Street entrance. "To-ba," Elsie called from the kitchen window, waving at Barney's daughter, and managing to get, at the same time, another quick look at Velda Reese. Toby waved back. "Hello, Pops," she said, kissing Barney on the cheek. "My sweetheart," he answered tearily, returning the kiss as a little of his drink spilled on the lawn. Meanwhile, Irwin stood aside, waiting for a greeting. They all stood aside, waiting, except for Toby and her father, who continued to chat together at their ease. While the group waited on the lawn, shifting from one foot to the other, they gradually formed themselves into a little crescent, which nevertheless did not quite hold together. A minute or two passed, as Toby gently raked her father with questions about his health, the same questions she asked him every day when she phoned him. Listening in, Mickey Schiller touched one of his sideburns and frowned. Standing beside him, Velda had to restrain herself from trying to fluff out her frizz, while also trying to think of something to say to Mrs. Scheingold. It was always hard for Velda at a first meeting. The half-circle shifted. The crescent grew ragged. It was very hot on Hilton Street, in the somnolent August way. The sun was still up over Powhattan Avenue in the west, a molten orange, almost

liquid, that burned everything in its path and brought an unconscious sigh of protest from Irwin, to whom Barney finally turned.
"Well," Barney said briskly, looking his son-in-law over as though
he had never seen him before. "What have we here?"

The picnic then began.

Mickey Schiller and Irwin Fedder were standing next to Barney's
fishpond in the center of the lawn, each holding a Tom Collins
in his hand, gently swirling the ice to help take the edge off their
uneasiness at the other's strangeness. The ice made a nice noise,
friendly and welcoming. Fortunately for Mickey and Irwin, and
a couple of the others, too, Vito's had come through at Elsie's
demand, even though it was Sunday, blue Sunday and against the
law, rushing a couple of pints of Dixie Belle to Barney on the
q.t., Barney being among the most steady and reliable of their
customers for all kinds of pharmaceutical products, including, on
occasion, alcohol. By now, the party was already confidently
sailing along on its own course, tacking easily in the mild currents
of small talk that seemed to swirl everywhere in the back yard,
whatever Barney's wishes might be. Not that he was being
thwarted. It was just that, as he told himself, he couldn't be
everywhere at once, he couldn't take care of everything and everyone. There was a congenial hubbub around him, however, a blur
of conversation from which he could pluck an isolated word or
phrase every now and then, just enough to convince himself that
everybody was happy. It was, he thought, easy and relaxed. It
was the way he had planned it, and he gladly allowed himself to
be buffeted, within reason, between one guest and another.
Meanwhile, he noticed, his heart was racing from pleasurable
excitement.

Within moments, the Safers had arrived in the rejuvenated blue
Chevy with Sylvan, whose appearance at the front door caused
Elsie's eyes to pop. And what's this supposed to be, she said to
herself, in a heavy, declamatory tone, when he walked in ahead
of Sigmund and Jenny, startling her in his navy shirt and white
ducks. The good Lord help us, she continued piously, there's

monkey business somewhere. Something must have happened, way back in the past. Something serious. The thought, flashing with electric energy, gave her profound pleasure; she could hardly keep from smiling with almost malicious joy. Monkey business, she loved it. Sylvan wasn't the first little Jewish boy who looked like that to Elsie. There was often monkey business lurking somewhere, she liked to think. And it wasn't just a matter of skin color; no, sir. The shape and thrust and dimensions of certain lips, noses, even haunches that she had noticed in her time in Forest Park sometimes suggested weird connections in the past. Even now, greeting Cantor and Mrs. Safer, who were among her favorites, she was wondering about that Miss Reese. With nappy hair like that, bleached as it was, you could never tell. Just because it was blond. As for the little Jewish boy waiting in front of her, well . . . Elsie was still trying to keep from smiling too smugly as she directed them out to the back yard.

"Where's Amy?" Barney asked, when the Safers appeared on the lawn. "I thought she was coming, too." Jenny's yellow dress glimmered brightly against the sweet green shine of Barney's grass, her hair, pulled tight after considerable effort, shone silkenly in the deepening light. Her nose, a thin arch, as thin as Sigmund's, was burned by the sun. She looked healthy and alive in the summer heat, as thriving and imposing as one of her husband's well-tended roses in its prime.

"You'll never learn, will you?" Jenny said, trying to sound good-humored about it. "It's not Amy, it's Annie. Please, Barn, for the last time."

"Anything you say, my sweet one," Barney said. "Whatever you want to call her, it's okay by me. But where is she?"

"She's on her way," Jenny said vaguely.

Then Barney turned to the Scheingold kid and reached for his hand, holding on to it for a moment or two, peering intently into his face. "You're Sylvan Scheingold," he said. "The boy from the choir. Your mother's already here."

"Yes, sir," Sylvan said. Lillian always insisted on "sir."

"I knew you right away. I could tell from all the descriptions. And I remember you from last year, on the pulpit. They tell me you're a star. If that's what they say, I'll go along with it. Maybe you'll sing for us today, give us a good time. How about it? Remind me to show you your room later, where you'll s'eep for the holidays. You'll have your own bathroom when you stay here. You like that?"

Sigmund finally spoke up, gripping Sylvan's shoulders from behind. "Mr. Fribush doesn't have any sons of his own," Sigmund said lightheartedly, as though that explained everything.

"Well," Barney said to Sylvan matter-of-factly. "I can certainly see why they call you 'Nigger.'"

At which, turning even darker, Sylvan scowled and pulled away from Sigmund, while the group around them slowly broke apart and separated. Where was his mother? Where was Mickey Schiller? Even Mickey Schiller was better than this. Even Stan the Gann.

"Barn," Jenny began to scold, in an aside meant for him alone. "Be a little tactful. Don't talk like that in front of the boy."

"I forgot. I apologize. A man sometimes forgets. So I forgot. But I'm happy you're here. That's all that counts, that all my guests are here," Barney said, his heart racing, but Sigmund and Jenny were already wandering off to pour themselves something cold to drink, while Sylvan left them without a second look, free at last to check in with his mother.

Now, still standing side by side at the rim of the fishpond, Tom Collinses in hand, Mickey Schiller and Irwin Fedder gazed at each other without speaking. Mickey was affecting a look of sophisticated boredom, eyes lidded (he hoped), blasé to the world, while Irwin nibbled at a monster pretzel and calmly sipped his gin. "Nice digs," Irwin finally said, nodding toward the house with a possessive air.

"Yeah," Mickey answered, as though it were all an old story to him. He didn't even bother to glance up. Behind his lidded eyes, he was still filled with the offer he had made to Lillian. It had left him with a powerful afterglow of good feelings about himself, which he was not quite used to. He had behaved well, he thought, he had said just the right things in exactly the right tone of voice, for a change; he hoped Lillian agreed, he hoped it would help her make up her mind.

"You from around here?" Irwin asked. "I don't remember seeing you before."

"I live downtown."

"How do you come to know Barn? You do business together?"

"Through my friend," Mickey said, pointing with his nose in Lillian's direction.

"And who is your friend?"

Mickey gave a little twitch of impatience. He didn't like inquisitions, he didn't like people who tried to position him. "Her name is Lillian Scheingold," he said. "She's the mother of that kid over there, the one in the white pants. He's in the choir. You know, at the House of Israel. He's going to stay here for the holidays."

"I think I heard something like that," Irwin said. "My father-in-law is very generous, always acting on impulse."

"I'm the same way," Mickey said, twitching again.

"You can be a victim or a beneficiary, you never know with Barn."

"I wouldn't worry about Sylvan Scheingold. That kid is one smart cookie."

"What line of business you in?"

"Lumber and building supplies. I run a yard out in Dundalk."

"Your own?"

"Right now I work for somebody else. But after the war . . ."

"Lumber must be a problem these days."

"Oh, yeah, it's a problem, all right. The army takes everything. But we manage. There are always ways, if you know the ropes." Then, after a weighted moment, "How about you?"

"I work for the army. I'm a civilian chemist," Irwin said.

Mickey looked blank.

"I'm in chemical warfare down in Virginia."

Without knowing it, Mickey took a half-step backward, snorting a little.

"It's a euphemism, of course," Irwin went on. "Chemical warfare, that is. I can't really talk about it. It's classified information."

Mickey didn't know the right question to ask. That was one of his social problems, he knew. What to say now? He had never met anyone who worked in chemical warfare. Almost everybody he knew was sweating it out overseas as an ordinary GI. Nor had he ever heard the word "euphemism" used in conversation. Worse, he was not absolutely sure what it meant. Nevertheless, the idea of chemical warfare gripped him. It had the ring of Buck Rogers about it. He thought he could almost see poisonous ether waves beginning to rise in front of him, the noxious fumes of chemical warfare ready to wipe out the rest of the world, especially the hated Germans. "Hmmm," he finally managed to say, barely breathing.

"At least I'm doing what I'm fit for," Irwin continued, nonchalantly. "And I like science. I like the detachment it gives you. No personal mess and all that. I especially like chemistry, with all its mysteries, all that smoky stuff, although it's my own opinion that physics is the wave of the future. Physics is tomorrow, you could say. You can't imagine what's going on in physics these days, even while we're standing here talking to each other, as though everything was the way it always was." Irwin shook his head at the mysterious implications of his own words. "It's just that the war puts a terrible edge on everything," he went on. "The stakes are too high. It's the whole world or nothing. If it wasn't for the war, I'd probably be doing serious research for the betterment of mankind. And that's not just high-minded talk, either. But I'm not complaining. Everybody has to deal with the war. It's fact of life number one. For all of us. We have to survive. And what about you?"

"You mean the war?" Mickey was a little dazed after listening to this speech.

"Yeah."

"I'm 4-F. I only have one kidney."

"How come you only have one kidney?"

"I was born that way. They say it's supposed to cut down your life span."

"If it's any solace, there's hardly anything that won't do that. And everybody's got something. With me, it's asthma. Ever seen an asthma attack? Believe me, it's serious business, the doctors don't have a clue. Anyway," Irwin added after a moment, clearing his throat noisily, "my father-in-law's not so happy at the idea of me being a scientist. Detachment doesn't interest my father-in-law. A doctor would be all right, somebody public and respectable like that, but research? Research is for the likes of Frankenstein. You know, creeps. Anyway, his plan was for me to join him down at the factory. I was supposed to take over Tiger Pads when I married my wife. In his mind, that is. Never in mine. He thinks I let him down."

"Your father-in-law owns Tiger Pads? *The* Tiger Pads?" Mickey forced a laugh and suddenly lifted his foot, showing Irwin the heel of his shoe, which carried the celebrated Tiger Pad logo. "And there are millions more just like me," he said, while they both laughed. But Mickey was impressed. Tiger Pads was big, it was really big. If you owned something as big as Tiger Pads, you just naturally became big yourself, and so did everyone around you. Including sons-in-law like Irwin Fedder. And for Mickey Schiller, big was always better. After a moment, he looked up at Barney's house. Then he looked at the houses that stood on each side of Barney's. Finally, he looked at Irwin. "You got to have at least twenty-five grand a year to live in one of these places," he said, already considering Irwin in a new light.

"I wouldn't know," Irwin said, sounding dismissive. "I never think about it." He started to move off.

But Mickey wasn't quite finished. He had found the right questions at last. "And what about your wife?" he asked, reaching for Irwin's elbow.

"What about her?"

"Is she a big success like her father?" Meaning, do you have a house like Barney's, a full-time maid, and all the other things?

Irwin raised an eyebrow. "Maybe you'd better ask her," he suggested, showing his teeth a little. "There she goes now, the one with the tray of pickles."

"I'm sorry," Mickey said, picking up the signals. "I didn't mean anything by that."

"She's getting her doctorate at George Washington, as a matter of fact."

"No kidding?"

"In psychology."

"Psychology."

"You know. Behavior. The way people act and think. How and why they do what they do. Conscious and unconscious. Dreaming and waking. I'm sure you know all about that." Irwin was smiling again, showing even more of his teeth, while his eyes narrowed with sharp pleasure.

All Mickey knew about psychology were the multiple-choice tests he sometimes took on the features pages of the *Sun*; the results always proved that he was loyal, dependable, and very hard-working. But he also knew in a vague way that psychology was in the air these days. If it was in the papers, it was important.

"Toby is a very serious student of human nature," Irwin concluded in a high, remote tone. "She cares about people. In fact, she's a very serious person herself in every way, in the best sense of the word."

If big tits were proof of being serious, Mickey thought, glancing peevishly at Toby across the lawn, knowing that somehow or other, without even realizing it was happening, he had been positioned by Barney Fribush's son-in-law, and that it had been easy. But before Mickey could think of something clever to say, something that this fatso would remember him for, Irwin was off to fix himself something to eat, rumbling across the lawn as slow and steady as the long summer afternoon itself.

"You've got a spot on your pants, sweetheart. It's really discouraging, I hate to nag, but after all the effort . . ."

"It's just chocolate."

"I told you, if you use salt and hot water right away, there's no problem. It washes right out."

"I forgot."

"Now they're ruined."

"Ma, it's as big as a freckle."

"That doesn't look like any freckle to me."

"Anyway, I hate these pants. They're too short. They pull in the crotch."

"One more season, that's all." She waited a moment for Sylvan to calm down, pretending to examine her fingernails. "Did you get to see the fountain in the front hall when you came in?" she asked.

"All that dumb water plopping around."

"It's very practical, for your information. It helps to keep the house cool. And it's always the same water, it just keeps recirculating, it doesn't plop around."

"Who needs a fountain in the house? Did you see all the dead bugs floating around?"

"You're in some mood. When you get like this . . ."

"Well, everybody keeps pulling at me."

"Oh, boy, I can tell, you're in some mood."

"There's Annie Safer over there," Sylvan said.

"Don't point, sweetheart, it's rude."

"She's really wild."

"What do you know about wild? All of a sudden. And she's not even wearing a brassiere, either. Who's the boy?"

"Some Italian."

"What's she doing with an Italian?"

"I think he must be a Jew."

"He can't be a Jew, Sylvan. Italians aren't Jews."

"Well, something."

"The cantor doesn't look very happy."

"He never looks happy."

"You better not bring home any Italians."

"Why, you think the Jews are so perfect?" Mickey Schiller's name was on the tip of Sylvan's tongue, but, catching his mother's threatening gaze, he decided to keep his mouth shut and maintain the family peace.

"To-ba."

"Hello, darling. I've been trying to get away from the crowd out there to say hello. I've been trying to get in here to see you. You feeling okay? Who are all those people out there, anyway? What's new around here? What's going on?"

"Nuffin' much." Elsie was stirring the pot of boiling franks with a soup ladle while Toby leaned against the kitchen sink, smoking a Lucky Strike, her short, narrow-hipped, busty body planted solidly on the bilge-green linoleum floor. The two of them had spent a lot of time together in that kitchen, in just that posture, most of it in intense family conference.

"He paying attention to the doctor's orders?" Toby asked.

"He pays attention to what's convenient."

Toby stirred and flicked an ash in the sink. Then she shook her head.

"Well," Elsie said, "he's a hard man to keep down. You know that better'n anyone. That nurse with the crazy hair is coming in for a couple of weeks to try. So he say."

"He told me. It'll probably be a good thing for everybody. An extra hand like that. You've been carrying a big load. Don't think I don't know it, either."

"That lady with the rouge's son is coming in, too." Elsie put the ladle down; it was pointless to stir boiling water. "You seen the boy?" she asked, looking at Toby peculiarly.

"They say he has a gorgeous voice."

"I don't know about no voice. But did you *see* him?"

"He's a nice-enough-looking kid," Toby said in a neutral tone.

"Hmmf." Elsie turned away and banged the ladle against the pot.

"Well, he'll only be here for a couple of nights," Toby said. "Just for the holidays. It's not the end of the world."

"It's still extra company. It's still work."

"Does he get enough rest?" Toby asked.

"Your poppa? Not as much as he thinks. Not as much as he needs. He went to the club last night with his friend Mistuh Metzguh."

"That's probably a healthy sign, a little socializing."

"Not the condition he was in when he came home."

"What do you mean?"

"Booze."

Toby thought for a moment, inhaling deeply. "Well, I suppose there's got to be an outlet somewhere," she said, blowing out smoke. "That's one of the rules of the game. A little forbidden pleasure occasionally."

"I don't know about no rules of the game. But you always sticking up for him."

"He needs protecting. He needs watching. You know my father."

"He gets all the protecting he needs right here, and you better know it."

"I do know it."

"Whassisname wants some salami," Elsie said after a moment. "I bought some special."

"Put it here on my plate. I'll bring it out to him."

"Just tell the folks the franks are on the boil."

"You sure did a nice job with that table. It makes me hungry to look at it. And the yard smells delicious, too. I never expected a picnic. My father . . . Now tell me, Elsie, the incision."

"I don't know about no incision. I know about his tush."

Toby laughed.

"Laugh all you want. It ain't a pretty sight, and it ain't funny."

"Maybe you shouldn't tell me," Toby said.

"Well, it ain't pretty. Depend on that."

"Those franks look done, baby," Toby said, peering over Elsie's shoulder. "Don't overcook them."

"You just go about your business, To-ba. Go talk to one of those strangers out there. Give your poppa a hand. That's the best thing you can do, help your poppa."

"You're looking very well, cantor."

"Thank you," Sigmund said stiffly, without meaning it. He wished that everyone would stop telling him how well he looked, when actually he was feeling abnormal again. If only somebody would acknowledge it. He began to sniff the late-afternoon air in a studied way, as though he were testing for a bad odor. The catarrh was back, it had started in again while he was having his disappointing little chat with the Scheingold kid over iced tea and brownies, thickening his voice and beginning to damp it. So was the hot wire from his shoulder to his thigh, which had lingered, insistently, since his busy morning at the House. And there were other unpleasant matters at hand that threatened his well-being, including the superior, aloof, and altogether sloppy presence of his daughter, Annie, who was standing not twenty feet away from him, alongside the other one, the thick chunky alien with the crepe-soled shoes and the magic hands. Where did she get that dress? Even Sigmund could tell that it was way too small for her. The top part alone . . . And everyone insisted on telling him how well he looked, if they only knew. The one thing that gave him undisturbed pleasure these days, he told himself, was his fish, where he wished he was at this very moment, with his gorgeous fish, whose aimless vulnerable lives he totally controlled. For the moment, he had even forgotten his reliable feelings for his wife, who had given him such an instant of joy just minutes before when she had entered the Safer living room in her yellow dress and who was now drinking a cold Pepsi at a single gulp, slouching under Barney's magnolia tree near her daughter, so involved was Sigmund with all the thin tight currents that were racing chaotically through him again. He was at the point, all too easily reached, where all he could think about was himself.

Me, he was thinking. Me.

Nevertheless, "Thanks" was what he said again to Irwin Fedder's greeting, in a deliberately thick voice meant to carry a message. "You're looking pretty good yourself. How's everything going down in Chevy Chase?"

"Chevy Chase is Chevy Chase."

"I really meant Virginia."

"Ah, Virginia, carry me back. If we don't blow it up one of these days."

"Still working on that stuff?"

"That's supposed to be a secret, cantor. What do you know about it?"

"Nothing. I'm guessing. I try to read between the lines, that's all. I touched a nerve, right?"

"I can't talk about it. It's all classified. I'm sworn to secrecy."

"Just so you get there before the Germans."

"We'll get there. But I'm not making any promises."

Sigmund clapped Irwin on the shoulder. That's what he did to everybody directly involved with the war effort, everybody who served. "Good boy," he said, sounding fatuous to himself but helpless to stop the words. In fact, like everybody else, he had no other words for a situation like this, all he could offer was a semblance of good will. "Just keep your eye on the ball," Sigmund added. "That's all anybody asks. We're depending on you. The whole country is."

"Well, I'm not making any promises," Irwin said again.

As soon as Bobby Fiorentino moved off casually, to check out the bathrooms in the house on Hilton Street, Jenny approached her daughter. "I thought he was just going to give you a lift," she said. "That's what you told me. I didn't know he was coming to the party."

"Well, you must have misunderstood. He's here, I asked him, what's the big deal?"

"The big deal is he wasn't invited."

"It's not all that important, so please don't blow it up out of proportion. I mean, Mr. Fribush doesn't even know my name. He doesn't care."

"I care," Jenny said, wondering whatever had happened to "Mummy." "Your father and I care," she added.

"I'll tell you what, we'll only stay fifteen minutes. Will that make you happy?"

"It's not a question of my being happy."

"What is it a question of, then?"

"It's a matter in general."

"Mother, nothing could be less important than the fact that Bobby Fiorentino ate a hot dog in Mr. Fribush's back yard as my special guest."

"What about your father's position?" Jenny asked. "Did you ever think of that?"

"That again."

"It's not that again. It's the most important thing of all. Your father's position is very delicate. Everything you have comes from your father's position. You should thank your lucky stars every day."

"My lucky stars."

"That's right."

"I swear, you're going to force me right into Bobby's arms."

"Where you're no stranger, I'm sure. I hear what goes on on the porch. I'm not deaf. And on the golf course, too," she added, trying a long shot.

"You're asking for it."

"And don't talk to me in that tone of voice. I don't like it. Miss hot and cold. What's wrong with you, anyway?"

Annie bit her lip.

"I thought you were going to get rid of that dress," Jenny went on, eyeing her daughter's body as though she intended to vacuum it. "And look at your sandal strap. Still broken."

"So tell me, young man, I didn't catch your name."

"Fiorentino."

"That's one name?"

"Bobby. Robert. Bobby Fiorentino."

"You got a little mustard on your chin."

Bobby dabbed at his chin with a paper napkin.

"Well, welcome to the Fribush back yard. It's always good to have a stranger around. You know what I mean?"

"I'm probably as strange as they come," Bobby said. "Ha-ha."

Barney stared at Bobby Fiorentino and began to wonder.

"I came with Annie Safer," Bobby went on. "She's my date."

"I know her all her life. A doll. Wonderful mother and father, wonderful family. A doll."

"I agree."

"Tell me, what *shul* you go to?"

"Forest Park. I'm a senior."

"*Shul*, not school."

"*Shul*."

"You don't go to the House. If you went to the House, I'd know. I know everybody at the House. What'd you say your name was?"

"Bobby. Robert. Now I get you. It doesn't take me long. Anyway, you probably never heard of it, I go to Our Lady of Lourdes, out on Liberty Road."

"That's no *shul*."

"It's a Catholic *shul*."

"You getting funny with me?"

"Sorry, sir. No offense meant." Bobby straightened up, hands at his side.

"I like good manners and respect all the time."

"Me, too. And so does my father. That's Dominic Fiorentino. You know him? The contractor? Good manners all the time. I'm honored to be here."

"You should be. You want a beer? You old enough to have a beer? Help yourself over there, there's plenty."

"Sweetie, what say we hang around a bit after everybody leaves?"

"I'd really like to get home," Toby said, smoking another cigarette. "I have that work to do on my paper."

"Just five, ten minutes. That's all it'll take. We really have to get the will settled once and for all."

"The will is settled," Toby said. "It's been settled for months, ever since he was diagnosed. I've been telling you and telling you, but you won't believe me. And it's none of our business, in any case." Smoke kept pouring out of Toby's mouth as she spoke.

"It's our future, that's all."

"But it's *his* will. And it's not called a will for nothing. That is a very precise word designed for a very precise context. My father has every right to do what he wants, legally and morally. If there's such a thing as a moral question about a will."

"And what about our children? That's a moral question. We have an obligation to our children."

She gave him a contemptuous look. "We'll worry about that when we have children," she said.

"Don't get so snappy." He began to wave his hand to clear the air of smoke.

"Irwin, you know how I feel."

"One more try?"

"No. My father wants his estate in trust, it'll be in trust. It's his affair. And besides, I don't give a hoot."

"That's because you've never been poor."

"I've gone without. I've been poor enough. You're not the only one. We weren't doing so hot during the Depression, before Tiger Pads took off. But that's not the point. You're not poor. And you're not going to be poor. You're just not going to be able to get your hands on the capital, that's all. I don't want to talk about it anymore. My father's not ready to be buried. Not yet. Look at him carrying on over there. Like a boy of twenty." She dropped her cigarette on the lawn and stepped on it.

"Okay, we'll forget it," Irwin said, gazing around the yard unhappily. "Where did your father find this gang, anyway?" he asked after a moment's silence. "The cantor aside."

"You got me. One of them is his nurse. You know, the blonde."

"I remember her from the hospital. That's some momma. Did you get a chance to talk to that guy Mickey?"

"I talked to his wife."

"It's not his wife."

"Then whose kid is it?" Toby asked.

"Hers. She has a husband somewhere. Another one of those stories. The kid looks like he's going to fall asleep on his feet."

"That's a pose. Don't let him fool you. He's eavesdropping on everybody. He's just pretending to be bored while he eavesdrops."

"I used to do that," Irwin said. "I used to hide under tables when I was a kid and listen in to the grown-ups talking."

"You always were a masochist," Toby said. "Daddy wants to bring out the portable so we can dance," she added.

"That's all we need in this heat," Irwin said. "Do me a favor. Discourage him. No dancing. They'll never go home if they start dancing."

"You know that I love you." He was whispering and laughing at the same time, even though the words sounded a little flat to him. After a moment's thought, he decided to change his tune; he knew a lot of tunes in many different keys.

"Barn, please, I beg you."

"As the lily among the thorns . . ." he sang.

She moved off without a sound, tucking herself away behind the magnolia tree.

"Come upstairs with me," he said, pursuing her.

"I wish I had stayed home. If I had known . . ." She found herself whispering, too.

"Thy lips are like a thread of scarlet . . ." he continued, enunciating slowly.

"If you don't stop talking like that, I'll go home right now. And I mean it, don't test me."

"Thy speech is comely . . . sometimes." He laughed again. Above them, a scimitar moon already hung low in the evening sky, and a few dusty stars suddenly appeared in a miniature spray.

"Barn, your hand."

"Thy temples are like a piece of pomegranate . . ."

The blood had risen to her cheeks, making her feel swollen to herself, larger than life, and she could sense a terrible flush there, which the whole world would soon see and recognize for what it was.

"We'll go upstairs for five minutes," he said. "You and me. I need you. What's the sin? I want to see what you look like in my house. In my bedroom. I want to see. I want to look. Oh, Jenny, I need you."

Jenny glanced at the moon, at its fragile curve. There was no help there. "Not now," she heard herself say. Not now? She was aghast. What could she mean? For the first time, it occurred to her that perhaps she was enjoying this.

"Of course, not now," Barney said. "I was only joking. Come tomorrow. Come tomorrow at three o'clock. I'll make sure Elsie is out of the house. I'll get rid of her."

"I think I'd like a glass of iced tea," she said, moving away again. "Do you think Elsie could manage that?"

"Thy two breasts are like two young roes . . ." he recited.

"My two breasts," she said, wistfully glancing down. She folded her arms in front of her. Her yellow skirt billowed for a moment.

". . . which feed among the lilies. Then something something, about a mountain of myrrh, I think. A mountain of myrrh and a hill of frankincense. Or vice versa."

"I don't know about all that, Barn," she said, suddenly sounding wistful, too. She was afraid that she was going to cry.

"Tell me, my darling, what is a mountain of myrrh, anyway? I never knew, and the book doesn't say. Is it what I think it is?" He smiled shyly and waited a moment. "Is it?" he persisted. "You'll show me, yes? Jenny? Yes?"

"Thank God, it's beginning to get a little dark at last."

"Oh, I'm sorry, you scared me. I didn't hear you come in."

They were upstairs in Barney's bedroom. Velda was staring out one of the front windows, gazing at the shimmering lake below, taking in the great reflected sheets of disappearing sunlight that came up off its surface. She was spellbound. Behind her, Lillian sidled into the room. Lillian wasn't sure what she might be interrupting; she hoped she wasn't interrupting anything. On the other hand, she had promised herself not to leave Mr. Fribush's beautiful, beautiful house, which was how she had begun to think of it, without taking a good look at every nook and cranny. Who knew when she would be back?

So far, Lillian had passed idly through each of the downstairs rooms (after turning down Elsie's hot dogs, just poking at the slaw and potato salad), wandering around at her own pace, tossing a penny, when she was sure no one was looking, into the front-hall fountain, feeling stupid as she made a wish, feeling like a child, but unable to resist the impulse. I wish, I wish . . . eyeing the heavy damask curtains hanging in the living room like domestic armor plate, the thick, the too-thick carpeting, the unplayed grand, six-and-a-half feet long, the Atwater-Kent radio standing like an icon in its own corner; then the dining room with its mirrored walls, in which you could barely see yourself because they were antiqued, and gleaming Sheraton pieces looking untouched and unused (which they were); the sun parlor with its rattan furniture, imported from Asia, and creamy venetian blinds; Elsie's dazzling white kitchen and the cozy little breakfast nook adjoining it, where all the meals on Hilton Street were taken; and finally, in the back of the house, overlooking the fishpond, the den, a small square claustrophobic room that held a leather-topped desk for Barney with its own telephone extension, pictures covering the desk of Toby at every stage of development, growing bustier each year, also a silver-framed photograph of Barney's late wife and Toby's mother, in solemn half-profile, looking dead already in the picture, holding on to her pearls as though she were afraid someone would snatch them from her as she stared without expression into her lap, and behind the desk, a shelf holding a few books from the Literary Guild. The only thing that Lillian had missed on her ramble was Elsie's wing, but that didn't bother her, she had been warned that Elsie's wing was private and out-of-bounds, and rightly, she thought. Now she was doing the upstairs, taking Mr. Fribush at his word. She was looking at everything, as he had urged her to do. So, apparently, was Miss Reese.

"It must be wonderful to live like this," Velda said. "To have the wherewithal."

Lillian joined her at the window and together they gazed at the scene below. "It's really gorgeous," Lillian said, taking a deep breath. "Imagine waking up to this every morning. It must make you feel like a million dollars. Look how much of the city you can see. It must make you feel that you own it. That has to be the harbor down there, where all the mist is coming from."

"We met downstairs when we first got here," Velda said. "My name is Velda Reese."

"I know who you are. I'm Lillian Scheingold."

"Your son is the pretty dark boy, isn't he? The one with the baby face?"

"Yes, he is," Lillian said primly, feeling a little piqued at Velda's compliment. Baby face? And dark, too, as though it always had to be said about Sylvan, as though nobody could leave it alone. "He's in Mr. Fribush's choir," Lillian went on, trying hard to sound pleasant. "I mean, Mr. Fribush's synagogue's choir. You know, the cantor's. Cantor Safer."

"I know the cantor from the hospital. I work at the hospital.

The cantor visits patients there a couple of times a week. He makes his rounds. He never misses. That's how I know Barney. I was his nurse."

"I wanted to be a nurse once," Lillian said, beginning to drawl her words like Velda. "It lasted about two weeks. It lasted until I saw my own menstrual blood for the first time."

"There's usually something like that," Velda said, stepping away from the window. "Most little girls want to be a nurse at some time in their lives. Then it gets spoiled. The feeling, I mean. The need. A shame, really. But it says something about little girls, doesn't it? Something good?"

"Maybe. I don't know. It was over so fast, I can hardly remember. I ended up behind the underwear counter at Hochschild's. Only they call it lingerie. That's a far cry."

Velda walked over to Barney's bed, sat, and bounced up and down once or twice with an appraising air. "That your husband down there?" she asked after a moment.

"A friend, that's all."

"I thought that was your husband."

"I don't have a husband."

"But the kid."

"I'm married, if that's what you mean, but I don't know where my husband is. My son and I live alone."

"You don't have to tell me anything."

"It's no secret. The whole world knows. My husband deserted us years ago."

Velda stood up. "Well, I don't have a husband, either," she said lightly. "And it's getting to be time. Yes ma'am, if I say so myself, it's more than time. I figure if I hang around the hospital long enough, something will show up. I've seen it happen before. Doctors. Patients. Why not? And I want to marry a Hebrew. Hebrews make good husbands. That's the word down in Knoxville, Tennessee, and from what I've seen it's the truth."

"You from Tennessee?"

"My whole family's there."

"I never knew anybody from Tennessee." Then, hesitantly, "I guess you're not Jewish."

"No."

"Well," Lillian said. Maybe she could introduce Velda Reese to Mickey Schiller or Stan the Gann. "You're probably talking to the wrong person on the subject of Hebrews. My husband was a Hebrew and he ran away." Lillian moved over to Barney's dressing mirror and began to comb her hair. "Actually, I never thought of him as a Hebrew," she said, laughing a little. "I never thought of anybody as a Hebrew. It sounds different from Jew." It sounds better, she thought, what with the gentiles giving the word "Jew" such a bad name all these years.

"Makes no difference," Velda said. "It's just a way of talking. I was speaking in general, anyway. About husbands. There are always exceptions. I know that." She ran her hand over the satin bedspread. "It's too hot to have all this stuff out in the summertime. Those drapes downstairs. These curtains. They should all be cleaned and stored away until the fall. That's the way we do it at home."

"It's a man living alone."

"But he's got a live-in."

"It's still a man living without a wife. But there's something about this room that still feels like a woman's."

"It's the satin. The satin and the curtains and all the mirrors."

"Give me a week," Lillian said, "and I'd have it looking right."

Velda laughed. "I'm going to have two weeks," she said. "I'm coming in to keep an eye on Barney. Postoperative stuff. All patients could use it." She couldn't resist a little anticipatory smile. "I'll shape him up soon enough."

"Hi, girls." It was Toby, standing at the bedroom door, blowing smoke into the room. "Having a look around?"

"It's gorgeous," Lillian said, feeling a little guilty at being caught. "I love it."

"You should have seen it when my mother was alive. After spring cleaning and the summer rugs were down and all that."

"It must have been just gorgeous."

"It really is swell-looking," Velda put in, suddenly shy in the presence of Barney Fribush's daughter.

"Would you like to see the rest?" Toby asked. "You can't leave the house without seeing the rest."

The three of them then trooped out of Barney's room in a

dutiful straight line, and, like a museum guide, Toby, still smoking, began to walk them through the three other bedrooms, the two baths, one green, one yellow, the vast cedar closets, now half empty, in each one of which you could hide an entire wardrobe, carefully pointing out the views from all the windows, to the west, over Powhattan Avenue, where the sun was finally giving up a last radiant burst in a cloudless sky, to the east, toward Liberty Heights, where the new scimitar moon rose slowly, to the south, where the city lay at their feet, which they had already seen and commented on, and down below, in Barney's back yard, where Toby's father and his guests were scrambling around the darkening lawn finishing off the last of the hot dogs and potato salad, strewing pretzel crumbs on the shining dry grass, and belching gassy fumes into the evening air, while, half hidden away, Elsie eyed them all from the kitchen window with heavy skepticism and a dyspepsia of both mind and body that came, at least in part, from chronically swollen feet.

I wish, I wish, Lillian thought, staring down at the back yard. Actually, they soon realized, wandering around the second floor, like a hunting expedition, it had finally begun to cool off.

"Where did you get that dress?" Sigmund asked in a tone that Annie wasn't sure she had ever heard from her father before.

"Bergdorf Goodman," she answered sarcastically, thrusting her chest out.

Sigmund had only a vague idea what Bergdorf Goodman was, mainly from ads that appeared in the Sunday *New York Times*, which the Safer family read every week, but he definitely recognized the arrogance in Annie's voice and in the way she was standing there in front of him. "You ought to be ashamed of yourself," he said. "Look at you. In public. It's a scandal."

For that, she stuck her chest out even farther and, glaring at Sigmund, still burning from their exchange at home that afternoon, Annie gave him her you-mix-with-me-and-you'll-live-to-regret-it look. They stayed that way for a second or two, not quite face to face. "Ugh," Sigmund finally said, feeling his soul shrink. He couldn't bear to look at her. His own daughter. Flesh and blood. Bone of his bone. And everybody was talking about her, too. He could tell. All the whispering and the sneaky glances in their direction. It was as he said. It was a scandal.

"Okay, if there's a God, then tell me why shit has to smell so bad. It could've been just the opposite, you know. Shit could've smelled sweet if God wanted it to."

Mickey Schiller blushed under his light summer tan. He wasn't sure he was up to this. "Come on, kid," he said, "what kind of question is that, anyway?" Mickey had just been about to confess to Sylvan that he wanted to marry his mother. He was going to tell him the truth. He saw a confession as a way of forging an alliance, and he suspected that he would need all the help he could get where Lillian Scheingold was concerned. Then the kid had brought up the subject of God. Jesus, God. What did Mickey Schiller know?

"I thought you wanted to be my mentor," Sylvan said.

"Sure I do, but what does that have to do with shit?" He had trouble saying the word to Sylvan. It did not sound paternal.

Sylvan waited a moment in order to keep Mickey off-balance. He had been feeling ornery ever since Barney had called him "Nigger." "Don't you see how important the question is?"

"What question?"

"Why God allows shit to smell like shit. If there is a God."

"Jee-sus, Sylvan." Mickey looked over his shoulder to make sure no one could hear them talking like this. He saw Irwin Fedder standing alone under the magnolia tree (served him right), Annie Safer lecturing the blunt-faced curly-headed kid, poking her forefinger into his chest with every word, and Barney Fribush drinking another rum and Pepsi as he stood next to the cantor. Velda Reese, who had just come out of the house, was helping herself to another beer. Where was Lillian? He needed her. He hadn't known how much he needed her.

"Some mentor," Sylvan said under his breath, but intending to be heard.

"Okay, then, why does shit have to smell so bad?" Mickey looked offended when he said the word.

"You don't know?"

"I don't even care."

"That's what I mean."

"What?"

"A real mentor cares about those things."

Mickey was sorry he had ever brought up the question of mentorship. This kid didn't need a mentor, it was Mickey Schiller who needed a mentor. "I care," he said in an unsure voice. "I do. But this isn't the place for such matters."

"All we're doing is having a little talk. What's wrong with that? I thought that's what you wanted."

"But it's a party, kid. Parties are for fun."

"You don't look like you're having much fun to me."

"Well, I'm waiting for your mother. Where is she?"

"What's my mother got to do with it?"

"You'd be surprised."

There was something teasing in Mickey Schiller's voice, something barely hidden, that forced Sylvan to respond. "How surprised?" Sylvan asked, tentative at last.

Mickey took one of his deep breaths before answering. "I want your mother to marry me," he said, looking down at his shoes. "I want her to be my wife. She is a wonderful woman."

"Are you proposing to me?"

"Come on, you better take it seriously."

"Ha," Sylvan said, but his stomach was uncurling inside him.

"I already asked her. Just so you know."

Now it was Sylvan's turn to take a deep breath, but he was afraid to speak, snakes might come out of his mouth.

"I asked her this afternoon," Mickey Schiller said, looking up. "While we were driving over here in the car."

Sylvan thought about Lillian sitting in the front seat of the car being proposed to. "What did she say?" he finally managed to ask.

"Nothing final," Mickey said humbly. "But she's sure thinking about it. Let me tell you. And you should think about it, too.

We'd make a good pair, you and me. That's my true opinion. And I'd see that you got out of that rattrap you live in, too. I'd make sure you had a little living space to stretch your legs in. We'd go uptown, that's my plan, maybe into a house out in Park Heights. You know where I mean, Glen Avenue, Menlo Drive, one of those spots, where they have those little colonial houses that match up on either side of the front door? How would you like that?"

Despite himself, a rush of possibilities filled Sylvan's head. "What about Henny?" he asked.

"Henny lives with his mother. That's the permanent agreement. I get him on the weekend. You'd have the whole house to yourself all week, except on Saturday night. On Saturday night, Henny sleeps in the house with the rest of us."

Sylvan looked Mickey Schiller square in the face, probably for the first time. What he saw did not please him. Mickey Schiller was not blond, he was not tall, and he did not wear a floppy hat and an air force uniform with medals all over it. Also, he needed a haircut and his sideburns were too long, like some Polack downtown, and he had one of those phony identification bracelets on his wrist, as though he couldn't remember his own name. But he was there. He filled space. Sylvan could reach out and touch him, if he chose. He was what was called reality, the inescapable thing that tyrannized the world. "All I thought was that you wanted to be a mentor," Sylvan said. Then, in the confusion of the moment, an idea occurred to him. "What about Stanley Gann? He wants to marry my mother, too."

"That jerk."

"But he does. He wants to marry my mother."

"Stanley Gann is a shoe salesman at the May Company. All he's got is fancy ideas. Come on, kid, have a heart."

They were silent for a moment. Then Mickey said, "After the war, I'm going into the construction business. I know all that stuff, lumber and building materials. Everybody's going to want a new house, especially the GIs. They'll all be sick of barracks and foxholes. And I'm going to build them for them. That's my plan. Me, in my own business."

"But you only have one kidney," Sylvan said.

"So?"

"Can you get married with one kidney?"

"I been married once already and it didn't stop me."

"Here comes my mother."

"She's adorable," Mickey said, watching Lillian head across the lawn from the house. "Look how adorable she walks." Sylvan didn't have to be told. How could his father have run away from such an adorable creature? As Lillian walked toward them, Sylvan's eyes filled with sentimental tears. The sight of his mother, the mere thought of her in imagined or real trouble, it hardly mattered which, always did that to him. Well, he thought, here comes Mrs. Mickey Schiller. That was real trouble. Mrs. Mickey Schiller. It sounded terrible. A grown man with one kidney and a name like Mickey, and a kid of his own named Henny who was scared of everything. It wasn't very promising, but it was what was called reality. And Mickey Schiller didn't even know why shit had to smell bad.

"What's wrong with you, you're looking so cranky?"

"I don't feel good." Sigmund tried hard to keep the self-pity out of his voice but was only partially successful.

"Then go upstairs," Barney said. "Lay down for a few minutes. Maybe it's the weather, it's got to everybody."

"I'm not myself. I don't feel right. I probably could use a checkup."

Standing on one of Toby's camp blankets in the back yard, Barney scrutinized Sigmund carefully. You never knew with these artistic types, even after all these years. Temperamental. Flighty. Living in a dream world. Barney knew all the characteristics and then some. He would go easy. "Is it the *shul?*" he asked.

"It's everything."

"What's everything?"

"I don't want to start complaining. It's a party. I don't want to spoil the fun."

"Complain a little, for God's sake. It's me, Barney, you're not talking to some stranger."

"All right, it's everything," Sigmund admitted. "The *shul*. Yes,

the *shul*. The rabbi, too. All that. And my family, my daughter."
Sigmund could hardly continue.

Barney threw a look at Annie Safer, sharing another one of
Toby's camp blankets with her boyfriend from Our Lady of
Lourdes, Mr. F-something, and pulled back a little. He thought
he knew what Sigmund meant. It was clear enough. He looked
again. "Well, most kids these days," he began in a hesitant voice,
thinking of the Shamer girl and her bathing suit at the club.

"And I have these dreams," Sigmund went on, having difficulty
getting the words out. "I'm living two lives, day and night, in
Poland and America, awake and asleep."

"Steady now."

"I told you, I'm not myself these days."

"Who is? You think I am? You want to see, maybe? I could
show you a thing or two."

"I don't compare myself to you, Barney."

"Cocks up, my friend. That's what counts. That's all that counts.
And put a smile on your face. Don't be such a sourpuss. Everybody
loves a smile. That's right, try it, it won't kill you. Smile, dammit."

"Well, I still have these dreams. I don't know what good smiling
will do."

"I'm beginning to think you're right, my friend. You could use
a checkup."

"But the holidays."

"But the holidays, what? Tomorrow you get a checkup. First
things first. You'll go to my doctor. I'll arrange it. I'll take care of
everything. Listen, I got this fire burning up my crotch all the
time. Think of that when you're dreaming at night. And stop
looking so cranky. Just remember Barney Fribush with his crotch
burning up alive. That'll keep you straight, believe me. So smile,
for crissake, smile, that's all anybody asks."

"Don't you ever get tired of looking down on people?" Sigmund
asked, hoping that he sounded facetious.

"I don't look down on people, cantor. I'm not that kind of
person."

"You're looking down on me now."

"It's not nice to point out other people's physical deficiencies."

"Deficiencies? I should be so tall."

"You think it's an advantage to be taller than the rest of the world? Especially when you're a woman? I don't like to look down at people, and I wouldn't want to have to look up."

The cantor had no answer for that. (He had no answer for that when Larry Adelman complained about the same thing.) He was looking up at Velda from the usual angle, his pince-nez tightening on his nose. The added strain this created, the sharp pull of his nerve ends, made him rise up on his toes, as though he were trying to reach for her. The bantering tension in their exchange also stirred him unexpectedly. It was like watching her stride off down a hospital corridor, clipboard in hand, white uniform crisp over her buttocks. He was aroused, no doubt about it, and surprised by it. A slight tumescence bulged at his front, to his amazement, and he made an awkward movement to hide it, letting his hands dangle casually in front of him. "Well," he said, "you're certainly a wonderful-looking woman. You know that, don't you?" He was trying to smile, just as Barney had told him to.

Velda smiled, too. Her thin red lips always parted at the merest sign of praise. And it wasn't the first time the cantor had told her that she was wonderful-looking. Every time he remarked on it at the hospital, she would head for the nearest washroom to confirm the statement in a mirror. Looking at herself in the glass, she really had to wonder. What did the cantor mean, anyway? She was too tall, everybody knew that, her mouth was too small, her shoulders too broad. It was obvious that she was plain Cumberland farm stock, a plain Scotch-Irish-German person with maybe a few other things thrown in who, uninvited, was looking for a place for herself in alien territory. A place of her own. As for her hair . . . "If you really believe that, cantor, and you're not just talking, why don't you help me find a husband?" she asked coyly.

"You should have no trouble in that line, my dear."

"I mean somebody at the hospital."

"A doctor?"

"Why not? A Hebrew doctor."

"You want to marry a Jew?"

"Why doesn't anybody believe me when I say that?"

"It's hard to be a Jew, Velda."

"Oh, cantor, come on."

"Do you know about the persecution of the Jews?"

"Find me a Hebrew doctor, cantor, then we'll talk."

"Now you're being flip," Sigmund said. "You have a tendency. Anyway," he added, after a moment's hesitation, "they say Catholics make good husbands too. What's wrong with a Catholic?" But he wanted to eat his words when he caught sight of Bobby Fiorentino lounging alongside Annie at the goldfish pond.

"My mother always said she'd disown me if I married a Catholic," Velda said primly. "And she would, too."

Sigmund was always shocked to discover how much the Protestants hated the Catholics. They were always eager to open up on the subject, if you brought it up first. He had been warned about that peculiar phenomenon from time to time by his fish pal, George Haney, who as a Catholic had always carefully noted all signs of Protestant hostility. Gentiles against gentiles, Christians against themselves. Maybe, in the end, it would help save the Jews. Divide and survive. He looked for a way to change the subject, it was making him uncomfortable. "Well," he began in a false voice that tried to hide his anxiety, "nobody can deny that you're certainly a magnificent-looking woman." He tried to smile again.

"Maybe you shouldn't get in the habit of saying such things," Velda answered.

"Why not? It's good to talk like that. We shouldn't resist such an impulse. We should always say loving things to each other." He looked around him, as though someone else, a total stranger standing nearby, had just spoken.

"Cantor," Velda said, "you're really hot stuff."

"You think so?" Sigmund tried to look skeptical, but his pleasure at her words broke through. "It's the greatest thing there can be between two people," he said fervently, "friendship, greater than anything else." He rose up on his toes again, responding to his own words, stirred by the sound of his own voice. And the fact that he was speaking in public, in Barney Fribush's back yard,

standing only ten feet from his own daughter and only a little
farther from his wife (whose name, for an instant, seemed to slip
his mind), aroused him even more. He looked around a little
desperately. The tumescence was still in place (one hand rested
on it), polarized by the presence of Velda Reese, sustained by
unsuspected feeling. Dusk was falling all around them. Two stars
gleamed over Velda's left shoulder, the quarter-moon was rising
almost imperceptibly. It was August, he told himself, Sunday
night, an amazing evening of rose-scented moments, of unexpected high bliss. Somebody shouted happily nearby, he heard
laughter from the house, Elsie's hoarse voice. He made a move
toward Velda. She stood there like a beacon of light, welcoming
him. "Maybe I better sit down," Sigmund said, suddenly feeling
dizzy in front of her. "I'm not my usual . . ."

"Get off your feet, cantor," Velda ordered, staring at him in
her probing hospital manner. "How many franks did you have,
anyway? You can't eat and stand up at the same time. It'll kill
you, you're not a horse. Look at your friend over there. Smoking
another cigar and yammering away. Come on, sit down, you look
like you're going to pass out." Velda was smiling her authoritative
thin-lipped smile as she ordered Sigmund around. Helping him
to a chair, trying not to appear to be helping him at all . . .

"I told you you'd enjoy it," Lillian said.
"I like this house. I could really get used to this."
"I knew it. I told you."
"You giving any thought to what I said before?"
"What did you say before?"
"Lillian."
"We talked about it enough for one day. Let's give it time to
cook."
"I can offer a lot, Lillian. I can make your life easy. I'm not
going to hang around Dundalk for the rest of my days."
"Please, Mickey."
"I even had a talk with the kid."
"What kind of talk? What kid?"

"I told him that we might get married."

"You fool, you."

"What?"

"You fool. He'll hate the idea. Oh, Mickey."

"You're wrong there, my friend. He wants me to be his mentor. He said so. He's got some crazy ideas, that kid. You should hear some of the questions."

"Oh, you fool."

"Say yes, Lillian. Say it now so we can tell everybody."

"I don't want to talk about it for at least a week."

"I won't last that long."

"You'll last."

"Oh, sweetheart, I love you. You want me to show you right here in front of everybody?"

"You're breathing in my ear."

"Jesus," Mickey said, "will you look at the boobs on that one over there."

"Stop it, Mickey. When you talk like that, you sound like some stupid Polack."

"Then what should I call them?"

"If you have to call them anything, say bust. Or bosom. But why do you have to say anything?"

"What's wrong with what I said? Men talk like that all the time. You should hear that son of yours. My God," Mickey went on, in an avid voice, "have you ever seen tits like that before?"

"Mickey!"

"Okay, nice weather we're having, if it doesn't rain." He had finally heard the threat in the voice of the beloved, but he couldn't help himself. "Jesus, Lillian," he continued, "the cantor's wife's not so bad, either. The daughter, too. Over there with the Italian salami. Hey, Lillian, where you going? Come back, sweetheart. Don't be that way. I'm only kidding around."

Dusk covered them all. A thin orange line appeared in the western sky, just above the horizon, and there was an occasional lightning flash, far away. But it was cooler, they all could definitely feel it. Downtown, to the south, a whitish haze had settled over Baltimore harbor, spreading toward the Patapsco. In front of Barney Fribush's house, Ashburton Lake gleamed steel-gray in the deep twilight. Leaves fluttered on the sycamores and oaks, roses bloomed in the gardens on either side of Barney's back yard, and all the great stucco-and-brick mansions on Hilton Street sat firm on their terraces, overlooking the rest of the world.

The street lights came on. In the back yard, Barney Fribush finally yawned. He didn't bother to cover his mouth. It was time for his guests to go home. It was getting late. Like Elsie's, his feet were swollen, and his face was red. He stood with his legs spread apart, to help ease the pain in his crotch. He had tried to suggest dancing to his guests, but nobody was interested. He had wanted to bring out his portable radio and show it off. But even the Scheingold kid, who might have been expected to care, wasn't interested. (Dancing didn't matter to the Scheingold kid tonight; his dancing days were over for the moment.) Soon it would be dark. Everybody would go home. But first, fatigue came down on him like a cloud of locusts. He could hardly stand up under its buzzing weight. Still, Barney kept his eye out for Jenny and her yellow dress. Over there, under the magnolia tree, the cantor sat in a canvas chair staring at the ground, looking old, looking as though he didn't know where he was. Velda Reese was holding his hand and talking to him. Where was Jenny? Why didn't everybody go home? It was time. It was as Elsie said. He shouldn't let himself get so tired.

"I just don't believe," Annie was saying, poking at Bobby, who was always a ready target, with her forefinger again. "I just don't believe in religions that demand obedience to faceless, anonymous authorities."

"You talking about Catholics again?" Bobby asked.

"If that's what you hear."

Bobby sighed. The argument never stopped. Annie wouldn't shut up. "I told you before," he said, sounding weary, "the Church is the will of God."

"Says who?"

"What God wills, the Church performs."

"That's exactly it, you're not a religion, you're a church. You're a manmade object, a thing. What does all that have to do with the idea of God and the rest?"

"The Church is the expressed will of God," he repeated stubbornly.

"Just take the whole idea of dispensation," she said. "Just one little thing like that."

"I never said anything about dispensation."

"You once said that if you married me you'd have to get special dispensation from the Church because I'm a Jew."

"Right."

"Well, I don't hear you talking about getting any special dispensation when you feel like taking a walk around Hillsdale golf course with me. Nobody has to give you the okay for that."

"Cut it out, will you? Just for once? Marriage is a sacrament, for crying out loud. . . . I don't want to talk about it, it's late, the beer is making me sleepy. Let's get out of here."

Annie checked her watch in the dim light. "Where's my mother?" she asked. "Where'd they all go?"

"Your mother's over there near Mr. Fribush. Your father was just here with that nurse."

"I guess we should say good-bye to Toby and her husband. Where are they? I like Toby. I always did."

"That kid is eating his fourth hot dog. Look at him stuffing it in. He's really weird. He keeps staring at the back of people's heads."

"It's hard to see anybody in this light. How'd it get dark so fast?"

"This is really a nice house. I like living across the street from a lake. Yes, sir, I could really bunk down on Hilton Street. But I bet there isn't an Italian within a mile."

"Well, the Italians have Ten Hills. And they don't allow any Jews there, either."

"You starting up again?"

"You need another shave already. Soon you're going to have to shave twice a day."

"Some days I already do."

There was a small commotion under the kitchen window. They could hear Elsie shouting something. "What the hell's going on?" Bobby asked, yawning again. Then there were two more shouts, one from the fishpond; they heard the sound of running feet, and a kind of slow-motion tableau began to unfold all around them, a light splash, Toby Fedder bumping past them, breasts swinging heavily, then Irwin, stomach pushing ahead of him, then a shriek. "Jesus," Bobby said.

Overhead, the whole sweeping arc of heaven passed across Barney's vision as he fell on his back. Blue, gray, orange, one pink streak, dusty in the evening light, but sweeping overhead to every corner of the globe. He reached out for it while a hand dabbed at his forehead with a damp handkerchief. Don't move, Toby said. Do as I say. Barney's eyeballs rolled to one side. A trickle of saliva dripped from one corner of his mouth. He hoped he didn't smell. He had a feeling he had pissed his pants. He felt wet everywhere. Somebody was moaning encouragement into his left ear. A star grew brilliant. The heaven was immense. He had never realized how immense it was. Somebody slipped a pillow under his head, there was a pain, he thought he felt a swelling. Just ahead of him, facedown in the fishpond, his friend Sigmund R. Safer lay gasping for breath. What the hell? Easy now, someone said to the cantor. They were trying to lift him up. Lying on his back, Barney watched his old friend struggling for breath in the fishpond. Don't move, Toby said. His friend's face was purple in the thick evening light. The nigger boy had the cantor by one arm, Mr. Scheingold by the other, trying to hoist him between them. The water washed off him. Daddy, someone cried. Jenny stood nearby, her fist in her mouth. The Catholic boy leaned over Barney and began to whisper to him. None of that shit, Barney tried to say, but no sound came out. In a second, Velda was back. Swallow this, she ordered. Then she paid attention to Sigmund. The sky began to fuzz a little at the edges. It was suddenly very cool. Moans, barks, coughing filled the air. The flies were back at the remains of the cole slaw.

Someone handed Velda a blanket. Elsie blacked out for a couple of seconds, then recovered, her eyelids fluttering. A flashlight went on. The Catholic boy whispered in Barney's ear again. Minutes passed, filled with disorder. More minutes. Then anarchy. Chaos. Apocalypse.

Seven

"Is there anything you need, anything I can bring you?"

Sigmund, propped up against two immense pillows, peered around him in the half-light as though he might find the answer to his wife's question in all the grim hospital paraphernalia, all the sterile metal equipment that was dimly positioned everywhere in the room. A skinny steel locker, for example, containing his personal possessions. A steel wash basin standing in a corner. An iron tank filled with oxygen. The bed itself, the bedside tables, the single ugly lamp with its gooseneck. It was all so ugly; he had never noticed how ugly it was before, when he was making his clerical rounds.

He shook his head no.

"The new *Life*?" Jenny asked, standing over him and speaking slowly, as though his hearing might have been affected by all the commotion of the past few days. "It should be out around this time."

Sigmund smiled up at her. "Maybe a new life," he said, also speaking slowly, while his smile turned down from the effort he was making. "That sounds pretty good to me."

"You'll have a new life. You have a new life now. It's already begun."

The truth of Jenny's words brought tears to his eyes, which he didn't try to hide. Already, after only three days, he had shed most of his inhibitions and physical quirks, all the commonplace restraints that he had always taken for granted, exactly as he had shed his soaking clothes, without resistance or question, on entering the hospital on Sunday night, alongside his old friend Barney Fribush, strapped to an ambulance stretcher. He had quickly discovered that he could cry in front of Jenny as well as strangers, and did so easily. He had cried briefly in Barney's presence on Sunday night, lying side by side in the ambulance, wrapped in blankets like two mummies. But other things had changed as well. He had stopped dilating his nostrils, without knowing it. He had not clicked his teeth once, even when there seemed to be a momentary doubt when he arrived at the hospital as to whether he would have a room to himself. And last night, at last, at the end of visiting hours, in the soft trance of the hospital silence, he had called Jenny his "dear heart," whispering the words in a shy half-voice from his bed as she was leaving the room with Velda Reese. It had been easy, unimaginably natural. It had been as though he had been saying it all his life.

"What I could really use is a radio," he now said. "I miss the news."

"They say in a couple of days. They don't want anything to agitate you."

"I miss Lowell Thomas. I miss his voice."

"You've got the afternoon paper right there beside you, you know."

Sigmund reached over and touched the front page. "It's not the same," he said. "I depend on the radio at night."

"Soon," Jenny answered in a comforting voice. "In a couple of days." She leaned over and kissed him on the forehead, her presence overwhelming him pleasantly. Lilac and talc; a faint Parisian scent that had lasted most of the day; the glisten of her hair, which he wanted to touch.

"I've made a decision," he said, breathing it all in. "I'm going to shave off my mustache tomorrow."

Jenny stood up straight again, trying to hide her satisfaction. "Let me do it," she said. "I've got a steady hand. I'll do a good job. I'd be your own Delilah."

They both smiled.

"You'd better go," he said. "You don't have to hang around like this. It's getting late. You need some rest, too."

"I'm in no rush."

"The kids are waiting downstairs."

"Another couple of minutes won't hurt them." She stroked his hand mindlessly a couple of times, then, surprising herself, and him, too, reached down and stroked his penis, once, through the hospital bedclothes.

"Not a chance," Sigmund said.

"Just so you don't forget," she said. She was laughing.

Velda stuck her head in the doorway. "I'm afraid . . ." she began hesitantly.

"I was just going," Jenny answered, gathering up her pocket-book.

"I hate to rush you," Velda said, entering the room.

"No, no, it's all right." Jenny leaned down and kissed Sigmund again, while he began to cry. "Sigi," she said.

"It's my fish," he managed to answer. "I can't stop thinking about my fish."

"Don't worry about the fish. Everything's being taken care of. Everything's in order."

"I can't help myself. They're always on my mind."

"They're all right. I promise," Jenny said.

After a moment, Velda began to straighten Sigmund's towels, which were already folded in a neat pile on the washbasin. She was embarrassed. "Sit up now, young man," she said, turning to him without warning. "You shouldn't slump like that. It's bad for the circulation." Sigmund lifted himself up on his elbows while Velda plumped his pillows. "Are you comfortable at this angle?" she asked. "Can you sleep at forty-five degrees?"

"If that's what I have to do." He lay back when she finished.

"Fresh water," she mumbled to herself, reaching for the metal jug on the bedside table. "Have you been taking the aspirin? And your angina pills?"

Angina pills. The way Velda said it, she made it sound like Mount Everest. "They said to take the pills if I have any pain."

"Just don't be shy about it. Don't play Mr. Brave."

"I'm going now," Jenny called from the doorway. "I'll see you first thing in the morning. Sleep well, dear heart. Don't worry about a thing. And do what Velda tells you. Good night, both of you."

While Velda arranged the top sheet, Sigmund blew a kiss to his wife. Then, with one motion, she was gone. The hospital silence fell on the room, something thick and pervasive and by now familiar, in which Velda continued to work efficiently, doing her nighttime chores. As she worked, she hummed a cheerful tune by Irving Berlin. "You're looking much improved," she said, glancing up at him after a moment. "Your color is beginning to come back. That's always a good sign."

"If it hadn't been for you . . ." He was too tired to say more.

"The reports are starting to come back from the lab," she went on. "It's all encouraging, although you didn't hear it from me. Anyway, there doesn't seem to be any permanent damage, that's what's important."

"So Dr. Rapoport said."

"Now, if you can learn how to take care of yourself . . ."

He grunted.

". . . there's nothing you won't be able to do. All in moderation, of course."

The phrase he heard ten times a day. All in moderation.

Velda continued to work, filling his water jug at the sink. "The weather's lifted," she said over her shoulder. "And about time, too."

He nodded.

"You'll be much more comfortable now."

He nodded again. He had been perspiring a lot.

She came over to the bed and stood next to him. "Well," she said, waiting.

He was afraid to ask.

She finally spoke up. "Our friend's not doing so great," she said in a small voice. "I thought you should hear that from me, so you don't have to listen to any gossip from the floor."

Sigmund turned his face away.

"A lot of it is the pain," she said. "The pain exhausts him. It eats up all his energy."

Sigmund raised one finger and shook it in protest.

"We'll see," she said firmly. "Everything that can be done is being done, you can be sure of that, and I've been around enough of these cases in my time not to be surprised by anything."

The room grew silent again. Velda reached for Sigmund's hand and stood there holding it for a minute or so. "Anything else you want before I go? Say the word. You know I'm just down the hall at the desk."

Sigmund smiled sleepily.

Velda checked the bedside table again. "If it doesn't bother you, I'll leave the little light on over the sink."

"Yes," he breathed.

"Water," she began to recite to herself. "Medication. Call button. Pan. Is this handy enough for you here? Don't get up during the night if you have to go to the bathroom. Use the pan. That's what it's there for." She took his pulse and stared into his eyes. "Pretty good," she said, scribbling on his chart. "Remember, I go off at eleven. Meanwhile, I'm just down the hall at the desk."

He slept for two hours, inside a blank enclosure, black and viscous, in which nothing moved and nothing appeared. When he awoke, it was to the faint smell of ether. He lay there without moving, trying to locate himself in the soft silence, waiting for the world to start up again. All his sleep was dreamless in the hospital, every night was like a vacuum. An hour passed swiftly. He turned on his right side, on his left, then again on his back, at the prescribed forty-five degrees. Over the sink, in a corner of the room, a dim blue light burned. In the strange light he could see white tiles and a silvery faucet shining. Outside in the hallway, there was a sound of hurried movement, the slap of rubber soles on the linoleum floor, then silence. He shifted again in the bed, floated the top sheet up and let it settle slowly. Even at this hour, he could hear sounds of traffic down below, outside on the streets of the city. Then he dozed a little, awoke to the same sounds of traffic, relieved himself awkwardly into the pan, spotting the floor, and fell back to sleep for another four hours. A black and dreamless sleep, a void in which nothing happened and nothing appeared, as though half his life had been left behind somewhere in Barney Fribush's back yard.

In the morning, there was another rush of activity. Breakfast at the crack of dawn (it seemed), temperature, pulse, heartbeat, bath, shave (he let his mustache go for another day), then, without respite, the doctors, just as he thought it might be time to move his bowels. Dr. Rapoport, an old friend from the House, so clean-shaven and powdered in the early-morning light that he seemed almost disembodied to Sigmund; Dr. Gundersheimer, Dr. Rapoport's tall, skinny associate, who carried a disdainful little expression around his mouth (in Sigmund's opinion); and Dr. Levy, a kid from Brooklyn fresh out of residency, who stood behind the other two during their visits, taking notes, occasionally asking a question of his colleagues but rarely addressing Sigmund directly.

The three doctors moved close to Sigmund, Dr. Levy remaining discreetly in the rear, and went to work, making bantering little jokes among themselves that Sigmund couldn't follow. They took his pulse, they listened to his chest cavity—even Dr. Levy listened to his chest cavity at Dr. Rapoport's insistence—they examined the pupils of his eyes, touched his thyroid, depressed his tongue, examined his swollen ankles, his knees, groin, armpits, thyroid again, then together silently tracked the information on his chart. An astringent smell came from where they stood at the foot of the bed, faces together. Dr. Rapoport smiled. "Not bad, my friend," he said, finally turning to Sigmund. "What is this, the fourth day? Not bad at all."

Sigmund hated it when Dr. Rapoport pretended not to know how long he had been in the hospital. This wasn't the first time. "And what's the condition of my heart this morning?" he asked, with what he hoped was obvious irony. "Remember?" he added. "My heart?"

"Actually, cantor, we're not even sure it *is* your heart," Dr. Rapoport said in bland tones. He waited modestly after delivering this sensational response, then went on. "Although we're sure enough," he added, "and we're certainly acting on that assumption. Anything else, of course, would be remiss. But it just might be a case of severe indigestion. Those things happen. You certainly wouldn't be the first."

Indigestion, Sigmund thought unhappily, his sense of dignity wounded. And there had been all those fat hot dogs on Sunday.

Dr. Gundersheimer bent from the waist and whispered something into Dr. Rapoport's ear. Dr. Rapoport nodded several times, then smiled again at Sigmund. "Let's say for today that you're doing remarkably well. Better, in fact, than we hoped at the start. But at the risk of sounding like a broken record, it's important that you remember . . ." And he went on to list all the orders and commands that Sigmund was to continue to obey without question and all the forbidden pleasures, mostly dietary, that were to be avoided forever, Dr. Levy writing it all down on his clipboard as though it were information that might disappear into thin air without his notes.

"How long . . ." Sigmund then began, after Dr. Rapoport had finished his catalogue of taboos.

"We'll know better by the end of the week. Anyway, it's too soon to be worrying about going home, if that's what's on your mind. You just got here, my friend." Dr. Rapoport laughed pleasantly.

"Because it couldn't happen at a worse time," Sigmund went on. "Rosh Hashana, Yom Kippur, you know what that means."

"In case there's any doubt, cantor, just so we understand each other, you're going to miss the holidays this year. You're not going to be on the pulpit at the House. No two ways about it. I know it's hard, but you'll just have to come to terms with that."

Sigmund's mouth tightened.

"Just put it out of your mind. Don't even consider it," Dr. Rapoport said, his skin almost gleaming in the morning sun. He waited a moment, as though expecting an objection, but Sigmund, brooding at this news although he had already guessed it, remained silent. "Anything else?" Dr. Rapoport asked, turning to his colleagues. Dr. Gundersheimer whispered something into his ear again, the little disdainful expression at the corners of his mouth beginning to annoy Sigmund. Dr. Levy moved closer, the astringent odor following him. "Cantor," Dr. Levy said in a confidential tone. "I hate to bother you like this, but they need your social security number downstairs. Would it be convenient?"

"Hand me my wallet. In the drawer there."

While Sigmund and Dr. Levy managed this transaction, Dr. Rapoport and Dr. Gundersheimer probed a little more, looking into Sigmund's ears, rolling his eyelids up one at a time, poking carefully at his ankles again, leaving their thumb prints on the swollen flesh, and taking a last swipe at his chest. Then, in a moment, chattering, they were gone, Dr. Levy trailing along behind the other two, still making notes on his clipboard.

Almost instantly, Sigmund fell asleep. When he awoke ten

minutes later, Annie was sitting in the visitor's easy chair. "There you are," he said. "I was wondering where you were. What time is it? Where's your mother?"

"Mummy's downstairs, talking to Dr. Rapoport. How do you feel this morning?"

"How should I feel? I'm okay, I guess. They say everything's hunky-dory. They're not even sure I'm sick." He pulled at the bedclothes. "I need a telephone in here," he said. "See what you can do. I feel shut off without a telephone. A radio, too. I miss the radio at night."

"Mummy asked. They said not yet. Just be patient. We're working on it. Are you in any pain this morning?"

He wasn't sure.

She stood up and approached the bed. She was wearing a new dress, one he had never seen before, very simple. Her hair was held in place by a gold barrette. She looked very neat. She looked just like his sister, Shifra Czaferski. She took hold of his hand and Sigmund began to cry again.

"Daddy," she said. "It'll be all right. You know that. They all say."

He turned his head away. "I'm like a girl," he said. "I can't help it. It's humiliating. This crying."

"Don't worry about it, it's good for you," she said. "It gets it out. You're lucky you can cry. Think of all the people in the world who don't know how to cry."

"You think about them," he said, blowing his nose.

Then Jenny walked in, carrying the *Morning Sun*, a copy of the new *Life*, a batch of mail, a list of telephone messages, and Sigmund's metal pocket comb, which he depended on to assure an extra-neat part in his soft fine hair.

They kissed each other on the cheek and quickly went through all the day's opening rituals, Sigmund trying to look bright-eyed and alert, and almost succeeding.

"What's going on down the hall?" Sigmund asked a few minutes later, once Jenny had settled in.

"I couldn't tell. The door's closed. It's always closed."

"Is Toby there?"

"I would think so. She's been sleeping at Hilton Street all week."

"Find out what's going on, please. Nobody seems to know anything."

"Why don't you start worrying about yourself for a change? It wouldn't hurt. Although Dr. Rapoport seemed pretty cheerful just now."

"I worry plenty about myself. I've got nothing else to do."

Sigmund began to smooth out the top sheet. There was a tremor in his left hand that he was trying to hide. The doctors had told him that it was probably inherited, his father had had a tremor like that, not to be self-conscious about it. But he didn't want his wife and daughter to see it. If they noticed it, he would have to answer for it, and he was tired of answering for things. Every day in the hospital, there were new questions. They called it his History. How old was his father when he died? What did he die of? And your mother? they asked. Living, dead? Anyone else, a brother or sister, ever have heart disease? A brother or sister; ridiculous. Anyway, how would he know? He had jilted them all years ago, mother and sisters. They were no longer his, except in his dreams. He wasn't even sure who was alive anymore. His History . . .

"Listen," he said, slipping his left hand under the bedclothes. "Now that we're all together, I want to review the money thing with you. Don't look like that, Jenny, it has to be done, we're always putting it off, and it'll only take a minute. Unfortunately." Sigmund pretended to laugh.

Then he forced Jenny and Annie to listen to his review of the money thing. As he had predicted, the whole review took only a minute or two. The shingled house on Granada Avenue (his perfect little estate, paid up and free of mortgage); the life insurance (not what it should be, but something); Annie's educational policy (limited but useful); his pension from the House (minimal); the blue Chevy, also paid up; social security. And the money sedately sitting in the bank (accumulated over the years at a caterpillar's pace, but with a consistency that had been almost compulsive). While Sigmund talked on, underlining each item by bending one finger back, Jenny and Annie pretended to be bored, yawning and staring out the window, although they were both paying careful attention to what Sigmund was saying. When he finished, Annie got up and rinsed out his water glass, just to keep busy, while Jenny began to sort out the mail at the foot of the bed.

"Do you have all that now?" Sigmund asked. "Sometimes I can't tell with you two."

"Sure," Jenny said, handing him a couple of get-well cards.

"I mean it," Sigmund said. "It's important."

"We know it's important," Jenny answered.

"We should talk about the cemetery plot, too."

"I know all about the cemetery plot. We'll talk about the cemetery plot in another twenty years," Jenny said.

"Jokes," Sigmund said. "Anyway, should I make a list on paper?"

"I know everything by heart."

"Go to Larry Adelman for any advice. If you need advice, Larry Adelman knows everything."

"Larry calls every day. He wants to come to see you."

"Even Mr. Metzger called," Annie put in.

Sigmund made a terrible sound and waved the name away.

"Dr. Rapoport said maybe by Sunday you can have a little company," Jenny added.

But even while his wife and his daughter were speaking, offering their daily reports from the outside world, wandering around the room rearranging things, Sigmund dozed off again, a brief submersion into the waiting void that lasted only a few minutes. When he opened his eyes, Jenny was reading the *Morning Sun* in the easy chair, and Annie was gone.

"Do you want to see the paper?" Jenny asked when she noticed that he was awake.

"I can wait."

"How about a little rubdown?"

"Later."

A nurse whom Sigmund had never seen before came into the room. She checked Sigmund's chart. "Everything all right, sir?" she asked. "Perfect," Sigmund answered. "You're looking better," she said, glancing at him. Sigmund nodded agreeably. "Well," she said, as though there were nothing left to talk about, and left the room, smiling at Jenny.

"I think about Barney all the time," Sigmund said.

"We all do," Jenny answered.

"I worry about him."

"I'll try to find something out," Jenny said, getting up.

"Where did Annie go?"

"She had a few errands."

"Dr. Rapoport said to forget the holidays."

"Well, of course. What did you expect?" Jenny sat down again.

"I never missed a holiday once. Not even when I dislocated my shoulder that time." Sigmund waited a moment, then added, "I have to see Volkonsky."

"You'll see him when you can have company."

"It's very important. There are a lot of things, a lot of decisions to make. Don't forget. Tell him I have to see him."

"When the doctors say so."

"Where is Patton today?"

"Who?"

"The Third Army."

"Here." She handed him the paper. "You'll see, the Orioles won."

"That's very nice," he said. He scanned the front page for news. Patton was heading east, the Russians were racing west. Tokyo was on fire again. There was also a big picture at the top of the page that showed a couple of laughing baseball players hugging each other and pouring champagne on each other's heads.

"They won the whole thing," Jenny said. "The city's going wild."

Sigmund restrained a yawn. "I hope somebody remembers to let Barney know," he said dryly.

So the fourth day passed, with a minimum of pain compared with the preceding three, punctuated by continuing tests, further doctors' visits, naps, meals, and the setting of the late-summer sun. Outside, it had finally begun to really cool off, just as Velda Reese had announced the night before. When Jenny agreed to leave for home at last, Velda was already on duty. Annie was waiting downstairs in the blue Chevy with Bobby, who would do the driving, who had been doing the driving all week (at his own insistence, without Annie's encouragement). As the room quieted down, Sigmund lay back and stretched. He was waiting for his supper tray to be picked up. For a minute or two, he practiced flexing his toes, then his shoulders. After a while, he began to sing softly under his breath, little sotto voce exercises followed by scales and arpeggios, culminating finally in a bar or two of Puccini, something from *La Bohème*. The afternoon paper lay beside him, still waiting to be read. He was discovering that the hospital days were strangely full, there was hardly time to sneak a quick look at the news. He had never known that when he was merely a visitor. Life went on like a whirlwind all around him, leaving him comfortably positioned, almost becalmed, at its very center. The truth tonight was that he was happy that Jenny and Annie were gone at last, happy to be relieved of the obligation of routine and responsibility, happy to be nestled alone in his mechanized bed, where for the moment he felt entirely safe.

In the morning, Sigmund awoke with an erection, feeling cruelly bound by his pajama pants as he lay there at peace in the early light, but sweetly happy, even joyous, at the idea. An erection, he thought to himself with a smile. A hard-on, as he had been told the kids called it, a boner. The blood must be circulating normally. An erection was clear evidence of normal circulation. The stoppages, if stoppages they were, must have opened up. As though he understood those things as well as Dr. Rapoport, Dr. Gundersheimer, and Dr. Levy. When Miss Schuster, the morning nurse, looked in, Sigmund was still smiling.

The implacable routine began. Everything moved fast, by the numbers. The staff had learned a thing or two from the way the army worked. Sigmund went limp, did what he was told, and lay there passively enjoying all the activity going on around him. The nurses liked him for that. He gave them no trouble beyond the expected. He made their lives easier. They didn't understand Dr. Gundersheimer when he complained that Sigmund was irascible. Such a sour face, Dr. Gundersheimer said, working the corners of his mouth. The nurses didn't know what Dr. Gunder-sheimer was talking about. To the nurses, whom he adored, the cantor was totally cooperative, practically the ideal patient.

Meanwhile, as the morning moved on, Sigmund thought about his erection. His blood, his own blood . . . it was so obviously willing, how sick could his heart be? At the thought, it even began to beat a little faster. He couldn't wait to tell Dr. Rapoport. Only the fifth day, and he had already produced an erection.

Around nine o'clock, there was a knock at the door.

"Come in."

A worn, disheveled face peeked in. It was Toby Fedder, wearing no make-up.

"Come in, come in. You're just the person." He hadn't seen her since the picnic, since the wild ride to the hospital.

Toby slipped around the door, glancing nervously over her shoulder, as though she were afraid she might be doing something forbidden. "You've got a nerve," she said to Sigmund, once she was safely inside the room. "Having a heart attack at such a time. I can't leave either of you alone for a minute." She shook her head in mock reproach at Sigmund.

A ghost, he thought as she stood there, distracted and unkempt, making facetious jokes, a ghost with a bloodless white face. "Toby, darling," he said.

"The wreck of the *Hesperus*, right?" she answered. "Well, I'm no beauty to begin with. But tell me how you feel."

"So-so," he said. "But better than yesterday." He smoothed out the top sheet. "Now tell me what's going on."

Toby sat down in the easy chair and crossed her legs, her top-heavy body seeming to sag momentarily. Sighing, she pulled herself up. Then she sighed again before speaking.

"It's not so good," she said.

Sigmund said nothing.

"He's in constant pain," she went on, "and half the time he's out of it from the medication they're giving him. It's making him crazy."

"And the doctors, what do they say?"

"Mumbo jumbo, hocus-pocus. After the operation, they said

he was clean. They bragged that he was clean. Who can believe them now?"

"They didn't want to upset you after the operation. They didn't want to discourage your father."

"It doesn't make any difference, anyway. What they say. Because here we are. Whatever they said then, here we are."

Sigmund nodded his head. A few moments passed uncomfortably.

"Velda tells me you're doing very nicely," Toby said, pulling herself up again.

"Every day is a little better."

"I just wanted to look in, while my father's still asleep."

"You're my first visitor."

"We're just down the hall."

"I know, two doors. So close."

"I don't want to tire you now with chitchat. Tell me if you're getting tired."

"Don't worry," Sigmund said. "All I see all day are white uniforms. It's a treat to have you here."

"My father is asking for you."

"I'll see Barney as soon as they let me out of bed."

"He would like that."

"Is Elsie there?"

"Ah, Elsie," Toby said, rolling her eyes. "Suddenly she can't move her right arm. Suddenly her right arm is like a board. The doctor says it's a sympathetic paralysis. Sympathetic for my father." Toby shook her head in disbelief.

They stared at each other for another moment or two, thinking about Elsie and other things, an old communal current of combined anxiety and kindness flowing eerily between them, so powerful that it soon became unbearable to both. When she couldn't stand it anymore, Toby got to her feet. Her skirt was twisted to one side. There was cigarette ash on the front of her blouse. "You don't have to go," Sigmund said.

"I just wanted to see you with my own eyes. You look better than I hoped."

I had an erection this morning, he wanted to say. "You know,

Jenny and Annie will be here any minute. If you need anything . . ."

"Thanks." By now, Toby was at the door.

"Are you getting enough rest?" Sigmund asked. "It's important
to take a break every now and then and get some rest."

"When you visit my father," she said, without looking at Sigmund, "there's sometimes a smell. You should be prepared."

"Yes."

"Ta-ta," she said and slipped out the door.

An hour later, Sigmund was able to tell Dr. Rapoport, who was
making his rounds alone this morning, about his erection and his
theories about it.

"That is a very positive manifestation, of course," Dr. Rapoport
said, not quite so close-shaven and gleaming this morning as he
had been the day before, and sounding tired as well; too many
overnight emergencies, Sigmund judged. "It's a good sign, all
right," Dr. Rapoport went on, "just as you say, and it certainly
won't do your morale any harm."

Sigmund blushed with pleasure. A-plus, head of the class.

"By the way," Dr. Rapoport continued, looking intently down
at the patient, "we're pretty sure now that it *was* your heart and
not just a false alarm. That's what all the test results indicate. We
can't always tell, you know. All those gullies and muscles and
rivulets in there are so delicately bound together that they sometimes fool us. I mean, we're not always sure. Everything relies on
everything else. Everything is interdependent. Yet everything has
its own mysterious right of way. That's why we hold our breath
every time we open up a patient. One palsied move . . . In any
case, we're pretty confident now about your condition. From all
the evidence so far, I think I've already suggested this, it seems
clear that the damage is not major and may not be permanent.
We can only hope so."

"Right," Sigmund said, taking in a long breath as he considered
the doctor's words. Not major, not permanent. Not bad. An unfamiliar feeling of elation passed through him; very sweet. "You

know," he added after a moment, "I still have this tremor in my left hand." He held out his hand to show the doctor.

"You'll probably have that for the rest of your life," Dr. Rapoport said, gently lowering Sigmund's hand onto the bed. "It's just a genetic thing. I've told you that before. It's very common. Let's say you'll probably have it for another thirty, thirty-five years."

"Oh, sure."

Dr. Rapoport smiled as he prepared to scold the patient. "That's not good enough, cantor?" he asked. "Thirty-five years wouldn't satisfy you?"

"I didn't mean it that way," Sigmund said. "I was being sarcastic. Thirty years would suit me fine."

"You'll have thirty years and more."

Sigmund pondered the prospect of three decades; that would get him to at least 1974, which at the moment seemed impossibly remote. But it was nice to think about, it had a substantial heft to it. "Will I have to measure out my life, bit by bit," he then asked, "the way I see other sick people doing? That would be hard. That would be hard on me and everybody around me. I'm not sure I want to measure out my life like that, a little here, a little there."

Dr. Rapoport began to chew on his lower lip. "Well, you might consider the alternative," he said, deciding to be tough. "Instead of complaining prematurely. And anyway," he went on, "we don't know yet how you're going to have to live. There's no telling at this point. Although your life will surely change, it's inevitable, and you'd better be prepared for it."

A fixed, very concentrated expression came over Sigmund's face, as Dr. Rapoport continued to lecture him.

"You're just feeling angry that you're a patient," Dr. Rapoport went on. "The 'Why me?' syndrome. It happens to everybody. It's practically a commonplace. You must see it all the time, in your position. People furious at reality?"

"I see enough," Sigmund said, beginning to quiet down. "Like you, I'm sure."

"Right, like me." Dr. Rapoport laughed for the first time that morning.

"Doctor," Sigmund began against his better judgment, as Dr. Rapoport made a move to withdraw. "I've been meaning to ask."

"What is it?" The doctor glanced at his watch.

"I don't want you to misunderstand, it's none of my business, every man has his own way, especially Jews, but it interests me. Someone in your profession. Tell me, do you believe in God?"

"Cantor."

"It's a serious question."

"Do I believe in God."

"That's the question."

"All piety is false, all belief is delusion," Dr. Rapoport said bluntly. "God is man's creation, probably his greatest."

Which was exactly Sigmund R. Safer's opinion, and had been all his life, yet hearing it stated aloud in his hospital room, he found his heart sinking bleakly at Dr. Rapoport's stony words. "That's what you believe?" he asked.

"That's what I believe. Isn't that what you asked me?" Dr. Rapoport waited a moment. "Had enough?" he asked solicitously, in the face of Sigmund's silence. "I could say more. About man and God, I mean. But I don't want to offend you, and this is a pretty silly conversation when you consider who we are and where we are."

"I'm not offended. Not at all. I'm interested. No crime in that. We'll have to talk some more."

"There'll be plenty of opportunity."

"So you think the erection is a good sign?"

"Cantor, the whole world was built on an erection. Where would we be . . ."

"I'm not talking about the whole world," Sigmund interrupted. "I'm talking about my erection. My heart. What else?" He made a little dismissive gesture. "And next time, doctor," he went on, "come again without your cohorts. We don't really need those other two, do we? Three's a crowd."

In response, Dr. Rapoport merely chuckled and reached down to pat Sigmund on the shoulder. "I'm running late this morning," he said, checking his watch again. "And it's your fault. All that fancy talk. I'll see you tomorrow. Keep up the good work. You're really coming along."

"Come over here, I've got a surprise for you."

Jenny moved slowly alongside the bed, weary tonight from having done single duty all day. Annie had stayed home to clean the house, to shop, to take telephone messages, to help do all the ordinary chores that lay dormant but urgent on Granada Avenue. Annie was very competent, Jenny had discovered, not for the first time—competent and decisive. It helped.

"What is it, dear heart?" she asked.

Sigmund took his wife's hand and placed it on the bedclothes.

Jenny smiled. "You *are* ambitious, aren't you?"

"Don't you think it's a good sign? Dr. Rapoport says so. It means . . ."

"I think I know what it means." She removed her hand.

"Still," he said, a little disappointed at Jenny's response. "You're tired, aren't you?" he asked. "That's it, you must be exhausted."

"I don't know why I should be exhausted," she answered. "I don't do anything all day."

"Except take care of me."

"What do I do? The nurses do everything."

"The waiting and the sitting and all the rest. The whole week, since Sunday. Why don't you take the day off tomorrow? Let Annie come in for an hour or two. Really. It would be good for everybody."

"We'll see." She was having trouble staying awake tonight.

"I'm worried about you getting home."

"There's always a cab on the street."

"You'll see, I'll be out of here in no time."

"What's the rush? You know that as soon as you get home . . ."

"It's just the fish. And the roses, too. I worry about them. There's a Siamese killer in the big tank, he could wreck everything."

"It's all in order. Bobby's taking care of the fish, and he waters the flowers out back every day with Annie."

"After the sun is down, I hope," Sigmund said unkindly. "And what does Bobby know about fish, anyway? I never heard him express any interest in fish."

"As long as he can read. There's directions on all the fish food, and your fish encyclopedia is there. He's even learning how to handle those awful worms."

"I'll bet."

"You see? You're not even home yet and you're aggravated."

"Make sure he doesn't overdo it. Tomorrow I'll write out a list for him. I don't want to see a bunch of swollen fish floating bottom-up when I get home."

"All set now?" Jenny asked, ready to change the subject.

"You'd better go."

"I am. And congratulations."

"Congratulations?"

"For rising to the occasion," Jenny said. "Get it?"

That was more like it. Sigmund waved Jenny off, smiling weakly, and stared at the ceiling as the hospital silence began to close in again. My Jenny, he thought, trying unsuccessfully to trace her image in the bland whiteness of the ceiling. Somehow he couldn't seem to find the necessary playful energy tonight. The ceiling remained absolutely blank. Friday night, he suddenly remembered. It was *shabbos*. The Sabbath. Holy of Holies. When Sigmund on his pulpit became King of Kings. He had almost forgotten, after only five days. It was his first Friday night in the hospital.

"You're some pal," Velda said, standing at the foot of the bed not long after Jenny had left. "I thought you were going to help me find a husband."

"It's not easy when you're stuck here like this, Velda."

"Come on, everybody beats a path to your door. You don't have to lift a finger."

"Okay," Sigmund said. "What about that Dr. Levy?"

"The little squirt? From Brooklyn?"

"He seems very smart, very nice. He's always writing things down."

"He comes up to my *pupik*."

Sigmund whooped, good spirits momentarily restored with

one word. "Where'd you get that? *Pupik?*" He whooped again.

"You can hardly work in this place without picking up a word or two. And I told you I wanted to marry a Hebrew. It doesn't hurt to have a word or two ready."

"I'll keep an eye out for you. I promise. As soon as they let me out of bed."

"You do that for me. Because I'm not getting any younger, you know." She began to poke at her frizz.

"Did they find somebody down the hall for my friend?"

"They've got two specials. At last. They're like needles in a haystack these days. You're lucky you don't need specials."

"I'm lucky to have you, you mean."

"To share."

"I don't mind sharing."

"Anyway, somebody relieved Toby this afternoon."

Sigmund grunted painfully. "Won't you get in trouble hanging around in here like this?" he asked.

"You've got five minutes coming to you."

"Because I have to go to the bathroom. And I don't want to use the pan."

"Important?"

"Crucial."

"Have you been regular?"

"On and off. My usual."

"Come on, I'll give you a hand." She came alongside the bed. "Just sit up slowly. Right. Slow. Now swing around," she said, waiting for him. "Not too fast there. Here, take my arm. Wait a minute now, while I put on your slippers. Just lift your feet a little. Good boy. Easy does it. That's right. One step at a time. One foot in front of the other. Feels like there's water where your knees used to be, right? Great. That's great. Don't get greedy, now. Don't push. You're almost there. Hold on. You're doing real great. It's almost a home run, cantor . . ."

They wanted to let him out of bed the next morning, as a controlled experiment. "Once up and down the hall," Dr. Rapoport said. "We'll see how you manage. But it's your decision, it's strictly up to you." Standing next to Dr. Rapoport, Dr. Gundersheimer nodded encouragement with a vacant expression on his face. Dr. Levy was absent today, off on a forty-eight-hour leave. Always in the background when the doctors were visiting, Miss Schuster, the morning nurse, was in and out of the room between chores, looking quietly pleased at the news. "Do you feel up to it?" Dr. Rapoport asked.

Sigmund wasn't sure. Last night's clandestine little excursion across his room to the lavatory had left him exhausted, far more exhausted than he had bargained for. He had had to wait for five minutes in the tiny enclosure, feeling dizzily claustrophobic, fearing he might actually pass out sitting there on a strange toilet, before venturing back to bed when his strength finally returned. And he had done it alone, not waiting for Velda's help, as he had promised, so eager was he for the comfort and safety of his ugly metal bed. It was as they said, everything had a price, every effort cost something. At this moment, while the doctors continued to wave their invisible magic wands over him, he felt like sending them away, dismissing them as irrelevant, as incompetent. For all their talk of a controlled experiment, he was too tired today to get out of bed. They should know that as well as he did, without explanation. This unexpected fatigue, this slowing of the blood again, this unwillingness of the muscles to respond . . . he knew he had to expect it. Yesterday's sudden renewed energy had put him off his guard. Yesterday was yesterday. One day at a time, they said at the hospital. It seemed like the essence of worldly wisdom to Sigmund. Certainly, he had not had an erection when he woke up this morning.

"I'd like to wait until after lunch," Sigmund said. "Maybe in another couple of hours."

"You're the judge," Dr. Rapoport said. "The important thing is not to overdo it. Moderation. That's the byword. If you don't feel like trying today, there's always tomorrow."

"I understand," Sigmund said. And where was Jenny this morning? he asked himself irritably. And Annie, too. They were late this morning.

"Cantor," Dr. Gundersheimer put in. "Your blood pressure has been normal now for two days."

"I'm glad to hear it."

"All vital signs are robust."

What was he talking about, with that expression around his mouth that had just turned disdainful?

Miss Schuster was now back in the room, waiting at the steel washbasin. Dr. Rapoport stepped aside. Dr. Gundersheimer checked Sigmund's chart for a third time. There was a flurry of activity outside in the hall, the soft purr of rubber wheels, a glimpse through the open door of a rolling stretcher, white sheets, a black orderly. Rev-run. Why didn't they all just leave him alone? He was tired. He was paying his dues for yesterday's high spirits. That was one of the things he would have to learn. Life would be erratic. And moderated. Already, it had begun to shrink. He closed his eyes.

"Okay, my friend," Dr. Rapoport said, all business today. He hadn't given a sign that he even remembered their exchange from yesterday, all that no-nonsense talk about piety and faith. "We're off," he added. "See you in the morning."

The two doctors left after a word with Miss Schuster. "Just yell for me," she said to Sigmund, "whenever you're ready to try."

"I meant what I said," Sigmund answered. "I'll wait."

"You're the judge," Miss Schuster said and left the room.

So all that was out of the way. The essential morning stuff, everything that was inescapable, the routine. The paper lay at his side, untouched; Miss Schuster had delivered it right after breakfast. The novel by Franz Werfel that had been his unread companion all summer sat on the metal table next to the bed, on top of Sigmund's copy of the new *Life*. A few get-well cards were scattered around and several vases filled with flowers sent by members of the House. Through the open window he could see the city slowly cooling off, even as the sun rose. It was a break, everyone needed it, the Baltimore heat made people crazy. Dr. R. had even suggested that it might have had something to do with his heart attack. The extra sustained pressure and charged effort for which no one was ever prepared . . . He placed the palm of his right hand over his chest and waited. Nothing. Then he counted to five. Not an echo. Should he ring for Miss Schuster? Then, with his palm still resting on his chest, an overwhelming urge came over him to write to his mother and his two sisters and tell them what had happened. My darling mother. I have something to tell you. Dear sisters, my beloved Bronya and Shifra. Now hear this . . .

His mind skittering, his heart palpitating quietly, if only he knew where to locate it, Sigmund lay there gazing out the window at the late-summer sky. An hour slowly passed. Where were Jenny and Annie this morning? His family had finally deserted him, leaving not a word, not a message, not even a warning. They were probably out having a good time with Bobby Fiorentino. They were probably all enjoying themselves in each other's company, driving around town in his blue Chevy, using up his gas coupons. Sigmund began to pull at the bedclothes, gasping as an avalanche of anxiety suddenly threatened to bury him. All the wicked familiar things, all the enemies, busy undermining him. It was too much for one morning, too much for Sigmund R. Safer, even though he easily recognized his poisonous old companion, paranoia, hard at work.

Ten minutes later, calm at last after a bitter struggle with himself, robed and slippered, his hair neatly parted and combed, Sigmund stood outside Barney Fribush's room. His knees were still like water, he felt as though he had no spine, he was even a little dizzy, but he had made the twenty feet down the hall alone, shuffling slowly, staying close to the wall. Already, resting there and gathering his energy, he felt stronger. He waited a moment before knocking. When he tapped on the door, nothing happened. He knocked again. The door opened a few inches and a strange face appeared. "Is Toby here?" Sigmund asked.

"After lunch," the strange face said.

"Are you the special?"

The strange face nodded. That was another thing about the hospital, it was filled with strange faces.

"I'm Cantor Safer. Mr. Fribush's friend. We came in together. In the same ambulance. Sunday night."

Another nod, touched by skepticism.

"We're old friends, for many years," Sigmund went on, as though he were explaining the creation of the world. "Can I have just one minute with Barney?"

"Please wait," she said and closed the door. Sigmund could hear the growl of a familiar voice inside the room. Then the door opened again. "Only one minute," she said, coming out into the corridor. "And don't bring up anything that will disturb him."

"Naturally," Sigmund said, stepping into the room.

There was the patient lying on his side, his back turned to Sigmund as it had been turned to him weeks before in a room upstairs. This time, however, his pajamas were in place and there was no ultraviolet lamp baking his flesh. A vaguely familiar odor hovered everywhere in the room, another pervasive hospital presence, acrid and soon unmistakable.

"Well," Sigmund said, moving around the bed.

"You're a fine one," Barney replied. His voice was hoarse.

"So."

"Everything I do, you have to do. It's always been that way."

Sigmund made a pained face.

"They tell me you had a heart attack. Is that what you were doing in my goldfish pond?"

Sigmund made another face.

"Say something, for God's sake."

"I don't feel natural with you down there and me standing here like this."

Barney drew up his right leg and slowly stretched it. He then shifted in the bed and did the same thing with his left leg, even more slowly. The whole exercise took a full minute. "I do this to stop the cramps," he said. "Especially in the thighs. It's worse in the thighs. Usually they want me to lay on my stomach."

"The question is how you feel."

"The question is how I am, not how I feel. With me, I'd say it's hopeless."

"Don't talk like that."

"I'm telling you. So you better pay attention."

"Barney."

"Don't give me an argument now. You're always giving me an argument." He began to clear his throat. "Now do me a favor, get me some water over there. With the ice chips. I've got this mucous."

Sigmund filled a glass with water and ice and, walking over to the bed, helped his friend take a few sips. Bending over, trying not to spill any water on the bed linen, he could hear Barney's gulps as though they were thunderclaps, but the mere action of holding the glass to his lips and helping him drink made Sigmund feel better. "What else can I do for you?" he asked when Barney had finished.

"Pray."

Sigmund winced at the edge in Barney's voice. "Beyond that," he said forcefully. "Something practical, something real."

"You can sing over my grave when the time comes."

Sigmund decided to change the subject. "Are you in a lot of pain?" he asked.

Barney rolled his eyes, like Toby. "I'm a dope fiend," he said. "Can't you tell? They made me a dope fiend in one week. That's how much pain."

The nurse suddenly stuck her head in the door, making deliberate noises to alert them. "I think that's probably enough for one day," she said. "Maybe you can stop in tomorrow for a couple of minutes."

"Whatever you say," Sigmund answered, ready to follow all her instructions.

"Toby says you're doing all right," Barney whispered.

"At least I'm standing on my own two feet."

Then Barney groaned, whether from pain or despair Sigmund couldn't tell.

"I think it would be better . . ." the nurse began, moving toward the bed.

"Right."

He left the room slowly, shuffling his feet again despite himself, and feeling embarrassed by it. He hoped Barney's nurse didn't notice. He hoped no one would notice. Staying even closer to the wall this time, he made his way down the hall to his own room, twenty feet, three minutes, looking at the floor the whole time. Counting each step. Measuring each breath. Thinking about his friend groaning in bed. When he got to his room, it took all his energy to push the heavy door open. Inside, Jenny was sitting in the easy chair, looking worried.

"What are you doing out of bed?" she asked. "Where have you been?"

"The doctors said," Sigmund explained, sitting on the edge of his bed, trying to get his breath back.

"Said what?"

"That I could go for a little walk."

"You look as though you didn't sleep all night."

Slowly Sigmund rolled over on his back and pulled up his bedclothes. He felt a moment's bliss. "I stopped in to see Barney," he said. "For a couple of minutes."

Sigmund closed his eyes and a lurid image of his friend appeared.

"Sigi? Are you all right?"

"Please. Don't nag me. It was only a minute. It did me good. I think it helped him, too. It was worth it. And why are you so late this morning?"

"I decided to go to services," Jenny said. "I wanted to be near people who know who I am. The rabbi made an announcement to the congregation. He made a nice little speech about you."

Sigmund waited a moment. "And who led the service?" he finally asked, unable to keep the jealousy out of his voice.

"Volkonsky. Sam."

"Volkonsky? Whose idea was that? Volkonsky doesn't have a voice."

"He can carry a tune," Jenny said. "He did all right."

"A tune. Is that what you think it's all about? A tune?"

"Look at you. Red in the face. So Sam took the service. It'll make the congregation miss you more than ever. Think of it that way."

But he was already asleep in the sudden silence, this time deeply. As he lay there on his back, mouth half open, making faint wheezing sounds, a huge angel fish swam across his vision, flicking its tail impatiently. Dozens of other fish followed, gorgeously iridescent, breaking formation, then reforming in straight-line patterns for the master's approval. It was Sigmund's first dream in the hospital. When he awoke, his lunch tray was being placed in front of him by an orderly. He blinked once, trying to remember his dream, but he was only able to feel a presence, a mood, shadowy and persistent, but not at all unpleasant; the details had already vanished into the bottomless repository of old Safer dreams. Sigmund examined the lunch tray. Fruit juice, a sickly yellow. Chicken, again. Mashed potatoes that were almost liquid. Something green. Bread as white as flour and soft as cotton. Slippery Jell-O.

"Let me help you with your napkin," Jenny said.

Sigmund sat up and leaned forward, while Jenny tucked his napkin into his pajama top. With his first hospital dream, he felt he had received an unmistakable signal of approaching well-being. From himself, to himself. He would be all right, the dream said. His heart would heal. Why not, he asked himself, why not Sigmund R. Safer, too, even in moderation? Sigmund stared at his food. From his vantage point, sitting up in a hospital bed wearing a bib, it looked totally disgusting, designedly so, he thought, more repellent than ever, yet he found himself beginning to eat with a relish that instantly gave him deep pleasure, even the white bread and the liquid potatoes, even the gray and flabby chicken, the green thing, and the slippery red Jell-O. Yes; he felt as though he had received an unmistakable sign of well-being.

"Thank God, you're alone this morning," Sigmund said, sounding pleased as Dr. Rapoport approached his bed without his colleagues.

"It's Sunday," Dr. Rapoport said. "Everybody has to have a day off. And how are you today?"

"Pretty good."

"Let me see your ankles."

Dr. Rapoport bent over, probing. As he worked, he made little grunting comments to himself. Sigmund lay still and tried to relax under his touch. A stranger's fingers, he thought; less strange each day. Dr. Rapoport was dressed for an event this morning. Navy-blue suit, white shirt, tie, silver tie pin. Early-morning translucent skin, gleaming. He poked at Sigmund halfheartedly, listened to his chest, thumped a bit, then stood up straight. He was smiling. Sigmund smiled back. "You're all dressed up today," Sigmund said.

"The Richman boy is getting married at noon," Dr. Rapoport said.

"I don't know any Richman boy," Sigmund said.

"From Seven Mile Lane," Dr. Rapoport answered. "Reformed."

Sigmund nodded and reminded himself about Reformed. He often forgot Reformed. Reformed was elsewhere, it was other people, it was free of dogma, there were no ritual obligations, there were no obligations at all. Maybe they had the right idea. "I've been thinking about our conversation," Sigmund said, sitting up straighter.

"Not much to think about," the doctor said after a pause, looking as though he clearly believed the opposite.

"I don't agree with that. Not at all. Those things are always on my mind."

"Well, given your position," Dr. Rapoport said. "But you shouldn't take everything I say too seriously. It was just one of those little outbursts that we're all prone to occasionally. If what I said was right, what difference does it make? If I'm wrong, we're all in for a nice surprise. Anyway, where does it get you?"

"It stirred me up."

Dr. Rapoport said nothing.

"What I mean," Sigmund went on, "is that I'm not sure I disagree with you."

"You're just feeling vulnerable, cantor, like anybody who's gone through what you're going through."

"No, it's more than that," Sigmund said, gaining confidence. "You and I know each other too well by now to kid about such things."

"You caught me in an off moment."

"I know the truth when I hear it."

"Okay, if it makes you happy," the doctor said resignedly.

"Now," he went on, brightening, "I'm told you were out of bed yesterday. How'd it go?"

"Just down the hall to see Barney Fribush."

"Out of bed is good. But I'm not so sure about Barney Fribush. Did it upset you to see him like that?"

"Of course it upset me."

"Maybe you should walk in the other direction next time."

"It was important for me to see him."

"I'm not sure you should let yourself be exposed yet . . ."

"It didn't depress me, if that's what you mean."

"I'm not talking about depression. I'm talking about strain. It's still early for you to deal with any strain. You haven't learned yet how to think about your own problem, much less Barney Fribush's."

"You keep saying that," Sigmund responded. "We have the same conversation every day. You know I'm a good patient. Everybody says so. And I don't have any illusions about what happened to me. I do everything everybody tells me to do. And everybody tells me. You know, there's too much lecturing going on around here. I hate being lectured. Everybody hates being lectured."

"That's quite a mouthful."

"And don't talk to me as though I'm a child. You have a habit, with all respect. You all do."

"Piss and vinegar this morning."

"Well, I'm feeling better. I'm feeling stronger. And I want a telephone in here. And a radio."

"Just ask for them."

"I have, but nobody listens to me."

"Then I'll ask, too. I have some influence around here."

There was only a moment's pause before Sigmund said, "When you're looking inside where the heart is, what do you see?"

Dr. Rapoport began to fool with the knot of his tie. "What do I see?" he finally asked himself, looking faintly alarmed. "Well, blood, mainly blood, then muscle, tissue, fat, a lot of fat, always fat. A few other things."

"And it's the same for everybody?"

"Given the usual variations among people. There are always

those, more extensive than you might think. In size, in length and mass, those things. Even inside, no two people are alike. I once saw a colon . . ."

"But that's all you see. Details."

"What are you getting at, cantor?" Dr. Rapoport asked, proceeding with care.

"What am I getting at?" Sigmund repeated, also sounding careful. "Actually, I'm not sure. Now that you mention it."

"I mean, the body is the body," Dr. Rapoport went on. "How much can you ask of it?"

"I'm not asking anything," Sigmund said. "But after all the body is the source of everything. Right? Mind, spirit, feelings, sensation. It's where the soul lives, yes? There's nothing as real as that."

"Or as beautiful," Dr. Rapoport added, after a moment.

"Beautiful," Sigmund repeated, looking down at himself doubtfully. "Yes. But don't forget sacred, too," he added.

Dr. Rapoport shook his head. "Beautiful is enough," he said.

"But not for all of us," Sigmund answered. He waited for Dr. Rapoport to respond, but the doctor remained silent. The exchange was apparently over. "Anyway," Sigmund said, "remember, I'm a cantor, a clergyman, a *hazzan*. Right? Why are you smiling like that? You think I'm joking? Sacred is important. Especially for me. I have a vested interest."

As Dr. Rapoport reached for Sigmund's hand, they looked each other in the eye.

And began to laugh.

"Why are you wearing those silly-looking glasses? They make you look old-fashioned. They make you look like a pedant."

"Cantor, I don't even know what a pedant is. And you're a fine one to talk. You wear a pince-nez. You're wearing them now."

"I'm going to give them up as soon as I get out of here and become modern. I'm going to get horn-rimmed. I'm going to be up-to-date like everybody else. And as soon as I have the strength, I'm going to shave off my mustache."

"I thought I was going to do that," Jenny put in from the other side of the room.

"All right, you're going to do that. What difference does it
make?"

"You look good with your mustache," Volkonsky said. "Everybody always says that. It's becoming."

"I'm sick of my mustache. I'm sick of my pince-nez. I'm sick of
the hospital, too, if you really want to know. And a few other
things. Okay, now tell me, what's going on? How are rehearsals?
You know, I'm not going to be there when the time comes. That's
the law, issued from above. I'm not going to be on the pulpit for
the holidays. For the first time. For the first time ever." Tears
began to form. "But that's not the point," Sigmund quickly added,
turning away for a moment. "The point is that the choir has to
do it alone. The whole thing. Under your supervision, of course.
That's why we have to talk. You'll have to learn how to improvise
and move fast. Everybody will have to be on full alert. Achtung!
You're in charge. No fooling around. No wasting time. That goes
for the kids, too. The kids especially."

"The kids I'm not worried about."

"The altes will have to carry the burden," Sigmund said. "Gozlov,
Frisch, and Bourne. And there's only one in that bunch you can
really depend on for the serious business."

"You mean Bourne."

"Correct. He's the only one. He should have all the repeats
and all my solos. Silent Devotion and everything else. He knows
it backwards, forwards, upside-down. He should do my part."

"I think the same thing."

"Of course, he'll be only too happy."

"If I know him."

"And it's nobody's business but ours. You understand that, don't
you?"

"How do you mean?"

"I'm the boss. You're the director. I know. You know. Nobody
else outside the choir has to know about Bourne until the time
comes. If the rabbi questions you about the service, you tell him
it's all peaches and cream, nothing to worry about."

"Sigi," Jenny put in, "you're beginning to overexcite yourself."

"It's business, my darling one. It has to be done." Then, turning
back to Volkonsky, "No one should know. Jeffrey Bourne does

my solos. Jeffrey Bourne takes over. For the holidays, Jeffrey Bourne is the cantor. Jeffrey Bourne does the Silent Devotion."

"Are you sure that's what you want?" Jenny asked, looking worried.

"Of course I'm sure."

"Maybe you should think it over a bit."

"For the holidays, Jeffrey Bourne is the cantor," he repeated. "He does Silent Devotion." This time, Sigmund called it by its Hebrew name.

Jenny, knowing when she was beaten, lowered her eyes and silently gave up.

Volkonsky was Sigmund's first real visitor from the world outside. Earlier, Annie had suggested that Bobby be allowed upstairs for "a sec," he had been so helpful, always ready for anything that was needed of him, all week long. But Sigmund had other ideas. He thought the blue Chevy was the perfect resting place for Bobby Fiorentino, out on the street. For the time being. For another week, at least. Certainly for the foreseeable future. When he had said no, Annie had given a quick little nod and made a quick little face that looked insincere. "He's really your friend, you know," was all she said with only a slight edge. But she didn't push it; she was still on her best behavior, and already she and Bobby were beginning to confront a future apart. Then, later in the day, around three o'clock, after Volkonsky had left with his orders, Larry Adelman showed up, bearing a copy of *The Brothers Ashkenazi* and a bouquet of yellow roses.

"I couldn't stay away," he said, seating himself in the visitor's chair with a long serious face, after Jenny had gotten up to pace the corridor outside, welcoming a break.

For ten minutes they delicately talked around every subject, the rabbi, Julie Metzger, Norman Sindel, that gang, and then, after making a wary circle and dispensing quickly with the question of Sigmund's will, which Larry reiterated several times was in perfect order, started in again on the same themes.

"Let's just forget it," Sigmund said, growing weary of the repetition. "Somehow, it doesn't mean a thing in the hospital."

Then, after Jenny rejoined them, they talked about the war,

the Orioles, and the question of the fourth term for FDR. This took five minutes. Whatever the subject under discussion, Larry Adelman never smiled, remaining ponderously enclosed in his furry, serious self, which was how he always was on visits to the hospital. Finally, pulling himself together before leaving, and making sure that Jenny heard, he said, "You know, you must not worry. The House is taking care of everything. There should only be one thing on your mind. Getting well." Then he said it again a few minutes later, hardly changing his words as he moved out of the room with obvious relief.

Two more faces showed themselves before evening. First, Toby's husband, Irwin, in for the day from Chevy Chase and chemical warfare. He stuck his face around the door of Sigmund's room and waved energetically. Hi-ya, fella, he called. Thinking of you, he said, always thinking of you. Then, when he saw how tired Sigmund seemed, he was gone. After Irwin, Bobby Fiorentino, none other, appearing somewhat daunted, unable to look the patient in the eye, showed up, with Annie in tow. I'm being punished, Sigmund thought when he caught sight of Bobby Fiorentino holding on to his daughter's hand. Bobby Fiorentino was wearing his Sunday clothes again, just like Dr. R., black suit, speckled tie, pink crepe-soled shoes. He looks like a yokel just in from the sticks, Sigmund thought. God help me. For the first time in the hospital, Sigmund clicked his teeth. His nostrils dilated and he began to turn his head from side to side on the pillow as though he were in excruciating pain. "I told you," Bobby said to Annie under his breath, clearly scared. They left quickly, tugging at each other.

Nevertheless, that night, after Jenny and Annie and Bobby Fiorentino had left for Forest Park, after Sunday supper and a quick bout with the Sunday paper, advances, retreats, air raids, the latest casualty lists, heavy today, and, of course, the Orioles, who were everywhere in the paper and about whose draft status Sigmund had just begun to wonder, Sigmund sat up in bed, reached for his slippers with his feet, rose like an emaciated ghost, put on his robe, and made his way, in spasmodic jerks, the twenty feet down the hall to his friend's room.

When he knocked on Barney's door, another strange face appeared. "Yes?" it asked.

"I'm Cantor Safer, Mr. Fribush's friend. I just want to say good night to him."

The special fooled with her bra strap while she considered Sigmund. "I don't even know you," she said.

"To say good night to my friend," Sigmund repeated impatiently. "To Mr. Fribush." Again he clicked his teeth.

"Hold it a minute." She closed the door in Sigmund's face, then quickly reappeared. "Make it snappy now," she said. "He's a little groggy tonight. And it's late. I'll wait out here. Don't overdo it."

Barney was lying on his side, facing the door, his cheek cushioned on his folded hands. He closed his eyes when Sigmund approached him, then slowly opened them. Sigmund saw him nod, by way of greeting. His eyes were bloodshot.

"I just came to say good night," Sigmund said.

"So good night."

"How do you feel?"

Barney closed his eyes again, then instantly opened them.

"I don't want to disturb you," Sigmund said.

"You're not disturbing me."

"Is the pain any better?"

Barney freed a hand, lifted one leg with a terrific effort, and pointed to his crotch.

"Is that where it hurts?"

Barney shook his head yes and lowered his leg.

A silence followed, contained within another silence. The room was dimly lit. An opened basket of fruit sat on the dresser, and the familiar acrid odor hovered everywhere. Sigmund made a move to leave.

"Want to make yourself useful?" Barney asked.

"Just tell me how."

"Rub my back with some of that alcohol."

"Would you like that?"

"Don't make me say everything twice."

Sigmund picked up a bottle of rubbing alcohol that was sitting on the bedside table and walked around to the other side of the bed.

"Just lift up my pajama top," Barney said, resting his cheek again on his two hands.

Sigmund did as he was told, staring at Barney's upper back, which was spotted with aging freckles and marked by two protruding angel wings. A stranger's body, Sigmund thought, pausing a moment—the skinny body of a boy, almost without flesh. Then he quickly poured some alcohol into his hands and, making small, firm, circular motions, the way Velda did every night, he began to rub Barney's back.

"Ah," Barney said.

"Am I hurting you?"

"No, no. Just slow. Go slow. Ah, that's nice, I can smell it, it's nice."

Sigmund then began to work on Barney's lower back, beginning at the base of the spine, where a faint tuft of hair sprouted.

"You should know I'm in love with your wife," Barney said.

"You're in love with everybody's wife." Sigmund's hands began to move in straight lines, up and down, pressing deeper into the bony flesh.

"I thought you should know."

"Thanks." A pinch of sciatica nipped Sigmund's left thigh as he worked.

"Also, I decided to turn down their offer."

"What offer?"

"The first president." Barney made a sound like a laugh, very moist, very deep in his throat.

"I should hope so," Sigmund answered. "And the same goes for me. And how."

So that was all done with.

"Also, I never slept with any other woman besides my wife," Barney went on.

To this, Sigmund said nothing.

"A little higher," Barney said. "Around the shoulders again."

Sigmund pressed harder on Barney's upper back, where the

freckles and the angel wings were. The smell of the rubbing alcohol was beginning to make him alert.

"You don't mind that I'm in love with your wife?" Barney asked.

"As long as she doesn't return the favor." Sigmund marveled at his own poise.

Barney thought for a moment. "No," he said. "Also, I once stole a couple thousand dollars," Barney went on. "From myself. From the factory. To pay off some goons. I never repaid it."

Sigmund shrugged, even though Barney couldn't see him.

"And I'll tell you something else. I've been voting Republican for four years, ever since that guy Willkie showed up."

"You and Joe Allen," Sigmund said, referring to a past president of the House who in his day had been the only Republican in the congregation.

"Actually," Barney said, "I slept with Cissy Sheer three times, once she gave me a blow job."

Sigmund began to work on Barney's lower back again, carefully avoiding the thin tuft of hair. He could almost count the knobs on Barney's spine.

"So if you add it all up, I'm a thief, a pervert, and an adulterer. Other things, too."

"It could be worse."

"For God's sake, is that all you have to say? It could be worse. Why don't you say you forgive me?"

"That's not my . . ." Sigmund began, but instead said, "I forgive you."

"Now I have this thing between my legs."

Sigmund was getting tired.

"I also drank a little. I was a *shicker* sometimes. Not like a bum, not like that, but I drank my share."

Barney's voice had suddenly become thick. It grew hoarse again, then flattened out. Sigmund could feel the back muscles relax under his hands, as Barney slowly fell asleep. Sigmund touched one of his angel wings with a forefinger, the sharp bone jutting up like a child's. Barney's body lapsed, he broke wind. Silently, then, without hurrying, Sigmund smoothed down Barney's pajama top, placed the rubbing alcohol neatly back on the table, and began to shuffle out of the room. Just outside the door, the special was leaning against the wall, eating an apple.

"He's asleep," Sigmund said. "He went off just like that."

"Enough morphine," she said.

"He didn't seem too uncomfortable to me."

"There are times when he doesn't even know where he is, or he's only half there, know what I mean?"

"It's hard to imagine Barney Fribush only half there. You should have known him before."

"Everybody tells me."

They both said good night and Sigmund slid down the silent corridor on the soles of his feet, only half there himself.

It was nine-thirty.

Velda was sitting in the visitor's easy chair when he got back to the room. She had the stiff controlled look of someone who was trying to stay awake against the odds. "Out on the town?" she asked, only half facetiously.

"This can be tricky," Sigmund said, edging toward the bed. "You can't push it. I can hardly stand up."

Velda nodded agreeably but made no move to help him. "Most cardiacs aren't out of bed for at least ten days," she informed him, yawning. "So maybe you shouldn't rush things too much. Maybe tomorrow you'll just take it easy."

Sigmund slid into bed, pulled the sheet up to his chin, and lay back at forty-five degrees. He began to gaze at the ceiling.

"You saw our friend?" Velda asked.

"I did."

"And how did he seem tonight?"

Sigmund thought about Velda's question, remembering the smells in Barney's room and the fading brown freckles on his upper back. "It's hard to tell," he said. "He's very alert, you can't pull the wool over Barney Fribush's eyes, but it's clear . . ."

"Yeah," Velda said.

"His life is what's on his mind tonight," Sigmund said.

Velda waited for Sigmund to go on.

"I mean, he's thinking about things. He's going over all the years. He told me . . ."

"Never mind," Velda said. "Better to keep it between the two of you."

The room grew quiet. Velda rested her head on the back of the chair. "Oh," she groaned, closing her eyes from fatigue.

Sigmund watched her, as sentimental feelings crept over him. His blond friend from Tennessee, his unwavering companion, *semper paratus, semper fidelis*, escaping her routine duties for a few stolen moments in a corner of his room. She deserved it, she deserved everything she asked for. She was working hard at losing her Tennessee accent. He could hear her trying every day. He was rooting for her. She wanted to sound like a Baltimorean, someone from Forest Park or Roland Park or one of those fancy places, not someone from the Cumberland Hills. She wanted to marry a Hebrew doctor in Baltimore. She had her mind set on it. He wished her luck.

Sigmund began to stare at the ceiling again. Even though the familiar hospital silence filled everything, there was still a faint stir of nighttime activity outside in the corridor. Footsteps, whispered conversations, rubber stretcher wheels. He saw Velda stirring in the chair. Her hand reached up to touch her hair.

"Velda," he said in a questioning voice that he could barely hear.

She stirred again, shifted position.

"Velda?"

"What is it?" She opened her eyes.

"Do you want me to tell you about Poland?"

There was no answer.

"Do you know where Poland is?"

Silence.

"I have two sisters there," he continued, but he couldn't go on, his voice broke. In Warsaw, he wanted to say. He began to cry again. He hadn't cried in two days. He closed his eyes and turned his head to the side so Velda wouldn't see. Outside, the city was coming to life; he could hear the Sunday-night rumble of incoming trucks and sputtering cars. In another moment or two, he was asleep. On the other side of the room, in the visitor's chair, so was Velda. Soon, the shy bristling sound of their snoring was the only thing that could be heard in the room. As he snored, a hair fluttered in Sigmund's nostril, and a whistling sound came through his nose. Even in his sleep, he was still a little sick from the smell in Barney's room. Soon, he began to dream. Melodies in heavy waltz time curled through his head bearing the thick aroma of the past. The perfume of olden times. Then a little Mozart. The sound of a tenor running silvery scales. The long breath, the one true bliss. No sweeter music for Sigmund R. Safer.

They were dancing again downtown that night in the skinny living room up front. Mickey Schiller was leading, with a firm right arm curved around Lillian's supple waist and his left hand holding hers, gripping it, fingers pretzeled together tightly so as to enhance the intimate feelings he was trying to express. "It's so uncomfortable like this," Lillian complained, trying to pull her hand away. "Can't we just dance like everyone else?" "Shh," Mickey said. "You'll break the mood. Just keep moving like you're doing. Heaven," he sang into her ear, along with the radio that was playing in the corner of the room, "I'm in heaven . . ."

Outside, on the front stoop, Sylvan Scheingold sat upright with his hands clasped between his knees. He could hear the music coming from behind him. How could he miss it? Heaven, he thought, his sphincter tightening. They're in heaven. Next door to the Scheingold row house, only ten feet away, the Hausner family sat sprawled on their stoop and on webbed beach chairs set out on the pavement, taking the air. The old man, the old lady, four daughters, and one son, who was wearing woolen bathing trunks and an undershirt. Every now and then they gave each other knowing glances as a snatch of melody came through the Scheingold living-room window. In the small park across the street, couples walked arm in arm, very slowly, while it was still light. Children batted a softball on the park lawn, watched by a small crowd, and the Good Humor truck continued to make its after-dinner way around the square, bell ringing. Two kids were stealing a ride on the back of the truck.

Sylvan was thinking about a couple of things at the same time.

In the back of his mind, the imagined silhouettes of Mickey Schiller and Lillian Scheingold flickered nervously as they danced together across the living room behind Sylvan. But he would not turn his head to look at them. He would rather sit on the white front stoop, imagining it, and let his fancy release the nervous trembling that moved from his clasped hands up through his shoulders. Otherwise, at the same time, he thought about the cantor, his mentor, as he had been thinking about him all week. Suppose he died? Suppose his damaged heart stopped and he choked to death? Is that what happened when the heart stopped? Sylvan's shoulders twitched. The vision in his left eye clouded over for a moment. He thought of the week's choir rehearsals, of Volkonsky's sudden assurance in the cantor's absence, of his authority; the new big boss in action. They were going to have to find another place for him to sleep for the holidays, too. Mr. Fribush didn't seem to be in such great shape, either. Old man Hausner next door belched loudly, then, as he passed a beer bottle along to his son, the family continued to talk among themselves, everybody at the same time. There was a new song on the radio inside, a new Les Brown that Sylvan had never heard before.

The old dreams weren't working anymore. They had run down, worn out by overuse. Louis B. Mayer and stardom. A mansion in the Maryland hunt country. Servants and swimming pools. An air force officer in a floppy hat. Louis B. Mayer lived in Hollywood and wouldn't be caught dead in Baltimore, Maryland. Not if he was in his right mind. A mansion in the country would remain just that, a mansion in the country, strictly for other people. And there was no air force officer wearing a floppy hat and natty uniform, there never had been, never would be, there was only the memory of a dim, silent, unshaved man, prone to anger, who had run away from his wife and his son years ago. A coward, a villainous coward; gone forever.

What was real was the image of his mother dancing with her boyfriend only five feet away from where he was sitting. The cantor also was real. Heart attacks might be unimaginable (if he hadn't witnessed it with his own eyes in Mr. Fribush's back yard), but they were real, there was no doubt about that. The sudden choking, the heavy, weighted fall, like an oak tree going down under the ax, the terror. Sylvan sat on the stoop, staring straight ahead, hands trembling. The trembling was relentless, he couldn't stop it, but he didn't care. The music behind him continued. So did all the life going on around the square in the fading summer light. Slowly, he began to cut himself out of it, to cut himself off from the music and talk and his own fancies, blind and deaf to it all for the moment, like an appendage that didn't belong or an excrescence, a foreign growth that would never take root in strange soil.

Night came down heavily, as relentless as his trembling, as relentless as all the laws of physics. Gonna take a sentimental journey, gonna get . . . Sylvan hated the song, it was so depressing, so deadening, like a funeral march, he was even beginning to hate Doris Day. Next door, the Hausners were snickering and drinking beer and Dr Pepper. Inside, Mickey Schiller and Lillian Scheingold were doing some convoluted stuff that involved dipping. Mickey Schiller still clutched Lillian's hand. Sylvan stared rigidly ahead from his marble step, seeing nothing but his own clear reflection in front of him, blotting out the park and the couples and the Good Humor truck, erasing the ball game and the orange bar of sun that was disappearing on the horizon, willing the future to begin, willing his life into being—the stupendous thing that would be his alone.

Waiting.

Eight

At the end of summer, a faint chill descended everywhere on the Atlantic seaboard as the earth's axis began to tilt ever so slightly, then settled in and took hold. Suddenly, it was fall. Three inches of rain fell in the Baltimore area, most of it during the Holy Days, disproving Elsie Thaymes's theory, which was widespread among her friends, that the Jewish holidays were always blessed by good weather and constant sunshine, as though the Jews had first call on heaven's rewards. (This theory, when expressed by Elsie, had always vaguely nettled Barney Fribush, who heard anti-Semitic overtones in it, or thought he did, but he let it pass unchallenged every year.)

Nevertheless, on the pulpit, the choir really did its job. No milk, no meat before services; no mucous, either. Volkonsky, temporarily number one, led them with all the confidence he needed, which was plenty. The thundering herd, the great unwashed, the tired and the poor, headed by the Scheingold kid, responded with full hearts; so did the grown-up gorillas. Jeffrey Bourne did as he was told—he didn't have to be told twice—singing the cantor's part, acting Sigmund's role, leading the Silent Devotion. Many wept, as usual, and, given the determining factors of Jeffrey Bourne's performance, there was hardly a word of complaint from the old-timers in the congregation; they were genuinely worried, in varying degrees, about the cantor and the condition of his heart. Besides, it was the Holy Days, time for spiritual reparations and worldly truces.

The rabbi himself also went along with it—he had to—flushing, however, with fierce emotion when he first realized what was happening on his pulpit. But he was unable to stop it, totally helpless in the face of Sam Volkonsky fervently signaling cues right and left to the members of the choir, wholly powerless at the sound of Jeffrey Bourne's gorgeous baritone filling the vast sanctuary with such transcendent sounds. But the experience left him with a residue of black resentment—and maybe even worse—that only reinforced his suspicion about Sigmund R. Safer's loyalty to his rabbi. That never resolved itself, never healed. It was like a fuel that kept the rabbi burning; and burning, as many knew, was one of the rabbi's favorite states.

But the cantor and his heart were doing all right. In moderation, of course. During the Holy Days, while it rained outside, the cantor lay in his bedroom on Granada Avenue, reading his books, daydreaming, trying to project himself, in imagination, onto the pulpit of the House (ah, Jeffrey Bourne, he thought, with a triumphant little smile), occasionally coming downstairs to have a look at his fish, sighing as he slowly took each step, like a child, holding firmly on to the railing. Then he would smile to himself again, he couldn't seem to help it.

Later, when Rosh Hashana and Yom Kippur had passed, Sigmund's recovery continued. Again in moderation, of course. Eventually, in due time, he returned to the synagogue—to services and committee meetings, weddings and funerals and the rest, all the demanding details of congregational life—but he paced himself quite differently now. He was unhurried, conscious all the time of the penalties of stress, strain, and overexertion (three of Dr. Rapoport's most cherished red flags). Sigmund, like Jeffrey Bourne, did not have to be told twice, either. He paid attention to the orders of the day. What Dr. R. said, he did. And even more, when his old pal Barney Fribush had to be buried, out near Dickeyville, when the president himself had a stroke and died in Warm Springs, Georgia (the ultimate casualty for Sigmund's daily lists), when the war ended in Europe in the spring and American troops began to uncover, one by one, the German camps, he took to his bed again, in the old way, for a couple of days each time. In the face of such events, it was little help. Nothing in fact seemed able to shield him against circumstance and history. His friend was dead; so was the president; and his sisters and his mother had disappeared forever, lost with the others; Czaferski ghosts. That part was over, it would not be spoken of again.

Over the next decade, even longer, Sigmund and Jenny remained much the same, ailments aside. Like everyone else, they seemed to go on in a way that was wholly faithful to themselves, bound by the need to be what they had to be, what they were (as though there were ever a choice). That, in fact, was pretty much what Sigmund R. Safer was thinking to himself, a few years later, as he sat in a canvas chair on the patio of his new ground-floor garden apartment, out in Pikesville in Baltimore County. He had retired now, semiretired, rather—the "semi" took the edge off it—with too much time on his hands, too much empty space around him, surrounded by aging Jews, an old friend here and there, his old library out of Europe, one tank of spiritless fish, and the fuller-bodied, still long-haired figure of his wife, who at that moment was arranging a bouquet of store-bought roses in a milky green vase in the living room behind him.

"What time are Annie and Seth coming for dinner?" Sigmund called through the screen door.

"It's the weekend, Sigi. You know Seth goes to his father's on the weekend."

"Well, sometimes I forget. It's so unnatural. Poor kid, pillar to post. Now I won't see him until Monday. I don't know if I can wait that long." Sigmund paused a moment, thinking about his grandson. He meant it when he said that he didn't think he could wait until Monday. "And what about Annie?" he then asked. "Is she coming?"

"She's not sure."

"Does she expect us to sit around all day waiting for her to make up her mind?"

"You should know your own daughter by now."

"I certainly should. I certainly do."

"Well," Jenny said, coming out onto the patio. She handed him a rose. "Watch the thorns."

Sigmund sniffed the rose. His nostrils flared, his eyes misted. Then he put the flower on his lap.

"How about some iced tea and brownies, the way you like them?"

"Why not?"

The afternoon passed, the sun began to go down. There was the sound of a passing freight train in the near-distance. Old Jews shuffled by, taking their daily mile, the newest rage, pursued with a near-frantic dedication on behalf of bowels and bloodstream.

An hour later, Sigmund and Jenny were still sitting on their canvas chairs on the patio, sipping and nibbling their tea and cookies in silence, waiting for the day to end, preoccupied by all the old things, the old questions, the blessed ongoing mysteries that never resolved themselves, never came clear (thank God for that, Sigmund sometimes thought), not if you lived to be a million.

A Note About the Author

Robert Kotlowitz was raised and educated in Baltimore. A graduate of Johns Hopkins University and the Peabody Conservatory of Music, Preparatory Division, he went on to become a book and magazine editor in New York, where he served as Managing Editor of *Harper's Magazine*. His first novel, *Somewhere Else*, published in 1972, won the National Jewish Book Award and the Edward Lewis Wallant Award for fiction. His subsequent novels were *The Boardwalk* (1977) and *Sea Changes* (1986).

Twenty years ago, Mr. Kotlowitz joined Channel Thirteen/WNET in New York and became Senior Vice President and Director of Programming and Broadcasting; upon retirement in 1990, he was named Chairman of the Editorial Council and Editorial Advisor to the station. He and his wife, Billie, have two sons and live in New York City.

A Note on the Type

The text of this book was set in Weiss, a typeface designed in Germany by Emil Rudolf Weiss (1875–1942). The design of the roman was completed in 1928 and that of the italic in 1931. Both are well balanced and even in color, and both reflect the subtle skill of a fine calligrapher.

Composed by PennSet, Inc.,
Bloomsburg, Pennsylvania
Printed and bound by The Haddon Craftsmen, Inc.,
Scranton, Pennsylvania
Designed by Irva Mandelbaum